THERE COMES A TIME

JACK NOLAN

Author of *Vietnam Remix*

Visit our website at **www.StillwaterPress.com** for more information.

First Stillwater River Publications Edition

Library of Congress Control Number: 2019920859

ISBN: 978-1-950339-69-3

1 2 3 4 5 6 7 8 9 10
Written by Jack Nolan.
Published by Stillwater River Publications, Pawtucket, RI, USA.

Publisher's Cataloging-In-Publication Data
(Prepared by The Donohue Group, Inc.)

Names: Nolan, Jack, author.
Title: There comes a time / Jack Nolan.
Description: First Stillwater River Publications edition. | Pawtucket, RI, USA : Stillwater River Publications, [2020]
Identifiers: ISBN 9781950339693
Subjects: LCSH: Young men--Conduct of life--Fiction. | Nineteen sixties--Fiction.
Classification: LCC PS3614.O4676 T44 2020 | DDC 813/.6--dc23

*"There comes a time
in the affairs of men when they must prepare
to defend not their homes alone,
but the tenets of faith and humanity
on which their churches,
their governments,
and their foundations are set.*

*The defense of religion,
of democracy,
and of good faith among nations
is all the same fight."*

—Franklin Delano Roosevelt

Contents

1

OH! WHAT A TANGLED WEB

On a wall of Colonel George Owen Donahue's office at the Headquarters of the 581st Military Intelligence Company on the southern edge of Saigon there hung a large map of the crescent-shaped Republic of Vietnam, which is no more. Too big for the filing cabinets, this Top Secret document was covered by a pale-green bed sheet whenever the colonel was not present, even though his office was windowless and well-guarded, as required by Army protocol.

Four white pins marked the Regional Headquarters of the bilateral intelligence operations in each of the country's four areas: I Corps in the north to IV Corps in the south, from the border with North Vietnam to the Mekong Delta. Dozens of red pins held labels in place to mark the scattered Field Stations of the bilateral effort, which made this map a useful instrument as these stations quickly came and went in changing conditions. After the massive, nation-wide "surprise attack" known as the Tet Offensive of 1968, for instance, ten of the three dozen stations moved because their locations were no longer considered safe. The map was a snapshot of the 581st MI Company's operations all over the country at any given time.

Bilateral operations were by necessity eccentric. Colonel Donahue was driven to work each morning in a black Citroën sedan and, like his driver, he wore a casual short-sleeved shirt and chinos. His driver leapt out and opened the rear door for him, but since neither was in uniform, there was no exchange of salutes. Headquarters for the 581st sat in the middle of a sprawling military compound, but the one-story building displayed a large sign over the entrance that read "Service International Corporation" and anyone who entered would see, beyond the high front counter, two dozen busy workers typing, filing papers, talking with each other or on the phone—all of them men in civilian clothes. Each of them carried a photo ID that said "Civilian Contractor, Service International Corporation [SIC]" and assigned the man a rank (GS-4 for young clerks to GS-15 for Mr. George Owen Donahue). Nothing seen from the front counter signified that this was a US Army headquarters, and any stranger who asked was told it was not. However, within the file cabinets "SIC" morphed into the 581st Military Intelligence Company and the young clerk was revealed to be an Army Specialist E-4 and Mr. Donahue became a bird colonel.

Why this elaborate and complicating subterfuge? It all followed "by necessity."

To protect the paid "Informants" who reported on Viet Cong (Communist militias, the "VC") and North Vietnamese Army (NVA) activities, their "Handlers," who were soldiers in the Army of the Republic of Vietnam, (ARVN), maintained civilian cover. They wore street clothes and, in order not to be themselves arrested as deserters, carried phony "civilian" identification. They recruited their Informants from the ranks of those who had access to areas where the VC or NVA were active (if not in complete control, as in Cambodia and

Laos and certain, shifting areas of the Republic) and trained these Informants to collect useful data, to develop cover stories to explain their activities, to practice counter-surveillance measures so they may meet securely with their Handlers, and so forth. These measures were exactly the same ones used by the VC and the NVA when they trained *their* Informants to spy on ARVN and the Americans—and both sides knew it. In retrospect, it might have been a win-win situation if all involved had held conferences where they merely exchanged the intelligence they were going to such great lengths to collect on each other, which would have saved everyone much time, trouble and expense. But such is not the tradition of warfare, which is "by necessity" a contest.

Informants recruited by ARVN Handlers were sometimes well motivated by patriotic enthusiasm or personal grudges against the Communists or by the excitement of being a spy, while others acted only to be paid. Some of them invented stories to tell their Handlers because they had nothing useful to report or because they hoped to mislead their Handler for personal reasons or for ideological reasons or to prove they were more clever than their Handler or they had grown tired of being nagged by him or because they were desperate for the money or from some slight they had received in life from someone other than their Handler or some experience that caused them to fear or favor the enemy or for no reason at all—and how was a Handler to sort all this out?

That's where the Americans came in.

Americans, who could not themselves "pass" for Vietnamese, and who spoke at best the street polyglot, pidgin-English, could not participate directly in field work of this nature and so never actually met any of the Informants. But they did nevertheless supervise the work, and that's because they paid the piper and, therefore, called the tune. The Vietnamese Army personnel drew salaries from ARVN funds, but the operating expenses for this elaborate bilateral effort were considerable: Informants by the hundreds, translators, security guards and typists all had to be paid, landlords charged rent for the Field Station houses and for the large villas for the four Corps HQs where dozens of people worked and, in some cases, lived. Office equipment, vehicles and supplies all cost money, and bilateral intelligence-gathering produced no income.

The US Army paid for all these things, by necessity, and, therefore, called the shots: Which Informants could be trusted—which retained and which let go—all these decisions were made by recent arrivals to this ancient, Asian country. It all would have presented a fascinating, perhaps even a comic spectacle to any objective observer. But objective observers were not allowed.

By necessity, of course, US Army personnel who were assigned to bilateral operations had to be "on civilian status" too. It would not have done for Vietnamese soldiers working in civvies, in order to protect their Informants, to work side-by-side with Americans in uniform. And US soldiers given the task of supervising Vietnamese in their own country—often in remote outposts, a modest house/office in a small town—would by necessity need to be carefully chosen for this kind of assignment and at least superficially trained in the craft of intelligence, in Vietnamese culture and history, and in independent problem-solving. All things being equal, bilateral intelligence might have produced reams of actionable information. But when are all things ever equal, especially in a war zone?

Among the Americans from Chicago and Nashville, Lake Charles and Clemson, who were asked to pull-off this intricate assignment were—from these towns, respectively—John Francis Mulcahey and Zachary Rosenzweig (assigned to the III Corps Headquarters in

Saigon), Mark Babineaux and Braxton Hood (at the Field Station in the beach-resort town of Vung Tau).

Soldiers since the time of Homer have developed loyal friendships. When men are far from home and family, living in an alien environment fraught with uncertainty and danger, clan-formation is inevitable and a vital part of what allows armies to function as they do. The four young men named above had joined a clique which called itself "The Greyhawk Six" during months of training and extensive field exercises at Fort Greyhawk Intelligence School. But during the half-year after they arrived together in-country—on 26 September 1967—Vietnam-at-war had thrown a phantasmagoria of jarring experiences at each of them, tearing at the fabric of the group. Mulcahey's wild temperament made him a danger to himself and others; Rosenzweig's compassionate heart had drawn him into an intractable love-affair that led to his house-arrest and demotion; Babineaux had fallen under the thrall of an ancient and diminutive but brilliant entrepreneur whom the Australians called "Itty Bitchy"; and Hood had participated in a series of scams that left him with many dangerous enemies and two large boxes of ill-gotten scrip money. And of the Greyhawk Six cabal, where were the other two?

Nine yellow pins on George Owen Donahue's map held labels denoting "special operations," and two of those pins accounted for Rick Singleton of Harlem, New York City, and Rene Levesque of Providence, Rhode Island, the other friends. It was clear whenever Major Cardenas was called into the air-conditioned office (Cardenas called it "freezing") of his commanding officer, George Owen Donahue (whom the major secretly thought of as "G.O.D.") that the colonel was bored by the set routines of the bilateral units but excited by the potential of these "special" operations, which he hoped would net the kind of higher-level intelligence that was usually the province of the CIA. Singleton, for instance, was recruited for his professional training as an actor to pose as a representative of the Goodyear Tire and Rubber Company, which might give him access to the plantation society at Xuan Song, where third-generation French Colonials were known to host upper-echelon Viet Cong and North Vietnamese leaders. "Imagine the potential for strategic and organizational data if our man cultivates *those* sources!" Colonel Donahue ranted, "And what have we got to lose? One measly private!"

"Corporal, sir" Cardenas corrected, while he thought to himself, *And the wrath of the Goodyear Tire and Rubber Company, if they ever find out.*

Another yellow pin marked the location, here in Saigon, of Rene Levesque, who was selected for a special mission because he was a devout Catholic who was fluent in French, or at least "Quebecois." He was assigned to pose as a Jesuit named "Brother Andre" come to offer his services in any capacity needed by the Holy Mother Church in this war-torn country. It was the colonel's hope that Levesque could ingratiate himself with the church hierarchy and become privy to the trove of secrets they knew, principally about officials in the Catholic-dominated government of South Vietnam. But wasn't this spying on our own allies? "Hey, intelligence is just something you know that you're not supposed to," the colonel hedged, "It'll give us some leverage with those big-wigs in the Saigon government, push-comes-to-shove. And what have we got to lose?"

"One measly corporal, sir," Cardenas anticipated, while he thought, *And if this comes to light, the wrath of the entire Roman Church, world-wide, and our heads on a platter for crossing the line.*

But Cardenas had nothing to fear on this front: The very qualities that made Levesque a perfect candidate to fit in with French-speaking Roman clergy also made him the very worst candidate. Within two hours of his insertion into this operation, he had consulted his God and his conscience and confessed to his religious superior, Father Martin, that he was not a Jesuit priest but an American spy. However, even if he had stuck to his cover-identity, the Roman hierarchy was as tough a nut to crack as there was. No new arrival was going to be made privy to that inner-circle, had he been native Vietnamese and carried a letter from Pope Paul VI himself. So deft was the handling of this matter by the Archbishop of Saigon that Levesque was merely assigned to a small parish near the Cambodian border and then, when the Tet Offensive made that assignment too dangerous for him, reassigned to lead the boys' choir from the Catholic orphanage in Saigon. He proved an energetic servant of the church, so why expose him as an imposter and create a fuss? US Army Intelligence had a lot of catching up to do to match the stealth of the Roman church.

Leading the boys' choir at Notre Dame Cathedral in Saigon was what Rene Levesque was doing when Mulcahey stumbled across his lost friend one afternoon in March of 1968. Since Levesque knew where to find Singleton, the six friends were reunited just in time for the departure of Major Shimazu, III Corp Commanding Officer, which was memorably celebrated for four days, 30 March through 2 April, in Vung Tau. It was a joyous affair, the reunion of these friends, featuring a Vietnamese parade marking "Whale Days" and by luncheons and dinners paid for by a wealthy, anonymous sponsor, ending with a grand party entertained by the boys' choir loudly mangling the lyrics of Broadway songs, with the talented Mulcahey at the piano. Not having been all together for six months previous, and knowing they had to go separate ways the next day, they sat on the beach deep into the night after the major's party, talking among themselves. Dawn would send them back to their secondary work—pulling the strings of the Army Intelligence apparatus—and their primary work—surviving the second half of their one-year assignment in Vietnam.

Levesque hoped to remain where he was, working with orphans while filing reports that vaguely suggested he was gaining the trust of his "fellow clergy." Singleton knew he would have a new assignment, since the Xuan Song Plantation he had infiltrated was now in the hands of Viet Cong militiamen who had executed the previous operators, Monsieur and Madam Guignon. Mulcahey and Rosenzweig would return to III Corps Headquarters in Saigon while Babineaux and Hood remained in the peaceful beach-town of Vung Tau, which on Colonel Donahue's map was designated a Field Station posing as a modest "office supply shop," marked by a red pin. The facts, had the colonel known them, presented a much more complicated picture. Ngon Bich, "Itty Bitchy," had taken over the office supply shop, adding it to her expanding business holdings, just after Braxton Hood spent the contents of one of his two boxes of loot to buy a large beach-front establishment he named "Bravo, Juliet!" This mansion now served as a combination bar, restaurant, whorehouse and intelligence-gathering operation—fully staffed by people working for Ngon Bich. It was thought better if Colonel Donahue and Major Cardenas were not made aware of these realities, since they may have become curious to know from whence the money for this investment had come, and the honest answer to that question would send Braxton Hood to jail.

During their time together in training at Fort Greyhawk, as they tried to grow accustomed to thinking of themselves as "soldier-spies," Singleton occasionally quoted Walter Scott's famous couplet: "Oh! What a tangled web we weave/When first we practice to deceive..." That became their motto. But it took on whole new levels of meaning in the second half of their year in Vietnam.

For they had all, so far, played individual parts in weaving that web, but each one was about to have his life altered by meeting the spider.

2

2 - 3 April 1968

IN THE PRE-DAWN DARKNESS

If only that magical night might have lasted forever!

Exactly one year from the day they'd met, six young men lay sprawled across the still-warm sand on the peaceful beach at Vung Tau, forty miles south of Saigon. A cooler piled high with empty beer bottles marked the axis of their half-circle under the panorama of brilliant stars doming the South China Sea. A rising land breeze calmed the pulsing waves that soothed them in their sleep—all of them but broad-shouldered Braxton Hood.

A welter of emotions kept Hood awake through the night: Major Shimazu's farewell gala had been a triumph—the formal dinner followed by a party at Bravo, Juliet! complete with balloons and ample food and drink for forty guests, while a chorus of Vietnamese orphan-boys led sing-alongs of Broadway tunes—all paid-for by the wealthy owner of the largest night-club/brothel on the beach. The wily Shimazu probably guessed that the generous owner of Bravo, Juliet! was none other than Braxton Hood, and that his loot had come from fraudulent schemes. But Shimazu apparently took the blame for

Hood's misdeeds upon himself, for he had assigned the young man
to work under Frank Monroe, whose genius for deception turned
out to be far greater than the major had anticipated. Now Hood's
concern was that Major Shimazu was leaving and what might happen
if his new Commanding Officer were to learn that he was sitting on
a pile of ill-gotten loot. The prospect of arrest, trial and conviction
under the arcane auspices of the Uniform Code of Military Justice
was one specter keeping Hood from sleep. Eighty or so wealthy
Saigon merchants and government officials who were bilked out of
tens of thousands in military scrip by Monroe, with Hood's help, was
another, even more unsettling ghost. If these powerful people were
ever to find him, their retribution would be more swift and violent
than the UCMJ's.

Hood's remarkable gift for mathematics (the weapon Frank
Monroe had employed to make them both rich) was also playing hell
with his mind. He could not abide unresolved problems. Just as last
evening's party was getting underway, Monroe's beautiful lover, Bian,
came striding into Bravo, Juliet! with a relic of a handgun and shot
several of the bar's best features to pieces, including a large mirror and
a delicately carved newel post. She had approached Pham Viet, the
head of the Translators' Pool in Saigon, and apparently intended to kill
him, then and there. They shouted at each other in Vietnamese, but
Hood distinctly heard Pham Viet say in English, "You have mistaken
me for someone else, madam," which had the desired effect of causing
Bian to back away, then turn and walk out through the doors. Hood
had known Bian well. They had dined together every evening for
months in Monroe's lavish Saigon villa. But why did she want to
kill Pham Viet? How did she even know him? And Rick Singleton
claimed he had met her, once, briefly, but knew her as Mademoiselle
Guignon, the daughter of a wealthy plantation owner executed by

the VC during Tet. Was she the same woman Singleton had met? Hood's obsession with the puzzle was working all the circuits of his disciplined brain, but there were just too many unknowns to solve it.*

For now, he comforted himself with his role in one of the best send-off parties ever!

Once Bian had gone, the guests crawled out from under tables and the little orphan-boys of Notre Dame Cathedral settled in and energetically attacked some of the best songs in the American canon: George M. Cohan, Rogers and Hammerstein, and others. They mangled the lyrics almost beyond recognition but with such enthusiasm that their mispronunciations only added to the fun. They rattled the light-fixtures with the chorus from "Oklahoma" and led the audience in "For He's A Jolly Good Fellow" while glasses were raised in the direction of Major Shimazu. That career-soldier's farewell speech, a tribute to the gentler sex as the faithful stewards of civilization in times of war—translated into Vietnamese by Pham Viet for the benefit of the bar-tenders, waitresses and prostitutes who comprised the staff of Bravo, Juliet!—had deeply moved everyone in attendance. Some shed tears. Hood thought about the major's wife and daughter, awaiting his return with open arms at his home in Los Angeles, and about the universality of that image for every returning soldier since Odysseus sailed back to Penelope (that bit of unpleasantness in the dining hall at Ithaca notwithstanding). Hood pictured his own modest home in Clemson, South Carolina, where his folks waited—mom questioning the postman on the front stoop each day—and he vowed that he would write them more often.

But Oh, this wonderful night! After the major's party, the six

---

* Years later, Professor Hood found a book, *Vietnam Remix*, in a bin marked "25 cents" that answered many of these questions.

young friends hauled a cooler of Australian beer to the edge of the South China Sea and under that glorious band of glittering stars, they celebrated this last night of being all together by sharing their dreams for the future, an intimacy encouraged by physical exhaustion and alcohol and shared experiences and an exotic setting. One by one, they trusted the group to know their secret hopes and plans without fear of the derisive ribbing that marked their usual talk. None of them expected such a sentimental moment, and it caught them all by surprise, as Braxton Hood remembered it.

When he challenged John Francis Mulcahey to tell what he wanted to do when he got home, the brash, combative maniac they called "Mad-dog" answered thoughtfully in a quiet voice, completely out of character. They leaned in closer to hear his words over the slapping of the unseen waves onto the pitch-dark beach. He told them how the victory of Jack Kennedy had made his Irish Catholic family and friends euphoric and he admitted that he began talking with the same Boston accent and quoting JFK at length. "I was in high school when they shot President Kennedy…" he said, pausing to get his voice under control, "so first thing I do when I get back in September, I'm going to work for Bobby's campaign. It's my chance to express how I feel about the only Irish president getting cheated out of his chance. Bobby will be the best president our country ever had!"

No one in the circle had ever seen their pugnacious friend show such vulnerability. Hood figured that's what set the tone for the rest. "How's 'bout you, Rosie?" he asked Zachary Rosenzweig, "You plan to take Nguyen Sang back to Nashville?"

Rosie was heard laughing quietly in the dark. "That might not work out, a Jewish guy bringing his beautiful Asian bride into the heartland. Do I think Sang and I will end up together? I don't know. Right now, leaving here without her come September… or if I extend in Vietnam to next year… it's something I try not to

Keep a secret? Major Shimazu gave me Army paperwork t

us to get married and he offered to set us up in Los Angeles, whe

of Viet immigrants live. But I'm not sure that's what she wants, s

don't know if it's what I want either. Truth is, she doesn't know about

the paperwork and we've never talked about it… I guess because we

both have enough problems as it is, day-to-day. I just don't know."

A silent minute passed before Hood asked Rick Singleton, "You plannin' to settle back in Harlem or you goin' straight to Hollywood?"

Singleton had a surprise for them. "I plan to give up acting for a while," he said, "My father and I have been corresponding about Reverend King's Poor People's Campaign. The idea is to take the Civil Rights Movement in a completely new direction. There are more white families living in poverty than black families, so King's beginning a grass-roots movement to bring the races together to fight economic inequality. They will oppose politicians and businessmen who drive wedges between the races on purpose for their own benefit. My father and Reverend King are friends from way-back and he can get me a good position with them. I think it would be exciting to be in on the ground-floor of something this big… and I have to admit, I've lost my appetite for acting in the last four months. Playing 'Ted Michaels, businessman' put me at the same dinner table with high-level Viet Cong and the French plantation manager that they shot against a wall during Tet. Day-in and day-out, I've been afraid I'd be killed or captured up there… I try not to think about how close I came… so the idea of going home and doing political work for a worthy cause will be a way to express my gratitude for still being alive."

Then Rene Levesque volunteered, "Like Rosie, I don't know what will happen when I get home. I've never been happier than these last few months, helping people who are suffering from the war,

Army gave me 'Brother Andre' for a
n than me. I'm going home to a family
me become a priest. But they will not
protestant girl-friend, and I don't think
rotestant. Any of you guys know how I
:over and do Good Works, move in with
family and the church… all at the same
time? Please let me know how that would work. Looks like there's no
way after September I'm not going to lose something important to
me."

"You've got nothing to cry about, Rene," Mark Babineaux said
from his corner of the night-blackened beach. "I've been living with
two beautiful young ladies… twins that will mix me any drink I want
any time of the day or night. I can't tell them apart, but why do I need
to? I sleep 'til lunchtime, read on the beach while the girls swim, go to
work in the hottest night-spot in town, pile in bed each night between
my girls… and you worry you might have to give up the priesthood?
Boo-hoo! Look at me! I'll have to give up everything I hold dear! Every
dear I hold! Before they put me in fatigues and march me around an
Army fort, I'll toss a rope over the rafters at Bravo, Juliet! and hang
myself."

Singleton rescued this special night for Hood by interrupting
Babineaux's diatribe, which had reverted to soldier-banter. "What
about you, Braxton? You have plans when you get home?"

He knew exactly what he wanted to tell them. "Shortly after we
get home, gentlemen, NASA plans to shoot some astronauts around
the moon and back. After that, they aim to land some on the surface
and bring 'em back alive. For the first time, a man's gonna step foot
on a different world than this one, our home-planet. My grand-pappy
rode a horse to school and didn't see a car 'til he was ten or twelve.

Now he rides in jet planes. Some awesome stuff is comin' our way. Good, solid science is gonna cure diseases and grow enough food and maybe keep us from wastin' so much energy fightin' wars. I'd love to be a part of all that."

Hood had never spoken this way before to the others. He savored his reputation as a big, physical man, a rough-and-tumble Son of the South who learned how to be a team-player on the gridiron. The aspiring scientist he harbored within surfaced tonight only because the others had owned up to their sincere hopes, so that cleared the way for him.

Recounting in his mind the hopes and worries that had been shared by his friends that night kept Hood from dwelling on the box of purloined money, his secret ownership of Bravo, Juliet!, the thought of dangerous men who were looking for him. But still he could not sleep. So he distracted himself by imagining the group-dynamics of the Greyhawk Six as a set of variables and constants that could be expressed in a formula.

All the experiences they shared would compose the common denominator. They were all college-educated and had scored high on Army exams, and they had volunteered for a three-year hitch to secure acceptance into the Intelligence Corps. Each of them had been offered Officer's Candidate School or a Direct Commission and had turned the offer down. None of them wanted a career in the military, but all of them grew up assuming he would be called to serve his country in uniform someday, just as his father had done in World War II or Korea. Their fathers had all seen first-hand how a dictatorship can destroy all resistance and enforce rigid conformity—Imperialism, Fascism, Communism—and they had instilled in their sons the ethics of non-conformity, warning them never to completely trust authority or to obey without questioning. These teachings they all had in common. None of the six knew hunger or poverty growing up, as their fathers and mothers had in the Depression, so they took a certain level of affluence for granted. They were all literate and read widely and shared in a common understanding of United States history, with emphasis on the Founding Fathers and the Revolution of '76, the Constitution, some version of the Civil War but The Winning of the West in great detail from Davey Crockett and Dan'l Boone and hundreds of hours of cowboy-and-Indian comic books and films. Each had been brought up to believe in fair-play and justice from an early exposure to childhood heroes: Each had rested his head on the kitchen counter where the radio told them stories of The Lone Ranger and Superman, even before they had televisions. The clarion call of "The William Tell Overture" or a baritone voice reciting "Truth, Justice and The American Way" stood the hair up on the back of his neck ever after. It was in his bones that good men always defended the helpless and won out, in the end, over bad men. Sitting in his father's lap at first, each learned about the wider world by watching John Cameron Swayze and later Walter Cronkite read the evening news. The smooth, reassuring baritone of President Eisenhower, the nation's greatest war hero, represented his first president. Before that, he knew the feel of *The Velveteen Rabbit*, the surging little engine that could, the heart-breaking story of Bambi, and, in the very beginning, *Dick and Jane Readers* and E-I-E-I-O. These things they all had in common to various degrees.

With this expansive denominator, Hood felt there was plenty to go around to each of the six numerators. All things being equal (which they never are), each of them would receive 16.666 of the whole, an equal portion to each of the six, given that their commonalities equaled 100. The individuals would vary as expressions of the commonality according to the portion each could claim to represent the Great American Mid-Century Consensus, "We hold these truths to be self-evident..."

Rene Levesque, for example, was in some senses of the word hardly even an American. His family immigrated to Rhode Island from French Canada and sometimes spoke Quebecois in the home. They were devoutly Roman Catholic in that primitive sense that Quebec had fallen under British rule in 1763, before The Enlightenment had found its way to the colonies. The saints were living and miracles could be expected momentarily in the Levesque household. Rene saw the common experience through Vatican-colored glasses, so as much as Hood liked Rene, these things detracted from his proportion of the denominator. Hood decided he could not grant him more than 12.333 over 100, representing only 1/8th of the six-man group. And that was being generous.

By contrast, because Rosenzweig was from a Jewish family, raised in Nashville, he had developed a critical understanding of American history from the time when he was seven years old and his grandfather, a refugee displaced by World War I, took him to the nearby battlefield of Franklin, Tennessee. Rosie had told Hood what a powerful feeling it had given him to stand on a field where, just four months before Appomattox, 54,000 Americans fought a savage one-day battle that piled acres of ground high with corpses and packed every building for miles around with the wounded and the dying. Rosie said that everafter, he assumed that peace was transient and human decency was conditional. His awareness of the vulnerability of civilization and of American history in depth, and his coming from a Border State, made it impossible to award him anything less than 24.333 over 100. That was nearly one-fourth and would make it unlikely that Rosie would end up on the same side of the equal sign as any other high scoring...

Immediately to Braxton Hood's right, Rick Singleton stirred, then arose, quietly brushing sand from his clothes in the dark. For a long minute he stood in silence before moving toward the lights of Bravo, Juliet!. As Hood watched Rick's silhouette cross the beach road and mount the steps of the hotel veranda, he reflected that Singleton was the one he admired most. During his South Carolina childhood, Hood had playmates who were Negroes (to use the term thought polite in those times). They went to separate schools but met over pick-up baseball and football games, choosing-up sides more on merit than on color. Rick Singleton, Hood learned, had grown up in a very different world from that: The son of a renowned Baptist minister, Rick was sent to private schools in Manhattan, where learning to fit-in with a privileged, white elite on one end of his subway-ride while maintaining his "Preacher's Kid" role on the other end turned him into a fine actor. He honed these gifts at drama programs and schools in New York, which led the way to his being a stand-out at Yale's prestigious School of Dramatic Arts. By the time he arrived at Fort Greyhawk, he was a polished professional, able to shape the expectations of others like wet clay in his talented hands. Hood had seen him under interrogation when he had transformed himself from one person into another, to the immense frustration of his interrogators. They would accuse him of pretending to be someone he was not— which, of course, was exactly what he was doing—except that he had the tools and the talent to "be" that person, completely. He did not act a role; he entirely inhabited a persona and could sustain the illusion for hours. Then he could switch roles in a flash and be someone else for hours. Everyone who witnessed these sessions found them weird, haunting and magical—even the counter-intelligence interrogators who were stymied by him. Many Greyhawk instructors, including the Program Commander, Major Alex Cardenas, attended the Interrogation Center when Singleton was being questioned, to observe his legendary performances. That is why Cardenas had chosen Singleton for a special assignment in Vietnam, and it is why Hood felt that Rick Singleton was the most remarkable person of any race that he had ever come across.

When Singleton's disembodied voice had announced out of the dark that he planned to join King's Poor People's Campaign, Hood had to bite his tongue to keep from objecting. Hood had grown up around Carolinians of every political stripe and persuasion, and he knew there were some among them who were violently opposed to the Civil Rights legislation recently passed, who hated Martin Luther King and everything he stood for, and who would oppose this Poor People's Campaign by any means, fair or foul. Rick Singleton didn't know what he was getting into, Hood thought. He was about to leave behind the cocoon of Harlem, elite schools, a promising career in theater in order to ride some political ideal into sure danger. Singleton might be a rich kid and a Yale graduate, but where Hood was from, he would be just a black trouble-maker from up North.

From his place on the beach, Hood watched with concern as Singleton disappeared into the brightly-lit interior of Bravo, Juliet!. The unruly pack of teenage war-orphans he paid to "guard" the prem-ises from midnight to dawn were making a noisy fuss over Singleton. Hood got to his feet and was almost to the edge of the beach road when the ruckus died down and a confrontation was avoided between those feral youngsters and him, the big American they called (but not without a sneer) "Boss."

The wise and all-knowing Ngon Bich—tiny, ancient "Itty Bitchy"– had persuaded Hood to employ the gang of street-urchins because, she said, "You no do that, those cowboys break-in at night, steal your booze. Pay fi-dollah, they be sentry you."

"Sounds fair," Hood conceded.

"Each," Co Bich added.

"Whoa! Five dollars each? No can do, lady! I pay one dollar each, that's it, and no more than fifteen cowboys, total, fifteen dollars." Months of negotiating with this wrinkled little dynamo had taught him great respect for her skills at taking scrip-dollars out of American and Australian pockets and delivering them to a vast community of war-widows, disabled soldiers and orphans who depended on her. Dozens of enterprises in Vung Tau, large and small, had been founded by her and each one occupied a building she owned and collected rent on. Hood had paid for the very lucrative Bravo, Juliet! nightclub, but Bich had served as general contractor, dealing with the carpenters, electricians and local officials, and she had managed all the employees, training them to run a first-rate beachfront bar and cat-house while also working their customers for military intelligence the Americans could use. She was, in short, not only directing the bar operation but also running the spy network that so-called "co-owners" Braxton Hood and Mark Babineaux were supposed to be in charge of. She was everywhere. She did everything. And so, it seemed natural and only fair that Bich would become the sole, legal owner of Bravo, Juliet! on 27 September 1968, the day after Hood and Babineaux were scheduled to return to the United States. They had already signed the paperwork for this arrangement drawn-up by her attorney.

He told her firmly, "You no bring twenty or thirty more cowboys to be sentry for me. Fifteen only, no more. Yes?"

"Fiftee-dollah and food," she countered, "You feed, they no touch booze. Deal?"

If Itty Bitchy had the power to keep that gang out of the liquor, Hood figured, then $105 in protection money every week was a bargain and feeding orphans was just fine with him. "OK, you tell them one dollar and food for fifteen. No more. Fifteen. Deal!"

Bich flashed him a stained-tooth smile and rewarded him for his generosity with a phrase she had picked up from Australian sailors: "You hard man but fair man, you."

"Yeah, well… tell them if they steal one drop of booze, I'll toss them out on the street."

"Bad idea!" Bich warned him, "They all have knife."

And that is why Hood worried when he heard his night-guards shouting at Rick Singleton and why he was much relieved when their voices went calm. He tilted his watch-face toward the lights from the bar. It was 3:30, too early to rouse-up the other four. He would keep an eye on them, as was his protective nature. He sat on the sand, barely able to make out the dark forms of his sleeping comrades, and he thought about Singleton. His community and family were certainly outside anything in Hood's experience and if Rick were white, wrangling an invitation to visit him in New York, to meet his family and friends, would be easy. But Armed Forces Radio and the papers were full of news about the growing civil rights and anti-war movements and Hood had misgivings about strolling the streets of Harlem, a white man with a pronounced Southern accent. He had read things about the Black Panthers and Malcolm X and Muhammad Ali joining the Nation of Islam. Until he could find out more about Northern cities, he couldn't see getting back home from Vietnam in one piece only to get taken-out by some angry militants in the Negro section of New York City or by some anti-war hippie mob. And as for having Rick visit Clemson, even his own father wouldn't go for having a Negro house guest. Some men he knew had witnessed lynchings not that many years ago for transgressions of a code of behavior that Singleton knew nothing about. So how could they be friends once they were out of the service? They could meet in Philadelphia or D.C. and hang out together, but that sounded more like "establishing liaison with an intelligence source" than a real friendship. Maybe it just wouldn't be possible back home.

Let somebody else do this poor folks' campaign, Hood prayed, *somebody who is not a friend of mine.*

3

3 April – 3 September 1968

SINGLETON'S REVEILLE

Each bounce up the veranda steps caved in the top of Single-ton's fragile skull. The only son of a well-known pastor could do nothing on the streets of Harlem—good or bad—that did not get immediately reported on the grapevine. So he learned early-on to be, or appear to be, as virtuous as Caesar's wife and later, at private schools and at Yale, he came to understand that his white classmates could be degenerate and popular at the same time. As "an example of his race," he could not. Besides, the drinking life never appealed to him. He preferred to be in control of himself and his surroundings. The friends he made at Fort Greyhawk were by far the most alcoholic he had ever chosen to run with, and he drank only enough to fit in.

Last night had been the exception. Major Shimazu's farewell party enticed him to indulge in four gin and tonics followed by a series of champagne toasts followed by the bull session on the still-warm sands. Strong Australian beers were handed around the half circle while Braxton Hood asked each of them in turn what direction they thought their lives would take when they returned to The World. That question was a challenge for him because he always tried to avoid explaining Harlem culture to his white friends. He found it irritating that people for whom he had respect didn't know that Otis Redding was black, or they liked Johnny Mathis but never heard of Lou Rawls, or as in last night's case, they were totally ignorant of Dr. King's Poor People's Campaign. As a consequence, four Tooheys poured over the other contents of his stomach last night gave him a colossal and well-earned hangover.

Singleton placed both hands on his head, pressing down firmly to keep his skull from exploding as the intense glare of Bravo, Juliet! pierced him through, even with his eyes tight-shut. When he was finally able to squint, he saw that every light in the place was on, just as during Shimazu's party. The large establishment was empty save for a dozen adolescent boys, a pack of roughneck war orphans called "cowboys" in pidgin English, playing a card game. As he came through the open door, they leapt to their feet and advanced on him, stop-sign palms up, pointing for him to go back outside, chattering Vietnamese commands. In no condition to win a bilingual argument, he retreated toward the beach but then decided to attempt a bribe. He dug into his front pants pocket for his wallet (no man who rode New York subways used a rear pocket) and pulled out, even better, the key to his upstairs room. He held the Bravo, Juliet! tag out for the youngsters to see, and at once they softened their voices and made gestures of welcome. They escorted him to the base of the stairway and waved him good night, smiling up at him like a page from a middle-school yearbook.

Singleton slipped into his room, grabbed his Dopp Kit and carried it quietly to the bathroom shared by all second-floor guests. He chased four aspirins with several glasses of water, washed his face, brushed his teeth, and combed as much sand out of his soft, curly hair as he could. He returned the Dopp Kit to his suitcase and dropped across his bed, praying that his headache would be better and he'd be able to eat something when he met Major Cardenas at breakfast in a few hours' time. But rolling around on the sagging bed, trying to find some escape from his throbbing head and the nausea churning his guts, memories of his four terrifying months at Xuan Song Rubber Plantation came to haunt him, reliving scene-by-scene those weeks when sudden death hung over him and the lingering puzzle of why he and his colleague, Le Duc, were spared. All of it worked on him together to create perfect misery and something happened for the first time since childhood. He wept. The disciplined actor gave over to genuine sobs—not the display he had mastered for the stage but a wave of overwhelming emotions: grief for the loss of his beautiful friend, Margot Guignon, guilt for having survived, fear he had been holding in check for months.

When daylight and the stirring of others awoke him three hours later, the last thing he wanted was food, but he had agreed to break-fast with Major Cardenas at 7:00 to receive his next assignment. He tossed aside the sweat-soaked sheet, crawled out from under the mosquito-netting and took his last clean shirt to the shared bathroom where he shaved, trying not to notice his haggard, red eyes in the mirror.

Walking the beach road, Singleton noticed that the spot where the Greyhawk Six had gathered was washed by the tide now, any sign of what had occurred there erased by the sea. As he understood it, his friends had done as he had—they pretended they were spies in a dangerous foreign country until they came to accept that they were just-that. Then, last night, the spell was broken by Braxton Hood's asking each of them to project a future for himself. What they had shared for the first time, beyond narratives of prediction, was their insecurities. Each man there had dropped his mask of invulnerability, the necessary fantasy of youthful adventure that death, loss and failure happen to others. Each one cast a horoscope for which the stars would decide the outcome. Singleton had felt his own rehearsed script drop away as he voiced in the dark his deepest hopes for the future. He acted one role with his childhood friends in Harlem, another for his privileged classmates downtown and at Yale, but unveiled his own voice last night and spoke from the heart. Playing "Ted Michaels" would be the last role of his acting career, he told them. From now on, he would be himself.

He arrived early at the café and ordered hot tea, a habit he had acquired at Xuan Song, and held the warm cup against his throbbing temples, carefully sipping, slowly feeling better. The worst time of his life was over now—had ended in last night's catharsis and his confession that he was turning a new page. He just wanted to get through the next six months doing what the other guys were doing, sitting at a desk, typing and filing Information Reports. Maybe he could join Hood and Babineaux here in Vung Tau and spend every evening on the beach. He deserved as much after his narrow escape from death or capture at Xuan Song Plantation.

Major Cardenas came sailing down the sidewalk wearing sunglasses, a printed, pastel shirt and white pants, looking every inch the tourist. Singleton stood and they shook hands.

"Son, I can't tell you how proud I am of you!" Cardenas said, keeping his grasp of Singleton's hand. He beamed with enthusiasm but kept his voice low. "I knew you had the makings, from the first time I saw your work at the school. You're a born actor!"

"I'm a trained actor," Singleton corrected him as they sat down, "but thank you, sir."

"You held your identity for five months, convinced Monsieur

Guignon you represented Goodyear, infiltrated the plantation infrastructure, developed rapport with two high-ranking VC field commanders and reported the presence of large numbers of Viet Cong posing as workers. I'd put you in for a commendation if it wouldn't get me a boot in the ass for running this operation. MACV wants CIA to handle strategic missions like this."

Singleton sensed danger in all this praise. He had just escaped a perilous situation, posing as a Goodyear executive on the thin authority of forged credentials and a few tailor-made suits, speaking high-school French and no Vietnamese and clueless about the international trade in rubber. Any momentary slip in his self-control might have burst the bubble and a trapdoor could have opened under the feet of "Ted Michaels." Monsieur Guignon, the hot-tempered tyrant who lorded it over Xuan Song, would have had him beaten or worse. And the upper-echelon Viet Cong he mixed with over cocktails could decide he was a prize worth taking and drag him across the Cambodian border into hell. He didn't want Major Cardenas' sparkly-eyed enthusiasm to plunge him into some other such dangerous and foolhardy mission.

"I don't think I did all that well, sir, to be honest," Singleton said. "Guignon was a Michelin employee with no authority to make deals with Goodyear. He would have had his goons toss me out on day one if his wife hadn't kept me around so she could practice her English. As for the VC, I didn't establish rapport with them. They established it with me. They wanted to know about American politics, the changing public attitude toward the war. I was the interrogated, not the interrogator. And it was Le Duc who reported that the so-called workers at Xuan Song knew nothing about rubber trees and a lot about combat. Posing as my chauffeur gave him access to the workers and servants and he never let-on he spoke more than a few words of pidgin-English, so they just thought he was one of them."

Cardenas countered, "In either case, two or three more weeks we could have rolled up that whole VC operation, but MACV took months to analyze your reports and Tet knocked them on their butts while they were screwing around with it."

"The VC saved us, you know," Singleton said casually.

"What do you mean?"

"Me and Le Duc. They had two companies of VC infantry at Xuan Song. They put themselves at considerable risk by warning us to get out. I don't know why. They warned us away before Tet started. It would have made more sense, from their perspective, to just put a bullet in us. When they brought the hammer down on Xuan Song, the Guignons were executed and everyone loyal to them, but why the VC sent us packing, I don't understand."

"Because they wanted to sell rubber latex to Goodyear when they took over Xuan Song."

"I don't think they were ever convinced I was Goodyear... they never asked me about business. They spent hours pumping me about The States, the anti-war movement and civil rights, LBJ, what it was like to be black in America... never anything about business. Glad as I am to be alive, it still makes no sense to me. They put a gun to Le Duc's head and ordered him in Vietnamese to drive me back to Saigon."

"We'll find out in time..." Major Cardenas beckoned the waiter and calmly ordered breakfast while terror spread through every limb of Singleton's being. Cardenas glanced expectantly at him while the waiter stood poised, pencil in hand. "What will you have?" Cardenas asked.

"You *cannot* send me back there!!"

Cardenas and the waiter were both startled by this outburst.

"My friend will order later," Cardenas said quietly, sending the waiter on his way.

"What do you mean, 'We'll find out in time'?" Singleton shouted. "The whole place is a VC camp. It's theirs now. I show up there again, Ted Michaels in a business suit, they'll use me for bayonet practice. I'm lucky as hell to be alive today, much less…"

"Keep your voice down, please," Cardenas broke in, "and get a handle on yourself right now! You've got the jitters, that's natural in a tough situation like this. When I was your age, my unit got overrun by the Chinese, at Pusan. I didn't sleep at night for a year afterward, so I know what it feels like, but that's what it means to be a soldier, son. You thought by signing up for Intelligence, you'd never have to face the enemy eyeball-to-eyeball. Well, you've done it and I'm damned proud of you. We have that much in common, except my enemy was firing a rifle at me at the time and yours was asking questions about LBJ over a dinner table. So cut me some slack and calm down."

"Now look, sir, I don't think I've been a coward. I've got friends who fled to Canada rather than serve, but I stepped up when you chose me for the Xuan Song mission. I trained for it and went there. I know what I'm talking about. Things are different up there now. So long as the VC were bringing in troops disguised as 'workers' and caching supplies for Tet, the Guignons and I were a necessary part of their cover. Business as usual. Nothing to see here. But they expected to win the Tet battle. The people were supposed to rise up and chase ARVN and the Americans into the sea. They told Le Duc and me to scram, shot Margot Guignon and her tyrant of a husband against a wall and prepared to rule. Now they're hunkered down at Xuan Song, ready to fight or flee if the 25th Infantry shows up. But if Ted Michaels shows up, he's just a wrench in the works, a risk they don't have to take."

"Taking risks, Mr. Singleton, is what soldiers do. It's what combat troops do every hour of every day. Hundreds of them die each week. You are in a position to greatly advance the war-effort, to save many of their lives by risking your own. That kid hauling his M16 through the paddies is counting on you to do your part. He faces the enemy every day… so must you. His mission is to kill the enemy. Yours is to burrow inside his mind, learn his intentions, reveal his strategy, earn his trust so you can turn your liaison with him into a battle-field advantage. Take that Yale education of yours and the months of training we gave you at Fort Greyhawk and out-fox these men. Will there be another coordinated, Tet-like offensive? When will they strike? What forces do they still have? They ask you about morale in The States? Return the favor: They lost 100,000 troops during Tet, so how's morale holding up in Hanoi and among their troops? Are they still getting well supplied by the Ho Chi Minh Trail?"

"I go asking those questions, they'll know I'm a spy and they'll shoot me then-and-there!"

"You're an American! They may well assume you and Le Duc are spies. But you, yourself, said they chased you back to Saigon before the fighting broke out. When I read your report, I saw just two possibilities: That they bought your cover and want to cut a deal with Goodyear that will bring them much-needed cash because war is damned expensive. Or more likely, they figure you're an agent, prob-ably CIA, and they hope to play cat-and-mouse with you, plant false intelligence through you, that sort of thing. In either case, you're no good to them dead, so sending you back to Xuan Song becomes an acceptable risk from an operational point-of-view.

"From my point-of-view, it's one-way to a dead end."

"Mr. Singleton, you've walked around in tailor-made suits too long, riding in a fine, chauffeur-driven Citroën. You've played the part so well, you think you're Ted Michaels! Time to face-up: You're an E-4 who is on a mission to infiltrate the Xuan Song operation, sniff-out the VC's intentions and level of strength in the area and engage the enemy in dialog. You've succeeded beyond all my expectations so far and you are now in a position to become a unique source of information that could help end this war sooner and in our favor. As your commanding officer, I'm ordering you to put yourself at risk to complete your mission, which could save thousands of American lives."

Rick Singleton slumped down in his chair, feeling nauseated, dehydrated, hung over and terrified. "Jesus" was all he managed to reply to Cardenas' eloquence.

The shiny, black Citroën itself seemed afraid as it crept toward the closed gates barring entrance to the Xuan Song manor house. Instead of being waved-through by a sleepy guard with a carbine slung over his shoulder, as happened many times before Tet, a dozen Vietnamese with AK-47s scrambled about, shouting excitedly through the steel gates at Singleton and his liveried chauffeur, Le Duc.

"They're telling us to wait here," Duke interpreted, his voice flat and calm as usual, which dampened only a little Singleton's growing urge to fling the rear door open and run for his life.

Both the men in the Citroën had been frequent visitors to Xuan Song for months before Tet and they were familiar with the smooth rhythms of its well-ordered day. None of that remained now. The strolling, chatting supervisors and white-suited servants had been replaced by ant-lines of men in peasant black dashing around with solemn purpose. The place had more the look of a teeming military

HQ—because that's clearly what it was. During the Tet battle, Xuan Song had ceased being a rubber plantation covering for a VC base and was now a military base covering as a plantation, with thousands of neglected rubber trees and an elaborate manor house.

At the end of twenty excruciating minutes in the sweltering car, Singleton's suit was sweat-soaked and what little courage he had brought with him was depleted. "Let's go," he ordered his chauffeur.

"I don't think they'd allow that," Duke answered softly, referring to a trio of gate guards whose eyes were locked on the Citroën, rifles poised over their forearms. "Our best move is to do what they tell us." Duke hardly moved his lips as he spoke, maintaining his cover as a servant who spoke only enough pidgin English to take orders from his boss.

Minutes later, a tall, pencil-thin figure in khaki shorts and white shirt appeared on the front porch of the house. He moved quickly, with the alert tension of a fox, barking sharp commands that sent guards scampering. The heavy gates were pulled open and the Citroën was waved into the courtyard. One of the men opened the rear door and the man stepped forward, made a slight, formal bow and offered his hand.

"I apologize for the delay, Mr. Michaels," he said. His tone was friendly, his English good. "It has been a busy morning. Please come in." Another barked command—in marked contrast to the gentle voice he used for English—and guards retrieved Singleton's suitcase from the car and hauled it into the house.

Singleton felt the series of knots that had been tying and re-tying themselves inside his torso begin to unwind as he conceded that this was not how condemned prisoners were spoken to, probably. The tall man helped him climb from the rear seat. "I don't believe we've met," Singleton managed, sounding far more certain than he felt.

"We have not, that's true. But you are familiar… is that the correct word? Familiar? To other people here."

"And you are?"

"I am Vo Danh. You may call me Mr. Vo, if you will. Now follow these men to your quarters and move in with comfort, please. I will call for you when lunch is ready so we may eat together."

Singleton did not move in with comfort, as a pair of armed men, one fore and one aft, led him to what had been the master bedroom for Monsieur and Madam Guignon, dropped his suitcase in the center of the room without ceremony and, as he could hear through the closed door, posted themselves just outside. Through a window beside the four-poster bed, he watched the Citroën being directed down a gravel road, past some out-buildings and out of sight. Nothing belonging to the Guignons remained in the room. Drawers, shelves and a medicine chest were bare. He hung his sweaty suit-jacket, shirt and pants over the doors of a wardrobe to dry and began the long, nervous wait for lunch. "I'm not dead," he reminded himself over and over. "I could be dead but I'm not, so this isn't so bad." One of the guards in the hallway dropped the stock of his AK-47 onto the floor with a thud.

The Guignons' bedroom was a convection oven, the ceiling fan merely re-circulating the heat. Singleton dropped across the bed and felt the morning's fear relent a little. Cardenas had been right. They wanted him alive and his orders were to confront them, to gather useful intelligence from them and build relationships that could be exploited in America's interest. No more dress rehearsals. His Grey-hawk friends were lucky. They sat in offices behind Remingtons, typing and filing reports all day. But it had fallen to him to do live-fire, high-risk espionage. For an hour, he slipped in and out of heat-induced sleep, with images of Mr. Vo threading through his dreams, reaching for his hand, helping him from the car.

When his watch read 10:30, he roused himself from the bed, washed in the bathroom of his friend, Margot Guignon, dried himself on the shower curtain she had used, then forced the ghost of her from his mind as best he could and dressed in his still-damp silk shirt and slacks, leaving the jacket and tie in the wardrobe. He sat in a wicker chair and practiced the details of his cover. He was Theodore Michaels, ambitious up-and-comer in Goodyear's International Division, hoping to steal Xuan Song's business away from Michelin. He had credentials and letters of introduction to prove who he was and he must stick to his story no matter what. If this "primary" cover should ever collapse—if they got Le Duc to turn on him, for instance—then he'd take a knife to his suitcase and slit open the leather, where he would find a new photo ID, press credentials and a contract with *The Baltimore Sun* for a series of articles on French colonialism in Southeast Asia. His name would become Rick Singleton and he will have been using "Ted Michaels" to gain access to Monsieur Guignon at Xuan Song. This "escape" cover would be about as likely to help him as a Mae West in the mid-Atlantic, but it was what he'd been given and being an American soldier out-of-uniform was not an option.

Singleton spent half an hour preparing himself for every imaginable situation or question. Then, needing the distraction, he took Ralph Ellison's new book, *Shadow and Act*, from his suitcase. His father had sent him Ellison's series of reflections on being an American, a Negro and an artist and Singleton had been slogging through it, finding it insightful but ponderous. He had been tempted to skip it but knew his father, the esteemed Reverend John Singleton, would be expecting a thoughtful response to the book from his only son. Singleton read, several times over, Ellison's concept of "Negro culture":

"It is not culture which binds the people who are of partially African origin now scattered throughout the world but an identity of passions. We share a hatred for the alienation forced upon us by Europeans during the process of colonization and empire and we are bound by our common suffering more than by our pigmentation… this identification is shared by most non-white peoples…"

The privilege and wealth of Singleton's family had paved his way from Harlem to elite schools where he was accepted on equal terms by most of his classmates. He never spoke of this adopted world to his Harlem friends, whose speech and interests he mirrored whenever the "A" train brought him home. Had his father sent him Ellison's book to challenge his thinking about his identity as a black man in a white world? If so, that challenge could not possibly have come at a worst time.

The bedroom door flew open and the two sentries beckoned him to come. He was escorted to the dining room, where Vo Danh sat alone at the end of the long table. Mr. Vo stood and beckoned him to take the seat opposite him.

"I have looked forward to meeting you for a long time," he told Singleton, "and I have many questions I wish to ask you. But today, I think it would be best for us to eat quietly together and afterwards, there is something I must tell you."

Attendants, men in peasant dress, served the meal, as uniformed servants had done when the French were in charge. Where there had been courses of French cuisine and flowing wines served to lively guests, there now was rice with chicken and a pot of tea brought to two men who ate in silence. Tet had come and gone and made Mr. Vo the new master of Xuan Song. Singleton studied Vo Danh's unhurried grace, his calm self-possession. The rooms and corridors around them were buzzing with activity and twice an attendant carried in a note for Mr. Vo, which was placed beside his place-mat. Vo Danh would glance at it, then stuff it into his breast pocket without setting down his chop sticks. By meal's end, Singleton had formed the opinion that Mr. Vo was probably about his father's age and, like The Reverend Singleton, one tough, disciplined customer, always in complete control.

When they'd finished, Mr. Vo nodded and the attendants pulled back their chairs and opened the doors to the veranda. They stepped into the oppressive heat of a tropical noon-sun. Singleton waved off the cigarette that Mr. Vo offered him. "Thank you, I don't smoke," were the first words spoken in half an hour.

Vo Danh lit one, took a long drag, and turned, reaching out to take Singleton's left hand in his right—a gesture of familiarity common among Vietnamese men but taboo among Americans. Singleton fought an intense impulse to snatch his hand away while a shiver of discomfort ran up his spine. He resigned his face and hand, showing Vo Danh nothing of his feelings, while the other held Singleton's gaze as firmly and steadily as his hand. "When I am your age," he began quietly, "I lose my father at Dien Bien Phu. I love and respect my father very much, then and now, and I suffer very much after that. But then the French surrender and we win independence and that help me. My father dies so our people can be free of colonial oppression, free of the French. In this war too…" Vo Danh paused, struggling to choose the right words, "I lose my brother, Thu, and many other friends. Do you lose friends in this war also?"

Singleton tried to keep his hand steady and his face calm. "No, sir, I have not. No one who is close to me."

Vo Danh took a drag off his cigarette, releasing a cloud of smoke into the breeze. "I tell you these things because I want you to know I understand about death… about violent death of someone you love."

"I'm glad you told me," Singleton managed, feeling fear about where this was going. Perhaps they shot Le Duc… or?

"I must tell you sad news…sad news for me also. They have

killed the leader of your people... this morning... a few hours ago. I'm sorry."

The horror of the Zapruder film leapt through his mind. First President Kennedy and now, "President Johnson is dead?" he asked aloud.

"No, my friend... your people, not your government. Reverend King, who leads the struggle of your people against colonial oppression. I'm very sorry."

You're LYING! Singleton wanted to shout, *That is a Commie lie to twist me around while I'm a prisoner here of you and your armed goons...* He pulled his hand out of Mr. Vo's grasp and glared at him.

"I'm sorry," Vo Danh repeated, "too much death."

Singleton felt pounded by rage, fear, denial—but not grief. Grief was the part taken by Vo Danh, whose eyes glistened with tears. Singleton followed Mr. Vo's beckoning on numb legs into the house, down the corridor, into the library, where he was motioned into Monsieur Guignon's overstuffed wing chair. A familiar voice filled the room with announcements from Armed Forces Radio about a sanitation workers' strike in Memphis, Tennessee, a balcony of the Lorraine Motel, Reverend King was shot by person or persons unknown shortly after 6:00 p.m. and was pronounced dead at 7:05 local time, 7:05 this morning, Saigon time. Singleton slumped in the big chair, his eyes squeezed tight-shut. The words spread through him, reviving vivid scenes of Dr. King and his wife sitting at his parents' table at home, the deep resonance of that famous baritone carrying everyone's spirits before it, filling the room with serenity, hope and warmth. Dr. King's laughter in private conversation, a contrast to the public man of stubborn defiance and indignant outrage, was a treasured memory given to the Singleton family. Buried in Singleton's belongings stored back at SIC HQ was the letter from his father, urging him to "turn your enormous gifts over to The Poor People's Campaign and devote your-self to Dr. King's righteous cause for a more fulfilling life than acting can ever afford you."

He pushed himself out of the depths of the wing chair and announced, "I'm going to be sick." But Mr. Vo had gone. He was alone in the room except for the voice on the radio repeating the same nightmare over and over again. So he climbed the stairs back to his room, trailed by the pair of guards, to spend the worst day of his life tossing over and back on the Guignons' bed in insufferable heat, seeking some sort of resolution to the incomprehensible.

"What am I *doing* here?" he prayed aloud. "What the *fuck* am I *doing* here?"

When the worst of the afternoon heat had passed, Vo Danh tapped quietly on Singleton's door and invited him to take a walk "for both of our sakes," he said. Not prepared for conversation, much less debate, Singleton was greatly relieved when Mr. Vo offered none. The two strolled side-by-side in a leisurely pace up a long, steep incline between straight, orderly rows of rubber trees until they stood at some height above the manor house. Circling the manor were large, stucco buildings where white latex from the bleeding trees had been processed into flat sheets of dripping rubber, drying on miles of racks. They stood some distance apart, in silence, until darkness began to overtake the scene, then Vo Danh started back and Singleton followed.

Vo Danh spoke when he took leave of Singleton at the door of his room. First, he barked a sharp command which sent the two sentries away. Then he said softly to Singleton, "I am very sorry for your loss, Mr. Michaels."

"Yes, sir," Singleton replied, "Thank you, Mr. Vo."

The following four months of Rick Singleton's residence at Xuan Song with Vo Danh marked the soul-defining epicenter of his year in Vietnam. As his trust grew that he was not going to be summarily executed, he came to understand that he was not only worth more alive than dead to the enemy but worth much more to them than Major Cardenas had guessed. Vo Danh and Singleton spent hours together each afternoon. And since it was, after all, Singleton's assigned mission to "develop rapport with and understanding of the enemy, to establish liaison and discover his strengths and weaknesses," Vo Danh made that very easy.

For the first three weeks, they took their simple lunch together in the library while Armed Forces Radio told them that Washington D.C. was in flames, with 1200 buildings set ablaze, mobs attacking fire fighters, troops in the streets, and machine gun emplacements on the steps of the Capitol. Mr. Vo had many questions: "Why do your people burn-down their own neighborhoods? Why not burn where rich, white people live? What are the goals of their rebellion? Who speaks for them?"

Singleton had few answers for him. "It's not a rebellion. It's just blind rage over Dr. King and from years of discrimination," seemed inadequate, even as he said it. He wanted to say, *Stop calling them "my" people. Those are not "my" people.* But he feared being asked, *Whose people are they, then? Weren't your ancestors slaves too?*

"Colonial oppression of non-white peoples!" was Mr. Vo's mantra, which derailed any kind of effective rebuttal from Singleton because it echoed so closely the passage from Ralph Ellison that he had memorized from the book his father had sent him. "What your people need is Marxist discipline! We Vietnamese have been beaten and harnessed like water buffalo by every colonial power. Now we have Marxist discipline and we can fight back against the oppressor! Your people need coherent ideology to focus your revolutionary energy!" Vo Danh argued, and Singleton felt a flash of anger and embarrassment that "his people" were smashing into liquor stores and appliance shops instead of organizing as Dr. King would have had them do.

Next it was Chicago, where hundreds were arrested and Mayor Richard Daley issued "shoot-to-kill" orders in the case of looters. "Where is the war, Mr. Michaels?" Vo Danh asked. "You are sitting here with me in Vietnam while government soldiers are fighting against your people in Chicago! Would you like me to pour you some more tea?" and he passed the tea-pot over, laughing.

Then it was Baltimore, where the National Guard came at crowds with fixed bayonets. Then Detroit, Kansas City, New York, Pittsburgh, Trenton, Wilmington and Cincinnati, the last of which was used by Mr. Vo to challenge "Ted Michaels." "Cincinnati very close to your home, right?" Vo said quietly, as an aside. And Singleton, with a fork raised to his lips, almost said "Nowhere near" before catching himself—an employee of Goodyear Tire and Rubber of Akron. "Yes, it is," he mumbled.

None of this terrible news was made easier for Singleton by Vo Danh's haughtiness about it. Vietnam had suffered violence and mayhem for generations—was still suffering—and now the high-and-mighty United States was getting a little of it back. Singleton had no effective defense against the arguments of a Marxist purist with well-rehearsed ideology and glib answers for everything. "Have you been to riots like these?" he asked.

"Me, personally? No! I stay far away from trouble like that."

"Good... very smart of you," Mr. Vo said, "because your people will never defeat the oppressor by stealing televisions. They must organize, like we have. They must have..."

"I know... Marxist discipline," Singleton anticipated.

When news from The States began to calm down, Mr. Vo brought two copies of a book to lunch, *Soul on Ice* by Eldridge Cleaver. "For many years, I study American history and culture. Very difficult for me to understand. But now you here so I ask you to help me. This new book, will you read it to me after lunch?"

It was Singleton's mission to establish liaison with the enemy and get inside his head so this was playing right into his hands. Perfect! Why then, did he wish for Le Duc to pull the Citroën into the driveway and take him away from all this, immediately? No such escape happened and for the next month, he read *Soul on Ice* aloud to Mr. Vo while the latter followed along line-by-line in his own copy but with many interruptions.

"Why you think Mr. Cleaver rape white women?"

"I don't know... Let's read more and find out."

"You and your friends rape white women?"

"Good God no! We don't rape anyone, ever!" Singleton shouted. "Almost never..."

"Mr. Cleaver say that all the suffering of Vietnamese peasants cancels out his debt to society for all his crimes."

"That makes no sense. What does one have to do with the other?"

"Still," Vo Danh took a sip of tea and scratched his chin, "I like he say that. I think some Americans like Dr. King understand colonial oppression and know we fight for our freedom. Don't you see white colonial oppression of all non-white people as world-struggle we all must fight together?"

"No, I don't," Singleton said firmly, ignoring the echo of Ellison's words that went rolling through his mind.

"But Dr. King fought against oppression of your people and you said…"

"Mr. Vo! Stop! I'm an American first-and-foremost! I'm a black American too, but we have fought for our country in all our wars, as patriotic citizens. America has to move toward freedom and justice as a whole, blacks and whites all together, see?"

"I see." Vo Danh was silent for a long minute, then added, "I see you very nice young man, but you co-opted. Oppressors give you bad education, make you think like oppressor, same-same white ruler who come over here, make war on us."

Singleton glared across the table at Vo Danh, who was blowing clouds of blue cigarette smoke toward the ceiling. A knot of anger and frustration choked the young man's throat and threatened to bring tears to his eyes, but he managed it by dissecting his adversary: How old was this Vo Danh? 50? 60? Where did he learn English? What were his weak spots? How could he, Singleton, get the upper hand in this debate and turn this stubborn, hard-core Communist into a double agent who would work on the side of democracy for political freedom and economic justice for "his people"?

"Have you ever read the Gettysburg Address?" Singleton asked Mr. Vo.

Fortunately for Singleton, the later pages of *Soul on Ice* softened the tone of their lunch conversations, as Eldridge Cleaver fell head-over-heels in love with his white defense attorney, Beverly Axelrod, and divisions within the black Muslim movement forced him to broaden his thinking. As Cleaver traced the development of his own maturity, Singleton and Vo Danh found ideas they held in common. They laughed at Cleaver's image of bald and crew-cut older men sharing a dance floor with mop-haired youngsters dancing the frug, the swim and the Watusi, dance-moves that Singleton demonstrated for Vo Danh. They agreed that the growth of monopoly and oligarchy were problems for any economic system, no matter what principles it began with. Vo Danh began to show more latitude: He admitted that "equality" in North Vietnam meant that nobody had much, including rights guaranteed in the U.S. Constitution, and he conceded that Singleton had the right to refer to all Americans as "his" people so long as Vo Danh could consider South Vietnam to be "his" country. The combat soldiers fighting on both sides, they agreed, were equally courageous, skillful and devoted to their side's cause. Over these many weeks of lunch debates, Singleton fought against any feelings of affection for his Communist adversary. He had been taught that Intelligence agents are con-artists, employing human emotions to gain advantage. But he had to admit that Vo Danh's persistence about race relations in America went beyond being a weapon he used on Singleton. His curiosity was genuine. He really wanted to understand America, as difficult as that was to do—even for Singleton.

The complex relationship that developed over these months of daily engagement might never have gone beyond an ideological chess match had it not been for the evening walks around the sprawling plantation. Singleton's mornings were long and boring, as he sprawled across the bed in his sweltering room, working his way with little interest through a stack of books assigned to him by Mr. Vo: James Baldwin, Malcolm X, Norman Mailer's *White Negro* and the like, all fodder for their lengthy lunch debates. But the evening strolls were the high points of Singleton's days. He carried an umbrella because monsoon season brought heavy rain most evenings, while Vo

Danh wore a broad-rimmed campaign hat and never seemed to mind being soaked through. The two men never spoke about politics then, but about everything else. At first, Singleton was wary that Vo Danh would use this time to probe his cover; however, "Mr. Michaels" was never asked about his work, Goodyear, or really much of anything else. Vo Danh, on the other hand, was surprisingly forthcoming about himself: His large, extended family had been merchants in and around Hanoi, but he found business too boring in his youth and so joined the Nationalists and spent years fighting the French and rising through the ranks. After Dien Bien Phu and the loss of his father, fighting was fierce between Nationalist and Communist units in the newly divided nation. Vo Danh came over to the Communist side at some point and was rewarded with a two-year stay in Moscow, where he learned English and "many other things about the world." He struggled with English, he said, but his Russian was very good. When what he called "the American war" began, he was assigned to interrogate enemy fliers who were prisoners-of-war. But over time the interrogation techniques he had learned in Moscow were discarded in favor of physical torture, which Vo Danh rejected as ineffective, so he asked to be reassigned and had been working in the South ever since, contacting businessmen and contractors who might be sympathetic to the cause of national unity and the end of colonial rule and might also be useful after the end of the war.

So, there it was. They often walked in silence, some distance apart, but would stop somewhere that was sheltered from the rain or held a scenic view of the manor house for a talk that would reveal another piece of the Vo Danh puzzle—until he had placed his personal story on the table, card by card, face up, in violation of every tenet taught about intelligence work at Fort Greyhawk. He wore no mask—and had not tried to probe Singleton's. He was a Moscow-trained agent working to recruit sympathizers to the Communist cause and the lunch debates were exactly what they appeared to be—indoctrination of a young, black American. Singleton knew from his own training that he would eventually be asked to perform certain tasks or—and this suspicion never left him—disposed of as a failed experiment and someone who knew too much about Vo Danh.

Nevertheless, the elixir of biochemistry is not subject to the conscious will. Over the days and weeks and months during which Vo Danh, who held all the power, was Singleton's only human contact, bonds of what could only be called "friendship" grew between them. Vo Danh had devoted his entire life to the cause of his nation's liberty—as a combat soldier, as a Nationalist then as a Communist. Singleton gradually acceded this view to his adversary: That the Communist Party was his means to end foreign interference in Vietnam. If Singleton wanted to argue that justice and equal treatment for non-white Americans could be achieved by organized political protest, education, the ballot-box and the court system, that was just fine with Vo Danh. If Vietnam could be made free of foreign control by treaty negotiations, that would be fine too. Vo Danh's core argument was that these gentler persuasions had been tried and failed, so that all-out warfare and Marxist discipline were the only effective tools left to bring freedom and justice to peoples who had been colonized.

During the four months of their intellectual jousting, Americans and Vietnamese were dying in greater numbers than at any previous period of the war. From the hilltop overlooking the manor house, they witnessed air strikes and heard artillery barrages, swarms of helicopters flew over and convoys roared down the highway near Xuan Song. By night, their sleep was disturbed by the thunder of B-52s, carpet-bombing the forests of Cambodia, not many miles away, while small arms fire often crackled in the darkness outside. Singleton often reflected on the irony that if this was a war "for the hearts and minds of the Vietnamese," then he was here, within the confines of a French colonial plantation, fighting that war eye-to-eye with Vo Danh, while all around him, savage exchanges of violence were deciding the outcome common to all wars: Who, in the end, would hold the ground.

The proof that Singleton and Vo Danh had "established liaison" came one sweltering afternoon in mid-July. Singleton had dozed off on his sweat-soaked bed with a copy of *The Autobiography of Malcolm X* across his chest. He was startled awake by an unfamiliar figure looming over him: It was Mr. Vo wearing peasant black silk and a conical hat. "Mr. Michaels, the Americans are here," he whispered, "I need your help."

Singleton threw on slacks and shirt and followed Vo Danh downstairs and through the foyer to the driveway. The half-dozen guards who normally toted AK-47s were nowhere to be seen, the gates hung wide open and GIs were piling out of a deuce-and-a-half truck and a jeep. Singleton crossed his arms and leaned on the doorframe, striking as casual a pose as he could.

While wary troops fanned out across the premises, M16s ready, a young officer with black captain's stripes on his helmet approached. "I want to see Mr. Gueeno," he barked.

Vo Danh, slouched down in the obsequious posture of the servant, the conical hat hiding his face, whispered "Saigon" into Singleton's back.

"Monsieur and Madam Guignon are in Saigon," Singleton announced.

"Yeah… right," The captain's sarcasm was easy to discern. "Well the French Embassy people think he's gone missing and by the way, who the hell are you?"

"I'm a civilian contractor for MACV, assigned to make a settlement with Monsieur Guignon." Singleton presented the captain with a photo ID of Theodore Michaels, GS-11, contractor for the Military Assistance Command, Vietnam. "The last time you guys paid this plantation a visit, you destroyed a lot of Monsieur Guignon's valuable rubber trees and he wishes to be compensated for them."

"And you think he's in Saigon…"

"Left two weeks ago," Singleton ad-libbed, "Asked me to keep an eye on things."

"Smells fishy to me, cap'm." The gristle-faced master sergeant at the captain's shoulder was glancing from the ID photo to Singleton's face and back again. "I peg this Negro for a deserter."

The captain placed his right hand on the butt of his side-arm. "I think my sergeant has a point here," he told Singleton, "Tell me why Mr. Gueeno would turn his ranch over to a colored boy?"

"He didn't," Singleton said with precision, "He asked me to supervise the operation in his absence, and I'm a MACV contractor whose GS-11 rank is equivalent to yours, captain."

"I still say deserter," the sergeant growled.

The captain handed Singleton the ID card and said, "You and your chink-friend mind if we have a look around?"

The rifle platoon searched every inch of the manor house and everywhere in the out-buildings of the rubber-latex operation, finding only dozens of peasants sweating under the burden of their work. More than half the men and women they saw were combat veterans of the 271st Regiment, but the Americans had no way of knowing that and it was better for all concerned that they didn't find it out because behind the forest fringe of the manor-house clearing a large force of armed VC lay hidden, watching for the attack signal from Vo Danh.

When the platoon had remounted and driven away, Vo Danh removed his cone-hat and said, "No one called me 'chink' since I was interrogating prisoners!"

"He called me a 'colored boy,' the racist prick."

"Colonial oppressor racist prick," Vo Danh amended, throwing an arm around Singleton's shoulders as they walked back inside, and he chuckled in relief that the confrontation had ended without bloodshed and that his student had performed so well.

During that evening's walk, they climbed to a spot where the whole of Xuan Song was spread out below. "This a big operation," Vo Danh said.

"Yes, it is."

"Takes lots of man-power, make it work."

Singleton nodded, fully aware of where this opening move was headed.

"Your grandfather, maybe he works on a big plantation like this one, yes?"

"No, not my grandfather. But my family back before him, maybe, sure."

"And now, you big-time businessman with a chauffeur."

Singleton said nothing, protecting any connection with Le Duc other than as his servant.

"You might still work on plantation, like your ancestors, except for an army from The North came down to The South to free the slaves from their oppressors, yes?"

"I understand what you're saying, Mr. Vo, but that wasn't the same thing." Singleton fished around in his head for what distinguished the Civil War from the "American war" in Vietnam, but there was the Xuan Song Plantation in the valley below, teeming with peasant workers who were not much better off than antebellum slaves, so he was relieved when Vo Danh changed the topic.

"My unit can't stay here," he said, "The Americans will come back in force when they can't find Guignon."

Singleton took a risk then, pressing a subject they had never spoken of. "So, you don't think Guignon is in Saigon… or fled to France?"

Vo Danh puffed at his cigarette for some moments, then confessed, "I was told by my predecessor at Xuan Song, the man you knew as Gia Trang, that you and Madam Guignon were friends, perhaps even lovers."

"No! We were good friends… but not lovers!"

"You tried to save her, I was told, to take her to Saigon with you when fighting broke out here at Tet."

"That's true. I did beg her to leave."

"Let's walk then," Vo Danh suggested. He led Singleton into an uncleared area of forest in the northwest corner of the estate, a mile from the manor house. Singleton was not unaware of where they were headed, but he didn't find the courage to say, "Stop… I don't want to know…" because he did want to know. Where brush had been cleared between trees, the earth rose over an area thirty feet square. Rubber-tree leaves lay in deep layers here, without rubber trees nearby.

"The decision was not mine, when we came here," Mr. Vo said quietly. Then he turned and walked back toward the manor house, telling Singleton over his shoulder, "Come back when you are ready."

But the young man did not stay long—just long enough to remember her beautiful face, her gently accented English and eager curiosity about all things American—and to imagine her dying here in this place that she loved and refused to leave, with the husband she had chosen for better and for worse. "So much death," he whispered to the forest, echoing Mr. Vo's often repeated phrase. "Too much death."

Their lunch discussion the next day, Friday, 23 July 1968, was their last.

Singleton carried his copy of *Malcolm X* to the table and opened it to the book-marked page, but Vo Danh raised a hand and told him, "Not today… today we must talk of other matters." A bottle of Monsieur's Sauvignon Blanc sat between them and Vo Danh proceeded to pour the first alcoholic drinks these rivals—if that's what they were—ever shared. He raised his stemmed glass in Singleton's direction: "Let us drink a toast to peace," he said.

Singleton tipped his glass and responded, "Hear, Hear!"

Mr. Vo swallowed and said, "Peace will come. The Americans cannot stay forever. Their losses are great and they grow weary of this war. The Saigon regime is not popular and our side will never stop. When peace comes.…" He drank from his wineglass and settled back in his chair looking, for the first time, contented and at ease.

Singleton drank, ignoring the bowl of soup before him. "And then, when the war is over, Mr. Vo, then what?"

"Why… then China will invade us, of course, before we can recover our strength, and we will ask Russia for help, which will upset the Americans and they will come back!" Vo Danh broke out in rolling laughter at his own dark humor, unlike anything Singleton had seen him do in their months together. He raised his glass and between bouts of cynical laughter said, "So let us drink to peace!"

Singleton tried to imagine what life must be like for this man: A 360-degree panorama of danger, war, loss, death, images of corpses, of wailing peasant women and villages burned by one side then by the other, French invaders then Japanese then French again then American and next the Chinese until—long after he was dead-and-gone, the unimaginable promise of peace.

Vo Danh refilled both glasses. "We must not hurry today, my friend. We must use this time to talk together." He drank from the wine, ignoring his meal, and offered, "If I believe someday my people will be their own masters... that they will own Xuan Song Plantation collectively and profit from it as the French have... then do you believe your people will see such a time in America when they have prosperity and authority the same as white men have?"

"I can believe that... I *do* believe that... yes!"

"And you believe coming here to fight us brings that day closer for your people?"

"We have always served our country in time of war..."

"As your people have done in all your many wars."

"Yes, and conditions for us have improved. Race relations in the United States are better than they were before the..."

A blast of cynical laughter cut Singleton off. "We sat together," Vo Danh said, "and listened to your people celebrating equality and justice in Detroit and Baltimore and even in Washington D.C. where they set everything on fire."

"That was anger because Dr. King was..."

"Yes, and because his killer was not found at that time. But now that he has been caught in Europe with a fake passport, do you not concede he has been helped by those in power?" Vo Danh lit a cigarette, blowing a cloud of blue smoke. "You very intelligent man, Mr. Michaels," he said, "but they teach you bad history and you think like the white oppressor wants you to. Your people need leaders like you to teach them how to win freedom through strength and unity. Not to go begging like dogs..."

"With all due respect, Mr. Vo, you need to understand..."

Vo Danh shouted, "Listen to me! We debate enough! Remember what I tell you! You will return home and see that I am right. You will be treated badly by white man. He will never respect you because he does not fear you. But one day, a man will ask you, 'Are you a friend of Vo Danh?' That man will be there to help you and your people in their struggle. Remember! 'Are you a friend of Vo Danh?'"

When no one tapped on his door that evening to invite him out for a stroll, Singleton ventured down to the terrace. The corridors of the manor house were deserted and just a handful of peasants, mostly women, worked around the rubber-latex buildings. They had gone, Vo Danh and his combat unit. They had begun their night-march toward their next encampment.

Waiting in the driveway, beside the Citroën, was Le Duc, or what was left of him. He had shed fifty pounds, so that his chauffeur's livery hung off his frame like a shawl. Singleton nearly shouted "Duke!" before catching himself. He walked casually toward the car until he stood near enough to whisper, "What the hell happened to you? Come into the house, man!"

"We're getting out of here right now!" Le Duc pleaded, "I can't stay here another second!" For appearance's sake, should anyone be watching, the chauffeur held his master's door then got behind the wheel and drove them through the open gate of Xuan Song Plantation. On the drive toward Saigon, it became clear that the Vietnamese-American was no longer the resolute, veteran Intelligence agent who had always been a calming influence on Singleton. Nguyen Le Duc's courage had abandoned him in these four months. Gone was his tempered baritone. In an odd, shrill voice, he sang-out the story of his captivity: "From day one they knew more about me than my own family! I played dumb for a couple weeks, speaking only in peasant

Viet and pidgin-English while they detailed all my CIA operations, complete with the cover-names of my colleagues and contacts, and my work for Army Intel. They knew what courses I'd taken at USC, for chrissakes! They knew what *grades* I got! When they got fed-up with my lies, they kicked my ribs in and withheld my lousy bowl of rice—a staple of the Asian diet, incidentally, I never want to see again for the rest of my life! I finally just came clean with them, assuming that would be it. They could have shot me anytime, so I tried to pitch them to be a double-agent. I told them I resigned the CIA because I couldn't stand working for the corrupt pigs of the rotten Saigon regime, that my heart was with the reunification of my native Vietnam and my people. I pointed-out that I'm completely bilingual with a degree from an American university and contacts in the CIA. I would be the best double agent they ever saw! I played this card for days of team-interrogation. I got panicky when I got nothing back! Zero! Nada! I'm looking at them, waiting for the pitch. They're looking back at me like I'm a bad joke! And finally, it occurs to me—it's *YOU* they want, Rick! They are after *you!* I would have been shot five minutes after we arrived if it hadn't been that blowing your chauffeur's brains out would have pissed you off and you were the point of the whole exercise. I was damaged goods, a turn-coat Vietnamese nobody could trust. It all made sense. An African-American kid with an Ivy League education was tabula rasa for them—young and pliable and ready to bend. Tell me that wasn't their pitch to you, man! They treated you like a long-lost cousin for four months while I was chained to an iron bed in the dark with bike-locks around my ankles, barely kept alive just to make you happy…"

"Slow down, Duke!" Singleton yelled from the rear seat, "You drive like this, you're gonna flip the car!"

The warning had no discernible influence on Le Duc, whose

lunatic tenor rose in crescendo: "Let me tell you something, *mein schwarzer Freund*! I'm getting myself a mammoth dinner tonight on the roof of the Caravelle with maybe three bottles of good wine then I'll put up with whatever debriefing Cardenas wants before I'm ripping my contract with the United States Army down the middle and hopping the next flight to California and for the next forty years I'll wake up thanking my lucky stars I'm alive and spend the rest of the day on the beach where I'll never think *even once* about this stinking hell-hole of a country because *life*, Rick, my friend, *LIFE* is *way-way-way* too under-valued by most stupid-assed people!"

"And your life is going to end in a car wreck, Duke!" Singleton shouted back, "if you don't slow the fuck down, NOW!"

On 3 September 1968, Singleton was putting the final touches on his long report to Major Cardenas in the quarters he shared with Nguyen Le Duc at SIC Headquarters. Le Duc's report wasn't nearly so long as Singleton's because being bike-locked to an iron bed in the dark for four months gave him less to report about.

"I'm telling you, you're making a big mistake, man," Duke said.

"Cardenas understands the game," Singleton argued, "He knows me and he knows the situation I was in. He put me there, remember?"

"Sure, Cardenas knows you. But I'm talking about how your report goes down when it leaves here. Higher-ups who never laid eyes on you will read this and say, 'Let's get a copy of this to the FBI. They're gonna want to know about this kid from Harlem who's been infected with the Marxist bug. 'Nothin' worse than a Negro Commie,' they'll say. Look what happened to me when the CIA found out I had relatives who were VC. Didn't matter I'm a California kid, a

USC Trojan who lives to surf. When they looked at me, even guys I'd worked with for years, all they saw was my gook-face and suddenly I was the enemy."

Singleton flipped through the pages of his detailed report, letting his eyes fall on certain exchanges between Mr. Vo and him that—Duke was right—could be taken out of context by men who didn't know him, white FBI agents in suits—men Vo Danh called oppressors—who might see only his black face and decide he was the enemy. He asked Duke to loan him his lighter and went outside to burn the pages of his report.

"Atta boy! Now you're showing some good sense," Duke called after him.

The report Singleton would submit to Cardenas would be much shorter and lacking in detail… lots and lots of detail.

Late in the night, a man leaned his elbows on the edge of a frail field table. Rain pounded the canvas above his head; a kerosene lamp lit the blank page before him. When his cigarette had burned down, he tossed it, took up his pen and wrote in Russian:

Top Secret

Eyes Only: KGB Department NS 54—Sub-Section 1115

Reporting: #7091

Preliminary recruitment of Corporal Richard Singleton has concluded with Level Two assessment. Corporal Singleton is highly intelligent but indoctrinated in capitalist and democratic patterns of thought and other illusions. His awareness of being a member of an oppressed minority is growing, along with his sympathy for the proletariat. He will develop as a valuable resource for operations in the

United States under these recommended conditions: 1) Initial contact must be made at a time when he is vulnerable, when the oppressors have stirred passions in him through personal loss, as in the case of Dr. King's murder; 2) He must be given sufficient time to develop trust in his control agent through Levels Three and Four; and 3) His control agent must use the Recognition Signal, "Are you a friend of Vo Danh?" It is a phrase he is conditioned to expect and is innocuous, as "Vo Danh" means in Vietnamese "Anonymous."

4

3 April – 4 July 1968

FOR GOD'S SAKE, MULCAHEY!

An hour after Rick Singleton left the beach, Braxton Hood watched with fascination as the sky began to erase all but the brightest stars, left-to-right across the horizon, and the breeze picked up steadily. The waves that had lapped his friends to sleep hours before retreated with the tide and were now barely audible. Hood became aware of whispering to his right, from Mulcahey and Levesque, and as their voices grew louder, he recognized the familiar duet of Mad-dog's tenor sarcasm answered by Levesque's calm, baritone counterpoint. These two were a puzzlement. The alliance they had forged in the misery of wintertime basic training at Fort Campbell had been sustained through seven months of intense field exercises at Fort Greyhawk during the heat of summer. Actively seeking each other out, they played a game in which Mulcahey's intentional and persistent mockery was hurled against the bastion of Levesque's serious nature and deep devotion to his religious beliefs. Hood wondered why they didn't just avoid each other. But the conflict seemed to energize them both. Perhaps it was a performance to entertain their friends, or merely a distraction from the boredom and anxiety of life in the Army, Hood figured.

The two had lost contact in Vietnam for four months, with Mulcahey assigned to III Corps HQ, Saigon, and Levesque taken under Major Cardenas' wing for a special assignment: To present himself as a Jesuit brother from the Diocese of Quebec, offering his services to the Archdiocese of Saigon as an errand of mercy in time of war. Levesque, who was fluent in French, carried a very convincing "Letter of Introduction" forged by document specialists, as well as all the accoutrements necessary for a successful infiltration of the Catholic hierarchy. It was Cardenas' idea that he would learn a great deal from his fellow clerics, who had a ready-made network of 1.1 million parishioners and close ties to high-ranking officials in the predominantly Catholic Saigon government. For months, Cardenas received reports from Levesque that were promising but vague, and he harbored a growing disappointment based on the lack of any specifics. Following the Tet Offensive, "Brother Andre" (Levesque's cover name) had been transferred from the parish church at Me Duc Tin in Tay Ninh Province to the Cathedral Church of Notre Dame in Saigon. He was now at the very heart of Catholic activity in Vietnam. He frequently spoke with the Archbishop of Saigon and priests from all over the country. Levesque's penetration of the church hierarchy had been a success! Why then, Cardenas wondered, had he not turned over one significant piece of useful intelligence, political, tactical or strategic?

The answer to Major Cardenas' question was a simple one: In the first two hours on assignment as Brother Andre, Levesque confessed to the French-speaking priest of Me Duc Tin that he was an intelligence agent for the American Army. A wise man—and absolutely desperate for an assistant—the aged priest congratulated Brother Andre for his honesty and devotion to the church, and he began the process of making him a Deacon. From that time until Tet forced his evacuation, Brother Andre labored night and day in service to the people of Me Duc Tin Parish. He was a godsend to Father Martin and the subject of discreet gossip among the clergy, so that at the time of his transfer to the cathedral, everyone understood he reported to the American military but that his heart remained with the Holy Mother Church. They assigned Brother Andre to lead the choir of orphan boys and Levesque, for his part, carried out his assignment with energy and diligence. He even recruited a talented American to be the boys' pianist.

That pianist, John Francis Mulcahey, meanwhile, continued to deserve the moniker "Mad-dog." To describe his conduct in just the previous six months: He had side-swiped a military ambulance while behind the wheel of Braxton Hood's Citroën (causing III Corp's second-in-command, Lieutenant Aaronson, to discharge a .45 caliber slug into his own boot, ending what had been a promising military career.) He had driven a powder-blue ("civilian-cover") jeep into the teeth of the Tet battle (because it was his turn to do the grocery shopping) and narrowly escaped death when nervous defenders at the main gate of Tan Son Nhut Air Base shot his vehicle to pieces (in what may have been an excess of caution on their parts—but combat situations do stir adrenaline). To his credit, he had returned to III Corps HQ with the groceries—but on a bicycle. Further, he spent many nights thereafter riding his bike through the streets and back alleys of war-time Saigon, dusk-to-dawn, out of loneliness and existential despair over not finding what he wanted, whatever that was (perhaps to have Jack Kennedy finishing up his second term). These excursions ended when happenstance led him to the Cathedral of Notre Dame one early morning to discover his best friend, Rene Levesque, disguised as a priest, conducting a choir of boys from the Catholic orphanage.

From that day on, Mulcahey—whose mastery of Broadway and Big Band songs was impressive—served as an accompanist for the choir. Mulcahey had found the outlet he needed for the excess fire in his blood, and Levesque felt that God had delivered the means for him to lead a choir, something for which he had no previous experience. It was a "match made in Heaven," as they say.

They worked the boys hard, six evenings a week, until they were ready to provide Sunday masses with high-pitched chants and responses in Latin and Vietnamese that echoed beautifully in the vaulted sanctuary of the Cathedral. As a reward for their diligent work on liturgical music, the boys had fun learning to belt out energetic versions of "Bali Hai" and "For He's A Jolly Good Fellow" and, their signature piece, the title song from "Oklahoma."

Braxton Hood was sorry to see this night of harmony and intimacy in the afterglow of the major's party ending now, under brightening skies, with Singleton already gone and Mulcahey and Levesque gnawing on each other.

Mulcahey's tenor: "They were terrific... everybody loved them."

Levesque's baritone: "What if they ruin their voices and are no good for plainsong anymore."

"They're ten to fourteen, for chrissakes, their voices can do anything at their age."

"The bishop said they sounded a little ragged last Sunday."

"What's *that* supposed to mean?"

"I agree with him. Their tonality wasn't pure. He said they were *en lambeaux,* ragged."

"Tell the bishop if he doesn't like it, we'll take them on the road, we'll play clubs and USOs and make a fortune."

"They're not our orphans, Mad-dog, they're his."

"Ever hear the term 'jail break,' Levesque? The church has

played warden over human prisoners for too long! It's 1968, man! Tell the bishop the times, they are a-changin'!"

"You tell him yourself, hot-shot. I'd really like to see that."

"I don't speak Vietnamese or French."

"It's a very good thing you don't."

"How do you say 'Kiss my butt, Your Excellency' in French?"

Levesque pulled himself up and brushed the sand off his clothes and out of his hair and set off for Bravo, Juliet! without answering the question. Mulcahey followed, chattering away just below Levesque's shoulder-level.

After breakfast, Hood, Babineaux, Mulcahey and Rosenzweig gathered for one last, sentimental farewell to Major Shimazu, who had been their mentor and protector. The Greyhawk Six, however, would all forever share the memories of their four-day reunion in Vung Tau to see Major Shimazu off.

Mulcahey and Levesque rode back to Saigon with the boys, passing the long bus ride by rehearsing plainsong and practicing correct enunciation in church Latin. The sixty-mile trip took over two hours as they crawled along heavily congested Highway 51, through areas that were not secure by night but were reasonably safe by day. By the time they arrived back at the orphanage, the bus had become a sauna on wheels and everyone was sweat-soaked. The boys, fired up by their adventure, merrily shouted their thanks and good-byes in Vietnamese and English to their choir director and their pianist. As chaperones led them inside, some shouted "Okra-homa!" over their shoulders, a word that conveyed everything they felt about their exhausting visit to a magical beach resort none had ever seen before, something out of their dreams, an Eden that helped them forget their shattered lives for a while.

X X X

Even for non-combatants, going off to war is bound to change a person in ways large and small. However, no one in III Corps underwent such an immediate and miraculous transformation as Louis Leffanta, son of a hard-drinking steel worker and the wife he battered. Louis was never a cheerful young man to begin with and disappointments had only deepened his woeful outlook on life. His dream was to escape Pittsburgh, where clouds of mill smoke bellowed over his playgrounds and penetrated into his house and school, coating every surface with a layer of graphite dust. But this dream was ripped from his grasp by vicious admissions officers who rejected his applications to every medical school east of the Mississippi on the flimsy excuse that his undergraduate performance was unimpressive and his letters of recommendation spoke too often of "potential" while omitting any mention of personal traits. Key adjectives were missing, such as "enthusiastic" and "hard-working," which, in the arcane lingo of admissions, doomed his chances. On the basis of Army exams, he squeaked into the Greyhawk Intelligence program and, by keeping his mouth shut, managed to pass muster. The Greyhawk Six first met "Bitter Louie" at III Corp Headquarters, where his nickname was well earned by the torrent of racist vitriol that poured forth from him. He had escaped Pittsburgh, the Third Circle of Hell, only to be plunged into the sulfurous pit of Vietnam, where hordes of little yellow people worked incessantly to perfect his misery. Oily fumes from millions of motorbikes assaulted his lungs and burned his eyeballs even worse than the open-hearth ovens and blast furnaces of Pittsburgh. ARVN convoys threatened to flatten his jeep. Armies of beggars attacked him everywhere he went. He was drowning in an ocean of aliens, every single one of whom he hated with an intensity the English language was inadequate to express. Bitter Louie wore out all the usual racist epithets and was forced to create new terms to describe the retarded, grasping masses of Asiatic Toads whose sole purpose was to be the scourge of his existence and the source of all his agonies.

Not to put too fine a point on it, Bitter Louie Leffanta was as devout a racist as there was in the American Army in Vietnam. That is what made his transformation—on the night of the Tet Offensive— so remarkable.

To improve the morale of the headquarters staff in Saigon—American and Vietnamese alike—Major Shimazu decided in December of 1967 to assign Leffanta to a distant field station. When the operation in Cu Chi fell to pieces due to the criminal fraud of a man who called himself Frank Monroe, the major took that opportunity to shift the station site to Tay Ninh and send Leffanta there as Station Chief. Mr. Ngo Nhat, a man with extensive contacts in Tay Ninh, was hired to be Leffanta's translator, but he quickly became much more than that. Once away from direct supervision, Bitter Louie fell into an even more dissolute state as a human being, so far as that was possible. To burning anger and boiling hatred, Corporal Leffanta now added unrestrained crying jags fueled by large quantities of rice wine. With more determination than he had applied to anything else in his life, Louie spent his first month in Tay Ninh discovering how loathsome a man could make himself.

However, Ngo Nhat in no way avoided the train-wreck to whom he'd been assigned. With the patience of a saint, Nhat served his station chief's every need. He got Tay Ninh Station up-and-running, working with Louie's Vietnamese counterpart to build a network of informants, then producing Information Reports that Leffanta barely scanned before signing. Nhat brought in food three times a day and listened patiently to Leffanta's flowing litany of complaints and racist indictments, including accusations that Nhat himself was plotting against him, taking advantage of Leffanta's unrequited generosity.

"I know what's going on here, buster!" Leffanta bellowed, "I'm onto the 'inscrutable Asian mind'! Which is just another way of saying 'pack of thieves'!"

"Maybe after you have this nice pho soup," Nhat would gently urge, "you feel like meeting with your counterpart, Nguyen Khan."

"Get this stinking bowl of chop suey off my desk and go tell old Noo-yen Can I'll meet with his lazy ass at Howdy-Doody time," Louie would respond, "Now go find me some ice."

And so it went.

When Nhat requested a week's leave over the Tet holidays, Bitter Louie threw a tantrum worthy of Ebenezer Scrooge. He yelled that North Vietnamese troops were flooding over the Cambodian border into Tay Ninh Province so Nhat would have to stay with the station in case it became necessary for Leffanta to flee for safety to Saigon. Nhat was puzzled as to why any man as wretched as Leffanta would fear losing his life. Nevertheless, he calmly explained that he was obligated to preside over important ceremonies at the *Cao Đài* Temple and that his presence there was required. Leffanta was apoplectic; Nhat was unapologetic.

The Tet Offensive that began 31 January 1968 proved to be the nadir of Louis Leffanta's life—and the apex.

In the morning, he watched a flurry of field reports pile up on Nhat's desk. The typist chattered at him in Vietnamese, waving the paperwork in his face and pantomiming her rising anxiety, but without his translator there, Leffanta could only guess at the content. He resisted the impulse to jump into his jeep and abandon his post, largely because if fighting broke out, he'd be less safe on the road than where he was. Instead, he thought about the situation calmly and rationally before taking resolute action: He sent the typist home at noontime and then methodically drank three bottles of rice wine. As evening fell, he staggered to the back porch of the small house to observe the growing crescendo of fireworks, large and small, near and far, mixed with the shouts of unseen celebrants all around him in the dark. The sudden flashes of light, the detonations, the shouts, every-thing tore away at his nerves, but with the aid of a bottle of cognac he found in the kitchen, he counter-attacked by loudly denouncing these savage people, their primitive country and this asinine holiday. Finally, exhausted, he felt his way back down the dark hallway and collapsed on his cot.

Rice wine and cognac in quantity must have disturbed his sleep because at some point in the night he was dimly aware of movement in the pitch-black room. He lunged for the revolver he kept at bedside, but strong hands grabbed him. He thrashed about, fighting for his life, until a voice whispered into his face, "Be silent, Mr. Leffanta. It is Mr. Nhat. You must make no sound and come with me."

Leffanta had little choice because there were other men with Nhat who pulled him to his feet and muscled him down the narrow hallway to the porch and then they were all running through the dark field, holding hands like children. The fireworks of Tet had been replaced by small arms fire and larger explosions from all directions. They ran a hundred yards to a line of trees between open fields and reached it just as Leffanta's house was blasted to pieces. They were all knocked flat by the concussion wave, followed by a shower of debris, roof tiles and bits of timber raining down on them. Leffanta peered back to see a bonfire where his house had been. Then they lifted him up and led him along paths that were familiar to them but which Leffanta—drunk, scared and confused—could only keep-to by following their white robes. Every step of the way, they gently held his hands as one would a friend's. Urging him to be quiet, they traveled several miles while intermittent gunfire crackled all around them.

They emerged onto a street that led to the enormous white temple Leffanta had driven past many times, honking the feeble horn of his rose-colored jeep and cursing pedestrians in his way. He was led to a cavernous, candle-lit room where hundreds of men in white robes slept in rows, apparently oblivious to the sounds of combat outside. He was given a straw mat and a thin blanket and told by Nhat, "You sleep now. We talk tomorrow."

"You saved my life," Leffanta whispered, but Nhat had already gone.

Against all odds, the sick-drunk bundle of rattled nerves that was Bitter Louie Leffanta rolled up in the blanket and slept more peacefully than he ever had since joining the Army. He awoke only a little hung over, as though running for your life at midnight was some sort of palliative for drinking to excess on an empty stomach. White-robed men were scurrying all around him and Nhat came to him with rice cakes and warm soup. "Big fight for Tay Ninh City last night," Nhat told him, "A field agent reported you were target for assassination, so we ran to get you out. We can keep you safe, but you will need to look and act *Cao Đài* in case VC come here." Mr. Nhat broke into a wide smile, much amused by the prospect of Leffanta in a white robe. "We must make you a sheep in the flock," he said.

Under the threat of being shot by the enemy, Leffanta put himself completely in Nhat's hands. His head and beard were shaved and layers of filth were scrubbed away with soapy water and a stiff brush. He was dressed in white robes and given a white head band and sandals made from motorbike tires. Nhat took his watch, keys and wallet from him so that within an hour of devouring the soup and rice cakes, he was kneeling in a row of *Cao Đài* worshippers, doing exactly what all the other men around him were doing. Nhat knelt at his side, quietly explaining to him the ceremony of which he was a part. Leffanta began the day this way, as a bald man in a light cotton robe, hiding from his enemies in an ocean of other men, learning chants and responses in Vietnamese and trying to get used to smelling of soap rather than alcohol and sweat. His rebirth began with these external changes.

But by day's end, holding a candle and repeating a chant, one man in a row of men holding candles and repeating the chant, no longer feeling hungry from a long day of fasting, the internal trans-formation of Louis Leffanta began to take root. The idea of living his life free of the fury and frustrations that gnawed on his guts— his disappointing family, his medical school dreams, his ending up in the Army, sent to Vietnam—why was he obligated to carry these grudges throughout his life when he could merely start over with a clean slate? The men around him, adherents of *Cao Đài*, were intent on bringing about the unity and enlightenment of the whole human family, accepting and combining all the great religions of the world, as Mr. Nhat explained, so that the race of man could pursue universal love and justice. This in the midst of a vicious and prolonged civil war! Leffanta felt an overwhelming release in the recognition that his life had been insignificant—that the grievances that obsessed him were of his own making. For hours he went through the motions of heeding God's call for universal love and justice among all men—until he knew he was no longer pretending. He tried to pray to *Cao Đài's* Queen Mother to nurture and restore him—until the heart within him began to feel nurtured and restored. He had carried the growing weight of his anger and self-disgust for many years, for too long. He now resigned from all of it. All that was petty and soul-destroying and voluntary. He let it go and felt a long-forgotten joy returning to him, the gift of childhood's sweet hopefulness.

For weeks following his brush with death, Louis Leffanta remained in the *Cao Đài* Temple, imbibing the complexities of his new religion under the tutelage of The Honorable Ngo Nhat, the man who had risked his own life to save a hate-filled foreigner. The contempt he had felt for all things Vietnamese dissolved day-by-day, as he learned the names and slowly began to recognize the faces of his fellow Caodaists, whom he now saw as his brothers. Soon, he forgot that he was a minority-of-one, the lone American in the temple. He devoted many hours every day to the study of documents translated into English for him by Ngo Nhat explaining the elements of Christianity, Buddhism, Confucianism, Taoism and Islam that were woven into the fabric of *Cao Đài*. He valued these pages both as sacred guidance and as a gift from his friend, whose impeccable handwriting spread across hundreds of pages by month's end, one man's devoted work to save the soul of another. Mr. Nhat found English editions of Sun Yat-sen and the novels of Victor Hugo, both considered Venerable Saints by Caodaists. Leffanta learned the chants and responses well enough to mutter softly along with the congregation, quietly enough not to disturb those around him with his imperfect pronunciations. Each day he awoke to the surprise of feeling peaceful and happy, setting about his chores in the kitchen with an irrepressible smile, glowing with gratitude for his new life, looking forward eagerly to studies, meditation and prayer.

Mr. Nhat paid him the greatest compliment of his life when he said, "Mr. Leffanta, you have a great gift for meditation. You become lost in time, an achievement that took me many years to accomplish." However, in the unique case of Louis Leffanta, things went far beyond his having a "gift." His spiritual powers were becoming incomprehensible even to the bearer of them and as ingrained in him as his pale blue eyes. Without any conscious intention on his part, he became a controversial figure among his fellow Caodaists.

One morning, as dawn broke, they found him in Lotus Position upon his sleeping mat, legs crossed, hands resting on his knees, thumbs touching index-fingers, apparently dead. His skin was ashen-colored and cold to the touch. Mr. Nhat came running and, full of fear at this strange sight, put his hand on Leffanta's shoulder and spoke gently into his ear. The body of Louis Leffanta toppled over onto its side, still locked in Lotus position, as though it were a statue. Nhat continued to shake him and speak to him to no effect. He pressed two fingers into Leffanta's neck, against his carotid artery and... nothing... then, just before letting go, a single pulse. In five seconds, another... and another... and the pinkish color of the American crawled into the parchment of his face and hands. Leffanta drew in a deep breath, as though emerging from under water. "Can you hear me?" Nhat repeated many times before his breathing grew deeper and then was replaced by faint, giddy laughter. His hands relaxed from their rigid pose and Nhat helped him to sit up as his giggles grew into full-throated laughter, tears rolling down from his blue eyes.

"I was with the Holy Mother," Leffanta calmed himself enough to announce. "I left here and went to be in her presence. She was as real to me as you are now, Mr. Nhat! It was not a dream. It is all true! It is! It is! It is!"

Nhat translated what Leffanta had said to the circle of white-robed Caodists pressing around them, and the anxious debate began between the believers and those who were sure the American intruder was faking it, making a mockery of *Cao Đài*.

Needless to say, of course, this state of affairs could not last.

On the morning of 5 March, Nhat again knelt beside him with a wallet, a ring of keys, a watch, a neat stack of laundered clothes and a check for $525.30 from the Department of Defense made out to Louis L. Leffanta.

"I don't need any of that," Louie said, "I'll donate it all to the temple."

"You must come with me to Saigon today," Nhat told him firmly, "Major Shimazu is angry with our field station… demands to know why we filed no reports in February."

"Tell him the truth, then. The station house was blown to pieces by a grenade the night of Tet, and I died."

Nhat laughed softly. "That was not a grenade, my friend. That was a satchel charge or maybe two of them. They try kill you fo-shu, GI. And Major Shimazu will too if we do not return to III Corps. We put aside *Cao Đài* robes now and put on office clothes, report to Saigon."

"I'm not putting those clothes on!" Leffanta said with intensity, "If I do, I'll go back to being how I was before. I'm *Cao Đài* now and I'm staying *Cao Đài* forever and Shimazu can throw me into Long Binh jail if he wants to. I don't care."

Implacable as he was by reputation, Major Shimazu nevertheless had trouble hiding his astonishment the next morning when Leffanta appeared in his office doorway. Clean shaven above and below his head-band, wearing a spotless white robe, the young man with a solid reputation as an angry, racist slob appeared happy and serene—and smelling of incense. Smiling like Alice's Cheshire cat, Corporal Leffanta tried to explain the nature of his epiphany. "They risked their lives to save mine," he told Major Shimazu. "I was too drunk to walk, so they hauled me like a duffle bag out the back door. Minutes later, the VC tossed a satchel charge through my bedroom window and blew the building apart. That would have been me in there, wasn't for my friends. I owe them my life."

"I understand," Shimazu said, "but that is not an excuse for the fact that not one IR has been received from Tay Ninh for a whole month... since Tet!"

"I have been working incredibly hard, sir," this transfiguration of Louie Leffanta said, "learning the ways of *Cao Đài*. God has founded our new religion to combine the teachings of Taoism, Confucianism, Buddhism, Islam and Christianity. Do you think that's something you can wrap up in a month?" The beaming smile that lit Leffanta's face was unlike anything the "Bitter Louie" who had been sent to Tay Ninh could have achieved. Shimazu had seen World War II and Korea bring about all kinds of profound changes in men, but never anything like this, and he found it both disturbing and fascinating. "There are 36 levels of Heaven and 72 planets with intelligent life aligned between Heaven and Hell," Leffanta went on earnestly, "Earth is number 68..."

"Mr. Leffanta," Shimazu interrupted. "Cao Đài may be wonderful, as you say..."

"It's pronounced *Cao Đài*, sir. They saved my life."

"Yes, I know..."

"The translator, Mr. Nhat, is my teacher and my friend. I wouldn't even be alive weren't for him, much less a disciple of *Cao Đài*. There are three million of us in the Republic, did you know that?" Laughter like a series of hiccups erupted, a sound no American in Vietnam had ever heard from Bitter Louie Leffanta.

That decided it for Major Shimazu. He would attend the budget meeting for the Tay Ninh Field Station—without including Leffanta or his counterpart or even Mr. Nhat—and announce to his own counterpart, Major Han, that there was no longer any need for a station in Tay Ninh and therefore no need to discuss a budget for it. In the meantime, he ordered Leffanta to pack up his gear and the office files and report for reassignment in two days' time.

"I don't have any gear to pack, sir," Leffanta responded cheerfully. "The VC burned-down the office the night of Tet, along with all the files and my stuff, so if you'll assign me a little corner for my meditation and study materials, I could stay here tonight."

In a month, on 3 April, Major Shimazu was scheduled to leave Vietnam, to fly back to the United States, where he would retire from the Army after 25 years' service. Being a Japanese-American had pretty much inured Shimazu to the human propensity for prejudice. Therefore, having an avowed racist like "Bitter Louie" at III Corps Headquarters had been unpleasant but endurable. But this new thing—this "Beatific Louie"—could be, he thought, something that might prove unendurable.

"Mr. Hood?" he called to the outer office, while Leffanta sat smiling at him.

"Gone to lunch, sir," Mulcahey called back.

"Mr. Rosenzweig?"

"Gone to lunch with Hood, sir."

"Where is everybody?" a thoroughly perturbed Major Shimazu whispered to himself.

Everybody was not where John Mulcahey wanted them to be either. Some men are loners; others at their best in company. Mulcahey was happy—or at least less insane—only when he was running in a pack of familiar friends. So March, 1968, began his descent into despair. Hood had left for Vung Tau to help Mark Babineaux develop the station in that resort town to its full potential. Zach Rosenzweig lived with his girlfriend, Sang, in a nearby apartment and reported into the office Monday-Friday, 9 to 5. Shimazu was intent on training his replacement, Captain Kearney, so that the dinners in the screened-in enclosure on the roof of the villa became quick and perfunctory—no longer the elaborate, leisurely evenings that brought everyone together. And Leffanta's blathering on-and-on about *Cao Đài* turned the enlisted quarters, after office hours, into a seething hell for the profoundly anti-clerical Mulcahey. He had no other choice but to escape—to unlock his bicycle after the dinner dishes were done each evening and ride off through the streets and back alleys of Saigon where he asked prostitutes to teach him Vietnamese and Filipino soldiers to teach him Tagalog, where he drank beer with old men who bragged in pidgin-English of their exploits when they fought the French in their youths. He was threatened by stray dogs and carbine-carrying security guards. He was invited to watch television in the lean-to of a soda merchant and his large family, so long as he paid for the soda. It was a different series of adventures every night. At dawn he managed to find his way back to the villa with the large sign—"Service International Corporation (SIC)." The guard would pull the gate open for him and he would go upstairs and catch a few hours' sleep while Leffanta typed and filed and served Major Shimazu's every need. At dusk on 23 March, he followed the sound of music into Notre Dame Cathedral and was stunned to find Rene Levesque leading a boys' choir, which led to his becoming their accompanist, which led to his teaching the boys Broadway songs, which led to their being the featured act at Major Shimazu's party in Vung Tau on 3 April. But what Mulcahey didn't know then and would never find out was what Louis Leffanta had done while everyone else was in Vung Tau.

The three days he was alone in the III Corps offices were happy times for Leffanta. Sadly, Mr. Nhat was back in Tay Ninh and Leffanta missed him sorely, since he was finding it easier and easier to transport his soul in the hours between midnight and dawn over to the realm of the Holy Mother and back again, and he needed Nhat's advice on how he should act when in her presence. But at least Corporal Mulcahey was not there to mock his religion, in remarks so sharp and insulting that Leffanta needed every ounce of his recently acquired Buddhist resignation and acceptance and his Christian love and forgiveness to keep from striking back. Even soft-spoken Private Rosenzweig had criticized the Star of David being prominently displayed in Louis' holy niche, a sheltered corner of the roof near the stairway. Mulcahey, though a lapsed Catholic, objected to the large, colorful picture of Jesus holding a heart ("probably not even his own," Mulcahey said) in his hand. But Jesus and the Star of David stayed put, closely guarded by the disciple of *Cao Đài*, and only the swastika was removed, by Major Shimazu's orders, because he associated it (Louis could not convince him otherwise) with Nazis. And no matter how often Leffanta tried to explain to them that the name of the eternal way was not "Cao Dai" but *"Cao Đài,"* they refused to pronounce it correctly by dropping their tone on *"Đài."*

Mornings, Louis worked diligently in the office not because he cared at all for the American military but to fulfill his Confucian obligation to impartially serve the state, and tried to finish his work so he could devote the remainder of the day to study and meditation. When the mail was delivered on Monday, 1 April, from SIC Headquarters, he opened Mad-dog's personal drawer to drop in two letters from Chicago and saw lots of others—dozens of unopened letters. Leffanta placed the new letters on top of the old and slipped the drawer shut, but for the next several hours, as he typed his way through stacks of hand-written IRs from the translation pool on his manual Remington, he kept turning over in his mind why any soldier in Vietnam would not want to read letters from his home, from "M. Mulcahey" on East 62nd Street in Chicago.

In the early afternoon, during his first deep meditation of the day, Louis knelt on a mat before the corner shrine where candles lit the icons and photos Nhat had given him, but immersion into timelessness eluded him. He couldn't shake those damned letters, Mulcahey's unopened mail! He arose after an unsuccessful two hours and because he was completely alone in the office from now until Monday, he decided to do something about it. He followed the procedures taught to him at Intelligence School for performing a "French slit." He sorted the pile of letters, newest postmarks on top, laid out an even bed of typing paper, and brought a new double-edged razor blade, a pair of tweezers, a box of Q-tips and a bottle of Elmer's glue to the desk. He sliced the return-address edge of each envelope, guiding the razor with a wooden ruler, removing an even, thirty-second-of-an-inch strip from each. He carefully collected each of the thirty-two thin strips and placed them in an envelope. Now the pile of letters had been reversed, oldest post-mark on top. He gently pulled the first letter from its envelope with the tweezers, read it attentively, and pushed it fully back into its envelope. He did the same with each of the thirty-two letters. Three hours later, when he was done reading, he used a clean Q-tip for each letter, painting a thin layer of Elmer's glue inside the slit edge of each envelope and pressing it closed until the glue took hold. In an abundance of caution, he wiped each envelope with a white t-shirt, to remove any fingerprints. Then he returned the envelopes to Mulcahey's personal drawer, oldest postmark on the bottom, newest on the top, and disheveled the stack, as it had been before.

For all the calm, methodical treatment he'd given the procedure, Leffanta's heart pounded wildly beneath his white robe as he pored over personal letters he had no right to read. The writer had signed each one "Yours in Christ's Love, Mom," and they etched a deep impression on the Caodaist's soul. Leffanta recognized elements of his own history in Mulcahey's—a blue-collar father and World War II veteran who drank too much, took it out on his wife, repented and apologized and then did it all over again. A wife who forgave him and struggled to understand the cycle, largely because she had no practical alternatives to making her marriage "work." But the glaring difference between Mulcahey's family and his own—and it gave Leffanta the explanation he had gone looking for—was that the priest was ever-present in the Mulcahey household, with no such counterpart in Leffanta's. Father Murphy was a cog in the wheel of misfortune that went round-and-round, receiving the contrition of Mulcahey's father at face value, making him swear to limit his drinking, control his temper, treat his wife with kindness—counseling Mary Mulcahey to be patient, understanding and forgiving. He would then give God's blessing to them both, leave the house, and wait for the phone to ring next time, in a week or two, as it always did. It was no wonder the wild Irishman heaped such vicious scorn on Leffanta's belief in the Highest Power, urging humanity toward love and justice, and in the Holy Mother, offering nurture and restoration. As much as John Francis Mulcahey could benefit from a belief in *Cao Đài*, Leffanta must seem to him just another form of Father Murphy. From now on, Leffanta promised, he would not speak to Mulcahey of his religious fervor but in all ways treat this suffering man, his brother, as the Highest Power would have him do, exhibiting love and justice toward him in every way, and he would bring him the comfort of the Holy Mother too. This, Louis Leffanta solemnly vowed.

When it came to mockery though, Leffanta was a side-dish for Mad-dog. Rene Levesque was the entrée. He and Levesque had slogged through the icy mud of wintertime basic training together, their jackets soaked and frozen, their ponchos little help against freezing rain in high winds. This was followed by seven months at Fort Greyhawk in the heat of summertime, which were exhausting and unsettling. But through it all, Mulcahey always had the pleasure of being able to stick it to his "fellow Roman Catholic," Rene Levesque, who was like all the other gullible sheep that swallowed all that horse-shit about walking on water and rising from the dead and the layers of Medieval manure on top of that having to do with the Trinity and wine that turned to blood and bread to flesh and Papal infallibility and all the rest of the crap spoon-fed by the sisters to stupid children. He got wise in high school when he realized that the church had beaten all the brains out of his own mother, a nice lady who deserved better than she got. He had stopped attending church during his last two years of high school but during college, he began attending again—not to worship but to ask impertinent questions of the parishioners: "Do you think God is in Heaven right now, looking down on you? What do you think he does up there, all day long, every day? Doesn't that sound a little boring?" Eventually, Father Murphy asked him to stay away and come back only when he could be respectful of others, and that was fine with Mulcahey.

In short, no one ever had to waste time trying to guess what Mulcahey was thinking. He had enemies and friends—very few unde-cideds—but they all agreed he was the most voluble and unfiltered human being they had met. Long before the term "hyperactivity disorder" came into use, they said he had "the gift of gab." Every stim-ulus, every sight or spoken word, needed his commentary. Many who knew him (Father Murphy, for example) avoided him like the plague.

Many others (Levesque, for example) delighted in his company. The small-town French-Catholic community of Rene Levesque's childhood was introspective, taciturn in the extreme, reluctant to give vent to their judgments lest they offend. So Levesque was greatly entertained by the flighty little man he dubbed "Mad-dog"—the chatterbox who took his mind off his trials and dark thoughts during basic training. He was the car radio that distracted Levesque with a fireworks display of verbiage, some of it even clever, during eight weeks of suffering at Fort Campbell. As for hanging out with a heretic, Levesque rested secure within the bastion of his own settled faith, impervious to Mad-dog's cap-pistol assault on it.

And so they waited in the choir loft on 7 April, four days after their return from Vung Tau, for the boys to be walked over to the Cathedral by their chaperones. Levesque arranged music sheets in the boys' folders while Mulcahey laid out a chord progression on the piano and rambled on in his usual way.

"How do you stand it, Rene?"

"Stand what?"

"The Great Liturgy of the Mass. It's exactly the same thing every time, word-for-word, like buying a ticket to the same play over and over with the same characters, the same ending."

"I like the formality… and the pageantry. It's very reassuring and restful to the mind. You should try it yourself sometime."

"I did try it, for seventeen years, and it put me in a coma."

"You play the same songs over and over… what's the difference?"

"I play different songs at different times. And I know I'm faking it when I'm pretending to be an Oklahoma ranch-hand or the King of Siam. Trouble with you is, you take pretending to be a Catholic far too seriously."

"I *am* a Catholic, Mulcahey."

"C'mon! There's no such thing in the past two-hundred years, since science came along. I took a survey back at my home parish, Saint Bunco's, and by actual count a third of the guys I talked to hedged on Mary being a virgin and way over two-thirds admitted 'Heaven' was not up in the sky. Yet every one of them stand up in church every Sunday and swear they believe 'He was born of the Virgin Mary' and 'He ascended into Heaven'. What a crock of hypocritical horseshit! As if the Divine Creator of the Universe... the *whole* universe... gives a rat's ass about people on some distant..."

"I would take it as a personal favor, my friend, if you would refrain from profanity while you are actually *inside* a Cathedral sanctuary."

Mulcahey banged out a few ominous chords on the keys. "Oh yeah? Or you'll do what?"

"Remember, you recited 'The Apostles' Creed' and 'Our Father' when you were growing up and how did that harm you, exactly?"

"Soon as they switched the mass from Latin to English, I was outta there! Before then I was a clueless child. I thought 'Et cum spiritu tuo' was God's phone number."

Levesque laughed. "You'll be back," he said confidently, to irritate Mad-dog, "Time will come when you need the church and, thanks be to God, it'll still be here for you... and for the sick and the poor, the grief-stricken and the stranger."

"Oh, sure I'll be back," Mulcahey leered, "when they serve pizza and beer at the altar rail and sing 'Climb Every Mountain' instead of 'Angus Dei'."

The orphan boys arrived, greeted their teachers with noisy enthusiasm and warmed up their soprano voices to a progression of chords Mulcahey played up and down the scale. Then they applied themselves diligently to plainsong and sung responses for forty-five minutes, having the enunciation of their church-Latin corrected by the choirmaster in the black robe they knew as "Brother Andre." As a reward, each received his own typed copy of "Do-Re-Mi" from *The Sound of Music* to put in his music folder, the lyrics typed in English and Vietnamese courtesy of Pham Viet of the III Corps translation pool. Mulcahey had them sing "La-La-La" through the melody and then "do-re-mi-fa-sol-la-tee-do," but time ran out before they could get to the more complex lyrics in English. Levesque worried that belting out "Oklahoma" would ruin the purity of his choir's tone, but he thought this more controlled melody was much easier on them.

"Grab a bite?" Levesque suggested when the orphans had gone back.

"Can't. I found a job playing in a bar. Rosie set up an audition for me, through Sang. It's a chance to perform real music for grown-ups instead of plainsong for children and imbeciles, earn a few bucks, and keep a piano between me and the booze on weekends."

"Beats riding a bike through the streets all night until somebody finally shoots you," Levesque conceded.

As always when such a suggestion was made, the Zapruder film of Jack Kennedy's final moments flashed through the mind of Mad-dog Mulcahey, but he said nothing.

Khung Quan Ba wasn't one of those more refined places on Tu Do Street where beautiful girls in ao dais talked lonely soldiers and sailors into buying them expensive "Saigon Teas"—then walked away if things got too intimate. The place where Rosenzweig's girlfriend introduced him to the owner was larger, louder, shabbier and closer to Saigon Harbor than Tu Do Street. But it did have an upright piano in good repair. Mulcahey thought it was a good place for American troops who wanted to forget the war, share drinks with friends and reminisce about home to patriotic songs by George M. Cohan and the Gershwins and the nostalgic classics of Rodgers and Hammerstein—the great American canon.

However, as Mulcahey himself wanted Levesque to tell the Archbishop of Saigon, the times, they were a'changin'.

His first night went well, comparatively. A rowdy mob of paratroopers from the 101st Airborne, on leave after the battle to recapture the Imperial City of Hue from the NVA, got totally wasted, outshouting each other over Mulcahey's vain attempts to deliver "America The Beautiful" and "It's a Grand Old Flag."

His second night wasn't so good. He was hoarse and exhausted from the night before and got only a few bars into "Look for The Silver Lining" before the hazing started.

"Hey, man! How about some Rolling Stones?"

"Baby, light my fire!"

"How's about something from this century!"

Mulcahey hammered out a few chords of "Light My Fire" but he didn't know the lyrics and was fading away when a trooper with a solid baritone yelled, "We gotta get outta this place!" which began the whole room wailing away at the chorus, shouting rather than singing, sloshing beer over each other. The third time through these lyrics, a fight broke out near the entranceway between the paratroopers and some Navy SEALs who came pushing their way into the crowd. By the time the brawlers were pulled apart, Mulcahey was a mile away, his music folder tucked under his arm, peddling his bike toward home.

At noon the next day, Mulcahey returned to tender his resignation and try to collect some pay. When he arrived, he found he had already been replaced by four teenagers pounding on amped-up electric guitars and an old trap set, making a racket Mulcahey would not have called music. The owner wasn't there and he figured *What the hell... he's not going to give me my twenty dollars without haggling about it for an hour...may as well just...* But on his way to the door he heard, "You're that piano-player, aren't you, from last night?"

The question came from a powerfully-built paratrooper in green fatigues, a sergeant, E-7, sharing a table with two much younger troops, both of them completely wasted. The sarge pushed a chair with his boot and beckoned Mulcahey to sit. Then he raised four fingers toward the bar and a girl brought over a round of "33" beers.

"I'm surprised you remember me," Mulcahey said, "I didn't play all that long."

"Men were blowin' off steam, is all. Don't take it personal."

But it was hard for Mulcahey not to take it personal when the wiry young paratrooper to the sergeant's left looked straight at him with wobbly, blood-shot eyes, showed him his middle finger and snarled, "Fuckin' pogue!"

"I'm sorry, was I talking to you?" Mad-dog shot back.

But the man kept his finger in Mulcahey's face and slurred, "Fuckin' pogue desk-jockey," then toasted his own wit by sloppily guzzling down his beer in one take. The E-7 put a hand on the young man's shoulder, clearly an "enough" sign, and his unsteady gaze went from Mulcahey to the passing traffic outside the door.

"What's 'pogue' mean, anyway?" Mulcahey asked the sergeant.

"Rear-echelon... you know, support. Guys like you who collect 'hazard duty' pay without ever taking fire."

"I'm a civilian contractor... road construction," Mulcahey improvised, as he'd been trained to do. "So I don't get 'hazard duty' pay, but I do get shot at now and then."

"Well, maybe you come with us tomorrow and get a taste of what my men go through, so you'll know why they get edgy sometimes."

The sarge took a swig of his beer. "We'll teach you to shove the NVA off a jungle hill…'cuz that's what your orders are… watch a bunch of your guys get killed and wounded… then get orders to leave the area so in a week or two you can do it all again, over and over. In this way, you'll be winnin' the hearts and minds of the people. You heard that phrase?"

"I have."

"And how do *you* think it's goin', Mr. Road-Construction Piano-Man? We winnin' any hearts and minds yet?"

Mulcahey didn't have anything to say for a change.

The sarge took another gulp from his "33" and snapped, "Hell, man! We're not even winnin' *our own* hearts and minds… all the protests and riots back home! These kids are over here fightin' to protect people who go around burnin' the flag and callin' us names. Somethin' fucked-up 'bout this whole thing." He waved four fingers toward the bar and drained his beer.

"This one's on me," Mulcahey said and fished some scrip notes out of his pocket.

The E-7 tipped his new bottle at Mulcahey. "I hereby officially invite you to come to II Corp with us tomorrow. We'll show you the heap of rubble that used to be the Imperial City of Hue. Marines pulverized that place but Charlie just dug in deeper. Rubble is the perfect battle terrain for an army of little, suicidal rats. He tunnels down and fights to the death and you get a bunch of your guys killed clawin' him out of there. When the smoke clears, you find a mass grave where he buried all the civilians he could get ahold of. But we torch an empty village with no people in it, it's called an 'atrocity'. We win every fight we're in, inflict massive casualties on the enemy and chase him off the field and know what they say back home? Fuckin' Walter Cronkite spends a week over here… talks to men in my company…

then goes on TV and says we're not winnin'... we can't win... we'll never win!" The sarge took a long draw on his beer.

Mulcahey tried to find some word of understanding for something he couldn't fully understand, some kind of encouragement. "Listen, Bobby Kennedy's in the race now and he'll win. When he gets into office, he'll get us the hell out of here."

The single "HA!" response rang with derision. "First place, nobody can 'stop' a war. We got a half-million men and so much equipment, it'd take 'til his second term just to demobilize this juggernaut. Second place, we promised the South Vietnamese we'd stand by 'em. We let the Commies take over, there'd be a blood-bath. They'd impeach Bobby Kennedy for treason and they should. Third place, try tellin' 25,000 American families that this was all a big mistake and their Johnny died for nothin', tell me how that works out for you, next election. And besides, goddammit! We *are* winnin'! We're kickin' Charlie's ass out there day-in, day-out, bombin' the crap out of him up-north. We quit now, we're not just quittin' on the South Vietnamese... we're quittin' on *ourselves!*" He jerked a thumb at the two E-4s on his left, both passed out across their folded arms.

Mulcahey was never a combat soldier. When anyone said of him that he was a Vietnam veteran, he would affirm that. However, if they said he was a veteran of the Vietnam War, he'd say, "No, I'm not... I watched the war on television, like you did." But thanks to the hour he spent with Sergeant Hollis, as his nametag said, E-7, 101st Airborne Division, he came closer to grasping the agony of the Vietnam War for those who fought it—their feelings of abandonment by their own countrymen, their victories disparaged instead of celebrated, their sacrifices ignored, their honor sullied—and why they could no longer find any pleasure or meaning in the patriotic, sentimental music that their fathers and grandfathers loved.

As they waited for the orphans to gather at the Cathedral that evening, Levesque asked how the bar-job was going and Mulcahey admitted to a broken heart. "They didn't like the music," he said, "In fact, they hated it. Guys our age, they've got no use for the American classics anymore."

"Maybe you should play The Beatles or Elvis."

"Right! Sure! Trade in 'South Pacific' for fucking yellow submarines and hound dogs! Hammerstein and Porter and Mercer wrote lyrics about life, man! Not stupid jingles about their blue suede shoes and five-thousand repetitions of the name Jude! Should I get some bell-bottom jeans and a vest with fringe, grow hair down my back, all that horseshit? Screw you, Rene!"

"I never said that."

"No, but they did!" Mulcahey stroked chords from Hoagy Carmichael's "Stardust." "I went over there today and drank beer with one of the troopers, and he told me why he can't stand 'Oklahoma'. He's seen a lot of fighting and he feels betrayed... like the home-town crowd walked out of the game at half-time. He's lost friends and risked his life because his country called on him and now they're declaring the whole war a big mistake, four years into it. Every other war, there's a victory parade with cheers and confetti... and he knows he's not getting that. They're going to get anti-war protests and riots. No victory, no peace, no end to it. He's just stuck in hell and he doesn't want to hear 'America, The Beautiful' or 'Oh, What a Beautiful Morning' because he thinks all that dreamy shit is what got us into this and now everyone's changed their minds and they're stabbing him in the back." He banged his fists on the keys. "They've got a bunch of apes pounding on guitars and drums over there now and I'm... I don't know... I'll just go back home and play 'Sentimental Journey' for old people in nursing homes who remember the 'good wars'."

The orphans began to file into their places, led by their chaperones, and Levesque said,

"Remember when you said I should tell the Bishop that 'times, they are a-changin'?' Well, Mad-dog, you can't have it both ways. If the Holy Mother Church is stuck in the past and can't get with the times, then so are Hammerstein, Porter and Mercer. Face it, you and I are rigid traditionalists, both of us, swimming against the tide."

"Listen up!" Mulcahey shouted at the orphans, "We're learning a new song today." And in his clear tenor voice, he sang, "Gonna take a sentimental journey…"

"Warm-up chords, if you will, Mr. Mulcahey," Levesque commanded.

It was just as well that Mulcahey lost his night job and that the demands of Levesque's orphan choir dropped off in the low Sundays following their exhausting Easter performances on 14 April because the work load at III Corps was picking up on growing evidence that the enemy was planning a May Offensive. Information Reports as numerous and alarming as those before the massive Tet Offensive were pouring in from the field and had to be typed up, correctly formatted and edited from hand-written manuscripts produced by Pham Viet's Translator's Pool. This time, unlike what occurred in January, MACV was taking them seriously and preparing for a major battle.

The enlisted men of III Corps—Leffanta, Mulcahey and Rosenzweig—worked feverishly throughout late April to organize and assess the volume of field reports moving up to the 581st MI HQ and the voluminous "Requests for Further Information" moving down from

HQ to the field stations. They worked "feverishly" also because the memory of Tet, three months before, was still fresh: Mulcahey's brush with death when his jeep was shot to pieces ("friendly fire"), Leffanta's vivid memory of his little house in Tay Ninh being obliterated by a satchel-charge seconds after he'd fled ("enemy action"), and Rosenzweig's suffering weeks of anxiety when he lost all contact with his beloved Sang in the chaos of war (SNAFU). All three still steered around the patch of dark earth where a corpse had rotted for a week in the alleyway outside their compound wall ("unfriendly carbine fire" from the ancient gate-guard they called Papa-san). So the fever that each felt at the prospect of another offensive was deep, personal, and the result not only of the rising humidity as rainy season approached.

Major Shimazu's replacement, Captain Kearney, who had arrived in country after the Tet fighting subsided, was much more confident than they were that American firepower could manage things and, therefore, much less concerned. He signed off on whatever analysis and assessment the more experienced enlisted men decided on and spent much of his time being driven over to the Officers Club at Tan Son Nhut Airbase, to various hotels, and to higher headquarters—the 581st or MACV itself—to politic and socialize. He had seen, in short, much less combat than Major Shimazu or even than his own office staff of two corporals and a private, and his focus remained ever keen on his mission, which was to be promoted to major. It irritated and depressed Captain Kearney that he went around in civilian clothing, gaining admittance everywhere with a "contractor's" ID. He longed to wear his starched, creased Class-A officer's uniform when he strode into a building, to be saluted by the sentry and called by his proper first name: Captain.

On the morning of 6 May, it fell to Rosenzweig to drive the captain to a luncheon engagement near Tan Son Nhut. It didn't exactly "fall" to Rosenzweig, as such, but Mulcahey was faking a migraine and Leffanta swore he couldn't find his ID card and because Rosenzweig had attacked an officer back in January, he held the rank of PFC while both his colleagues were corporals so had "command authority" over him. Though terrified about driving around when an attack was expected, Rosie slipped behind the wheel of a jeep (painted rust-brown and inscribed "SIC" across the hood) and drove through the gate with Captain Kearney perched on the back seat in a business suit, despite the heat.

They drove north-west through swarms of blue-and-yellow taxis, pedicabs and motorbikes, toward Plantation Road, where twenty young men had gathered over the course of the morning, hauling heavy baskets of fish and rice, made heavier still by small arms, ammunition, and explosives buried under the food. The men were members of the 9th VC, a unit which had been appearing regularly in the reports coming into III Corps. Their mission was to gather these supplies in two houses rented for them where Plantation Road came nearest the Tan Son Nhut perimeter and wait for darkness, when they would be joined by their main force, bringing in weapons and more supplies for an attack through the perimeter fencing. Aircraft, fuel and ammunition storage areas were their objectives and they had trained for weeks for this night. Across the street from one of these houses, an old man sat patiently sharpening a box of knives with a whetstone, smoking one cigarette after another, pretending not to notice what he was seeing on his street.

At noon, Mulcahey and Leffanta locked the second-floor office and mounted steps to the screened-in roof enclosure to eat and to seek some relief from the afternoon heat. It had not rained in five months, but now clouds were building up each afternoon and ceiling fans were turning the offices into steamy convection ovens. For Mad-dog, this was a break from pounding on his Remington, rolling three pages with carbon-paper under the first two through the platen, careful to make few errors because they needed burdensome "correcting" of all three copies. He looked forward to a couple cold beers (maybe three, since the captain was away), a ham and cheese on rye, and stealing an hour to read J.P. Donleavy's *Ginger Man*. For Leffanta, who normally skipped lunch in favor of prayer and study, this was much more—a chance to speak privately with someone he had taken under his spiritual wing, a man he had vowed to the Holy Mother he would nurture and protect, perhaps eventually convert to *Cao Đài*.

Mulcahey was well into his first beer and his book when he realized that Leffanta was riveted on him, smiling like the lunatic he was, studying him with pale blue eyes that belonged, Mulcahey thought, in a pretty girl's face. Holding his own gaze on his book, he said, "You're giving me the creeps, Louis."

Leffanta remained silent for a long time, seeking inspiration, then said quietly, "I've been demonstrating an example… of nurture and eternal love."

"Oh Jesus Christ, Louis! Don't start with me on that shit!" was the response emanating, Louis knew, from Mulcahey's tortured soul.

"Have you noticed your shoes or your bed lately?"

"What about 'em?"

"I shine your shoes every night, when you're sleeping. And make your bed…"

"Mama-san makes my bed."

"She used to, but now I do it before she arrives."

"You are one freaky weirdo, Leffanta, I'll hand that to you. I would say 'thanks' for the shoes and all, but instead I'll just say 'stop it right now!' I don't know what your game is, but I'm not playing it, so count me out."

"I understand you, John Francis…"

"My mother calls me John Francis. To you it's 'Corporal Mulcahey'."

"I understand you more than you know, John Francis… and my sacred obligation is to love you eternally and unconditionally…"

"OK!" Mulcahey leapt to his feet, "That does it, faggot-face! Keep the hell away from me or I'll kick your teeth down your throat!"

Leffanta remained seated, smiling his smile of eternal love. "Your inner demons are speaking through you, John Francis," he said quietly, "but that changes nothing. You can let go of all that, like I did. I can show you how."

A half-mile away, Zach Rosenzweig and Captain Kearney had no warning of danger before it was too late. The old man still held a knife in one hand, a whetstone in the other, when he pointed out the suspicious houses to an American patrol of the 719th MP Company responsible for perimeter security along that stretch. Their approach to the suspicious house brought a hail of small arms fire down on them. As the MPs ran for cover, rifle rounds hit the rust-brown jeep behind them, breaking the windshield. Roof tiles on both sides of Plantation Street shattered, sending shards of red clay flying everywhere. MPs laid down covering fire on the house so their wounded could be dragged to shelter and fortunately—or so it seemed at the moment—when they called for reinforcements, they were told a flight of the new Cobra helicopter-gunships were headed in from the field. If they marked the target with smoke, they would get all the support they needed. Two men crawled along low walls until they were close enough to lob smoke grenades at the intended house, and as the wind drove the red smoke drifting back over them, all hell ripped loose. Two Cobras hanging low on the horizon blasted every house on the entire block with four Gatling guns firing 600 rounds per minute each, causing Americans of the MP 719th, Vietcong militia of the VC 9th, and the civilian residents of Plantation Road to run for their lives in every direction.

With a half-empty beer can in one hand and a half-eaten sandwich and a paperback book in the other, Mulcahey went stomping across the open roof toward the stairway. He turned to warn Leffanta, "Stay away from me, you frickin' homo, or I swear to God I'll mess you up." But the screen door of the enclosure opened and Leffanta followed him onto the roof.

"You are my brother, John Francis. Love transcends time and space…"

The ricochet hummed past Mulcahey like an angry bee and, thud, punched a clean little hole in the center of Louis Leffanta's snow-white robe. He looked down at it and said, 'Oh!'" then sat down and pulled his legs in, hands on knees, placing himself into an imperfect assimilation of the Lotus Position as blood spread down his robes and onto the roof.

Days later, as the paralysis of shock, confusion and helplessness subsided, Mulcahey convinced himself there was nothing he could have done that would have made any difference. Pounding his fists at the Translators' Pool where everyone had gone to lunch, shouting into the phone for the operator to send an ambulance to the SIC building in an alley off Cong Ly Street when he didn't know the address, too full of fear to go back up those stairs to "administer first aid" to Louis when he had already watched him die, unable to do anything but scream against it "NO! GOD! NO! HELP! SOMEBODY!" Helplessness, he discovered, is profoundly embarrassing. In his own close call with dying—when his jeep was shot to pieces outside Tan Son Nhut— he had shown exceptional courage. However, that was the courage of innocence. The infant who crawls to the top of the stairs then starts down or the toddler who reaches for the stove are not acts of courage, and Mulcahey's "going shopping" into the active battlefield of 1 February 1968 was an extension of his childhood. However, the end of Louis Leffanta's young life altered John Mulcahey's consciousness forever. Rosenzweig and Captain Kearney were caught in the core of a chaotic battle, but both of them came home unscathed except for some cuts on Rosie's face from flying glass while Leffanta, who was only dimly aware of distant gunfire, caught a random ricochet that missed Mulcahey by inches, and he died. In that instant life ended for Leffanta and awareness was born for Mulcahey. Now there was happenstance in the world, at least. And there was mortality. Perhaps there was even fate.

The work of the III Corps offices would never return to "normal" so long as those who had known Leffanta were still there. Mulcahey and Rosie wrote the letter Captain Kearney signed for the Leffanta family. Praise for Corporal Leffanta's work ethic and compassion for the Vietnamese people did not stretch the truth, but no mention of *Cao Đài* was made and the box of his "personal possessions" included a few short-sleeved shirts and chinos from Rosie's wardrobe, which were the right size, while his collection of white robes and the religious artifacts and photos from his makeshift shrine were boxed up for Ngo Nhat to have.

Unlike Mulcahey, Rosie had no previous experience of being shot at, so the Plantation Road fire-fight left him jumpy. Any loud noise or the sudden appearance of someone in a doorway made him flinch now. Not so Captain Kearney, who thought of combat experience as another feather in his cap toward his promotion to major, although his "experience" consisted of lying face down, curled up behind the front seats of a jeep, his heart in his throat, swearing a blue streak, while his corporal turned the jeep around and sped away from the scene as fast as the bullet-riddled windshield allowed.

For Mulcahey, who was a flincher to start with, the events of 6 May robbed him of his sense of security in the III Corps suite of rooms where he lived and worked. Lincoln's phrase "hallowed ground" went through his mind each time he gave wide berth to the section of the roof where Leffanta died. As soon as the funeral detail had removed the corpse, Mama-san matter-of-factly scrubbed the area clean on her hands and knees with a bucket and rags, as she would have spilled soup. But Mulcahey saw her cleaning out the bucket in the shower on his, the enlisted, side of the villa and from that day on, he washed himself as best he could at the sink, head-to-foot, without ever stepping into the tiled shower. The corner of the roof at the top of the stairway where Leffanta had constructed his shrine, too, Mulcahey never passed without feeling a tinge of fear, as if removing the artifacts did not, somehow, remove the shrine. A hollowed-out church is still a church, even to a self-proclaimed atheist like Mulcahey.

Every night, when the dishes were done after the supper they ate together in the roof-top enclosure, Rosie quietly slipped out to join his beautiful French-Vietnamese lover, Sang, in the apartment they shared. "Cohabitation" was strictly against Regulations, but "SIC civilian cover operations" required lots of things that violated Army Reg's. Captain Kearney returned to the officer's side of the villa's second floor and Mulcahey was left to sleep by himself in a small room with three cots—one assigned to Rosie, technically, and the other assigned to the former Corporal Leffanta. The only chance Mulcahey had to avoid tossing about on his cot all night, sweltering under mosquito netting that blocked the breeze from the overhead fan, was to haul gin, tonic and a bowl of ice to the front office and sip away until he was cross-eyed and exhausted from typing letters to every friend for whom he had an address—those who wrote him back and those who never did. He never wrote about what was happening to him (not even about being "on civilian status") but rather about plans when he got back home to work as hard as he could in whatever time the Army wasn't controlling him to get Bobby Kennedy elected president. He wrote the Kennedy campaign headquarters in Washington and in his hometown, Chicago, at least twice a week, asking how they could use him. He would do anything. He could play piano. That RFK would win the nomination and the election, he had no doubt. Bobby was smarter, better looking, more articulate, and a better human being than Eugene McCarthy and Hubert Humphrey combined plus whatever ape the Republicans came up with too. "Everything is out of kilter," he wrote, "Soldiers here are feeling betrayed in a war that will never end, mobs of rioters and protesters are in the streets of every city, somebody shot Martin Luther King and they can't even find out who did it, but all this can be set right when Bobby Kennedy is our president. He can lead us out of it, I know." Then he would drain the last of the gin-and-tonic and stagger off to his cot for a few hours before starting another morning of pounding out reports in triplicate on his Remington, hung over and bleary eyed.

The third week of May brought some relief to III Corps when replacements came in. Fresh from Fort Greyhawk, Corporal Danny Goodman was cheerful and buoyant, which Mulcahey found annoying because it reminded him of himself before Tet and Leffanta and all the rest that had happened to him in his nine months in Vietnam. Corporal Goodman sparkled with the unalloyed happiness that a man has before he is shot at. But Mulcahey was much relieved to have company, especially in the evenings after Rosie left, and to watch the new man sleep in the former cot of the former Leffanta and walk over the "hallowed ground" on the roof with no ill effects. He and Rosie agreed not to tell him anything about what had happened two weeks earlier.

Captain Kearney was not at all pleased with the new officer assigned to III Corps but he hid it well. His view was that he had borne the weight of command nobly and without complaint after Major Shimazu's departure. He judged that he had ruled with a light hand, making few demands, bearing his authority with a natural grace. His unit had endured a combat loss with equanimity under his mentorship. He deserved, in his own judgment, to retain command. Corporals Mulcahey and Rosenzweig saw it differently. Major Shimazu had delighted in cooking a delicious dinner every night whereas Captain Kearney came to the table to be served dinner over his shoulder by his overworked underlings. The captain signed every report, assessment and analysis that crossed his desk without comment (usually without reading them at all) and only intervened in the function of the office to make demands. He required to be driven everywhere, so it wouldn't appear he was a nobody who had to drive his own jeep, and to be served over his left shoulder, with empty plates removed over his right shoulder. It was clear that the captain considered enlisted men to be expendable, interchangeable parts, given that he had never said a word about the loss of Leffanta. Be that as it may, Major Zorth Wills by virtue of his rank would be the new commanding officer at III Corps with Kearney serving as his second-in-command. Wills proved to be more affable than the captain but no more useful. No one expected him to cook dinner just because Major Shimazu had chosen to do so. While he contributed no more support to the operation than Captain Kearney, he added this: There were now two officers to be driven around instead of one. They soon learned that Major Will's passion in life was crossword puzzles and he required to be driven to the Tan Son Nhut Post Exchange several times each week to choose new books of puzzles. But this kept him busy and out-of-the-way so these puzzle-runs were a small price to pay for having a contented and sedate CO.

Meanwhile, because he had refereed the test of wills between Mulcahey and Levesque all across the frozen roads and fields of basic training and throughout the ordeals at Greyhawk, Rosie figured he knew Mad-dog Mulcahey's every mood. The obstreperous Irishman went through life making everything about three times harder than it had to be, which Rosenzweig found an oddly endearing quality in his friend. So, he didn't like what he was seeing in the hectic month following Leffanta's death. The most uninhibited loudmouth Rosenzweig had ever known had become conspicuous by his silence.

They were padlocking confidential materials into file cabinets before heading off for lunch on 5 June 1968 when Rosie couldn't wait any longer for things to self-adjust. "You go ahead," he told Goodman, grabbing Mulcahey by the sleeve, "We'll catch up with you."

When the door closed, Mulcahey barked "What?!"

"It's been awhile since we talked, one-on-one."

"That's because you take off every night and every weekend to be with Sang."

"True enough… but what's up with you, man?"

"Nothing's up with *me*! What's up with *you*?"

"You've been deaf and dumb for weeks and that's not like you, Mad-dog. Goodman thinks you're a nice guy, man! What's happening to you?"

"What d'you care? You're gone every night and weekend to your girlfriend's place. Maybe I do all my bitching when you're not around."

"OK, three things: First, Sang is my fiancée, not my girlfriend. Second, it's our apartment, not 'her place'. Third, Goodman says you lie around with paperbacks all weekend and don't ever go anywhere, no bar-hopping, no trips to shantytown for girls. So there's something rattling around inside your rat-infested brain. What is it?"

"How about you leave me alone?"

"OK. I will. But first tell me how stupid people from Tennessee are… especially Jews from Nashville."

"Fine, OK! You're all a bunch of illiterate hillbillies who marry your own cousins when they turn twelve. Happy now?"

"C'mon, Mad-dog. You're a big-city kid. You can do better than that."

"Sure, fine! The best thing ever happened to you was when the Union Army marched down there and stomped your asses for treating your slaves like shit."

"That all you got?"

"Hell, NO! I just hope you-all get electricity someday so you-all can buy a table lamp and see to chase the chickens and pigs out at night and maybe a radio so you-all can listen to music that's not played with a washer-board and a banjo."

"That's more like it! Feel better? Now… what is going on with you?"

"Your people are so poor that…"

"That's enough, Mulcahey, now the real thing on your alleged mind is what? Spill it!"

"I don't like playing piano anymore… not since that run-in with the soldiers in the bar." Mulcahey averted his eyes to study his own folded hands. "Maybe I feel the same way they do, what with all the race riots and war protests back home… and there's a thought I keep having, too, about…"

Rosie waited for it in silence.

"… about Bobby Kennedy. The California Primary is today and he's gonna win it."

"And that's what you want, right?"

"Sure… but then he'll have the nomination sewn up… and look what they did to President Kennedy and what they did to Reverend King. I'm scared Bobby will be next."

"There will always be lunatics with guns," Rosie said softly.

"I don't believe that… the 'lunatic with a gun' theory. Some-body set Lee Harvey Oswald up… and they don't even know who killed Reverend King. Nobody's even been arrested and it's been two months."

It was Rosie's turn to study his own folded hands. "No point worrying about what might never happen," he said but he realized at once that offered no comfort. So, he said, "I'll bet you ten bucks he wins and we'll be back home by then and we'll go stand in the freezing cold on The Mall, all wrapped up in scarves and gloves and heavy coats and attend his Inauguration together. Deal?" Given that it was 98 degrees and humid in the office, the image of a freezing-cold day did draw a smile from Mulcahey.

"Deal," he said, and they set off for lunch.

It was 7:00 p.m. Saigon time with the dishes all washed and dried and stacked on the shelf in the roof-enclosure before Mulcahey tuned into Armed Forces Radio hoping to hear election results but heard, instead, the account of Bobby Kennedy's being shot, appar-ently by some lunatic with a gun. By then, Rosie had left for the apart-ment he shared with his fiancée and so no one was there for Corporal Mulcahey except kind, naïve Danny Goodman, who could say only "Oh, my God," over and over and over.

For the following four weeks, the murder of Robert Kennedy was the reality John Francis Mulcahey lived, while his daily life was not actual to him. Each morning, even on weekends, Rosie nagged him out from under his mosquito-net, he stumbled across the hallway to pee wearing the same clothes he passed out in, then across the other hall to the desk he had once shared with Leffanta. There he drowned his hangover with ice water Rosie brought him from the fridge and pounded ineffectively on his manual typewriter, but the newspaper photo of Bobby stretched out on the floor, arms flung wide, a kitchen-worker kneeling at his side, appeared across every page he was supposed to be typing. He slept away lunch time on his sweaty cot, pounded on the Remington until dinner, then numbly stuffed down enough food to get him through doing dishes and the sipping of gin and tonics until he passed out in his clothes. Every other day, without saying anything about it, Rosie handed him clean clothes, a towel and a cake of soap and walked him to the bathroom, closing the door behind him. The memory of Mama-san rinsing bloody rags in the tiled shower precluded that option, so Mulcahey stripped and washed himself at the basin as best he could. Each moment of each day, the reality was Bobby Kennedy's murder. The present was a fogbound dream-state.

Wednesday, 3 July, seemed to Rosie a tropical steam-bath, even by the Saigon norm. By the time he dropped Sang at her school and pushed the Suzuki through heavy traffic to III Corps, his shirt was soaked and the alleyway was still deep in mud from the previous afternoon's downpour. As Papa-san swung open the courtyard gate, Rosie saw Mad-dog leaning on the railing of the second-floor balcony with a coffee cup cradled in his hands. He was about to call up to him when a shot rang out, very near-by, and the coffee cup shattered on the cement of the courtyard. Rosie and Papa-san raced up the interior stairway and found Mulcahey lying on his back, arms stretched out. They crawled low getting to him and Papa-san, the veteran warrior, went to work, running his hands over him, his head, torso, limbs, searching for an entrance wound. He pulled the limp body over and

searched with eyes and hands for an exit wound. Then he flipped
Mulcahey onto his back again and slapped him hard across the face.
Mulcahey opened his eyes and mumbled something under the torrent
of Vietnamese curses Papa-san laid on him. Then the old man went
to the railing and shouted angrily at three ARVN soldiers who were
yelling back, mocking and laughing. At length, they shouldered their
carbines and moved off and Papa-san descended the stairs, muttering
angrily to himself.

"For God's sake, Mulcahey!" Rosie screamed. "Why did you do
that? You scared the shit out of us!"

"I didn't know they were there. They fired in the air to scare me
and I felt like it hit me. I felt it hit me in the chest."

"Look, I know this has been a hard time for you," Rosie said,
"It's been a hard time for lots of people, not just you. Guys are dying
every day. So, I'm giving you exactly twenty-four hours to pull yourself together here, then I'm not cutting you any more slack, you got
that?"

Early the following morning, before dawn, whatever it was that
happened, happened.

Mulcahey remained at the long table in the roof enclosure after
the dishes were stacked, Goodman had retired to his cot and Rosie
had left to be with Sang. Mulcahey sat alone, with the lights out,
drinking gin and tonic, nursing a fantasy that tortured and soothed
him at the same time. His imagination projected a vivid scene onto
the facing wall—the crowded, chaotic kitchen of the Ambassador
Hotel in Los Angeles on the night of 4 June. He heard the cheering
of the triumphant crowd in the ballroom and then Bobby Kennedy's entourage pushed its way into the kitchen, NFL legend Rosie
Greer leading the way and a wake of staffers following behind. The
moving images were three-dimensional and in color and they became

a reality, so that Mulcahey was no longer trapped in an Army Intelligence villa in Saigon but was there, in person, a volunteer for Bobby's campaign. When the assassin stood up on the counter and drew his gun, Mulcahey leapt between him and his intended victim. Shots were fired but they entered his body instead of Kennedy's. As Mad-dog lay dying, Bobby knelt beside him, cradling his head in his hands. "It's OK," Mulcahey told him, "Now you can win the election and save our country." Bobby wept.

The flight of stairs was precarious for a man as drunk as he was, but he managed. The advent of the rainy season marked the return of clouds of mosquitos at night, so he put a match to a coil of incense that was almost as obnoxious to humans as to insects, then pulled off his clothes and slipped under his netting. He tried to revive his redemption fantasy but soon passed out.

What happened began as a monotone sometime in the night. A sustained, irritating note that slowly penetrated his sleep. Eyes still shut, he tried to identify it. Machinery? A truck engine? Overhead fan bearings going bad? He tried to ignore it for a long time but it pulled him from sleep, finally, to the point where he was fully aware of it and he opened his eyes and saw the fan-blades slowly turning in the glow of a dim yellow light. *It's Goodman,* he thought, *with a flashlight, reading in bed.* But across the room, through his mosquito-netting, he clearly saw Goodman lying face-up on his pillow in the golden light. *OK then, what?* He sat up, slipped out from under his netting and stood up.

Huddled at the foot of his bed, the source of the monotone knelt there, glowing, golden, three-dimensional. The human form had no distinguishable face but the robed figure held the Lotus Position just as Leffanta did in his lifetime. Mulcahey felt intense excitement at this spectacle but no fear. Rather, he felt strangely comforted by its presence. He held his ground for a full minute or maybe two, absorbing the image and steady monotone, then like a candle guttering out at the end of its wick, whatever it was faded and was gone. Mulcahey placed his bare foot in the space where it happened and verified that there was nothing there, no warmth or cold, only the tiled floor. He walked calmly to the stairs, descending to the courtyard. Papa-san opened the gate and spoke to him in Vietnamese as he rode his bicycle out. He flew through the semi-deserted streets as fast as he could go, six miles to the doors of Notre Dame Cathedral. He padlocked his bike to the usual street sign just as dawn was breaking and jogged across to the building where Levesque stayed. He got the night-guard to understand "Brother Andre" and was permitted in. He wrapped on Levesque's door, whispering "Brother Andre!" Levesque's cell was so tiny, the two of them barely fit into the space between bed and wardrobe.

"I had a visitation! This morning! Just now!" Mulcahey whispered. He was out of breath from his dash across town but to his own amazement, he felt serene and although he was bearing an insane message, he felt sane for the first time in weeks. "It was Leffanta, the weirdo I told you about from III Corps who got shot during the May Offensive, that's who it was, sitting cross-legged like he always did. I saw him, man! He was glowing and flickering like a candle-flame. But he was real!"

Levesque ducked his head out the door and checked the corridor, left and right. "That's good, I'm glad," he said, "But let's get you a shirt and sandals. You can't go in boxer shorts. Then we'll go somewhere for coffee."

"Don't blow me off on this, Rene! I'm serious!" Mulcahey said much too loudly.

"OK but pipe-down! I'm running some cover here, remember? I'm not even supposed to know you except as a piano-player for the choir. This place is a bee-hive, so let's get out of here."

Huddled over coffee and croissants with Rene's shirt hanging off his shoulders, Mulcahey laid out everything in detail, just as it happened, then said, "You're the only one I know who might believe me about this, Levesque."

"Of course I do. Why wouldn't I?"

Mulcahey stuffed a whole croissant into his mouth and said, around it, "Man! I feel… I don't know… I feel better… I feel GREAT! I should be scared out of my tree, shouldn't I? But I'm not!"

"Why shouldn't you feel good?" Levesque said quietly. "You didn't know you had a Guardian Angel, now you do. Angels pop up all over the place in Scripture."

"Yeah, well… if it really was Leffanta, he's still a creep. I hope it's some other ghost!"

"Angel," Levesque amended.

"Don't tell anybody about this. I don't want everybody to think I've gone nuts!"

"You've been nuts a long time, Mad-dog."

"But I do feel like some huge weight has been lifted off me! It's all gonna work out, somehow, isn't it, Rene. The last thing Leffanta said was love transcends time and space… weird, huh?"

"Not really," Levesque sipped his coffee and smiled. "It's what I've been trying to tell you all along."

5

15 October 1967 – 24 September 1968

A NEO-COLONIAL TANGO

Like most young men of his time and place, Zachary Rosenzweig had to learn about love in stages and without much guidance. Respectable families of the mid-twentieth century practiced discretion around children and by the time it occurred to them the children had somehow grown, well, explanations were obviously no longer needed. So, like most his Nashville friends, Rosenzweig muddled through the stages of romantic love by tapping a white cane down a dark path.

He first noticed "Pam" (no need to use her real name) in eighth-grade English class when she began wearing tight blouses with three buttons open between her white throat and her brand-new cleavage. Rosie always liked her—she was a friendly girl—but now he couldn't keep his eyes from drifting toward her while the teacher droned on and on in the airless classroom. His "A" in English became a "C" as he scribbled long, extremely amusing letters to Pam during class. He bought her a red and gold bracelet at Kresge's that he knew she would like and a 45 RPM record of Nat King Cole singing "It Was

Fascination, I Know." But in the crowded classrooms and hallways, he never managed to catch her alone and he felt feverish about the idea of giving her these things in front of people, so she never saw them. At the end of the year, he dug everything—the letters, the bracelet, the record—out of the bottom of his green canvas book bag and dumped them into the cafeteria garbage pail because by then, of course, Pam had a boyfriend. He never mentioned any of this to anyone, not even to his best friend, Buzz O'Malley.

It is a fair but unanswerable question to ask if Rosie's being of the Jewish persuasion was the cause of his timidity in the "Pam" stage. The Rosenzweig family was quite secular, though they did observe The Seder and Chanukah in their home with a small number of invited guests. When as a child, Zachary caught any playground flack about being a Jew, he took a head-count and figured being a defender of his faith was not a viable option in an elementary school that was 97% Christian, 2% agnostic and less than 1% Zachary Rosenzweig. Affable and easy-going by nature, he developed pacifism to an art form, which served him well both before and after he grew to be a six-footer with broad shoulders. He loved high school—played a trumpet in the marching band, won quarter-mile races as a member of the track team, was well liked—but there was something missing.

What was missing, exactly, was the chapter of his freshman biology textbook entitled "Human Sexuality." There it was in the Table of Contents, but the School Committee had voted unanimously to have it razor-sliced out of each copy of the book and that the teachers be instructed not to mention the topic, ever. Rosie ran his thumb over the stubs of the fourteen missing pages and tried to imagine what had been there. He caught a few glimpses of *Playboy* magazines some seniors on the track team hoarded to themselves before the coach confiscated them. But his curiosity on the matter was like a hole in his pants pocket that, as Twain famously observed, was impossible to keep his finger out of.

He was tapping his white cane down this dark path during his sophomore year on the day he was inducted into the Lettermen's Club at a pep rally and that's where "Rhoda" first saw him. "Who's that?" she shouted to her friends over the blare of the pep band, "He's adorable!" "Don't waste your time. He's Jewish!" someone yelled back. "Rhoda's" big, almond eyes flashed and her nifty little body shivered with excitement. "Not for long!" she shouted, and the game was on. Rosie was puzzled to find an invitation to the Sadie Hawkins Day Dance taped to his locker from someone he didn't know.

"The girls get to ask the boys on Sadie Hawkins Day." Buzz O'Malley told him.

"I know that, Buzz, but who is she?"

He fretted about it until someone pointed her out to him in the cafeteria, then he felt like the luckiest kid in the school.

They danced every dance together on Sadie Hawkins Day and when he walked her to her door and nervously bent down to offer a kiss, he was overjoyed when she returned it eagerly. Finally! A real, live girlfriend to help him solve the riddle of the missing chapter! He held her hand and kissed her everywhere they went, teasing and bantering and joking with her, with growing trust in her affection for him, taking a lot of ribbing from Buzz O'Malley about being "Rhoda's" love-slave."

Two months into it, after he was conditioned to expect a charge of adrenaline at the mere sight of her, Rhoda sat in his lap at the drive-in movie with her arms around his neck and announced that she had a very, very important question to ask him. "Seriously," she said, "seriously… have you found Jesus Christ?"

"I didn't know he was lost," Rosie jibed.

And that began their first real quarrel. Rosie spent the next two years trading conversion promises for kisses. He read the New Testament with her and discussed it earnestly between making-out sessions in his car. He attended prayer groups but avoided telling his parents. He lied to Rhoda about family obligations to get out of attending religious retreats. All that time, her remarkably beautiful face and tight young body held for him the kind of bliss that she promised awaited him if he came to The Lord. They broke up senior year because she despaired of ever winning him for Jesus and he concluded religion would always be more important to her than lust. By then, Rosie had learned what he needed to know about human sexuality—far beyond what was offered in the plumbing diagrams sliced out of his biology book—and it had left him more worldly wise and cynical than he should have been at eighteen.

"What'd I tell ya'," the still-unattached Buzz O'Malley said, "Women just want to get their hooks in ya'."

With this for his education, Rosie was content to run with groups in college, hanging out with friends but avoiding serious attachments. There was, though, "Sheila"—lithe "Sheila"—who fascinated him his junior year. But she made it clear that finding the right partner to start a family with was her passion, which seemed somehow to leave passion itself out of the whole equation. Rosie left college with a degree in U.S. history, lots of ribbons for winning quarter-mile events, a high GPA, many excellent friends, and his virginity. He knew that he was in a small and shrinking minority as a 21-year-old virgin, but it was not that uncommon in the years before the sexual revolution shifted the ground under an entire generation. And Rosie was a moral guy in the traditional way. He wanted his first True Love to be perfect. He didn't want it rushed or haphazard. Besides, this Vietnam thing wasn't going away and his draft board was making noises. He could do a hitch in the military and then settle down and find the girl of his dreams.

That's not exactly how it went down.

Rosenzweig's meeting Nguyen Sang was the single most shocking, life-altering event that ever happened to him. Nothing in his experience could have led him to anticipate it, yet his whole life had prepared him for it. It was his destiny.

His first week posing as a "civilian contractor" in the noisy, exhaust-choked bake oven of an Asian city filled him with terror. Recurring nightmares of MPs dragging him from under his mosquito netting, demanding to know who he *really* was, alternated with VC firing squads executing him for being a spy, which of course he really *was*. Belmont, a larger-than-life man of experience (six months in-country), had been teaching John Mulcahey and him how to run III Corps Headquarters, how to stay alive in Saigon's roller-derby traffic and how to bicker over prices at the market, as well as the locations of all the officer's clubs, gyms and pools where their rank-inflated civilian ID cards gained them access. The finale of all this on-the-job training was how to manage the sprawling world of "shantytown."

"There are rules," Belmont warned, "Never go alone. Stay out of there at night. Keep an eye on your watch and wallet and stay alert. But be prepared for a *great* experience. When you get back home, you won't be as well received by your family as you are in shantytown. Here you are a gold mine and a godsend to 10,000 desperate refugees. A few of them will feed their families tonight because you graced them with your presence. So bargain your girl or her mama-san down to $5, as I taught you in the market, and when you kiss your girl goodbye, give her $10. Hell! Give her $20! It's only money to you. It's bread on the table and shanty rent for her. Now go and do as God has bid thee and love thy neighbor as thyself."

Swarms of children, shrieking like parakeets, pulled on Rosie's hands and pushed him like a water buffalo into the warren of shacks, dozens of small salesmen from hell vying for his attention. "My sistah, she numbah-one beau-ful, come with me!" they begged him. But Rosie soon turned against the human stream and tried to make his way back toward the jeep. He didn't want his first sexual experience to be like this, in this muddy flesh-market conducted by preteen pimps. This was not for him. But this horde of children had gone to bed hungry too often to give up landing this big fish. Rosie was losing the physical fight, so he waved his wallet high over his head and yelled at them, "I give you dollar, you take me jeep, OK?" and he began putting paper scrip-notes into grasping hands, 25-cent note here, 50-cent note there, then dollar notes, repeating, "Now *you* take me jeep, OK? Now *you* take me jeep!" Unfortunately, but predictably, his tactic released some invisible pheromone and a floodtide of frenzied beggars, not all of them children, descended on him from every direction. Feeling the panic of a giant caterpillar under siege by an army of ants, he twisted his body left and right, trying to wrench free of clutching hands until in his struggle, he slammed smack into a good-sized adult. In his blind panic, he thought it was Mulcahey coming to his aid, Mulcahey in a simple straw hat with a bright blue silk ribbon, grabbing him by his shirt and yanking him through the mob and into the doorway of a shack. He was shoved inside and the door was pushed shut against the rabble. Then she turned toward him the most strikingly exotic face he had ever seen, large, wide-set almond eyes above high cheeks, flawless olive skin, an abundance of softly flowing dark-brown hair pouring over the shoulders of her white silk au dai. She was taller than any other native person he had seen—she seemed Vietnamese but not Vietnamese. She stared into his face calmly, seriously, for a long moment that left an eidetic image burned permanently into his memory.

"If you give away money like that, they will eat you for lunch. What were you thinking?" she asked in barely accented English.

He tried to find an answer but was thoroughly rattled by his narrow escape and completely awed by her appearance, her fluent English, the deliberate, confident way she had intervened and taken charge of him. "I don't know," he finally managed, "I just wanted to go home."

An American civilian, young, new to the country, money in his pocket and he can't keep his eyes off me, Sang thought. *This could work out, but he is scared and I must not press him too hard.* She flashed him a big, mirthful smile and said, "You can stay here for awhile and they will go away out there. Then you can go home." She put on a performance for him, lifting the straw boater that Captain Blake had given her, shaking her luxuriant, brown hair over her shoulders and breasts as she waltzed across the room to the bed, the only piece of furniture in this corrugated-tin shack, placing her hat on the bedstead. His eyes followed her every move. She sat on the edge of the bed and patted the mattress beside her. "Come sit down," she told him, "I won't bite you." He did as he was told but put two feet of space between them. *He is a very skittish bird*, Sang thought, *I must be patient.*

She began by saying something that would convey to him that she was not a shanty-whore, despite appearances. "I would offer you something, but I don't have anything," she said, careful to use correct English, as Captain Blake had taught her. She waved her delicate hand in a graceful gesture at the room, ten-by-ten of packed earth with only this ancient, creaking bed and a fifty-gallon drum for catching rain water through a hole in the tin roof. "This is not my house. It belong to... *belongs* to mama-san."

The young man was clearly uncomfortable and not feeling

THE TIME WILL COME 117

oriented. "Where is your house?" he asked.

"I have an apartment... I *had* an apartment," she corrected, "near Cholon. You know Cholon, the Chinese part of Saigon?"

"No, sorry. I've only been in Saigon for a few days," he said, which did not surprise her.

Young men did not wander the alleys of shantytown unless they were looking for a street-girl, so she tried to let him off the hook by saying, "So you got lost and you were paying money to children to find your house?"

He had a very nice laugh. "No... not exactly. A friend drove me over here to..."

Now he had cornered himself, so she said for him, "... to find a girl."

"Well, OK, yes."

"Did you find one?" she teased.

"No... I changed my mind." He flushed like a schoolgirl, which Sang found endearing.

"Yes, but you did find one... you found me!" She played with him in this way to test him, to find his chemistry. Captain Blake had always been so confident, but this younger man seemed vulnerable and sat there so rigidly!

"Yes," he said, "but I think you were the one who found me. So, thank you for helping me. I felt like I was getting in trouble out there."

"You *were* in trouble out there."

"I was... yes, I was," he admitted, "So thank you for helping me..." He lapsed into an awkward silence.

She assumed by the way he looked at her that he was not a boy who preferred boys, probably, but he was not coming on to her, as any other American she'd ever met would have done. In a minute or two, he would make some excuse and walk out the door, casually taking away her chance at a good life and never knowing it. Fighting back a rising sense of panic, she made her play. "If you want to make love to me, you can... you could."

"I... I don't feel ready yet... for that," he stammered and at once, Sang relaxed her fears. She understood him now. *He's cherry!* she thought. *Captain Blake made me his mistress when my step-father died, when I was 13, but this man is 20-or-so and has never had a lover! He has as much need of me as I have of him!*

Rosie realized he had confessed to this young woman something his best friends did not know about him. He twisted himself around to look full-on into her face, to see how she was responding to his admission. She held a slight look of amusement—her chestnut hair cascaded over her shoulders and caressed the white au dai—and it occurred to him that if he did not make love to her, as she said he could, here and now, he might be making the most colossal mistake of his life—one that would haunt him into old age. He began to say, "OK... let's do," but the words that came out were instead, "So your apartment near Cholon... you don't live there anymore?" Sitting on a rusty iron bed in a shanty, as he was, it was an idiot's question.

Sang knew what to do now. She would lay it all out for him—who she was and what she wanted from him. Then if he walked away from her, he would at least know from whom he was walking away. "I show you," she told him and knelt beside the bed to retrieve her box of things. She put a hand on his knee for balance and he flinched, so she looked up at him with her big brown eyes and laughed playfully. She pulled the few clothes she had from the box for him to see and placed them aside, then opened the manila envelope of her photos and letters. "This is my house," she said, handing him a glossy 4x6 photo of the apartment she shared with Captain Blake, "... *was* my house." She ran her lacquered fingernail over pictures of the art pieces that adorned the wall above the red sofa, the matching black end tables and the middle-aged Caucasian on the sofa wearing Air Force blue. "This my friend, Captain Blake, who taught me English," she said, "We are friends for two years before he have go back home to Auzona." To make certain this young man did not misunderstand what she was telling him, she nestled into him while she pointed out each of the refinements of her recent past. *This could be your apartment,* she was telling him*, and it could be you having your picture taken by me, the pretty girl who is pressing herself against you now. This could be us.*

As he stared at the picture, Rosie was acutely aware of the warm pressure against his thigh, his hip and ribs, and that he was being asked a question for which he had no answer. "You must be a good student," was how he shaped his evasion, "Your English is excellent."

"This is me on Captain Blake's scooter… and this is me in Phoc Tho, where my mother and brother live," she continued excitedly, laying her life out for this young American. "This my brother Huy. He is brave soldier in ARVN, in artillery." And then she gently caressed a tattered, cracked black-and-white photo of a soldier, smiling from under his service cap, his arm draped across the shoulders of a pretty, young Vietnamese girl half his size. "This is the only one pic-shah I have my father, together with my mother. He was French soldier, very brave. He is why I have light hair and am so taller as other girls. He die fighting Viet Minh and they take him home to France. So sad, my mother cannot visit grave…"

They were startled by someone pounding on the flimsy door, shouting, "Rosenzweig, you decent? Time to go, man." Belmont had paid an urchin to point out Rosie's location.

"My friends," he said awkwardly as she pulled out from under the arm he didn't remember putting around her. "We need to…"

"You want to go home, I know," she said and smiled to hide her fear.

"Maybe I can come back sometime… to see you," he offered.

"Sure… OK. That would be OK," she said.

He crossed to the door, lifted the latch and pulled it open, then turned to see her standing by the bed in her long, white ao dai, photographs in one hand, envelope in the other, an expression of sadness, he thought, but wasn't sure. Then he raised a hand in a parting gesture and slipped the door shut.

As she slid her cherished photos back into the manila envelope, the tears began to roll down her cheeks despite her efforts to fight them back. Grief at her accumulation of losses was one part of her flowing emotions: Her dreams of escaping life in a village where she was scorned for being a half-breed Euro-Asian—of becoming a nurse, a professional woman in the big city—all of it slipping away when her step-father worked himself to death trying to till enough rice to keep her in Catholic school. Her appearance, which made trouble for her in Phoc Tho, was what drew Captain Blake to her. She was tall and exotic-looking with flowing hair, which caught his attention in a café, and he spoke just enough French to seduce her. She did not "live with him" so much as she sneaked away from her boarding school to be with him. He, in turn, taught her English and paid her tuition, room and board.

And this was at the heart of Sang's sorrow: She was furious at having to grovel at the feet of rich Americans for the right to have a good life. Captain Blake treated her well. Perhaps he even loved her, as he said. But he did not treat her as his daughter. He treated her as his mistress. When he left her "to go back home," she had sold their furniture, the motor scooter she never learned to drive and the art work, which kept her in school for a semester, but she was reduced by degrees to desperation, living in a hut in shantytown with just enough cash remaining to last a few months then, if no other man came along to replace Captain Blake, she would return to Phoc Tho to help her mother in the fields and that would be that. She was an excellent student, hard-working and dedicated to her studies. Why couldn't that be enough? Why did she have to be some rich foreigner's mistress to continue in school? She had to lay out her life before that young man just now and plead for his help, to offer her body to him to gain his sponsorship—*why*? Because he was born a rich American and she was born a Euro-Asian outcast in a peasant village.

She knew the tapping at her door was the American. He was a decent, well-meaning young man, also an astoundingly naïve virgin-idiot, but he would do. He would want to help her and she desperately needed help. He was a man and, therefore, would try to be possessive and controlling and shape her to his ideas. But Sang knew herself and this one, unlike Captain Blake, was malleable. She would flirt and cajole and persuade and have her way. In the end, she would have a life of her own. She dried her cheeks on the sleeves of her au dai and opened the door.

His eyes were dancing in his head and he was grinning like a maniac. He thrust a fistful of blue and purple scrip at her and barked, "OK, listen. Can you find a place for us like you had in Cholon?"

She took the money, the down-payment on her being his mistress, and told him, "I knew you were a good man. I knew when you say you want to go home. You same like me." And tears came again to her eyes as she sealed the deal that would preserve her dreams. He told her he would meet her again, noon next Sunday, here at shantytown, but just to make sure he didn't get distracted in the meantime, she pressed her body into him and kissed him on the cheek. That would keep him thinking the thoughts she wanted him to be thinking until then.

Before she could hide the money away among her things, he was back in the doorway, shouting, "What's your name?"

She laughed and answered, "Co Sang."

"Hi, I'm Rosie!" he said, "Rosie like the flower." Then he was gone.

As she tucked the scrip papers into her hiding place, she realized she was feeling something almost forgotten, a hopeful, cheerful mood she had not known since Captain Blake left her. "This will be OK," she whispered to herself, "He is a nice boy and a long way from the worst American I have met."

"Co Sang!" Rosie announced as he rejoined Belmont and Mulcahey in the jeep. "Her name is Co Sang and she's half French, really tall, maybe five-eight, with amazing hair."

"Quite a bargain for 40 bucks," Belmont assured him, "We're proud of you, Rosenzweig. Aren't we, Mulcahey?"

That following week was nerve-racking for Rosenzweig. Belmont had warned him that she might take his $40, come across a better offer, and be gone for good. When Sunday came, he drove the powder-blue SIC jeep through a downpour, the canvas over his head dripping onto his lap, his heart pounding in his chest, to find her waiting for him as she had promised, her ao dai and cardboard box soaked through, long strands of wet hair hanging from under her straw hat with the blue ribbon. Before he could say, "You remembered!" she jumped in beside him and shouted, "You remembered!" She directed him to the small, second-floor apartment she had found for them with a little balcony overlooking Tu Do Street. It was more expensive than where she'd lived near Cholon, but this new man was a civilian and everyone knew they made more money than military men.

In the pseudo-military realm of civilian-cover Intelligence, cohabitation with a Vietnamese woman was forbidden and, also, not uncommon. If your commanding officer was Major Shimazu, you were required to dine in the roof-top enclosure each evening then, after dishes were stacked, if you discreetly departed for Tu Do Street, that was your business. If next down in the chain-of-command was Lieutenant Aaronson, a disciplinarian who took Army Reg's very seriously, it was an offense worthy of a court-martial. But fortunately for you, majors outrank lieutenants.

So, the eleven weeks following 22 October 1967, when Rosie and Sang moved in together, was a period of unblemished bliss for them. He gently, patiently corrected her English—she gently, patiently instructed him in the arts of love-making and of using latex contraception. Sang found pieces of used furniture and negotiated the prices. Rosie roped these onto the top of the jeep and they lugged them with Mulcahey's help up the stairs to their apartment. He made sure the red couch and lacquered tables were like the ones she had before. And he used up all his savings to buy a portable Olivetti Lettera 32 typewriter he taught her to use and a used Suzuki motorcycle which, this time, she learned to drive. Her school texts and notebooks were neatly shelved between two six-inch-high lacquered vases painted with golden birds and fishes that they bought as gifts for each other. His corporal's pay was wiped out by their expenses, but he kept that to himself and tried not to look too relieved when Sang got a job running a sewing machine in the afternoons, which brought home a little money as well as steeply discounted au dais.

This three-month honeymoon encountered just one slight speed-bump. In their third week together, Rosie insisted that they celebrate her birthday in style (though she tried to explain to him that in her village, New Year's Day, Tet, was when birthdays were celebrated). They would dine on the roof of the Caravelle (Sang spared his feelings by saying she had never been there before, let alone often, let alone with Captain Blake). With money he borrowed from Mulcahey, he splurged on a bottle of champagne, but when he raised his flute and said, "To Nguyen Sang, the most beautiful girl in the world on her... what birthday is this, actually?" she smiled brightly and answered, "Sixteen." His glass hung in mid-air while he absorbed the unexpected news that he had been sleeping with—was in love with—a child! Her exotic Euro-Asian face and height and her expertise in bed had tricked him into guessing her to be, like him, in her 20's. He managed to smile, sip from his glass and get through the meal, but he was subdued for several days afterwards while he worked through the implications: First, the Army would jail him in a heartbeat for statutory rape if this arrangement came to light. Second, he had not yet considered where this blissful affair was going, but now it was not going toward a happy homecoming, bearing a war-bride back to The States. Even if he extended his tour of duty in Vietnam, his enlistment would be over before she was 18. And third, if it was criminal and immoral for Captain Blake to take a 13-year-old into his bed, what made it the most wonderful thing that ever happened to him that he had fallen in love with a 15-year-old?

Eventually, the depth of his feelings for her overwhelmed all other concerns. And thus it was that, after some days of doubt and ethical brooding, Zachary Rosenzweig came to be "all in" with Nguyen Sang and could not imagine life without her. All things being equal, the two lovers might have lived in Eden forever—Rosie chaining-up the Suzuki in the alley beside their home each evening, bringing left-overs from Major Shimazu's meals to Sang, sipping a cold beer on the red sofa while reading a newspaper or a book to stay out of her way while she studied (he would like to have helped her with her schoolwork but it was in French), trying her patience by taking candid pictures of her with his noisy SLR camera ("Stop it, Zachary," she'd scold, "I'm trying to work."), bringing her tea, falling asleep each night with an arm draped over her, gazing into her beautiful face as she slept. He had been sent here to win the hearts and minds of the Vietnamese people and, dammit, he was doing his best!

For Sang, Eden held out a different kind of bliss. She was working full-tilt, full-time to achieve her dreams. Her first class began at 7:00 a.m. and she needed to be on time, beautifully dressed and academically prepared. She would need not only top marks but enthusiastic recommendations from her teachers to advance into the profession of nursing. Classes ran until 3:30 p.m., then she walked two miles to the sewing shop and labored there until 7:00 p.m. She arrived back at Tu Do Street to see what Zachary had brought her to eat while she did her homework and studied for the next day. She was coaxed into bed sometime after midnight and reluctantly closed her books, feeling behind in her work. She worried that Zachary might become bored, as little time as she had for him, so she made love to him whenever she found the strength, but he seemed to be happy and said he loved her over and over. Her sleep was disturbed by anxious scenes in Vietnamese, French and English: she failed an exam and was expelled—or the school authorities discovered that the aunt she introduced, with whom she said she lived, was in truth a mama-san from shantytown who was paid to play the part and that Sang was actually cohabiting with an American civilian—or the school was invaded by the VC and the Americans bombed it to smoldering ashes. But she never dreamt, waking or sleeping, that Zachary would suddenly leave her.

Eden's fall was on Tuesday, 9 January, beginning with the first full-scale fight of their affair. Sang was bent over her algebra text early that morning, cramming for an exam she would take later that day. Zachary had been hounding her ever since she mentioned that she would be visiting Phoc Tho for a few days during Tet, when school was out. Why this upset him so much, she did not know, and taking him to bed on Sunday afternoon seemed to have no good effect on his mood. He stood on their little balcony now, pouting, while she struggled to solve for two unknowns.

He turned into the room and said "Sang" in a commanding tone she did not like.

"She is my mother!" Sang barked without raising her eyes from the text or her pen from the notebook.

"We *know* things!" he exploded. "People in my company are very well connected and they are telling me that heavy fighting is coming! Bring your mother here! Phoc Tho will be a very dangerous place! And when you lived there, they didn't want you around because you were half French... so why would you *ever* go back?"

Her eyes remained on her textbook while she said, "We do this every year at Tet, Zachary. It is never a problem. Everywhere in Vietnam, North or South, we all go home to family at Tet every year... always... before you Americans ever came here. There is a truce and, for one week, peace and joy of family together..."

"Not this year, Sang! I'm telling you the NVA is moving down from Cambodia and the VC..."

"Why this not on TV? Why Ho Chi Minh himself is announce truce for Tet? You people don't know Vietnamese people..."

"We'll talk about this later," he cut her off, "after you calm down."

"*I* calm down?!" She slammed her book shut. "*You* the one who go diên cái đầu! I go see my mother every year! Captain Blake never tell me no-can-do!"

This was the first time she had mentioned the name of her previous lover since the day she met Zachary and she could see it had the desired effect, if what she wanted was to win the fight and break her opponent. His face red, his jaw clenched in fury, he took his keys and wallet from the shelf and went out, slamming the door behind him. This was not what she wanted. She wanted him to understand how unfair he was being, to admit that she was right to want to visit her mother over Tet—so she yanked the door open and yelled after him, "*Every night,* you go to dinner with your boss! *Every! Night!* But I cannot see my mother in Phoc Tho *one time*?!"

She waited at the top of the stairway, hoping to hear him returning, coming to take her in his arms and say he was sorry for being so angry. Why were men like this—arrogant, possessive, always needing to be right about everything? She heard the motorcycle start, drop into gear and fade into the ever-present traffic noise of Tu Do Street. She splashed water into her face from the basin, dried off, gathered her notebooks and lunch into her book bag and hurried off, lest she be late for her 7:00 class. She would speak softly to him tonight, put her body close to him and ask him to explain, patiently, why he felt so strongly about this? They would settle things. If she could solve the formula for two unknowns in algebra, she could do the same in life.

That day was grueling even by the standards of Sang's normal weekday. She ran the last two blocks to be on time for her first class, arriving sweat-soaked and out of breath. She skipped eating her lunch to cram a little more algebra into her head, then the exam was an ordeal: It was given in the airless bake oven of midafternoon and Sang couldn't shake off the memory that connected math studies to the fight with Zachary that morning. While running the sewing machine at her job, she ached with regret for throwing Captain Blake's name at him. Perhaps she should beg Zachary's forgiveness for being so angry with him. He was, after all, worried about her safety and wanting to protect her, even if he didn't know what he was talking about.

She was glad he was not yet home when she got there. It gave her time to change into fresh clothes and brush out her abundant hair.

When she heard him coming up the steps, she set the straw hat with the blue ribbons on her head, which he always said made her look beautiful. But he didn't use his key. He knocked. When she opened the door, his strange friend Mulcahey stood there looking nervous and embarrassed and behind him, the biggest American she had ever seen stood silent as a statue. Mulcahey thrust an envelope at her and said, "I'm supposed to give you this." She opened the envelope, with $40 in scrip notes inside, and read,

Dear Sang,

My company has sent me on an important assignment to Thailand for a week or two. Enclosed is money for you to visit your mother. I am sorry we had a fight about it. I just want you to be safe. I love you very, very much.

Zachary

Her voice was shaking when she said, "Thank you, Mad-dog. Tell Zachary I will miss him very much" because she was quite certain of what his note meant. He was gone. She had thrown Captain Blake in his face, compared the two of them and said she preferred the life she had with her former lover, who never told her "no-can-do!" She had lost her temper, injured his pride, and underestimated the strength of their bond. And now, with all his money, he had sent her only a symbolic $40, the same amount with which he began their affair.

By the last full week in January, Sang decided she must take the landlord's rising threats to heart. He really would evict her if he didn't receive overdue rent by the end of the week and paying him would leave her penniless, with no way of retaining the apartment.

So she split, packing two cardboard boxes with her treasures—several new au dais and sandals, her textbooks and notebooks for school, her Olivetti typewriter and the two black lacquer vases with golden birds and fishes painted on them—hauling them by pedicab to shantytown, where she gave mama-san $25 for a month's rent on a leaky plywood shack. Sang tried to avoid thinking about Zachary's leaving her, in order to meet all her obligations to class attendance, her studies and her afternoon job. But as she packed up her boxes of things, she turned herself over to sorrow while sorting through dozens of photographs Zachary had taken, choosing a dozen of her favorite ones to place in her manila envelope. She permitted herself to cry, then, at the loss of the young man, aware that she had loved him after all more than she had admitted to herself, more than she had shown him. He had treated her with kindness, allowing her to call him by his given name instead of his rank and family name, buying her a typewriter and teaching her to drive his Suzuki, and by his gaze and voice and touch, showing more affection for her than she had recognized at the time. Americans came and went and, in the end, always had to "go back home." You could not allow yourself to become too strongly attached, for your own survival, but when you found a good man, like Zachary, you had to nurture that relationship—because without him, you lived in shantytown until your money was gone, then you had to give up your dreams and go back to Phuc Tho to spend the rest of your life in the fields.

The week before Tet was a test of Sang's strength. School was a long commute by jitney from shantytown and making sure she arrived with a clean au dai and a groomed appearance was a challenge. She began each day lined up to relieve herself at the women's communal trench and because monsoon season had ended weeks ago, lined up again with her water jug, waiting her turn at the community tank, then she trekked her water through two hundred yards of twisting alleys back to her dimly lit hovel. She filled the basin with water that was unsafe to drink, washed herself with it and scrubbed any dirt off the au dai she would wear that day. She lined up again at a road-side bakery where she bought a baguette loaf the length and thickness of her forearm, which would provide breakfast and lunch. She competed with many others on the main road for a seat on a jitney going toward the harbor, then was jostled, pushed and bounced for forty minutes, during which she rarely succeeded in reading much from her text-books. She arrived at school dizzy and nauseated from dehydration and the cloud of oil-laced exhaust created by the jitney and the sea of traffic around it. If she had time, she went to the restroom to chew on her bread loaf and drink enough water, cupping her hands under the faucet, to clear her head and steady herself. Then a day of classes, an afternoon at the sewing machine, and forty minutes of jitney ride back to her neighborhood while the sun was setting. She took her only real meal each day at an open-air shop where she nursed her rice, *pho* soup and tea for as long as she could because they had fluorescent lights that allowed her to study. Soldiers and civilians came and went from her table, sometimes breaking through her reluctance to make conversation, sometimes asking her polite questions or not-so-polite questions. Sang told them she was waiting for her uncle, to put off any suggestion that she wanted more from them than to be let alone. But the shop owner became more and more suspicious of the pretty Euro-Asian girl who lingered for hours over her food and her books with no uncle ever coming for her. She brushed off young men who tried to talk with her, but if she was not a street-girl, then what? On the fifth straight night of her loitering in his shop, he confronted her with sharp words. Sang told him the truth, in part, that she was a poor student living in shantytown and that when she left his shop to go home, she had no light to study-by, so had to cease her work and sit idly in the dark. The truth she avoided telling him was that she was praying someone like Zachary would come in, man or woman, Vietnamese or American, who would for whatever personal reasons they had, sponsor her dreams, provide her with food and shelter and a place to study so she could someday be a nurse, a professional with a substantial income to provide for herself and her mother. She had once dreamed too of a husband and children, but over the years of her schooling, if she succeeded, she would likely have to be the mistress of a string of rich Americans who would come and go, each one "leaving for home" when his time in Vietnam was up and so, realistically, who would want to marry her then? The shop owner had plenty of his own problems, but he convinced himself it would be less trouble to clear a foot of counter-space in the kitchen where this girl could study than to have men coming on to her, causing trouble. Sang introduced herself by name, thanked him profusely, paid for her meal, and carried her books back to the kitchen, where she stood by the counter until closing time, taking notes and writing pages under the bright fluorescent tubes. Then she returned to her dark shack, hung her au dai from a nail and, lacking a mosquito-net, slept under a sheet to keep from getting bitten on her face.

The bus dropped her on the main road, four miles from Phoc Tho, when she made her pilgrimage home for Tet. She toted two heavy canvas bags of her belongings down familiar roads, feeling happy for this much-needed holiday and its reunion with family and the neighbors of her childhood. The very first words her mother said when she opened the door of their small house were, "One letter in four months! How do I know you are alive?" The next words were, "You skinny like snake! You pay school to feed you, but they steal your money and starve you!" Sang's mother ran to the kitchen to stoke the fire and put on water for rice. For an hour, Sang told her mother all about her studies, her teachers and her friends, how smart they all said she was and how successful she was in school, how much she enjoyed working as a sales person in the tailor shop that paid all her expenses—tuition, books, room and board. Sang's mother said nothing, so it was hard to tell whether she believed what she was being told, was proud of her daughter's achievements, or was silently rejecting it all as a pack of lies. She knew nothing about life in Saigon except that it was not, as her daughter thought, a paradise of opportunity but a pit of evil. Sang spread across the table proof of her accomplishments, papers with high marks and glowing school reports, but Sang's mother was illiterate so couldn't have distinguished the French from the Vietnamese in these documents. Sang cleared the table for the special meal—stir-fry vegetables mixed with rice and chicken, the sign of her mother's love—and she devoured it like the starving girl she was and then fell asleep on her mother's bed.

At dinner-time, Uncle Chieu came in from the field and Sang enjoyed her second large meal of the day. He was the third-born son in her mother's family, so had no stake in the fields handed down to his brothers. Therefore, he had worked as day labor for others until the death of Sang's father (step-father, but that was a family secret well known by everyone in the village) made room for him as his sister's necessary business partner on this small plot. He worked and took his meals here but slept in the house of his brothers. He dearly loved his niece but shared his sister's opinion about Saigon. They both thought she should come back home, where she was needed by her family and where she would be fed properly and not become as skinny as a snake.

And yet, had it not been for Uncle Chieu's influence on her, Sang might never have left. For he was a talented story-teller with a huge repertoire of folk myths and heroic tales about Vietnamese history. He had filled her mind with powerful images of adventure. Without intending to, he had planted the seeds in her of curiosity and a hunger to know the wider world. Although from a Buddhist family, Sang had been strong-willed about attending the Catholic school six miles from her home, where the sisters put ideas in her head that she was intellectually gifted and should pursue higher education. Sang's mother and Uncle Chieu recognized this as a plot to steal her away from her village and her people, but she was, after all, half French so perhaps the French-speaking Catholics were her people also.

However, it was Tet now and harmony was the order of the day. Sang's mother brought out the crumpled letter Sang had sent in late September and recited it word-for-word, as a literate neighbor had read it to her until she knew it by heart. This was chastisement but done gently and with affection. The "one letter in four months" was a family treasure. They gathered with neighbors to enjoy firecrackers provided by the more prosperous families of the village and later, Sang received money wrapped in red paper, twenty Dong each from her mother and her uncle, a great deal of money for them to give. This reminded her of Zachary's birthday celebration for her at the rooftop restaurant of the Caravelle, which cost a hundred times more than forty Dong. There, she had been the English-speaking lover of a rich American, an elegantly dressed and sophisticated young lady, urbane beyond anything her mother or uncle could imagine. Here, she was a peasant farm-girl, still a child who received gifts of money in red paper in celebration of her birthday.

Who I am is determined by my circumstances, she told herself as she fell asleep on a mat on the floor, *but who I will be is a matter of self-determination. I will sacrifice whatever I have to, and I will fight to become what I wish to be.*

The Tet Offensive may have changed the course of the war, the strategic thinking in Hanoi and public opinion in the United States, but it made very little impression on Sang. The fighting never came near Phoc Tho or her school in Saigon. For her, life in shantytown went on much as before, with one noteworthy difference: Sang was running out of money. Her job at the sewing machine paid most but not all her shanty-rent and everything else came out of her reserves. She considered giving up the jitney rides each day, but that would mean arising at 4:00 to get to her 7:00 class on foot and sacrificing most of her study time on the café's kitchen counter in the evenings. Mama-san was not willing to lower her rent and the café owner said he didn't need any more employees. She stopped buying a baguette, which had little effect on her financial decline but much effect on her stamina. She studied during lunch at school so the other girls wouldn't notice she had nothing to eat. Still, she didn't see how she would make it through the end of the term unless things changed—but oh! were they about to!

As little as Rosenzweig understood the young lady he loved, she knew even less about him. He was not a rich American civilian but a lowly corporal who had sent her his last $40. He was not free to come and go, as a contractor would be, but a soldier who, with the help of his friends, was hiding his liaison with Sang. He did not live in a villa at this time, as he claimed, but in a military compound, assigned to share a six-bunk room with other soldiers. He wore civilian clothes as required by his assignment to bilateral operations, US Army

Intelligence, but were he to be reassigned, he could be back in Army fatigues in the blink of an eye. He didn't tell Sang any of this in part because he wanted to command the respect that was due a rich American civilian who was not a lowly corporal—and in part because telling her that SIC was a cover organization for military intelligence would, if discovered, land him a court-martial followed by jail time.

Wise and observant Major Hideo Shimazu had noticed Corporal Rosenzweig coming and going on a motorcycle, never with the other men who lived in the compound but by himself. And he suspected he was living somewhere else, probably with a woman. Lieutenant Stephen Aaronson, neither wise nor observant, knew only that the enlisted men were defiant, disrespectful and much in need of correction at III Corps HQ. He was too often overruled by the major when he tried to impose order on these unruly corporals and, as Tet approached, with reports flooding-in from the field that made for frightening reading, he became desperate to crack down on them. His chance came on the very day that Rosie had the blow-up with Sang over her plans to visit Phoc Tho during Tet. All that day, Rosie was trapped—between sorrow about his fight with Sang, about storming out, slamming the door, her screaming down the stairway at him as he unchained the Suzuki—and a growing anger with his stubborn lover. An attack was coming and it was going to be big, nation-wide, and she wanted to walk right into the middle of it. Why wouldn't she listen to him? Who paid for their apartment and her tuition and books? Who bought her a typewriter and all the food she ate? She owed *everything she had* to him! Without him, she was just a peasant girl in a shantytown hovel with nothing but a box of clothes and old photos! He had lifted her out of all that, so she could be a successful student with a future, a nice home, an American civilian contractor (sort of) who loved her and wanted her to be safe!

These were the obsessions raging through Rosie's fevered brain as he sat at the dinner table in the rooftop enclosure, numb, deaf to the conversations going on around him. And this is when Louis Leffanta—when he was still an angry racist who had never heard of *Cao Đài*—got good and drunk and blew the lid off it for Rosie.

"To Braxton Hood," Bitter Louis mumbled, raising his eighth glass of wine to the newcomer, "Finally, someone to sleep in Rosenzweig's empty bed!"

Lieutenant Aaronson pounced at once. "Where does Corporal Rosenzweig sleep then?"

"Damn-fino," Leffanta slurred, "Out with the gooks somewhere." Never before had he let slip any of his rich vocabulary of racist terms in front of his Japanese-American commanding officer, but he was angry and drunk so reverted to habit.

"A different room in the compound... downstairs... temporary arrangement..." Mulcahey chimed-in, too late.

"Exactly where DO you sleep, corporal?" Aaronson demanded.

Rosie blinked, startled, as someone waking from a sound sleep. "I have my own place... a rental. I can't sleep in the compound... too noisy."

"If I find out you've been shacking up with some Vietnamese slut, I'll have you up on..." Aaronson didn't finish his threat before he was on his back, sprawled on the floor with his shirt-front gripped in Rosie's left fist, trying to shield his face from the right fist. The efforts of both Hood and Mulcahey were required to drag Rosenzweig off his prey, while the lieutenant picked himself up, sputtering promises to file assault charges, blood running down his shirt.

This, then, was the origin of Rosie's curt note to Sang, wrapped around his last $40, telling some improbable tale about being abruptly sent to Thailand, delivered to her by Mulcahey and Hood. What else could he have told her? That he was under house-arrest for striking an officer? That he had been busted back to PFC, with a reduction in pay that would preclude supporting their life together? That he could not write to her or visit her because he was under confinement and perhaps headed for a term in Long Binh jail? And then the Tet Offensive distracted everyone from these mundane concerns.

The very first morning of freedom after his thirty days' house-arrest, Rosie drove the motorcycle hell-bent for Tu Do Street but, just as Mulcahey had reported, their apartment had been leased to someone else. Neighbors he showed her photo to didn't know the whereabouts of the girl in the straw boater with the blue ribbons. Did he want to pursue her until someone finally told him she was killed during Tet, on her way to Phoc Tho? Would it give him any comfort to discover that she was living with some fifty-year-old Lieutenant General on the MACV staff? He had screwed up, and he had lost her, and that was that.

Nine days later—Sunday, 18 February, to be exact—is when Braxton Hood's keen mind and considerable resources changed everything. Hood had been desperately hoping for a new field assignment—in part because there were powerful merchants and Saigon government officials who, if they found him, would want his head on a platter for stealing money from them—and in part because that money was in two heavy boxes under Hood's cot at III Corps HQ and he needed to find some way to spend it. Also, his Greyhawk classmates, Rosie and Mulcahey, were driving him insane: Rosie because he was mortally depressed over losing Sang and Mulcahey because he was Mulcahey.

Shantytown was the world's largest and cheapest outdoor whorehouse for Mulcahey, who had as yet no soul to consider (in these Halcyon days while Bobby Kennedy still lived and no conscience about refugees and their desperate circumstances. So, beside the road at shantytown, Hood parked the jeep and relieved Mad-dog of his wallet, sunglasses, watch and belt. "Your belt holds up your pants, so you won't be needing it," Hood jibed, "and they stole it from you last time." Then a gaggle of barking children dragged Mad-dog into the warren of shacks with his chinos held up with one hand and waving $10 in scrip high over his head with the other. "If I'm not back in twenty minutes, come find me," he shouted over his shoulder.

"You're on your own, pal," Hood answered, not meaning it.

Hood worked the jeep through the heavy traffic, across the busy street, finding a shady spot on the other side away from the army of children, accomplished salesmen all, with more needs than anyone could meet. He dallied with reading a paperback but kept watch through the moving traffic in case Mad-dog needed to be rescued. The swirling street was the same dirt-blown inferno it always was, and Hood had grown used to it. He decided when he got back to III Corps, he would declare by the authority vested in him by his superior physical size and strength that his troubled friend Rosie was going out bar-hopping with him along Tu Do Street, end of discussion. *No More Moping!* he would command. And it may have been merely because of this confluence of thoughts—of Rosie and Tu Do Street and being here at shantytown—that when a jitney pulled out of the traffic twenty feet to his right, he thought he saw someone he knew among the passengers alighting from it. He had seen her only once, briefly, accepting Rosie's letter from Mad-dog and—OK, maybe all Vietnamese look alike to Americans—but this girl was unusually tall with flowing brown hair, and Rosie said he had met her at shantytown.

Hood leapt from the jeep and hollered, "Lady! Hey, ma'am! Miss!" But she gathered up her canvas bag, paid the driver, and began crossing the busy street. Hood started toward her but realized he couldn't abandon the jeep without chaining it up, and she was moving away fast, so he jumped back in and drove straight across her path.

She was startled by this sudden obstacle in her way, but she nimbly danced around the rear bumper while the stranger shouted at her, "Ma'am! Lady! Wait a second! Come back!" She picked her way through the maze of fast-moving vehicles, thinking to herself in her native language, escaping the annoying man who was yelling at her, who nearly ran her down, the fourth or fifth American today who had said something to her, trying to pick her up. This kind of unwanted attention was a condition of her daily life and surfing through it was something she had gotten used to… then she heard "Zachary Rosenzweig" and she stopped at the roadside and turned back, switching her mind from Vietnamese to English. The large, powerfully built stranger was standing beside his jeep while taxi and motorbike horns beeped at him like barking dogs. She had no memory of seeing him before, this man. But he was shouting over the orchestra of annoyed drivers, "You're that girl, right? Aren't you that friend of Rosie's?"

And she stepped further back, out of the traffic, and nodded her head as the Americans do, and her little straw hat with the bright blue ribbons bobbed up and down.

The reunion Hood planned for the star-crossed lovers was every bit as joyful and dramatic as he hoped it would be. He parked Sang with Mad-dog at an eatery a couple blocks from the III Corps villa then fetched Rosie, telling him he needed help moving some furniture. Rosie and Sang fell into each other's arms, crying and shouting explanations in front of a dozen startled customers. "You disappeared for weeks! Our apartment went to strangers! What was I to think, Zachary?" Sang protested. "I was under arrest! Thrown into jail by my enemies! I lost my income!" Rosie hedged, telling Sang a version of the truth that didn't broach the US Army or mention covert operations. Hood was deeply moved by their love for each other and it endeared the couple to him, then and there. He promised himself he would help them in any way he could.

Braxton Hood's vow was almost too easily accomplished. He had never undertaken the daunting task of actually counting the money Frank Monroe and he had fleeced their victims out of, but the bundles of scrip in the two large boxes under his cot made them incredibly heavy. It was in everybody's interest—not least of all his own—to lighten them as expeditiously as possible. By week's end, he had found them an apartment on Cong Ly Street, not far from III Corps and, with Sang's help, he had negotiated a two-year lease on it, paid in cash and in advance. The landlord was grinning from ear to ear as he counted out the bundles of scrip, but to Hood, the blue and purple notes looked like play-money and he had a whole lot more where that came from.

For Rosie and Sang, life seemed miraculous! Late January through February had been hell for each: Rosie condemned under Article 15 of the Unified Code of Military Justice to a month's house-arrest and stripped of his rank; Sang living in grinding, hopeless poverty in shantytown, fearing her school days were about to end. And each one thought they had lost the other forever. Reunited now, benefiting from Braxton Hood's generosity, they were again in bliss. Without rent due, Rosie's PFC pay met their living expenses and his mortal enemy, Lieutenant Aaronson, was in Walter Reed Hospital, undergoing multiple surgeries on his foot and being interrogated about whether his gunshot wound had been intentional, to escape the war. Sang was dropped off a block from school so no one would see her riding on a Suzuki behind an American civilian, and she arrived in her class clean and rested and academically prepared. Her book bag always carried enough food for several lunches and a playful note from Rosie. The small lacquered vase with the golden fish rested on a shelf close beside the one with the golden birds and every day was sunny.

The first cloud to cast a shadow over this unblemished world did not appear until the first week in April. Despite howls of protest about how much schoolwork was due, Rosenzweig insisted that Sang take four days off to vacation with him in Vung Tau. "All of my best friends will be there," he told her, "and I want them to meet you. Braxton Hood is hosting a big party to say goodbye to Mr. Shimazu, who's been the boss at SIC since I got there."

She scowled and said, "That sound like Japanese name."

"He's an American. His grandparents came from Japan."

"Japanese no good. Uncle Chieu say they invade Vietnam, starve our people to death."

"Mr. Shimazu feeds people... you eat left-overs from his cooking almost every night," Rosie said, "He's an American... born in California... doesn't even speak Japanese."

"He look like Japanese?"

"Yeah, I suppose he does *look* Japanese, but what difference does that make?"

"It's in the blood, Zachary. I look Vietnamese because I *am* Vietnamese. Uncle Chieu say you can wrap a dog in pig-skin, is still a dog."

Rosie walked to her and wrapped her in his arms. "You're adorable, you know that? You're a racist but such a beautiful racist." He pulled back and looked her in the eye. "Come with me, Sang. You can sit in the hotel room in Vung Tau and do your homework all day, but first you have to meet my friends. And someday, we'll go to Phoc Tho and I'll meet your uncle."

The idea of Zachary coming to Phoc Tho filled Sang with horror. She would be mortally ashamed to be seen in her village with her American paramour, the man who paid her way because he "loved her," he said. She was not a street-girl. She had never traded money for sex with some passing stranger. But her village would see that as a distinction without a difference. And maybe it was. She told Zachary "I love you too." She had missed him terribly when she was left alone. He was her friend. They each loved living together and sleeping together. But if he were suddenly transformed into a dirt-poor Vietnamese peasant, would she decide to starve with him in shantytown for the sake of their relationship? Or would she look around for a rich American? These were questions Sang tried never to think about, but they were not easy to avoid if he was going to drag her to Vung Tau and show her off to his friends. It was not about having too much homework. Not knowing how to communicate her feelings about this to him, Sang eventually caved-in to his demands and agreed to go with him to Vung Tau—as his what? Many Vietnamese phrases came to her mind, but she didn't know the English equivalents for all of them. *I will tell them I'm a nursing student and then I will ask them lots of questions, so I won't have to answer any*, she decided.

But immediately upon arriving, the magic of the scenery relaxed her tensions. She had never been to any of the beaches on the South China Sea and the immensity and beauty of Vung Tau was overwhelming to her. She would never, herself, have stretched out on the sand, almost naked, sprawled under the sun or splashed around in the waves, laughing and shouting. But that so many others were doing so seemed an innocent and joyful pleasure in this special place. They were like children at play. Once they checked in to their room at a beach-front hotel, Bravo, Juliet!, Sang changed into her brand-new, blue au dai and followed Zachary down to the dining area near the bar, where a sea of loud Americans awaited her. She recognized Zachary's twitchy friend, Mad-dog, sitting beside their wealthy benefactor, Mr. Hood, and she headed in their direction. Mr. Hood shouted something to her in his strangely accented English that she didn't understand, while he pulled a chair out for her. They exchanged a greeting that was familiar to them both. She said, "Thank you, Mr. Hood," and he responded, as always, "Please call me Braxton, ma'am." The address "ma'am" reminded Sang of a Vietnamese word borrowed from the French, "madam," which had a very unfortunate connotation, but Mr. Hood could not have known that. On her right side, Mad-dog was bouncing around in his chair, staring at her with great intensity. He was a good friend of Zachary's, but he always made Sang very uncomfortable and she did not like him. She thought him rude. They were all drinking beers, pouring glasses from a common pitcher. Mr. Hood asked Sang if she wanted something, and she requested a soft drink. Zachary introduced her to Rick Singleton, who was well dressed and soft spoken and the first black person Sang had ever seen up close. Then she met a tall man named Rene Levesque, skinny as a snake and alabaster-colored, like the statues in the chapel at her school. Finally, across the table from her, a man with red hair and dancing blue eyes introduced himself as Mark Babineaux. The men chattered away among themselves, several speaking at a time, high-spirited on this special reunion and drinking beer at a fearsome rate. Sang was greatly relieved that none of them asked her embarrassing questions, as she had feared, but she was having trouble following English spoken at this rate. She sipped her soda and began to feel giddy about how alien they were, these Americans! A black man and one with red hair! A thin, alabaster statue-man and her own broad-shouldered Zachary, whose hair was dark and curly. Mad-dog, the nervous little one who was an inch shorter than Sang, sitting beside the gigantic bear-man,

Mr. Hood, whose hands and head were huge! If she were sitting with
Vietnamese men, they would all have straight, black hair and brown
eyes and would be within a narrow range of sizes and skin-tones.
These Americans were as varied as wild birds!

Over their four days together, Sang was often happy to be left in
the quiet bedroom overlooking the beautiful beach, catching up with
her school work and away from the cacophony of Zachary's circle of
friends. But when she joined them, she began to play a game with
them that became of great interest to her. No one ever asked her about
her studies or the delicate question of her age. They were too caught
up in their party mood to bother. So Sang began to ask discreet questions of each of them, when she caught a moment with one alone.

"What do you do at SIC," she asked Mr. Singleton.

He hesitated for longer than it should have taken to answer a
simple question, then said, "I solve problems for rubber plantations…
you know, transportation issues, mostly."

"That sounds interesting," Sang lied.

"Yes, it is. It's very involved… trucking and shipping and the
like."

"And what work do you do for SIC," she later asked the tall, thin
Mr. Levesque.

It took him a while to gather his thoughts, then he said, "I'm
doing a lot of liaison work with the Catholic church." He paused,
looking thoughtful, then added, "Mainly I work with the orphans,
arranging adoptions and seeing to their care."

"Orphans," Sang said, "That must be very sad work."

"Yes, ma'am, it is. But we do teach them to sing in the choir."

"Sing in the church choir?" Sang asked.

"Yes, ma'am, in Latin. Mad-dog helps us out by playing piano
for the choir."

"How interesting!" Sang prodded, remembering that when she asked Mad-dog, he said all he did was type and file reports, "mostly financial." He had said nothing about playing piano for orphans.

Sang was taking great delight in this game even before she stepped beside Mark Babineaux during the Whales Day Parade. "What work do you do with SIC?" she asked, smiling broadly out of the sheer anticipation of humor.

"Office supplies. Furniture, mostly. Braxton and I have a store here in Vung Tau, up the hill from the beach."

"Office supplies," Sang echoed, "Is that how Mr. Hood got to be so rich like he is?"

Mr. Babineaux looked stunned for a moment, then said, "Oh, no. That's all his own money. He was rich before he ever worked for SIC. He comes from a very wealthy family."

"And now he sells office supplies in Vung Tau?"

"Yes, ma'am. That's what we do."

Sang was having increasing trouble during this round of questioning not bursting out into gales of laughter. She didn't want to be disrespectful but neither did she want them to think she was as stupid as they apparently thought. She was, after all, the best student in her class.

These men are a pack of spies! she concluded, *Zachary and his friends and SIC are all part of the CIA that Uncle Chieu told me about! Otherwise, nothing they say makes any sense!*

She was never tempted, thereafter, to ask Zachary what it was, exactly, *he* did for SIC. They told each other enough little lies as it was, lies of omission, without tainting their friendship with outright, spoken lies. Zachary had asked her once about the "Asian custom of 'saving face'." He had been taught, he said, that Asians avoided placing themselves in embarrassing positions. Sang hoped to avoid that conversation with him ever again—or she might be tempted to ask how he and his friends had managed to provide themselves with so much potential embarrassment by all their ridiculous stories—and why, then, avoiding embarrassment was an "Asian" custom.

Sang's suspicions were confirmed on their last night in Vung Tau, when they all gathered for the party celebrating their boss, Mr. Shimazu. An elegantly dressed woman burst into the party, firing a gun and shouting that her parents had been murdered by Pham Minh, but the man she tried to shoot was Pham Viet, the polite young man who directed the translation office at SIC. She had mistaken his identity, apparently, and soon left without doing any harm except for a shattered mirror. But this kind of thing wouldn't happen to a "service organization." It would happen to a pack of spies.

The party, however, was one of the most wonderful events of Sang's young life. The choir of orphan boys, with Mad-dog helping them on the piano, turned out to be a true story and their energy and eagerness, singing in very bad English, made everyone laugh. Mr. Shimazu certainly was Japanese after all, but despite Uncle Chieu's stories, he turned out to be a very nice man, who offered an eloquent tribute to the importance of women in keeping society civil in times of war. His remarks were translated into Vietnamese by Pham Viet, who didn't speak English as well as Sang, and she felt she could have done a better job if called upon.

When the party was breaking up, Zachary said he wanted to walk on the beach with his friends, asking if Sang would be OK with that. When she said "OK," she didn't think he would be gone all night, so she waited up for him, studying until well past midnight, then, a little worried about him, she slipped under the mosquito netting and listened for him for a long time. Men always made it clear, by their actions, that no matter what they said about love, their men friends came before their girlfriends in their hearts. She wondered if it would be the same if Zachary had an American girlfriend. Or if they were married. She fell asleep feeling sad.

Their lives together in the Cong Ly Street apartment went on as before for a month after the weekend in Vung Tau. Monsoon Season picked up toward the end of April and often she would take a jitney home from the sewing shop and laugh when Zachary came home on the motorcycle and stood dripping in the hallway while she brought him a towel and dry clothes.

"Zachary! What happened!?" she shouted at him when he came home on 6 May with lacerations across his face.

"There was fighting out by Tan Son Nhut, on Plantation Road. Somebody shot out the windshield of my jeep, but I'm OK," he said, but she could hear in his voice that he was not OK.

He refused her advice that he have a doctor look at him, to give him stitches if needed, and he was brooding and silent throughout dinner. She prodded him with gentle questioning, studying his expression more than his words, until he admitted to her, "One of the guys at our office was killed today, Louis Leffanta. You never met him. He was a harmless little guy who liked to dress in white robes and study some weird religion he called Cao Dai. He just caught a stray bullet and died." He pushed shrimp and noodles around on his plate without eating.

Sang was quiet for a time, then said softly, "And you are alive and having dinner with me. Is a problem for you."

"What do you mean, Sang? I'm just feeling sorry for Leffanta, that's all."

"Yes, a little, you are. But your strong feelings are because somebody shoot bullets through your jeep window and you still alive, eating shrimp and noodles with me."

"That's how it turned out. I was lucky."

"Yes, but just one bullet to the left or right a few inches and you be dead like Mr. Leffanta. I see this many time in Phoc Tho, when my neighbors die in war because helicopter shoot them or VC come at night, take them away, never come back. The dead people are big problem for other people because they still alive, eating food, playing with children, working in field. Every hour, all of life, they think of dead neighbor and they feel bad because they still alive." Sang stood and walked over to him, placing her arm around his shoulder and leaning down into his cut-up face. "I think of my friends Khanh and Le every day. They Phoc Tho girls same like me, but they die and I live. Khanh very beautiful. If I step on mine instead, she maybe here, eating shrimp and noodles with you. Now you have Mr. Leffanta to carry with you every day. It very sad. But because of Mr. Leffanta, you must love life more."

Sang's soft hair was falling over his face and neck and he began to choke back tears of guilt—she was right, that he still lived while Leffanta did not—and of fear, that he had come so close today to being among the dead. He was in awe of the comprehension and wisdom of his teen-aged lover. How did she know about these things at her age?

Wise beyond her years, perhaps, but Sang might also have been older than she seemed—for in a drawer of Rosie's desk at III Corps rested a perfect forgery, done by professionals, of a birth certificate that could prove she was nineteen on her last birthday. It was a gift from Major Shimazu to Rosenzweig, in compensation, perhaps, for having to discipline the young man under Article 15 for the crime of striking an officer. The major had no choice, even if he believed in his heart that Lieutenant Aaronson had it coming. He explained to Rosenzweig that this document, along with permission from his commanding officer and the consent of the lady, would allow him to marry Sang—which was precisely why Rosie had placed the forgery in a file folder in his desk and never told her about it. Each week, it was that, well, he hadn't bought a ring… or she had exams… or it was that budget meetings at III Corps meant getting home too late… or it was raining. He had to face it, as wild-in-love as he was with her, he wasn't sure how it could actually work out. Could they end up with an apartment in Los Angeles in the area where Vietnamese immigrants were settling—Sang working in a hospital and he teaching history in a high school? If he knelt before her with a ring in his hand, he was not at all sure what she'd say. So, the file remained in his desk drawer.

A week after his windshield was shot to pieces, Information Reports began pouring across Rosie's desk about the Battle of Coral-Balmoral, an attempt by Australian forces to cordon-off escape routes needed by North Vietnamese Army units that had infiltrated Saigon during the May Offensive. He traced the coordinates where the heaviest fighting was taking place, 25 miles north-east of Saigon in Binh Duong Province, and realized his finger was pointing at Sang's village of Phoc Tho. Each evening for a week, he promised himself on the way home that he would do the right thing, reveal to her that the 141st Regiment of the NVA was clashing with Australian infantry, supported by Centurion tanks, across the fields of her home—and each evening he feared that would cause her to board a bus and place herself in the middle of the fighting. Their life was good. She was safe. Why ruin it?

But if you do love someone, honesty is often, if not a perfect policy, at least less painful in the long run.

On 26 May, the day the 165th NVA Regiment launched an all-out assault on Fire Base Balmoral, Rosie paid for his two weeks of cowardice. Sang was running late for class and asked Rosie to drop her across from the school gate. As he pulled the motorcycle to curbside, an old woman with a cone hat dangling from her neck ran at him, shouting angrily and shaking her fists. Rosie showed the palm of his hand to her in the universal sign for "stop!" and braced for impact. She halted six inches from his face and yelled in Vietnamese, *"Every young girl who comes to Saigon falls prey to a whore-master like you! How much you pay this school girl to lie in your filthy bed, you ghost-white foreign devil!?"*

"This kind gentleman gave me a ride to school because I am very late," Sang yelled back, *"He saw me running and offered to help me so I can be on time."*

Sang turned to Rosie, bowed slightly with her hands together and said in Vietnamese, *"Thank you very much for your kindness, sir. I shall remember you in my prayers."*

"What's the old hag pissed-off about?" Rosie asked in English.

"She thinks you have hurt my reputation, but we are strangers. Go away!" she told him.

Sang started toward the school gate, but the old woman followed her into the busy roadway, yelling at her, *"So now you will go to your school and leave us here on the street? Where will we go? Is this what those Catholics teach you—to treat your people like dogs?!"*

Sang turned back and saw that Uncle Chieu was there too, standing by two large bundles tied up in blankets. *"Dieu aie pitié de moi,"* Sang muttered to herself and walked back to deal with this shocking development, giving up on attending her first class. She put a hand on her mother's elbow and guided her back through the heavy traffic, then demanded stiffly, *"What are you doing here? Did I ask you to come here and scream at me in the street in front of this nice gentleman?"*

"We cannot stay in Phoc Tho. Northern soldiers take over everything and the Americans try to kill them with artillery, tanks, shooting everywhere. We had to run to stay alive!"

"Well, it so happens that this gentleman told me he is a landlord and he might have a place for you to stay, but you must be nice and not shout insults at him... or at me either!"

Sang led her over to Rosie and said, "I have a... we have a problem here. The old hag and her brother, over there by the bundles, need to stay in our apartment for a little while and you will need to find somewhere else to stay. Would you be able..."

"What in hell are you talking about? You can't bring refugees to stay with us... street-people... look at them!"

"Zachary, I will introduce you to my mother and Uncle Chieu later... after they have calmed-down..."

"Your mother and uncle?" Rosie glanced over at them, peasant-refugees like hordes of others who crowded the streets of wartime Saigon. And in his embarrassment at calling her family "an old hag" and "street-people," Rosenzweig had a small moment of epiphany—for wasn't every refugee hauling a bundle through the streets someone's mother or uncle? Didn't his own grandfather once escape from war with whatever he could carry?

"Would it be possible for you to bring a jeep here and help them get to the apartment?"

"Of course, I will. Tell them I'll be back in half-an-hour."

"And Zachary..." Sang glared at him, "Don't be too friendly, please. It's very American to be too friendly but my people are proud and do not want to beg for a place to stay or for food."

"Is that an Asian thing?" he taunted and she narrowed her eyes. "Tell them I'll be right back."

Sang was nowhere to be seen when Rosie returned in the rust-brown jeep with the shattered windshield, but he remembered her instructions and tried to be as unfriendly as he could. He loaded her mother and uncle and their bundles into the jeep without a word said.

When he led the way into the apartment on Cong Ly Street, he carried a bundle in one hand and with his free hand he grabbed two framed photos—one off the wall, the other from the table—showing Sang and him together. He made awkward gestures of welcome, presenting the apartment to them like a real estate agent, while they warbled at each other in Vietnamese. They made no eye contact with him neither as he quickly gathered an armful of clothes from the armoire and a Dopp kit from the bathroom, nor even when he bowed slightly, hands together in prayer position, and let himself out.

Braxton Hood had been long gone from the makeshift bedroom at the III Corps villa, so Mulcahey cheerfully welcomed Rosenzweig's moving back in. "Don't get used to it," Rosie told him, "I'm only gonna be here a few days, until things quiet down in Phoc Tho."

But combat between large units—as any Gettysburg tourist knows—can take on a life of its own. The Battle of Coral-Balmoral raged across Binh Duong Providence for a month, as Australian forces kept tripping across supply dumps that the NVA judged were worth fighting over. The largest military action fought by the Royal Australian Army in the whole of the Vietnam war set off a much smaller but heartfelt skirmish between Rosie and Sang. For a young man in the throes of his first serious love—already doomed to a short life-span by the context of a military assignment—sacrificing one day in the company of his beloved or one night in bed together seemed a soul-wrenching tragedy, and this grief he suffered day after day and night after night throughout the month of May and into June. His few stolen moments with Sang when he picked her up from the sewing job were often spent shopping for food and necessities for her mother and uncle. Then a quick hug in the alleyway as he dropped her off would be all the nourishment their relationship received. In these hot days of Rosie's manhood, the sexual frustration alone was beyond tolerable, setting aside his loneliness at seeing so little of her.

The torment of these days was every bit as intense for Sang as it was for her paramour, but she experienced it differently. Shouldering the burdens of her daily life gave her no leisure to reflect—or even perhaps to *feel*—the loss of Zachary's presence. Indeed, those things she most needed from him, he still provided. She had a home, she had food and the opportunity to pursue her studies, continue down her path to the professional life, all because Zachary was still there for her. He had not "gone away," except in the sense of his physical presence, which (she had to admit) had often been a distraction from her work and a drain on her energy. She was very fond of him but had only so many minutes each day to get things done! In his place stood her anxious mother—in constant fear for the crops and animals and small house she left behind in Phoc Tho—with nothing to occupy her all day in the midst of a teeming city that was alien to her. Each day, she posed a thousand questions that had no answers, including invasive inquiries into Sang's personal life. How could she afford this apartment? What crazy ideas were her Catholic teachers putting into her head? And, repeatedly, why didn't she come back home where she was needed? Even Uncle Chieu, who was much less intense in his tone, asked questions about her life in Saigon which could not be truthfully answered. Thus, the apartment on Cong Ly was no longer a study-hall for the ambitious student but a battlefield where her two irreconcilable worlds collided, her double life laid bare. In brief, Sang was as stressed out during the extensive battle in Binh Duong Providence as Zachary, but she had no time to ponder it.

Rosie had too much time to ponder it. Days still ended with dinner on the rooftop enclosure, but since the departure of Major Shimazu, they had become cursory affairs, with little conversation and no camaraderie. Major Zorth Wills brought his book of crossword puzzles to the table and Captain Kearney read *The Saigon Daily News,* noisily folding and unfolding the pages. The whole tradition, which had been such an elaborate social ritual when Hideo Shimazu presided over it, might have been called off altogether had it not been that the enlisted men shopped, cooked and cleaned up seven nights a week, serving their two seated officers in silence. No one said anything about the decline in menu quality with Mad-dog Mulcahey as chef.

After dinner, the ever-restless Mulcahey went out on the town and, after several failed attempts to sit alone in the villa and read, Rosie began to tag along on Mad-dog's well-rehearsed rounds: To the Cathedral for choir practice, to nearby cat houses where he drank and flirted with coteries of pretty, young women, whether or not he chose one or two for the back rooms, to several humble dwellings in the dark alleys where large families welcomed him for animated conversations in pidgin-English and sign-language and where Mad-dog passed out candy and danced about with the children, being more or less one himself. None of these places did Rosie want to be. His heart remained on Cong Ly Street all the time his body performed the duties of the dinner ritual or trailed along after John Mulcahey, as a diversion until he could be back where he belonged.

The Battle of Coral-Balmoral eventually ebbed and the Australians began to withdraw forces from Binh Duong Providence. So plans were made for Rosie to drive Sang's family back home on Saturday, 15 June.

On the Thursday before the anticipated trip, Rosie experienced a firm reminder of how far life at SIC differed from being "in the military." He and Mulcahey drove to the Army scrap-yard on Plantation Road to have the shattered windshield on the rust-brown jeep replaced. They plugged their ears as they walked past the giant hydraulic machine that smashed vehicles—large trucks to little jeeps—into compact cubes that were stacked by a magnetic crane, six-deep, like a child's set of blocks. The brawny sergeant in charge of the operation had a vocabulary consisting entirely of two phrases: "No can do" and "Army Reg's." Ten minutes of reasoning with him— pointing at the line of damaged jeeps with perfect windshields that were awaiting the crusher—elicited only echoes of his two phrases. Suggesting that he might get busy with paperwork and not notice anything but the $20 someone left on the counter caused him to snarl through clenched teeth, "NO CAN DO!" and "ARMY REG'S!"

"What the hell's the matter with that nut case," Mad-dog asked as they drove out.

"He's in the Army," Rosie said, "He's not like us."

Meanwhile, two days of arguing with an exhausted, stressed-out Sang resulted in Rosie's finally squeezing out of her a reluctant invitation to dinner in his own home.

"Sitting down to eat with my mother and Uncle Chieu will not be what you expect," Sang warned him, but she was too tired to fight about it and he was, after all, going to drive them home the next morning.

Rosie was in a buoyant mood all day Friday. Major Zorth Wills hardly looked up from his crossword when Rosie told him he had a dentist appointment, so would miss dinner. He bought a new Oxford dress shirt with button-down collars and succeeded, after a few tries, in tying a brightly colored silk tie into a double Windsor. He gathered up his gifts and a bottle of rice wine and headed out feeling like it was Prom Night.

Sang, when she opened the door, seemed to share his anticipation, dressed in her prettiest blue ao dai over white silk pants. Her mother and Uncle Chieu, well dressed but somber, had lost their street-refugee raggedness. Rosie put his hands together and bowed to them and they nodded slightly in response. Sang bade him sit at the table and assumed her role as servant to a guest and her elders. She poured them each a rice wine, adding some water to her mother's, and Rosie, the only one in the room grinning like an ape, raised his glass in their direction. They nodded again, solemnly.

"I've brought a little gift for them," Rosie said quietly, trying not to look at his beautiful Sang, "Shall I give it to them now or wait until later?"

She said, "Now would be fine, Zachary."

Rosenzweig drew two packages from his shopping bag, each wrapped in the red paper which he had learned was traditional for gifts of money, very much in keeping with Vietnamese custom. Rising up, he reached across the table and set a package before Sang's mother, first, and then another before Uncle Chieu.

The reactions of the recipients were very different. Uncle Chieu unwrapped his first and found four rubber-banded stacks of Dong, each about three inches thick. His eyes went as wide as a kid's at Christmas and he broke into a smile to match Rosie's. Nodding vigorously, he repeated "cảm ơn, cảm ơn" over and over, one of a half-dozen words Rosie knew: "Thank you."

Sang's mother, by sharp contrast, barked in Vietnamese, "*Is this for you!?*"

"*No, mother, it's a gift for you.*"

"*I mean, is this the price the ghost-white devil is paying for you–so he can take you away to The United States forever?!*"

"*Don't be ridiculous, mother!*" Sang whined, "*I'm not going anywhere! And you have to learn something! For an American, this is very little money. If he wanted to buy me for his wife, he could fill this room knee-deep in Dong!*"

Sang's statement made Uncle Chieu's eyes and smile grow still wider. "*This room... knee-deep in Dong?!*" he asked.

Rosie could not mistake the fury of this argument, which raged heatedly between mother and daughter for some minutes, as any version of "Thank you." "What's wrong?" he asked quietly, "Did I insult her?" But he was ignored by Sang, who was exactly what she would have been in any other language or culture: A teenager in combat mode, fighting her mother to gain her independence.

While Rosie was being ignored by the combatants, he was, in turn, ignoring Uncle Chieu, who raised his wine glass in one hand, his stacks of Dong in the other, laughing until tears of gratitude flowed down his cheeks, hailing Rosenzweig as if he were Caesar.

The mother-daughter fury continued in loud, razor-edged Vietnamese while Sang served the meal, slapping bowls and utensils (one fork, three sets of chopsticks) onto the table, flinging drawers open and slamming them shut, her face a mask of petulant defiance. Rosie watched her closely for clues, helpless to know if he was the subject of the debate—or his gift—or something else entirely. He had seen her like this only once before, the day they fought over Sang's visiting her mother during Tet, and he was jolted by the realization that this was Sang "acting her age." She was not—when it came to her family— the woman he loved. Not yet. Sang became before his eyes a bright, precocious adolescent, struggling like any other adolescent to discover who she was becoming. The rest of it—his lover, the fashionable young woman dining at The Caravelle—were costumes she tried on to see how they might fit her.

Had Rosie been fluent in Vietnamese, he would not have been flattered by anything being said, beginning with, *"If he wanted to buy me for his wife, he could fill this room knee-deep in Dong! He was just making a small gift to you, to get you to like him... to make you happy!"*

"I am happy!" Uncle Chieu said, *"I DO like him!"*

"Keep quiet, you!" both women shouted at him.

"This no small gift, daughter! Look at it! It would choke a water buffalo!"

"He makes ten times that much every day! This is nothing to him! A gesture!"

"He makes TEN TIMES this... ?"

"Stay out of this, brother!"

"Yes, shut up, uncle!"

"He buys you then, with all that money?"

"He is just a friend... He sponsors young students, boys and girls... it's a hobby for him!"

"You LIE! I see how he looks at you, daughter!"

"THAT Is None. Of. Your. BUSINESS!"

"Soon, he steals you for a war-prize, takes you away!"

"I'm not going ANYWHERE! Not EVER!"

"Easy to lie to me, the mother who gave you life!"

"You've had too much wine! Eat your shrimp binh-cake!"

"You think I'm stupid because I live in a village, work in fields! I remind you NOW, daughter... Jean-Luc promised to marry me, take me home to France, but he..."

"He died and left you with me!"

"You make same mistake as me! I see it!"

"I'm not YOU, mother! No one's taking me anywhere!"

"Why not go with him? You can have big villa in San Francisco.*"*

Both women stared at Uncle Chieu, stunned by the words "San Francisco," which neither one of them had ever heard before.

"I can come visit you there!" The wrinkled peasant-face broke into a huge smile.

"Don't be ridiculous, uncle! I am Vietnamese! I am BORN in Vietnam, I will DIE in Vietnam! I will serve my people as a nurse in a big hospital someday and I will give you four stacks of Dong every single month!"

"Money no good if my daughter is a whore for Americans!"

"You talk? Who was a whore for the French?"

"How dare you! Jean-Luc wanted to marry..."

"How do you know that? Because he said so? This American—at least he doesn't tell lies about marriage and taking me to The United States.

Sang stopped slamming utensils and food on the table top. She dropped into her chair and looked at Zachary, whose wrinkled fore-head and raised eye-brows asked the broad question: "What is going on here?" She let out a deep breath, put her hands beside her bowl, palms down, and looked her mother straight in the eye. *"So please leave me alone,"* she said calmly, *"I know what I'm doing. I don't want to go to America. I don't want to be an American. And I don't want to grow rice and feed chickens in Phoc Tho. I know what I want and I know how to get it. If I need help from a rich American for a little while to succeed, then that's what it takes."*

The domestic storm blew itself out, for now. Sang slid a mouthful of rice and chicken from the raised bowl with her chopsticks, then reached over and put her right hand on top of Zachary's. *"And besides,"* she told her family while she chewed, *"This particular rich American is a very generous, kind and gentle man. He is my friend and I like him. I want you to be kind to him while he is here, a visitor in our country."* She smiled at Zachary and he dared to smile back, at all of them, a big, happy all-American smile.

But the long, mostly silent drive to Phoc Tho on Saturday was a sad time for Rosie. The dinner with her mother and Uncle Chieu was not what he expected, as Sang had warned him. It broke the spell of his love affair with Nguyen Sang. She was beautiful and the lover he had been searching for since his high school days, but now when he looked at her, he could not help seeing the girl at the dinner-table. She was a daughter and niece of a tight-knit family, a teenage high school student, and above all, Vietnamese to her core. He had never imagined that Sang—that anyone—would not want to forsake this war-ravaged, poverty-stricken, ever muddy or dusty tropical furnace for the world capital of pleasure, opportunity and security. He had wanted to rescue her, to be her savior. But as he watched her holding hands with her mother in front of their one-room house in Phoc Tho, the two of them talking quietly with their heads together, he understood the hubris of his claim on her. This was her family, but Vietnam was her home. The future he once imagined for Sang—as an American immigrant war-bride—simply substituted his vision for her mother's. To find her way, she needed to be free of both.

Sang began to cry as soon as she slipped into the passenger seat of the jeep. She used the flowing silk of her ao dai to dry her tears and Rosie held his peace until she felt like talking. When she was ready, she announced, "I want my mother be proud of me!"

"I'm sure she is," Rosie offered. But the embarrassment of the dinner hung over them both, his looming presence at the table, a rich man who handed out stacks of money, the foreigner who had barged into a family fight, who didn't even speak their language, the smiling stranger who wanted to steal their daughter away from them. That he and Sang were a metaphor for the American incursion in Vietnam was not lost on the history major from the border state of Tennessee.

He took her to eat at their favorite restaurant, near their first apartment on Tu Do Street. And when they got back to their Cong Ly Street apartment, he flipped through his dog-eared copy of *You Only Live Twice*, about the woman-loving spy James Bond, until Sang put away her textbook, changed into her pajamas and went to bed. Then he went to her, ducked under the mosquito net and kissed her. "Good night, Sang," he said, "I'll come get you for school in the morning."

"OK, Zachary. That will be good." She squeezed his neck with her thin arms and whispered, "Good night."

Then he locked the door behind himself and pointed the Suzuki toward III Corps Headquarters.

He took her to school and brought her home from work, he paid her expenses, they ate together each night, and he tucked her into her bed with a kiss at the end of each day. Sang seemed happier this way and Rosie loved her even more intensely than he had before.

On 26 September 1968, PFC Rosenzweig, in uniform, flew out of Tan Son Nhut Airbase, leaving as much money as he could spare with Nguyen Sang. The rent on the Cong Ly apartment still had a year paid-in-advance through Braxton Hood's generosity. Rosie sent letters to her address for months but got no reply. Perhaps they never reached Nguyen Sang, for whatever reason.

In 2003, Dr. Rosenzweig, professor of history at the University of Memphis, joined a group of fellow veterans for a tour of Vietnam. From Hanoi to Ho Chi Minh City, Rosie visited every hospital and clinic along the way, showing a letter in the Vietnamese language and the photograph of a young girl to any staff members who would listen. Though he failed to find her, he was certain that she had succeeded in her dreams and that somewhere in this rising, energetic, independent nation, there was a nurse serving her people.

6

VUNG TAU RHAPSODY

I f the purest definition of communism is that it's an economic system in which the state controls the marketplace, then the purest definition of capitalism may have been Ngon Bich, called "Itty Bitchy" by Australians and Americans serving in Vung Tau during the Vietnam War. Diminutive, weather-beaten and ancient, she padded around the streets of her town in peasant black pajamas and rubber sandals, chattering away at everyone she knew, which was pretty much everyone. If you paid attention, though, there was a swagger in her walk, a determination and certainty of purpose. Soldiers and sailors idling on the sidewalks instinctively got the hell out of her way.

She had learned how to marshal the resources Vung Tau offered in abundance: War-widows, orphans, refugees of all ages who were drawn to this place that was immune to war by virtue of being a narrow peninsula surrounded by warships. This horde of misplaced persons supplied the raw material to Co Bich, who brilliantly matched them to opportunities for them and for herself. Mark Babineaux made her acquaintance the night he was rescued from a street gang by Itty Bitchy, wielding a machete, and the next day she matched him up with beautiful Co Hang who became his live-in lover and maid. He paid her six dollars a day in military scrip until, after three weeks, Hang bought a used sewing machine and moved out. Co Ly took Hang's place under the same arrangement and by dint of great talent and incredibly hard work, she developed the "office supply business" (which was supposed to serve Babineaux as a cover for his bilateral intelligence operation) into a busy and profitable store with several paid employees. At that point, Ngon Bich explained to Babineaux that Co Ly would be taking over the enterprise and would be buying him out of his share over time.

Distraught and confused by this fait accompli, Mark Babineaux locked horns with the world's tiniest mergers-and-acquisitions genius. "Tell Co Ly she can't have it! It's MINE!" he howled.

But Itty Bitchy planted her sandals an inch from his size-12 work boots and scolded, "Ly do everything in store! You do nothing! You pay six dollah day. No good! You numbah ten lazy dog! She want you out of store today, Mr. Bahno!" Then she dangled the carrot. "You stay with Co Qui. She have good house. Make you happy!" Qui was standing there, beaming a radiant, eager smile, an offer too attractive to turn down. So he traded in a tiny room in a retail store that had become a commercial beehive and an operational headache for a good-sized house he shared with a woman much younger and prettier than the entrepreneur, Co Ly. And though Qui would cost him six dollars a day, he would now be receiving an income from Co Ly for his half of a lucrative office supply store. The worm in the apple, of course, was that he could be sent in handcuffs to Long Binh Jail if Major Shimazu found out he had sold his "cover story" for hard cash, while the Army continued to pay rent to his landlord (Co Bich) for the

"Vung Tau Field Station." *So who's gonna tell him?* Babineaux thought to himself as Qui took his hand and led him away.

Lithe and lovely Qui, it turned out, was an extraordinary athlete who could and did outswim and outrun Mark Babineaux on a daily basis. He reached a point where he could no longer bear losing so many races by land and by sea, from having his hand slammed to the table while arm-wrestling and his shoulders pinned to the sand in the incessant contests that Qui loved. Each day ended with Qui proving she could outlast him in bed as well. The competition had put him into the best physical condition of his life, but he was a broken, defeated, exhausted man, mentally and physically. Therefore, when Babineaux faced another rotation of girlfriends, it was with eager anticipation and relief.

So he offered only token resistance when Qui went to work in the Australian Military Hospital and was replaced by young, petite and lively identical twins, Phuong and Long. There were powerful incentives at work in this new arrangement. Babineaux now had two live-in lovers, adorable, deferential and cheerful, neither of whom could outrun or outswim him. There were two downsides however: He had to pay each of them six dollars a day (which came to more than Co Ly was paying him for the store) and he continued to get absolutely nothing accomplished for the almost-forgotten Army Intelligence mission that was supposed to be his occupation. His translator, Duong, and his counterpart were of little help and the few Information Reports he was filing were testaments to his non-performance. Babineaux suffered a rising sense of panic about how long he could dwell in this Eden of a beach-resort before it all came crashing down on him.

In a desperate attempt to cling to his paradise, Babineaux fabricated an elaborate fiction he called "A White Paper on the

Near-Term Course of the War." From whole cloth, he invented a prostitute spy-ring that had seduced Hanoi's most important agent into disclosing a change of war plans. Following the failure of the Tet Offensive to overturn the government in Saigon, the ruling party in the North was rethinking its strategy. Their focus would shift from attacking ARVN to creating American casualties for the purpose of energizing the anti-war movement in the United States. This would force Washington to open peace talks that would lead to the Americans abandoning the war. All of this insider intelligence was gained by the liberal use of scotch and the allure of beautiful whores named Hang and Qui and Ly, who plied their charms with this high-level source.

This ploy worked almost too well. The "White Paper" did salvage a future for the field office in Vung Tau, but it led to Babineaux's having to present it, dressed in a tailored suit and posing as a GS-16, at a top-level MACV briefing. Having painted himself into a corner, he had no choice but to carry it off. He was proud of his performance at MACV and, when nothing further came of it, he was more than happy to forget all about it.

Hood's arrival in Vung Tau the next month was a godsend for Mark Babineaux, whose obsession had become training Phuong and Long in every aspect of mixology so they could go to work behind a bar and produce an income. They proved to be a flashy and adroit bartending duo that would be irresistible to soldiers and sailors in their matching au dais. All they needed was a place to ply their skills, but Co Bich had declined to finance any such venture. Then on 6 March, Braxton Hood showed up behind the wheel of a luxurious but damaged Citroën with two heavy boxes of military scrip in the trunk—well over $100,000 in ten-, five- and one-dollar notes. Wars have ever been costly to some and lucrative to others. In this case, Hood happened to be standing where it rained lucre and his problem now was to get it spent without getting caught either by U.S. authorities or the well-connected victims of his (correction: of Frank Monroe's) elaborate fraud. Hood's interests, then, were nicely aligned with Itty Bitchy's and Mark Babineaux's. One of the two heavy boxes was emptied for the creation of the most beautiful and prosperous beachfront establishment in Vung Tau. Hood doled out over $50,000 to convert a large villa into "Bravo Juliet!". Ngon Bich employed and supervised an army of craftsmen who repurposed the home into a bar-restaurant-hotel complex, with a large wrap-around veranda over-looking the spectacular beach. Legal documents drawn up by Bich's attorney, Mr. Chồn, made Bravo, Juliet! the joint property of Braxton Hood and Mark Babineaux until 26 September 1968, on which date the firm of Ngon Bich, Ltd., would acquire the property as sole propri-etor. Also on that date, Corporals Hood and Babineaux were due to rotate back to The States. So half of Hood's problem was solved—he was down to one heavy box of scrip—and Babineaux's dream of a beach-front bar had come true. Also, a number of Itty Bitchy's widows and a few wounded veterans found employment as waitresses, cooks, maids, and maintenance workers—including Phuong and Long behind the bar—and as for the long-neglected intelligence work, she became the de facto chief of the field station's bilateral operations. Both CIA agents in town and half the Naval Intelligence men were already living with young women she had assigned to them (for six dollars a day) and she knew within a week of Babineaux's arrival that SIC was a front for US Army Intelligence. Nothing happened in Vung Tau that remained a secret for very long from her widespread network of affiliates and it gave her great pleasure to point her gnarled finger at a passer-by and say, "That one, he CIA chief here from Saigon, talk his two men. They live import-export store near dock. Vietnamee man in blue shirt, see? Over by tree? He keep eye on CIA man all-way, maybe for VC. I find out, I tell you." Without being asked, she had every waitress who served customers at Bravo, Juliet! and every hostess who entertained men upstairs on alert for useful information. These sources produced lots of very reliable information about American and Australian matters, useless to Hood and Babineaux, but Ngon Bich had many other sources in town and was a vital contributor to a half-dozen IRs each month. "Communis' numbah ten no good!" she preached, "Bad business! I pay bribe police, gov'men', taxman, they take care me. Communis' come, no more bribe! Close business! No good!" It made sense, then, for Hood and Babineaux to get out of her way and let her recruit, train and debrief "their" spy network with a minimum of interference. III Corps in Saigon was paying for information, they were getting information, much of it timely and valuable to MACV, and life was good. The fact that no one at III Corps had ever heard of Ngon Bich (including classmates Mulcahey and Rosenzweig) and that they assumed an office supply store was the cover, so be it. Knowing the whole truth was in no one's best interest, up in Saigon, really, was it?

From early March, 1968, nothing drew more attention from Vung Tau's inhabitants than the strange sight of Braxton Hood (six-foot-three, 290 pounds, powerful physique) strolling along in animated conversation with an ancient woman (four-foot-nine, 95 pounds, peasant dress), she taking three steps for each of his. They might well have been thought to be separate species. But in fact, as they struggled through hours of difficult conversation, they built a solid relationship based on trust, common purpose and mutual respect. While Mark Babineaux was happily engaged with the day-to-day details of running Bravo, Juliet! Hood preferred to spend most of his time following Ngon Bich from point to point in her growing enterprise, fascinated by her cunning and raw energy. His grasp of her rudimentary English grew to the extent where she could explain most things to him, using gestures and facial expressions where the spoken words failed.

Standing in the courtyard of the sprawling compound that served Bich as an orphanage, a widow's shelter, a school, a dispensary, her home and heaven-knew-what-else, Hood asked her, "Where do you get the orphans?"

Bich cocked her head as though she had trouble hearing him. "From war," she said.

"I mean, does the government bring them to you, the military or the Catholics?" Hood asked, "How do they get assigned to you?"

"People bring offen here. No fami'y. No home. Vung Tau good place, no fight here."

"What becomes of them, when they leave here?"

"We teach read, write. Girl cook. Boy work. Maybe woman have no chi'ren, she can have offen." Bich broke out in her betel nut-stained smile. "She can have fi' offen or sik! How many as she like!"

"And the women just wander in here too? No home, no family?"

"People talk. Come Vung Tau, stay with Co Bich. Be safe, you."

"Damn!" Hood shook his head, awestruck by the informality, the person-to-person grapevine that had sprouted, through word of mouth, a place of shelter for seventy or eighty orphans, dozens of unattached, unsupported women of all ages, with more coming each week.

"War end someday," Bich told him cheerfully, as though it might happen tomorrow, "I put all women in business, they pay me rent, I teach them all make money," she smiled.

"I can help you with the orphans here," Hood offered. Brilliant mathematician he certainly was, but he had only a general idea of how much scrip was in the large box under his bed. His goal, to spend it all before he left the country, was being frustrated by the success of Bravo, Juliet! plus allocations from SIC for maintaining bilateral intelligence operations. He had three Army paychecks stashed in his wallet because cashing them would only add to his problems.

But Bich told him, "Offens bad business. Give money! No get money! No good. Give money women. They take care offen and do business. Pay me rent." She eventually agreed to take $150 each Monday from him to be used to set women up in various businesses. He trusted her to use this money wisely because it would extend her holdings, her pride and joy. And he suspected she didn't ask for more because she walked around with a master plan in her head for spending every last dime she could get out of him, strategically directing it to where it would do her the most good—exactly what he wanted her to do.

Striding along the beach road, Bich asked, "You have boocoo beau'ful beach, same like this your home?"

"Sure, yeah," Hood assured her, "We have lots of nice beaches like this, but not hot every day like here. Sometimes in winter, we have cold days, snow."

"In winter, cold days..." Bich tried to grasp what he was talking about but without success.

"We have sailboats... and speedboats. Boats just for fun." Ahead of them was an area where the local fishermen were restricted, to keep them away from the vast collection of USN and Royal Australian Navy craft of every shape and size swarming around—every vessel in sight serving a purpose—not one "just for fun."

"Vung Tau, no boat for fun," Bich said wistfully, "Maybe someday war end."

"At home, we build whole... towns, I guess you'd say... on the beach just for fun."

"No fun, build town! Hard work!" she scoffed.

"I mean, the whole reason for the town is fun! Down in Myrtle Beach… boocoo beautiful beach same like Vung Tau… they just built the Family Kingdom Amusement Park with all kinds of rides and games for people to laugh and play and have fun. Children, families come and there's nothing else to do there but play games and ride cars and trains in circles and have fun!"

For the next ten minutes, while beach-dwellers stared at this strange couple, Hood shaped images with his hands and drew sketches on the beach sand with the toe of his shoe, delivering as best he could for Ngon Bich the idea of an amusement park. He concluded with what he called "the grand-daddy of 'em all" in California. She listened intensely, following his every gesticulation and word with rapt attention. When Hood finished preaching the gospel of fun, Bich responded with enthusiasm, "Good idea! OK! War stop, we make dizzylan Vung Tau. People come from *all* Vietnam, have fun all day, spin fast in circle, ride car in sky. Eat shrimp and rice, drink Ba-Me-Ba, good beer, no Lave La Rue, rice wine and funny hat and shirt and stay nice villa like Bravo, Juliet! but nice lady, no bar-girl, maybe Buddhis' monk tend bar," which idea made her burst out in laughter. "Touris' come here too, spend boocoo money," she paused to consider then said, "but no Japanee or Koree… maybe French and Chinee, one or two, no many. Vung Tau be numbah one for Vietnamee people firs'. Touris' come later."

They returned to this topic often during their long walks together, how to build a dizzylan in Vung Tau, a paradise of peace and security full of laughing children and their serene, well fed parents on holiday, former soldiers from the disbanded armies with their girlfriends, rich merchants spending rivers of money that would flow to Ngon Bich, who would see to it that farmers, fishermen and workers were made prosperous by all the commercial activity. It was a vision that grew each time it came up, the mere mention of it filling the tiny Asian lady with happy anticipation and setting her off on an idyll about the future, "when war stop."

It was during one such recitation that Braxton Hood realized that he had come to love Ngon Bich, meaning nothing improper. He simply conceded that he was awe-struck by her complete dedication to the people who were depending on her and the impossible vision she carried in her heart, despite the suffering and despair all around her, of a prosperous, safe and joyous future. She seemed amazing to him.

In the meantime, it was a very fortunate thing that Hood and Babineaux made a good, complementary team because the work required to keep it all going was extremely challenging. The day-to-day details of managing Bravo, Juliet! were never-ending: Hood kept accounts for the busy establishment, switching out the bar till three times a day, dispersing the tip jar evenly among all employees so that pretty waitresses wouldn't monopolize it, paying the cowboys each morning who guarded the premises all night (in part against their own depredations) --- one dollar each for fifteen of them plus a good breakfast—paying the tradesmen who supplied food and drink for twenty-odd staff and two hundred customers (the laundry bills for the beach hotel/cat-house were considerable, given the amount of towel theft), and, each Friday, determining that week's net profit, which was dispersed evenly among all employees. In a separate ledger, Hood kept track of a phantom budget for a bilateral intelligence opera-tion that existed entirely within a four-drawer file cabinet. Bilateral counterparts and translators in South Vietnam ran the whole spec-trum from heroic patriots and dedicated professionals to ineffective featherbedders, among whom Babineaux's counterpart and his trans-lator, Duong, dropped outside the visible array of colors. Neverthe-less, they were given half of the field station's allocation to buy their continued silence and neglect, and Ngon Bich was given the other half in exchange for her steady flow of military information. What any of them did with the money was their business. Hood tried not to think of himself as a small-scale Frank Monroe as he did this, but III Corps dispensed only about $800 a month to Vung Tau, a fraction of the $3,500 Monroe had collected, and the point of the exercise, from Hood's point-of-view, was to get money spent as quickly as possible.

Mark Babineaux's contribution to their joint effort was hands-on. He typed up the Information Reports and delivered them in person to III Corps Headquarters. He had to drive to Saigon anyway to obtain a long list of retail goods from the Tan Son Nhut Post Exchange for the office supply store, but he put in the personal visit to III Corps, spending time with Major Wills and Captain Kearney, to discourage them from thinking they needed to visit Vung Tau themselves. Only four people on earth knew who owned Bravo, Juliet!—Hood, Co Bich, her attorney and himself—and he had to keep it that way. He served as the ever-present maître d' of Bravo, Juliet! making sure the regulars were happy and keeping order between bar-girls and any fellow on holiday who forgot his manners. (A soldier on leave could flirt with the petite twins who tended bar, but he kept his hands to himself or was shown the door). Babineaux managed supplies, giving the bills to Hood, oversaw the kitchen and resolved the myriad interpersonal issues inherent in this multi-service operation.

Seven days a week were crowded with this exhausting work, each day ending in the wee hours with Hood cautioning the preteen posse of cowboys to behave themselves and be faithful sentries before plodding up to his room to collapse on his bed as Babineaux and his tired-out twins dragged themselves three steep blocks uphill to their bungalow. Each day began with a sea breeze off the serene, blue South China Sea, bringing the coolest hour of the day to the tropical resort town, and they arose and began the cycle again. Hood and Babineaux did not understand until later that they had been lulled into a false sense of insulation from the troubles of the world. Their work hardly gave them time to read about the King and Kennedy assassinations, rioting in dozens of American cities, the rising tide of anti-war emotion inspiring mass protests and the retirement of Lyndon Johnson from the Oval Office. Even those things that happened close-by, the May Offensive that cost some corporal they barely knew his life and got Rosie wounded, made but a momentary impression on them, distractions from the pressing and immediate problems they had to deal with each day. Events that were life-altering for their Greyhawk classmates seemed from the perspective of Vung Tau to be occurring on some other planet, to some other species. They were walking a high-wire, trying not to look down, moving one tense step at a time toward the day when that last box of scrip was empty, Bravo, Juliet! became the property of Ngon Bich, and the last Information Report was hand-delivered to III Corps. They were too exhausted in body and spirit to dwell on the series of disasters described in *Stars and Stripes* or the English-language newspapers from Saigon. Their sole concern was to arrive at Tan Son Nhut on 26 September wearing the simple tan uniform of US Army corporals and leave everything but their duffle bags to the redoubtable Itty Bitchy. They dreamt of that day as a little girl does of being a bride. All things being equal (as if they ever were), it would thereafter be as though none of this had ever happened.

On 3 August 1968, in the bowels of MACV Headquarters, Captain Charles Atwood was having his head handed to him by his commanding officer, Colonel Claude Witherspoon.

"I told you, captain, that I wanted that report on my desk no later than noon, did I not, goddammit?! What time is it, Captain Atwood?"

"1317 hours, sir!"

"It was a rhetorical question, you idiot! I don't need you to tell me what time it is! Listen to me! You are not to eat or sleep or take a piss until that goddamn report is on my goddamn desk, is that clear?!"

"Yessir!"

"What are you standing here for?!"

"Yessir!" Captain Atwood spun a 180 in proper fashion and left. He jogged down a long hallway to the records office, where two of his enlisted men were searching through file cabinets, closely supervised by record-office clerks. "Anything?" he yelled. When they shook their heads, he echoed his colonel. "Goddammit!"

"I remember he had a French name, sir," PFC Fontenot offered, "Cajun, I think."

"How the hell could you know he's Cajun?" the captain bellowed.

"I don't know, sir. Just a hunch," Fontenot said.

"So, you think you were at this guy's presentation... but you're not sure?"

"I wasn't allowed in, sir. Top Secret clearance. But I remember him. I brought him a coffee while he was waiting and we chatted about Louisiana."

"Think, private! What was his name? When was he here?"

"Just after Tet... a few weeks after I got in-country, so February sometime."

"What else! Anything!"

"He was a civilian, had on a nice suit."

"He wasn't CIA," the second PFC said, "I been through all their stuff, sir. Nothing."

"OK, then look for something from civilian-cover military, unilateral, bilateral. Start with the 135th CI Group, 149th Collection Group, 519th MI, 581st MI... Find that son-of-a-bitch!"

"And no scattering files!" the lieutenant in charge of the records office hollered, "Leave every file exactly where you found it!"

Thirty minutes of silent work later, PFC Fontenot found it buried among Information Reports filed by the 581st MI Company (SIC) in the bilateral operations section. The cover sheet was dated 17 February 1968 and was stamped in red "Top Secret—Eyes Only" above the title: "White Paper on the Near-Term Course of the War." As Captain Atwood scanned through the four pages, his memory of that morning returned to him. The presenter, "Marcus Babineaux, GS-16," had been a red-headed young man, much too young in fact to have earned a GS-16 rank, with a buoyant, nervous enthusiasm and the tight body of a well-conditioned athlete. The report referenced "Operation Big Fish" and was based on IRs filed by agents posing as prostitutes who targeted sources in the resort town of Vung Tau. One in particular, code-named "Co Ly," had developed a liaison with a high-ranking North Vietnamese official in hiding who, under the influence of her charms and a day of drinking, confided to her that Hanoi was altering its war strategy. They were giving up any hope of toppling the Saigon government of President Thieu. Instead, they planned to focus on American forces, inflicting increasing casualties in order to fuel the rising anti-war movement in the United States and drive the Americans to the negotiating table in a mood to end the war on Hanoi's terms and at Saigon's expense. This report—one of a series of briefings that morning—floated away on the river of paperwork that flowed through MACV and would have been forgotten forever were it not for a lull in the dinner conversation at General Creighton Abrams' quarters on 2 August 1968.

Seven weeks earlier, Abrams had replaced William Westmoreland at the head of MACV and he was still getting his bearings, meeting as many of his staff as he could, peppering them with a barrage of questions. Colonel Witherspoon was among the dinner guests that evening when Abrams opined, "This may be our last chance to win this thing. He's taken a pounding at Tet and another shellacking in the May Offensive, we're building up ARVN's capabilities and we've got him on the run in I Corps. But the president who comes into the White House in six months, no matter who wins, might start pulling our plug. Our casualties have been soaring all this year and it's making the commie-sympathizers at home look like heroes. 'Bring our boys home' looks better with every casualty. So how do we finish the war now, while we still can?"

That's when the lull occurred. The senior brass up and down the long table all reached for their drinks in unison as seconds ticked away. Colonel Witherspoon had the flu. He should have been home in bed with a thermometer in his mouth and an ice pack on his head. But colonels don't send "regrets" to a general's dinner invitation. So "We finish it in Paris" shot out of him before he realized he'd said anything at all.

"What's that colonel?" Abrams demanded.

Witherspoon looked around sheepishly at the rows of expectant faces. He bought time by saying, "Permission to speak freely, sir." Then he spoke as confidently as he could. "I recall an intelligence briefing some months back, just after Tet, that predicted this would happen, that it was Hanoi's strategy... ignore ARVN, drive up American casualties even at great cost to themselves, and wait for war-weariness and political change at home to force a settlement that would take us out of the war and shove Saigon off a cliff."

"I'll speak freely too, colonel," Abrams said, "That sounds to me like they expect us to admit defeat and surrender."

"Let the politicians spin it to look like a victory, sir. That's their job and they're good at it." This brought a few chuckles from around the table, which Witherspoon mistook for encouragement. "But it's been four years, sir, and as you said, the enemy is taking a pounding. But he hasn't quit. He'll never quit. He's got nowhere else to go, so he'll just hunker down and generate as many American casualties as he can and wait... six years? eight years? ten?...for us to develop an 'exit strategy' that we can pretend is a 'peace treaty' to be signed in Paris."

Colonel Witherspoon's fevered brain had spun out, he thought, a brilliant analysis that would catch General Abrams' attention and begin, perhaps, a long and fruitful partnership between them, marked by mutual respect and even a promotion. However, the expressions up and down the table gave him pause. Perhaps he had said too much. Perhaps he ought to have been at home in bed with a thermometer in his mouth.

"I want to see that report," Abrams said quietly. "In fact, bring me the man who presented it."

In Vung Tau, 3 August began like any other day, with Mark Babineaux's adorable and indistinguishable twins bringing him coffee and croissants on a tray. In the afternoon, in the gap between the Bravo, Juliet! lunch crowd and the party-all-night stampede, Babineaux was floating on his back in the warm waters of the South China Sea with Long and Phuong in matching bikinis splashing around him like playful otters when he heard a familiar voice calling his name. There on the sand stood the hard-working proprietor of the office supply store, Co Ly.

"They call you," she yelled, "Saigon!"

"Take a message," he shouted back, "I'll call them back later."

"You come NOW!" she insisted. "Your boss, Mr. Will, very angry you!"

The last thing Babineaux wanted was for Major Zorth Wills to end up in Vung Tau, so he reluctantly swam ashore, dried off and pulled on a shirt and sandals. At the office supply shop, the "Vung Tau Field Station telephone" was the last vestige of bilateral intelligence still there. The phone worked but the connection was third-world.

"I want the truth, Babineaux!" Major Wills hollered from what sounded like the bottom of a well, "Have you been reporting directly to MACV, making an end-run around me?"

"No sir! Never!" But something tugged at the base of his brain stem before working its way into his conscious mind. "Well… one time, months ago, before you came, but that was under Major Shimazu and he was there with me… he approved it."

"MACV is calling here for you! They want you to report to some colonel over there *immediately*! *Within the hour!*"

"Sir, it's a four-hour drive from here!"

"Grab a chopper! I don't give a damn! Report to me at once… we'll go over there together… do you hear me?!" The line went dead.

Babineaux's hand was shaking as he cradled the receiver. "Eight more weeks," he muttered to himself. "I just need eight more crummy weeks without any trouble and I'll be out of here."

"You don't remember it, do you?" was Babineaux's guess when he tried to tell Braxton Hood about what created the mess he was in. He had never seen any reason to confess his past sins to Hood and he'd never asked Hood the details of how he'd come by two boxes of scrip and a Citroën. They were both forward-looking men in that way.

"Can't say's I do," Hood admitted, "I was havin' a lot of my own problems back then."

"Well, in January, Major Shimazu threatened to close down Vung Tau if I didn't score something big, intelligence-wise. Duong and my counterpart were no help and Bich had me working on special projects for her, so I had nothing going. I was about to be chucked out of paradise and sent some place where they shoot at people. I had just then…" he searched for the right word, "inherited the twins and I would have lost them too so… what I did, Braxton… what I did was I spun a yarn, one I thought would keep me here, keep the field station open. I don't even remember how it went, exactly… it was based on James Bond, with beautiful women and a high-level North Vietnamese big-shot spilling his guts over a bottle of scotch. Major Shimazu loved it and I figured I was off the hook, at least for a while. But then, it kind of took on a life of its own. MACV wanted me to present it at one of their bull sessions and Shimazu bought me a silk suit and made me rehearse it with him and Lieutenant Aaronson. Man, Braxton! I wasn't looking for anything like that! One thing just led on to another and I got sucked in! You end up in the middle of the river, all's you can do is keep swimming for the other shore!"

"I been there myself, Mark," Hood admitted, "I know what you mean."

They found a copy of "White Paper on the Near-Term Course of the War" and read it through. Hood laughed out loud at Babineaux's using the names of his girlfriends, Hang and Qui, as agents in the "Big Fish" spy ring and the no-longer-young and never-beautiful Co Ly as the temptress who seduced a high-ranking agent of Hanoi into betraying state secrets. But Babineaux wasn't laughing. He was scared out of his wits—a vision dancing in his head of the whole fabrication landing him in the Binh Long stockade.

Hood said, "Well it's gonna be dark in a couple hours, so no matter what Wills wants, you best wait 'til sunrise if you want to get there in one piece."

As was his style, Babineaux had tossed the tailor-made silk suit onto the floor of his closet in February and it was in no condition to be worn. They were walking together, talking strategy, on their way to Co Hang's clothing shop to see about having the suit cleaned and pressed when Ngon Bich caught up with them. The tiny woman was running full-tilt, sandals flapping on the roadway, distraught, shouting.

"Very bad!" she panted, grasping for air, "Big trouble you!"

"We're working on it, Itty-B," Babineaux told her, "Calm down and catch your breath."

"I not talking YOU, you wambat! I talking Mr. Hood!" She tilted her head up at the towering Braxton Hood, like a squirrel about to climb a tree. "Bad man! Very bad man! Make trouble you!" she gasped. Neither American had ever seen her like this, not even when she was waving a machete at a street gang, as on the night she met Mark Babineaux. "I tell you he numbah ten bad man! This man have gun!"

Hood began to get a creepy feeling that his own past sins—like Mark's—might have finally caught up with him too. "Is this man from Saigon?" he asked, "Maybe a rich merchant?"

"He know you! Say you steal money him! He call you Fray Morrow!"

"He calls you what?" Babineaux asked.

"It's a long story," Hood muttered, "This guy may not know my name, but he's got me pegged for a friend of Frank Monroe, this guy… he… it's a long story."

"You come BravoJulie! Pay money. Tell him didi mau, go back Saigon, no more come Vung Tau!"

Hood needed time to plan his next move, so he said as calmly as the adrenaline coursing through his veins allowed, "Tell him I'm on my way. I'll come as soon as I can."

"You come NOW!" Bich shouted, "This man have gun!"

"I will… very soon," Hood said. Bich headed uphill, away from the beach front.

While Co Hang's people worked on the wrinkled suit, Hood outlined in broad terms the part he had played in Frank Monroe's final scam. "We traded a truckload of counterfeit scrip for the real thing, tellin' 'em a conversion to new scrip was comin' and they'd be stuck with the old scrip. Monroe didn't tell me it was counterfeit, that there was no conversion comin', and by the time I figured it out, he was long-gone, left me his car and 150 pounds of small bills and a hundred cheated big shots lookin' to get even. Hidin' out in Vung Tau was workin' pretty well 'til now."

"What are we gonna do?" Babineaux asked.

"You're gonna stay the hell out of it, Mark. It's my problem."

"Not the way I see it. We co-own the bar, don't we? And we've got fifteen cowboys on the payroll, itchin' for a fight…"

"Forget it. That ain't gonna work. This guy is the first of a long line, once word gets out. Others'll come on his heels tomorrow and the next day. Bich is right. This is big trouble."

Hood stood in a corner, brooding, while Babineaux slipped into his clean, neatly pressed suit. Then Hood said, "Only chance I've got is to cut a deal with this guy. He gets his money back and then some, then I'll pay him more each week so long as he keeps it all to himself. Once word gets out where to find me, then all payments stop and there won't be any more money to give because a hundred other guys will be comin' at me and he won't get any more, I'll tell him. It's blackmail, but if he plays along until 26 September, we turn into uniformed soldiers in a sea of uniformed soldiers and disappear into the sky."

"I still say we could…"

Hood barked at him, "Let me do all the talkin', got it?"

The scene at Bravo, Juliet! was every bit as bad as Bich's limited English conveyed. There were five of them arrayed behind a circular table: A rotund, middle-aged antique dealer whose elaborate collection of rare and valuable artifacts impressed Hood on several visits to his store; behind him stood two body guards who had been lifting a lot of weights, sports coats over their shoulder-holsters; a young man with a goatee sat to the merchant's left and Mr. Chồn, the lawyer who had represented Ngon Bich in the purchase arrangement for Bravo, Juliet! sat to his right.

"Won't you take a seat, Mr. Hood," the goatee said in a clipped British accent, "I believe you know why my employer, the honorable Tham Giá Bán, has been looking forward to meeting you."

Hood sat facing them, his anger mixing with fear at this carefully laid ambush. Thanks to Bich's lawyer, that weasel Mr. Chồn, they knew his name and doubtless that he had purchased this beach-front bar with cash, stacks of scrip in small denominations. Hood was further unsettled when Babineaux, despite being told not to, pulled up a chair and joined the meeting.

"I reckon he's huntin' for Frank Monroe," Hood said in a drawl that was neither clipped nor British.

"To be specific, Mr. Hood, he is 'huntin','" the goatee paused to sneer at this term of American slang, "for the money you and Mr. Monroe took from him under false pretenses. Mr. Chồn has informed us that you, not Mr. Monroe, purchased this establishment with

THE TIME WILL COME   183

Military Payment Certificates in great quantity."

Babineaux whispered through cupped hands, "This clown sounds like David Niven."

"Shut up," Hood whispered back.

The body guards tensed like Dobermans on a short leash.

Hood told the goatee, "Tell your boss I'll make things right for him, on account of what Mr. Monroe did to him. It wasn't right and I aim to fix it. But all the money I have is invested and I need time to cash it out. Today's Saturday. How's about I come up to Saigon next Saturday and buy back all the bad scrip Monroe stuck him with and pay him $5,000 besides that in cash. Tell him that."

The goatee held a quiet conversation in Vietnamese with his boss and Mr. Chồn then said, "Your offer demonstrates the proper spirit, but it does not satisfy the honorable Tham Giá Bán. He proposes… rather he insists that you come to his place of business at noon on Monday, two days from now, and bring to him the fifteen thousand dollars you took from him and also the deed for this beautiful property, to which the honorable Tham Giá Bán has taken a fancy. Mr. Chồn will be there to oversee the transfer of the property. I will be there to see to it you pay your debt in full and in exchange, you will receive a suitcase full of the worthless scrip you and Mr. Monroe are so fond of. That will be your reward for your evil deeds. If you fail to comply with any of these conditions, we will send some very persuasive men to bring you to terms. Is that clear?"

Hood saw that any counter-offer he made would go nowhere, so he uttered a defiant "Clear as mud" and left it at that.

"We will see you and your cohort in Saigon at noon on Monday then. Mr. Babineaux as co-owner of this property will be present to sign the paperwork prepared by Mr. Chồn." He slid business cards across the table for each of them that gave the contact information for the antique store. Then the honorable Tham Giá Bán led the group out to the waiting cars, flanked by Mr. Goatee and Mr. Chồn, and last, his bodyguards backed out, eyes locked on the Americans.

"Got no choice," Hood admitted, "Monday's just a down payment. He aims to take it all down to the last red cent. But if he doesn't, there's others who will. So that's that."

"I say we fight it out, Braxton! We can't just roll over on this."

"Duke it out with the Saigon mafia? We'd both be dead... not the way I want to go." Hood looked around at all they had built together. "Damn it all!" he burst out, "I don't feel so bad for myself. All this stuff and the money, it's all stolen goods anyway, just gonna move from one thief to another on Monday. But Bich and the people workin' here, that pig will probably turn 'em all out and turn this into his beach house. We at least tried to make it into somethin' good for everybody, and now he's gonna take it all to make himself richer than he already is. The little guys always lose out in the end. *That's* what galls me!"

Hood shoved his chair back and started for the stairway. "Tell the twins to make room," he said over his shoulder. Without another word, Babineaux followed him up the stairs to help him pack up his office and bedroom for the move uphill to the bungalow.

Babineaux drove the yellow jeep onto the beach road at daybreak Sunday morning, having defied a direct order from his commanding officer to drive to Saigon in the dead of night. "If I get ambushed by the VC, tell that MACV colonel I won't be much good to him," he'd shouted over the phone at Major Wills, "and besides, if I leave now, I'll arrive up there at two a.m.? Nobody'll be in their office at that hour."

"You are ordered to be here no later than 0600 hours, corporal, or I'll have you busted back to…" Babineaux just hollered "Yessir" into the phone and hung up, having no intention to leave at two a.m. to arrive at six a.m. and no intention to start using the Army's 2400-hour clock either.

The breath-taking sunrise was wasted on him as he drove the familiar route, his mind racing wildly through different scenarios to deal with Major Wills. The only outcome he could see to any of these scripts was being led off in handcuffs for dereliction of duty or insubordination or some other article of misconduct that he'd yet to hear of. A military tribunal followed by years in a stockade were his secondary considerations. His primary one was that if he failed to show up at the antique dealer's shop Monday at noon because he was under arrest, those thugs would figure Hood was trying to pull a fast one and break every bone in his magnificent body one-by-one. It had all happened so quickly—like Eden's Fall—paradise on Friday, banishment and the gnashing of teeth on Monday! He was so distracted that he nearly ran through an ARVN checkpoint at the neck of Vung Tau Peninsula—one of the troops fired a carbine into the air in warning. *The final irony,* he thought, *avoid the VC and get shot by ARVN.*

This was it, the day of reckoning. His "White Paper" was a fabrication from end to end, not a true word anywhere in it. He may as well just confess it all to Major Wills and save everybody an embarrassing trip over to MACV.

At nine a.m. he climbed the stairs at III Corps, bracing himself for the onslaught. Major Wills did not fail him. The normally sedate aficionado of crossword puzzles flew at him in a rage. He was being hammered by some colonel he never met at MACV and defied by a mere corporal under his command. He became inarticulate with anger, piling one incoherent half-question on top of another without waiting for an answer to any of them.

"I don't know, sir," Babineaux stammered, "I don't recall, sir. Co Ly is no longer available to us, sir. She's a prostitute. She doesn't have an address. She drifts around, like a hobo. No, sir, she's not a hobo, she's a prostitute. She refused to name her source, sir. She feared for her life if she did, sir. There is no 'Big Fish' network anymore. It dissolved. No, sir. Yessir. It disbanded when all the working women went their separate ways, sir. NO, SIR! I am NOT making this up! I stand behind my report one hundred percent!"

When they arrived at MACV, Babineaux driving the jeep with Major Wills and Captain Kearney interrogating him about the Vung Tau Field Station, they learned that Colonel Claude Witherspoon was a devout Catholic. He was attending 10:00 Mass at the Cathedral, which he did every Sunday because they had a superb boys' choir. They stewed in silence until the colonel returned at 11:30. It was only as they were being ushered into his presence that Wills and Kearney realized they were standing there in chinos and short-sleeved white shirts while Babineaux was nattily attired in a tailor-made silk suit, off-white. They etched one more vendetta against him in their minds. Major Wills introduced himself and his second-in-command then said, "This is the agent you're looking for, colonel, who wrote the 'White Paper' report."

Babineaux first fought the urge to salute the uniformed colonel, then the impulse to stick out his hand and say "Nice to meet you." Instead he smiled and said, "Yessir, that's me."

Witherspoon looked him up and down and said, "Yes, I remember you now. Same suit." He dropped into his desk chair but had given no one else permission so they remained standing. "General Abrams is up-country today. He wanted to speak with you personally."

"With me, sir?" Wills' eyebrows shot up. "*The* General Creighton

Abrams?'"

"Yes, major, *that* General Abrams and no, not with you. He wanted a word with Marcus Babineaux about the 'White Paper'."

"But colonel, this man is a... *corporal!*" Wills whispered that last word, as though it were a profanity.

"Perhaps another time then," Babineaux suggested, taking a step toward the door.

"I will convey to him what he needs to know," Colonel Witherspoon barked, "Principally, he wanted to verify the reliability of the report and he wanted to know, in light of steeply rising casualties, that it is an intentional shift in Hanoi's war policy and, if so, how Mr... Corporal Babineaux had come to know about it immediately after Tet."

"Happenstance, sir," Babineaux offered by way of explanation, "We got the right girl in the right bed at the right time. One in a million. Lucky break." Babineaux beamed at the colonel, hoping he had answered the question. But Wills and Kearney were glaring at him and Colonel Witherspoon was grinding in his chair as though sitting on a burr.

"The girl in the bed," Wills tried to intercede, "that prostitute has moved on... like a hobo."

Colonel Witherspoon rose to his feet, his face flush. "I'm not asking you about any whores, goddammit! I'm asking you about the source of the information."

"He doesn't know who it was," Wills said, "She wouldn't tell him... feared for her life."

"Not *one more word* out of you, major!" Witherspoon thundered, "I didn't ask you! I asked *him!*" The colonel's long index finger pointed unmistakably at Mark Babineaux's solar plexus.

"We have code-names for all our sources, sir. I'd have to ch-check my f-files," Babineaux said, shivering. He had not been exposed to air-conditioning for ten months and the colonel's office was a meat-locker compared to the tropical heat outside.

"Don't hand me any spy-craft bullshit, corporal! I've got the general breathing down my neck about this, goddammit! I want a straight answer out of you here and now! You presented that report based on intelligence you had gathered and it turned out to be accurate—so who was the base-line source of that information!?"

It was a close call. Mark Babineaux, cornered, all eyes on him, shivering from cold and fear, took in a deep breath to say, "I made it all up" when his right hand, in the pocket of his silk jacket, felt the sharp edge of a business card and he was inspired to say: "The source is running deep cover as an antique dealer out of a store down on Truong Đinh Street. I can tell you where to find him, but he's an experienced operator and one tough cookie. He'll stick to his story and deny everything, no matter what you do to him."

"We'll see about that!" Colonel Witherspoon said firmly.

Babineaux was feeling warmer now. "He runs an extensive network with deep roots in the Saigon government. He can pull levers all the way up to President Thieu. So, if you move on him, don't use ARVN."

"We know what we're doing," the colonel insisted.

"Right now, he's sitting on his first shipment of counterfeit scrip, MPCs, the first of many that his network will use to flood the market with phony bills, destabilize the economy."

"How do you know all this?" Witherspoon demanded.

Babineaux was nice and warm now, confident, on a roll, and his reflexes told him he should avoid talking about what Witherspoon called "whores." He bit his lip for effect, then mumbled, "We have a mole, sir... a man trusted by Hanoi's agent, the antique dealer, but he was educated in England and we flipped him to our side. He must be handled with the utmost discretion, sir. If they find out he's been working for us, it could cost him his life."

"That's not my problem," Colonel Witherspoon barked, "We're going to smash this den of spies with a ten-pound sledge and let counter-intelligence sort them out."

"Well, good luck, colonel. This man is a hard-core Communist son-of-a-bitch. I doubt you'll get anything out of him, but if you succeed, he knows more about the inner-workings of the Hanoi regime than anyone this side of Ho Chi Minh. And, sir, make sure your people know he's probably got a cyanide pill on him, disguised as a button or a piece of jewelry. So grab him fast and strip him down before he has a chance to use it!"

In the outer office, Babineaux carefully copied from the business card, hoping to get all the diacritical marks right: "Tham Giá Bán/ Rare Antiques/Đồ Cổ Hiếm/1409 Truong Đinh, Saigon." Below this he wrote, "The man with the goatee is fluent in English and requires special consideration because he is a double agent, an informant for US Army intelligence." His pen moved smoothly across the paper and he felt confident and powerful. As he was walking back toward the jeep behind III Corps' bewildered officers, however, his hands began to shake, then his legs, uncontrollably. He was soon trembling all over and had to be lifted into the rear seat. Captain Kearney drove them back to III Corps.

The story that Babineaux told Hood of his harrowing experience at MACV was not much embroidered, but it was redacted here and there. He omitted relating that he was within a breath of breaking down and admitting that his "White Paper" was a figment of his imagination—and he left out the part where he practically fainted and had to be lifted into the jeep by Captain Kearney. Hood was beaming with admiration for him and the whole truth would have ruined the moment.

"I'm feeling pretty good about this," Babineaux concluded, "The colonel is a man of action and I expect he's got a hair-trigger."

"But we don't know that."

"Not for sure."

"Then while we hope for the best, we better plan for the worst," Hood cautioned.

Late into Sunday night, they pulled together paperwork on the real estate they co-owned and laboriously counted out $15,000 in scrip in 10-, 5-, and 1-dollar notes, stretching rubber bands around each bundle of $500.

They hardly exchanged a word early Monday morning as Hood guided the Citroën through heavy traffic toward Saigon. There was nothing to be said. Either MACV would have "smashed that den of spies with a ten-pound sledge," as Witherspoon said he would, or the antique dealer and his thugs were going to get everything they demanded before upping the ante and demanding more. The Americans had waved off Ngon Bich when she asked about the "very bad man," but she had ways of finding out everything anyway, always, so she either knew who he was and what he wanted or soon would know.

Hood parked the Citroën on the Cathedral Square, keeping it blocks away from the bargaining table, and they walked toward Truong Đinh Street, Hood carrying a leather briefcase full of paperwork and Babineaux a pillowcase bulging with bundles of scrip. From within the tall brick Cathedral of Notre Dame, pure voices of a boys' choir echoed through the rafters and onto the boulevard outside.

"Levesque," Hood said quietly.

"Brother Andre," Babineaux corrected him.

They stopped into a bar near their destination and ordered beers, cradling their burdens in their laps, under the table, waiting it out until the appointed hour. To the bar girls they shooed-away, they appeared to be indolent civilians, Monday morning drinkers, idle and lazy. The opposite was true: They were hyper-alert and wound up tight. The minutes crawled by until Hood stood up, placed a five dollar note on the table and drawled, "Reckon we best go."

They maneuvered through blocks crowded with pedestrians before they arrived at the most thrilling sight they ever hoped to see: 1409 Truong Đinh was dark and dead, a steel security gate covered the entrance and inside the show windows, floors and walls were bare— no art work, no furniture, not a living soul. The ten-pound sledge had landed on Tham Giá Bán! They walked another block in silence before Babineaux threw his arms as far around Hood's torso as they reached, trying not to spill bundles of scrip out on the sidewalk. "Jesus Christ!" he swore in amazement and joy, "I almost feel sorry for him!"

"You ain't got the right to," Hood said, laughing, "You're the one who did it to him."

They strode back to Cathedral Square with the jaunty bounce of condemned prisoners who had been suddenly pardoned.

"I'll tell ya' what else," Hood said when they were closed up inside the car, "When word gets out what happened to this douchebag, I figure nobody else will come to Vung Tau lookin' for Frank Monroe."

"Or for Braxton Hood," Babineaux added merrily.

All things being equal, Monday, 5 August 1968, looked like

it would end in celebration, the gates of Eden thrown open to the returning sinners, MACV, Major Wills, Ngon Bich and Jehovah Himself having forgiven all their transgressions, and only eight more weeks to hang on until the "Freedom Bird" would carry them home.

But when are all things ever equal?

Duong, the almost-forgotten translator for the almost-forgotten Vung Tau Field Station, was perched on the sofa in the bungalow, sipping a can of soda from the fridge, grinning like he owned the place. "I have important Information Report for you," he announced to Babineaux.

Finding Duong making himself at home in the bungalow, where he had never stepped foot before, gave Babineaux the creeps. "Have one of the girls type it up and I'll look at it," he told him.

"Not that kind of report," he told the American, the same smug look on his face, "Different kind."

Babineaux carried the pillowcase, bulging with $15,000 in bundles of scrip, into his bedroom, shoved it under the bed and returned to ask Duong, "OK then, what's so important?"

"Two young ladies, Co Phuong and Co Long, say tell you they live with Ngon Bich now. Work at bar, OK, but no live for you here."

This was too much for Mark Babineaux, after all else he'd been through. He felt as though he had ridden in from a three-day battle, seventy-two hours of continuous violent combat against dragons, giants and enthroned kings—now he had come home exhausted but victorious to find no parades, no banquets, no medals and no twins— just betrayal and abandonment. His body and mind became numb, as though Duong were speaking from a great distance to someone else.

"Co Phuong, Co Long, they tell you Mr. Hood, big man, is friend Ngon Bich. Co Bich, very little, is friend Mr. Hood. But you are friend Co Phuong? No! You are friend Co Long? No! You do not talk them! You do not see them! Co Long is NOT Co Phuong! Co Phuong is NOT Co Long! But they same-same both to you. Even they sleep your bed, you not know them!"

Duong stood and walked to the door as Babineaux's exhausted brain tried to recall what the Bible said about knowing a woman.

It was apparent that Duong was enjoying this opportunity to set a foreigner straight. He set his empty soda can on the tile floor beside the door and got off a parting shot. "Vietnamee very proud people, Mr. Bahno. You must treat with respect!"

Braxton Hood, stock still, hadn't even set down his briefcase during Duong's tirade. He wanted to say something comforting to his friend in this difficult moment but he felt embarrassed because, in his heart, he agreed with Duong. Mark Babineaux did indeed treat the two sisters as "adorable," interchangeable toys.

A half-minute of stunned silence passed before Babineaux muttered, "I need a drink!"

"Well, pardner," Hood said, "I reckon you'll have to pour it yourself."

7

20-26 September, 1968

THE FLIGHT OF THE FREEDOM BIRD

The Date of Estimated Return from Overseas—DEROS—was fast approaching, which meant a return to the United States and to life as soldiers in the US Army. Their anticipation of this magical date, 26 September 1968, began building from the first day of their year in-country. Fantasizing about it was pleasant. But the gritty reality of it gave them chills as each one struggled to disengage from the identity civilian-cover work had assigned him. There was no Army Manual explaining how to do this.

At a French restaurant in Vung Tau, an elderly woman in a spotless yellow and white ao dai sat between two Americans, her new leather sandals not quite touching the floor, sipping champagne for the first time in her long life. Over a two-hour period, they ordered six courses from the high end of the menu, consumed several bottles of expensive wine, laughed and reminisced together like grandmother and grandsons. Finally, over litchi nuts and tea, they became quiet and choked with emotion as she was handed the keys to Bravo, Juliet! They strolled at a leisured pace up the hill to the compound that was her home and tried to find the right words to express what they felt. Finding none, the Americans each awkwardly bent down to embrace her, which she returned with her strong, wiry arms. Then she went inside. As the Americans ambled back down the hill, the old woman shut the security gate behind her and stood gazing with moist eyes at the large sign that would soon replace "Bravo, Juliet!." It read "Những Ngày Vàng Son." She would have a matching English-language sign made soon: "Golden Days."

Zach Rosenzweig adroitly wove his Suzuki through heavy traffic with Nguyen Sang poised side-saddle behind him, hanging on to him with one arm and swaying with the motion of the motorcycle like a bird on a moving branch. It took them hours at the Vehicle Registration Office to get the title transferred from his name to hers before, laughing and shouting, they set off for the apartment on Cong Ly Street with Rosie straddling the padded seat and Sang learning to navigate traffic with a heavy passenger on board. "Lean with me, Zachary, dammit!" she shouted over the whine of the engine, "When you drive, I lean with you!"

That night, as he bent under the mosquito netting to kiss her goodnight, she felt warm tears drop onto her cheek. He turned to leave, but she held onto his hand and asked him to stay, to sleep with her. "It will be OK," she told him. Rosie had gone back to his cot at III Corps after tucking her into bed every night since their trip to Phoc Tho to deliver Sang's mother and uncle to their home. This was good-bye, the last hours of their year together, so he stripped to his underwear, slid under the netting and fell asleep with his arms around Nguyen Sang. At dawn, he nearly slipped away without waking her, but as he locked the door, as usual, he realized this apartment was no longer his. He jiggled the key off the tight ring, reopened the door and reached in to set it on the shelf. Sang grabbed his hand, tugged him inside as she had done the first time they met, when she saved him from an excited mob, and now it was her turn to cry. She hugged him and told him through her sobs, for the first time and the last, "I love you, Zachary. I always love you before and after now." "I love you too, Sang," he whispered. When she had cried herself out, he released her from his arms and said "Write to me," without knowing if that would be possible outside of military channels, and she replied, "You write me too."

Then the apartment door closed between them.

Mulcahey was even more wound-up than usual on the weekend before 26 September, the Thursday he was estimated to return from overseas. "Short-timer" nerves were as unavoidable as the monsoon rains that came down every afternoon and, therefore, it was a great relief to have unexpected company.

Short, bald Jerry Dodd, known as "Petite Buddha" by his many Vietnamese friends, and his partner at the Khap Noi Field Station, Belmont, arrived at III Corps with orders granting them a one-month leave. "Hey, man! We volunteered to extend our tours in 'Nam," Belmont said happily, as though it was some sort of reward, "and we get to fly stand-by on military flights anywhere in the world, so long as we're back at Tan Son Nhut by 24 October."

"I say Paris!" Dodd said.

"And I say Rio!" Belmont countered, "Amazon women in bikinis will carry Dodd down Copacabana Beach like a teddy bear!"

"I've got to side with you, Belmont," Mulcahey said, "The Commies are rioting in the streets of Paris and you'd just get tear-gassed and beaten by the cops."

"You mean like in Chicago, right?" Dodd said.

Mulcahey was happy to process them through, to distract himself from all the bad things that could keep him from boarding the Freedom Bird next Thursday. He drove them to SIC HQ to get them travel documents, open-ended through 24 October, and for medical clearance and shot records. Then they headed to the shipping container where their duffle bags had been stored with all their military gear when they went on civilian status. The steel containers were technically waterproof but that didn't prevent mildew from getting established among canvas bags that hadn't seen daylight for a year.

By Monday night, Mulcahey had them ready to go, but they still hadn't decided on a destination.

"We've got to start by putting in an appearance at home," Dodd argued, "Then we can get together and decide where to go."

"We've only got four weeks to see the world, Jerry. If you want to spend your time holding your mommy's hand, suit yourself."

"India!" Mulcahey shouted, just to confuse them further. He put the last few stitches into the corporal's stripes on Belmont's Class-B khaki uniform. Dodd and Belmont had both been corporals for many months but their uniforms still carried PFC stripes that had to be carefully removed with the razor blade he had found in his desk drawer, under his unopened letters from home.

"You do nice work, Mad-dog," Belmont jibed, by way of saying thanks, "You'll make some guy a wonderful wife someday."

The contest of wills about travel plans grew edgier as they faced the fact that they would carry open-ended travel orders out to Tan Son Nhut in the morning and still couldn't agree.

"I know how we decide this," Belmont announced, "Come with me."

Mulcahey and Dodd trailed him up the stairs to the screened enclosure, dark and vacant since the end of supper. Mulcahey switched on the lights and Belmont switched them off. Then he sat by the screen and in the vague glow of the city's ambient light, he expertly poured three generous lines of marijuana onto papers, licked the edges and rolled them, lit one with a lighter and passed it to Dodd, another to Mulcahey.

At the first whiff of smoke, Mulcahey said, "This is the same crap Papa-san uses in the waterpipe we got him, to keep him from punching holes in aerosol cans of pesticide."

"Ganja!" Belmont exhaled, coughing slightly.

"God's own incense," Dodd said before taking a drag.

Belmont instructed Mulcahey, "Take it in deep and hold it as long as you can." That wasn't long. Mulcahey coughed it all out at once. But he felt honored that Belmont, his guide to officers' clubs and photography and market-bartering and shantytown, was sharing yet another secret with him.

"Now," Belmont sprawled back in his chair, "What do you say we take the first flight we can on stand-by and let the fates decide it for us?"

"Works for me," Dodd said and began a fit of giggling for no apparent reason.

"That settles it then." Belmont took another sustained toke, let it out slowly and added, "We should never try to decide anything unless we get high first."

Mulcahey had been struggling to hold the smoke in his lungs, as instructed, and was having some success but didn't feel "high" or anything else aside from a dry, sore throat. He asked, "What is this stuff supposed to do, Belmont?"

"Mellow you out, man. Expand your understanding."

"Well, so," Mulcahey took a last drag from the dwindling cigarette, "It must work for some guys and not others because it's wasted on me. I don't feel anything at all from it."

"Takes practice, Mad-dog," Belmont said, rolling another round of three fat roaches.

John Mulcahey never got around to admitting to his friends that after they had come down from the darkened roof enclosure and had turned-in, he had gone to the office to type some letters but someone had altered the overhead fluorescents, which now threw a sort of golden luminescence over the desk tops so that papers and files took on a magical glow, as if lit from within. The overhead fan blades now moved in extreme slow motion, sending a rhythm through his whole being as he gazed up at them—whoosh... whoosh... whoosh. He stood in the office doorway for some minutes, his body swaying in perfect sync to the undulation of the fan-blades across the glowing lights. He broke this trance by turning off the wall switch, then followed a powerful urge that returned him to the roof enclosure where he stood alone in the light of the refrigerator and wolfed down an entire loaf of white bread, no butter, no jam. And strangest of all these phenomena, Mad-dog went to his cot feeling remarkably calm and serene.

At Tan Son Nhut Airbase the next morning, they stood beside the jeep trying to say something conclusive, but only formulas came to mind. Mulcahey said, "Thanks for everything, Belmont. You've been a great teacher" and "Take care, Petite Buddha." They firmly shook hands because men, in those times, did not hug each other in public. "You guys gonna have the same APOs when you get back here? Last thing I want is to lose touch, so if you don't hear from me, write me at the 250th MI Company at Fort Meade in Maryland."

They made solemn vows to stay in communication with each other and they sincerely meant it. But they never did. John Mulcahey wondered about Belmont and Dodd often, years after no one ever called him Mad-dog anymore.

The next time he went to his footlocker, Mulcahey found a shoebox half-full of weed and papers placed there with a note from Belmont: "Have fun. Give anything extra to Papa-san."

In appearance the Pham twins were so similar that even family members often could not tell Viet from Minh. This could work to their advantage, as when Pham Viet secured from III Corps SIC a photo ID that established him as an ARVN corporal (which he was not) and gave it to Pham Minh, who used it to travel around in an ARVN uniform and with forged "leave" papers. Or it could work to their disadvantage, as when Co Bian Guignon nearly shot Pham Viet at Major Shimazu's party because she mistook him for his brother. The key physical distinction between them (which saved Viet's life at the party) was a scar Minh carried on the back of his neck since he was ten, when he was pushed down onto a jagged piece of corrugated tin during a violent street fight.

The differences between them were otherwise fundamental. Viet made his living as head of the Translators' Pool at III Corps. He not only worked with Americans, he genuinely liked them and longed to see the United States for himself someday, perhaps to study at one of their great universities. Minh was, by contrast, an ultra-nationalist even before becoming a Communist and he despised the whole long list of foreigners who had raped his people, as he put it—the Chinese, the French, the Japanese, the English, the French again, and now the Americans and Australians and Koreans and Thais. Minh did more than philosophize about it. He was an aide to Colonel Vo Minh Triet and a respected combat leader in the elite 271st Regiment of the Viet Cong. When he wasn't using the ARVN cover his brother had supplied him to gather intelligence for Colonel Vo, he was leading combat units in attacks against "the Saigon puppet regime and its foreign masters."

That the Pham twins had chosen opposite sides in the war did not diminish their genuine love and respect for each other, founded on their common devotion to and identity with the family. The numerous and widespread Pham clan had members on both sides of the national conflict, as well as many who tried not to choose sides. They all, however, measured their worth by their status in the family and their loyalty to its patriarch, Grandfather Thanh, who resided at their central compound in Tra Vinh in the Mekong Delta. Americans bought life insurance, health insurance, and paid for unemployment insurance, social security and a pension plan—all so that they could enjoy the safety net provided to the extended Pham clan by their family. It was an article of faith that, ultimately, each person's success, perhaps even survival, depended on the family's cohesion and mutual support. For Viet and Minh, this translated into an understanding that if Hanoi won the war, Minh would rescue his puppet-regime brother and if Saigon prevailed, Viet would protect his Communist brother. Grandfather Thanh would demand it.

The power Pham Viet derived from his family was invisible to the Americans at III Corps. "Mr. Viet," as they called him, appeared as a polite, deferential factotum in their office, a pleasant young man who was useful as the bilingual bridge to their bilateral counterparts.

Their evaluation of him would not have changed if they had visited his home, the small, rented ground-floor apartment in Cholon where he lived with his wife and two small sons. One spacious tiled room had six wooden chairs and a simple table which held a small black-and-white television flanked by photographs of family members (one of which appeared to be a picture of Viet standing beside himself). A rear door opened onto a brick patio featuring a wash basin and clothesline, a charcoal fire-pit and little toy trucks. In the rear of the yard, Viet's wife grew a small but flourishing vegetable garden. A bedroom adjoining the main room had a wardrobe and a bureau, and the bathroom featured a toilet with a bidet built into the tiled floor and a wash basin with a cold-water tap. This family home was kept as clean as anyone could make it using a straw broom, a stiff brush, a pail and rags. Viet brought home the equivalent of $26. per week and owned a new motor scooter, which he kept inside the front door. At 27 years of age, Viet was proud of his home and in it, he ruled with a strong, commanding voice—an assertiveness he never showed at III Corps—so that his wife and sons would know that they had a husband/father who could protect and provide in a dangerous, uncertain world. However, no middle-class American reared in a three-bedroom house lined with electrical outlets and wall-to-wall carpeting kept clean by an electric vacuum, with an appliance-laden kitchen the size of Viet's main room and an attached two-car garage, would have been any more impressed by Pham Viet after visiting his home than he had been before.

Yet, if knowledge is power—as they were fond of saying in the Intelligence business—Pham Viet was by far the most powerful man in III Corps. As direct descendants of Grandfather Thanh—not mere cousins on outlying branches of the sprawling family—he and his brother stood to inherit the considerable property and, more importantly, the mantle of authority of their revered ancestors. This considerable potential was visible only to the initiated. In the meantime, it gave the brothers an intelligence web that would have been the envy of MACV.

Through cousin Diem, Viet knew more about Frank Monroe and his various scams than anyone in the US Army, even Braxton Hood! Diem had supplied the counterfeit "new scrip" Monroe used to fleece the Saigon elite out of hundreds of thousands (and Diem himself walked away with a sizeable chunk of the proceeds). Viet was the only man at III Corps who knew, for a fact, that Hood owned the Bravo, Juliet! and where he had gotten the money to buy it.

Because cousin Diem had long served Co Bian Guignon, whose parents had managed the Xuan Song rubber plantation, Viet also knew more about Rick Singleton's situation there before Tet—and through his brother, Minh, more about the extensive efforts made by Vo Danh to recruit Singleton to the Communist side after Tet— than even Singleton himself knew! The Pham brothers were vastly amused by Singleton's confusion when the III Corp translator seemed to resemble Colonel Vo's companion at Xuan Song dinner parties— who was none other than Pham Minh! Viet could even have told Singleton, if he wished to, Vo Danh's real name, Chu Le. It would be an understatement to say that Viet knew more about Rick Singleton's activities than any of his American friends in Saigon or Vung Tau— because none of them knew much of anything about any of it.

Rene Levesque, the man who led the boys' choir, remained a mystery to Viet. No one in the extended family under Grandfather Thanh was Catholic and few even knew a Catholic, so Viet had no way of learning more about Levesque. But how any American agent could hope to gain anything from embedding himself in the Byzantine labyrinth of the Vietnamese Catholic church bewildered and intrigued him. It seemed a fool's errand.

After work one night, Rosie's Suzuki blew by Viet's scooter on the crowded streets, so out of curiosity, he tailed him to an apartment on Tu Do Street. An hour's quiet surveillance was rewarded when a young woman climbed the stairs and let herself into the apartment with a key. Thereafter, Viet could never see Rosie in the office without breaking out in a big, happy smile. Rosenzweig just assumed that Mr. Viet was a naturally cheerful fellow.

Pham Viet never used or intended to use any of his knowledge for personal gain. He acquired as much intelligence as he could about these Americans because he was deeply and genuinely curious, fond of them and hugely entertained by their simplicity and kindness. In a world of mean-spirited, violent men intent on war, he cherished the time he spent with the Americans he knew—basically decent and well-meaning men his own age, whom he thought of as friends who were far from home and family, caught as he was in the never-ending war that was Vietnam's fate. His offer to host a farewell dinner for John Mulcahey and Zachary Rosenzweig was extended for the purest of reasons. He felt sincere sadness at seeing them departing forever, Mr. Rosenzweig and Mr. Mulcahey, colleagues he had worked beside every day for a year. It would cost him the equivalent of three days' pay, but he wanted to express his fondness for them and gratitude at the sacrifices they made to keep the Communists from, as he saw it, ending freedom of expression, capitalism and democracy, such as it was, in the Republic of Vietnam.

This note in Viet's stylized hand was placed on each of their desks on Tuesday morning: "This evening, 24 September, I be honored and pleased to invite you as my guest to dinner at Bò Vàng Restaurant for celebration of your year of service and hope for your safe return to your country. Pham Viet, Chief Translator."

Rosie pondered it but, in the end, couldn't bear giving away some of his last hours with Sang. He shook hands with Viet and told him, "I very much appreciate your invitation, but I have another appointment I cannot get out of. Thank you for inviting me."

Viet gripped Rosie's hand firmly in both of his and said, "I understand, Mr. Rosenzweig, and I wish you the best of luck." Indeed Viet did understand, more than Rosie knew, but he was disappointed to have his dinner party spoiled.

Mulcahey accepted Viet's offer, although he harbored some suspicion that this office-worker was probably going to ask him for some favor in return—suspicion nurtured by a year of haggling in the local market over the price of seafood and rice and at shantytown over the price of a girl.

On Tuesday, the last afternoon Mulcahey would spend in the III Corps villa, he presented the ancient gate guard they called Papa-san the gift of his treasured bicycle, along with the chain and padlock and his keyring with a University of Chicago medallion. They spent some time together adjusting the seat for the diminutive new owner, then Mulcahey shook his hand and told him, "You saved all our lives during Tet, so a used bike may be an insufficient reward." The old soldier may not have caught the gist of these words, but his gratitude for the bike was clear in the weathered face and many nods of the head. An hour later, the maid they knew only as Mama-san brought them the tan uniforms they would wear on their Thursday flight and Mulcahey carefully razor-cut the PFC stripes off his sleeves and sewed on corporal stripes he had bought at the PX. Rosie's PFC stripes were still, unfortunately for him, valid.

When everyone else climbed the stairs to the roof at suppertime, Mulcahey descended to the courtyard and straddled the passenger seat of Pham Viet's scooter. Viet often wedged his wife and two small sons onto the scooter for a ride through Saigon's hellish traffic, so hauling one American only ten kilos heavier than himself presented no problem.

Bò Vàng featured golden bulls on the sign and door and menus. It offered a variety of small French and Vietnamese dishes, which Viet expertly ordered for them, with watered-down cognac to clear their palates between each of the twelve courses. Mulcahey was thrilled to see that he was the only Westerner in the room and he made every effort to keep his voice down, even after the cognac had its full effect on a man with no hollow leg.

"What will you remember about Vietnam when you go home?" opened their conversation on a serious note.

"Being shot at!"

"Of course, when you went shopping for food during Tet fighting!" Viet laughed. "I am very happy they killed your jeep and not you!"

"Shimazu would rather had his jeep back than me."

"I don't think so. Major Shimazu is a good man."

"These are delicious. What are they?"

"Those Vietnamese spring rolls… you dip in sauce like this. You have Vietnamese restaurants in your home?"

"We've got everything you can imagine in Chicago… Chinese, Italian, German… but no, I don't think we've got any Vietnamese food, not that I've heard of." Mulcahey stuffed half a spring roll in his mouth. "Maybe you could come home with me, start the first-ever Vietnamese restaurant in Chicago." *Oh, Oh,* he thought, *I shouldn't have suggested that.*

"I would like very much to visit the United States someday."

Here it comes… I knew it! Can you sponsor me? Can you help me get a visa? There's always an angle with these people, Mulcahey thought, while saying, "Sure, you should do that."

"Will you tell your friends at home Vietnamese ladies very beautiful?" Viet teased.

A scene flashed into Mad-dog's mind: He's at his favorite bar on East 62nd Street bragging to his friends that he's gone to bed with fifty or sixty refugee peasants he paid $5 or $10 for and the thought struck him that they might believe him and walk away in disgust. Better to say nothing about it back home! And it might be a good idea to get checked out for every disease in the book as soon as possible. He mumbled, "Oh, sure. Girls in au dais, very nice. What is this?"

"Cat fish, you call it, in wine sauce. I'm glad you like it."

Mulcahey sloshed down cognac and said, around a bite of fish, "Man, Mr. Viet, I'll tell you, I can't wait to walk down Michigan Avenue again! The sun coming up over Lake Michigan! Shedd's Aquarium! The Natural History and Science and Industry Museums! Comiskey Park and Soldier Field! Man! No place like the Windy City!"

Viet understood what was being said without knowing all the specific references. "Perhaps I will visit you in Chicago when war ends. It must be very beautiful."

"Sure. I'll show you around," Mulcahey said, while thinking, *'You give me money for ticket... let me stay with you.' There's no such thing as a free dinner at the Golden Bull.*

"You have beaches like Vung Tau at your home?"

"Oh, yeah! Sure! We've got lots of beaches. And you can drive over to the Indiana Dunes and climb up mountains of sand higher than the Caravelle, right there on the beach!"

Viet was struggling to keep this dinner a happy event for himself against this tide of comparisons between the wealthiest, most powerful country on earth and his own poor homeland. Was there nothing about Vietnam that this man, after a year in-country, found praiseworthy? "Your family will be very happy to see you," he said.

"They sure will," Mulcahey said, washing down pho soup with cognac, "My mom writes me a letter every week. She can't wait to have me back home."

"And your father? Is he alive?"

"The old man? Well, let's just say he and I don't get along."

"But one must always honor his father, no matter what. That is true of all families, everywhere."

"Maybe here, not so much in America. My old man tries to tell me what to do, but I don't have to listen."

"But who among us can say that he is a better man than his father?"

"Around my house, 'father' refers to the priest. I just call my dad 'the old man'. And the priest tries to tell me what to do too and I don't have to listen to him either."

Viet felt anger rising in his chest as his dinner guest loudly denounced everything that he valued—loyalty to family and reverence for its elders. He asked quietly, "What holds your family together, Mr. Mulcahey, if you have no respect for the authority of your father?"

"Screw him!" Mulcahey took a gulp of cognac. "He shows no respect for my mom, so I don't have any for him."

Then the chain is broken, Viet thought to himself, *and you may have a great country to return to, Mr. Mulcahey, but without family harmony, you have no home in it.*

Viet endured the rest of the evening as best he could, making small talk about office matters and reminiscing about the grand weekend they all shared in Vung Tau, including the strange incident of the crazy lady who mistook him for someone else. Then he paid the bill, put Mulcahey into a pedicab and rode his scooter home cautiously, a little drunk and very unhappy.

When he arrived home, his brother was there, an unpredictable but not a rare visitor. "The Americans work you very late," Minh said, stubbing a cigarette out in an empty tea cup.

"I was at dinner with a friend, an American. You'll be happy to know he's leaving tomorrow."

"They can all leave tomorrow… that would make me very happy," Minh said. "I don't understand how you can be friendly with them."

"It's not easy sometimes," Viet conceded. "They can be arrogant, like the Chinese. You have to accept they are informal in their speech, often vulgar, and they do not show respect for anyone or anything, not even themselves. They can be insulting without knowing it. But they are also high spirited and generous. The Japanese stripped us of everything—the Americans bury us in mountains of material. They are richer than they know."

"You've been drinking their wine, Viet. You ramble on like a fool when you drink."

"I'm also very tired, brother, so let's not argue. We will talk tomorrow."

"I must leave at dawn. They are moving us to the highlands near Dalat. We may not see each other for a time."

"I worry about you, Minh. Please be careful."

Minh let out a burst of laughter, more in derision than in jest. "There is no safety for any of us until we are free! They buy you a dinner and fill you with wine and call you their friend. Do friends bring soldiers and helicopter gunships and tanks into your home? You've been co-opted, my brother. You are nothing to them but coolie labor!"

"Please, Minh…"

"Very well, let's not argue. It's late and I have far to travel tomorrow to rejoin my unit. One practical matter, first, about the American spy at Xuan Song. You gave us his name and rank in April. Now we need contact information for him in the United States, if you please."

"Corporal Singleton? His records are not kept in my office. I saw him in Vung Tau with an older man from SIC Headquarters. They are running him directly out of there, not through us."

"Do what you can, Viet. It is an urgent request from high up. They need to contact him when he goes back home."

Viet pulled a mat into the main room and bedded down at his brother's side, afraid that it might be the last time they saw each other. It was silent for a long time before Viet made one last, useless plea to his stubborn twin. "Please consider coming home soon, Minh. I will quit my job and stop working for the Americans if you will resign the 271st while you are still in one piece. We can live with Grandfather Thanh in Tra Vinh and help the family."

Silence followed. Viet thought his brother may be asleep. Then Minh said, "You remember that bully, Chien, when we were children? He beat me and gave me the scar on my neck. I got up, blood running down my shirt, and I went at him. He won the fight that day, but he let us alone after that. The Americans will too if we go at them and don't give up."

Viet answered, "This is not the same. I know the Americans. They will never give up until Hanoi agrees to their terms. In the meantime, the terrible firepower they command will rob me of my brother."

"Maybe," Minh conceded, "We'll just wait and see."

The night before their flight home, they were held in a gray, five-story building on busy Cong Ly Street, undistinguished except for the twelve-foot wall of sandbags across the front topped with coils of barbed wire and by MPs in turrets. The "Off Limits" sign stretched across a stairway attracted Babineaux's attention and it was he who ignored it and discovered the rooftop haven that allowed the Gray-hawk Six to discreetly escape the airless, eight-bunk cells where there was nothing to do. One-by-one, each of them was let in on the secret and led to the back stairway where they ducked under the sign and pushed the crash-bar at the top of the stairs to escape the teeming masses of excited soldiers buzzing about tomorrow's flight, the stench of sweat and cigarette smoke, the trite lyrics of what they would do when they got back to the USA. The building MPs who used this roof-top space had left chairs and tables around and a Coleman gas-lamp that pierced the darkness with a singular point of glaring white. In a far corner of the roof was an open-air shower, a cold-water pipe with no head, wooden pallet and drain but no walls or curtain, since privacy was not an issue. Mulcahey set up shop beside the white brilliance of the Coleman lamp where he razor-cut PFC stripes, replacing each with corporal stripes. Mad-dog had kept aside a goodly stash of Belmont's weed and Babineaux proved as artful in rolling joints as Mulcahey was at sewing insignia—so on this strange night, in this weird, ungodly light, Levesque, Singleton and Rosie experi-mented with pot for the first (and for Singleton, the last) time. Braxton Hood declined, as he had the dubious pleasures of shantytown, as a matter of personal preference. By turns, each of the six padded across the roof to the makeshift shower, dropping his clothes in a heap and experiencing the shock of cold water striking hot, dry skin under the night sky. Men in various stages of nudity were ambling about in the lantern's glare, soaking wet or almost dry, smoking joints, throwing shadows across each other and the low wall along the roof edge, chatting quietly among themselves for three hours which, they ever afterwards agreed, was a most other-worldly and haunting memory.

Oddly enough—and unlike the men on the floors below them—they didn't speak at all about the United States. There had been lots of civil unrest in their absence and they knew it, to varying degrees, but how it would feel to walk through an airport or down a busy street in uniform was something they couldn't predict. For them, the familiar and knowable was Vietnam, which was—like the sheltered doorway is to the homeless man or the jail cell to the prisoner—the environment they had learned to navigate.

Hood and Babineaux told the others about life in Vung Tau and "Itty Bitchy"—but not about who owned Bravo, Juliet! or that the bar-tending twins had walked out in anger.

Rick Singleton explained the plantation society at Xuan Song and described the tyrannical manager, Monsieur Guignon—but did not mention his lovely friend, Margot Guignon, and certainly did not utter a word about Vo Danh.

Rosie would only say about Nguyen Sang that she was doing well in nursing school and they planned to stay in touch—but nothing about the hole in his heart.

Mulcahey and Levesque told some anecdotes about the boys' choir—but omitted recounting that their final farewell took on the aspect of mass hysteria on the part of the orphans and embarrassed sobbing in response on the part of the musical conductor and his accompanist. Absolutely no mention was made, by prior agreement, of Corporal Leffanta, much less any reference to ghosts or visions or angels or any other spiritual phenomena.

In short, then, the intimacy of the Grayhawk Six on the occasion of this weird reunion on the lantern-lit rooftop with the open-air shower was renewed entirely on the basis of superficial anecdote—with nothing revealed that might have been regarded as intimate.

The closest anyone came to a passionate statement was Mad-dog Mulcahey's repeated exclamation: "Please stay out of my goddamn light, goddammit! I stuck myself with the needle AGAIN!"

They were called for their flight by some system understood only by the personnel in charge. When the order came to advance single-file onto the tarmac, the six friends jockeyed in and out of line until they were all together, a clique within the mass of enlisted men identifiable by their having a number of corporal stripes sewn onto their khaki sleeves at seventy- and sixty- and, in one case, forty-five-degree angles off true vertical. Almost three million Americans felt the same adrenaline-rush they did as they approached the massive Boeing 707, their flight home. They dropped their heavy duffle bags at the foot of the long stairway and climbed to the small doorway at the top, squeezing into the belly of aluminum and scrambling for a window or aisle seat.

This flight, though, got off to a shaky start. The volume of merry chatter dwindled down and then ceased as the big jet taxied a couple hundred yards—then abruptly jerked to a halt and cut its engines. No announcement was made. Concern grew quickly among the 219 passengers and crew, wedged in tight together. In complete silence, they listened to three muffled explosions in the distance. They feared more were coming, perhaps closer. After five tense minutes, the engines whined back to life again and they continued to taxi. The take-off was as close to vertical as the four big Pratt & Whitney turbofans could deliver. When word passed from window to aisle that the coastline of Vietnam was passing under, a great cheer went up, with sustained applause, and everyone aboard was thrilled except the crew members. They had seen it all before many times, over and over. They would be back soon for just another load of sweaty, pumped-up soldiers, a tedious, monotonous and nerve-racking job for them. For the soldiers, a year in the tropics had thinned their blood, so there were many complaints that the cabin temperature gave them goose-bumps and shivers.

Corporal Mulcahey, who began reading Joyce's *Ulysses* on the flight to Vietnam, was being overstimulated now by Ken Keysey's *One Flew Over the Cuckoo's Nest* and he would not stop interrupting Rene Levesque's concentration on the series of meditations offered in *Are You Running With Me, Jesus?* by Malcolm Boyd, no matter how many times Rene asked him nicely.

PFC Rosenzweig appeared to be deeply engrossed in Bernard Malamud's *The Fixer*, but the truth was his mind was drifting from his book to an apartment on Cong Ly Street, and he checked his watch often, worrying about her driving the Suzuki from school to the tailor shop then home, envisioning her reading a textbook while cooking rice on the hot plate, then eating by herself, perhaps glancing up from her book at the empty chair, wondering what he was doing at that moment. It was well that Rosie sat between a soldier who slept for most of their sixteen hours together and Rick Singleton, who put aside *The Confessions of Nat Turner* only to eat or nap or make a bathroom run. Neither Rosie nor Singleton felt like talking.

Not so Hood, cramped in his aisle seat and restless, and his business partner of late, Mark Babineaux. John Updike's *Couples* was not holding Babineaux's attention, so the two spent most their waking hours discussing stories from a stack of used *Newsweek* magazines Hood had found in the departure lounge. Vung Tau had provided a busy, insulated bubble inside of which world events passed with little notice. They were eager to hear more than vague rumors about the "Battle of Chicago" in which anti-war demonstrators fought police and military in the streets outside the Democratic Convention that had chosen Hubert Humphrey as their candidate for president. Another issue profiled Republican candidate Richard Nixon (again?) and his choice of Maryland Governor Spiro Agnew as his running mate. Other issues covered massive demonstrations across the US and in Paris and outright warfare in Prague when Russian tanks and troops invaded Czechoslovakia to crush a rebellion. "How come the mob in Prague are called 'Freedom Fighters' and the one in Chicago isn't?" Babineaux asked. Hood didn't know.

The moment of their flight home when one might expect a great cheer to go up was instead one of quiet awe and whispered exchanges. Hours of bored confinement in a narrow seat had induced a torpor, an exhaustion of all the eager anticipation built up over a year of waiting for this moment. The nighttime lights of San Francisco lit up the ceiling of the dark cabin from below with the power of search-lights. Even soldiers from Saigon or major military bases had not seen this much nighttime light in a year, and they had forgotten how amazing it was. "Man!" Braxton Hood muttered, "You could walk down the street readin' a book down there."

The shock of returning from a Third World country to a First was just beginning. They all knew that the homeland to which they were returning was not the one they had left. Recruited in the winter of 1966-67, none of them had ever seen the kind of mass demonstrations and riots that had become commonplace, none knew a "hippie" from a "yippie," but they were now about to be dropped into all of this from out of the sky—in uniform and carrying personal experiences that were inexplicable, even to each other.

8

26 September – 25 October 1968

ALL WE LIKE SHEEP

Lake Charles, Louisiana

The four-hour bus ride from New Orleans to Lake Charles just about froze Mark Babineaux to death. Several of the white riders sitting up front asked in vain if the driver could adjust the air conditioning. Black riders in the rear made no complaints. Other than that, Babineaux was savoring every moment of the ride home—the lush greenery, so unlike Vung Tau, cranes and herons fishing in the ditches and swamps beside the highway, occasional lazy gators lying in the mud. To warm himself and to settle his nerves, he shouldered his duffle and walked three miles home from the Greyhound Station, inhaling the almost forgotten scent of pines, sweat-soaking his uniform shirt under the heavy load. He stood on the cement porch of the single-story brick house and stared at the doorbell for a spell, then took a deep breath and flung the door open. He stepped into the spacious front room and shouted, "Hey, y'all! What's for dinner?"

He had expected his parents to be home—three cousins, a niece and her husband, he had not. They raced in to mob him from the kitchen and back patio, where the answer to his question was barbequed steak and shrimp, potatoes, red beans and cold beer. The way was cleared for his mother to give him the first hug, then his hand was shaken and his back slapped as they all yelled at once: "Why didn't you tell us you were comin'?" and "Where's all your battle ribbons, corporal?" and "Look at you! You've put on weight!" His father hung back in the kitchen doorway, watching, so Mark went over to him and shook his strong, calloused hand. "I'm glad you're back safe, son," he said quietly.

They ate on lawn chairs and drank beer until mosquitoes chased them indoors. Through the course of the evening, Mark noticed something: All the explanations and evasions he had been preparing in his mind since leaving Tan Son Nhut were unnecessary. His kith and kin chided him about "all those Oriental women" and asked how he had gained weight on Army food and how soon was he "getting out"—but they asked him not one specific question about what he had done, how he had lived, and in fact, the name "Vietnam" was not uttered. The talk soon turned to LSU's chances of winning the SEC, then to an uncle who had left his wife of twenty-nine years for a woman half his age and to rising property taxes, to finding a babysitter you could trust and gas prices. These people, a few of his many relatives in the area, were intelligent, caring people. But the world beyond Calcasieu Parish appeared to them as flickering images they caught glimpses of through the keyhole of their television sets. Mark had been away, now he was back, they were glad.

He went to bed in the room that was his since childhood and lay awake for a long time wondering how his own family could care so little to know about the life-changing things he had witnessed, what he had done in Vietnam—and still be said to care about him. But what if they had pulled chairs into a circle and grilled him? Would he have told them about weaving an elaborate web of lies at MACV—or that he would give a year of his life to spend tomorrow watching Qui running along the beach, see beautiful Hang happily buzzing around her clothing shop, put his elbows on the bar and ask the twins for a Tom Collins, and end the day at dinner with Braxton Hood and the redoubtable Ngon Bich? Had they wanted to know, he would not have told them anything. And on the horns of that dilemma, he finally slept.

His father was off to work by the time he came into the kitchen. His mother poured him a coffee and asked if he wanted eggs and grits. She propped a paperback romance in front of her face while he ate, but he caught her glancing at him. She waited for him to push the empty plate away before saying, "I never wanted you to go, Mark. I want you to know that."

"You never said anything one way or the other."

"How could I? Your father, you know…"

Mark tried in vain to decipher that before giving up. "What about him?"

"He told me to stay out of it, that it would do you good. You'd learn more about life in Basic Training than in four years of college. You'd come back a man, he said."

For reasons he couldn't understand, this simple narrative was putting his mother into an emotional state, so he tried to placate her. "OK… well… maybe he was right. I did learn a lot."

"I can just imagine…" she said, choking back tears. "If you ever need to talk about it, I am here for you, Mark!" She got up and retreated down the hallway, sobbing.

Jesus! he thought, *No wonder nobody says anything about Vietnam around here. They all just assume I burned huts and shot villagers!*

The talk Mark had with his father, in the neighborhood bar two days later, went an entirely different direction but was no more comforting. Mark carried a pitcher and two iced mugs to a dimly lit corner booth and said with a grin, "Mom thinks I've been traumatized by war!"

His father, still in work boots from the refinery, wasn't grinning. "I don't," he said seriously.

"Good… because I think she's about to set me up with a shrink over at Tulane." Mark poured their mugs full and they sat together in silence as he pondered the meaning of his father's "I don't." In his late teens, Mark awoke to the realization that his father was as taciturn as he was thoughtful. He said very little and meant every word. Before that, he had just been the powerful, silent presence who came and went from the house, to work, on hunting and fishing trips, attending church at the Cathedral of the Immaculate Conception by himself on Sundays. A couple of men came in who were supervised by his father at the refinery and greeted him as "Mr. Babineaux" while Mark examined "I don't" for the intention. Then he came at it obliquely. "Anyway, I'm beginning to understand why you never talk about the war… your war."

His father responded with a rare chuckle, which Mark took as agreeable. It wasn't. "You ever heard of John McKeithen?" his father asked.

"Sure. He's the governor."

"Well, when I was your age, John McKeithen was my lieutenant in the 77th Infantry. We fought our way together across Guam and then Okinawa. We shot, torched or blew hell out of every Jap we saw. No prisoners, which worked out 'cuz they didn't want to surrender anyway. We won our battles. We dropped the bomb and won the war and occupied Japan. So, you see?"

Mark felt pretty sure he saw, as visions of pretty girls on the beach at Vung Tau danced through his mind. He said, "I guess you don't agree with mother about my being traumatized, then."

"I've never much liked that word," he said, refilling their mugs. Then, "Look, don't get me wrong, Mark. I'm as glad as anybody that you're home safe and it's OK with me if you didn't have to do what we did. But it makes me sick to my stomach to watch these pussy-footed politicians wasting American lives over there. The firepower advantage we've got today? We could roll-up those fucking supply lines through Cambodia and Laos, shoot our way into Hanoi then mop up the South and get the hell out of there. They've had four years to get it done… longer than it took us to chase the Japs out of the whole Pacific!"

This was the longest and the most passionate statement he'd ever heard from his father, but his pleasure at being talked to man-to-man was spoiled by the disappointment about Vietnam—his war. He thought of debate points. A very different situation: Thousands of farmers by day who turn into VC militia by night, China and Russia poised to intervene if the North is invaded. But he would lose the debate and spoil their time together, so he turned the talk to cousins and uncles.

As they drove home his father said, "When your time's up, come out to the refinery. I'll set you up with a good job that'll put some muscle on ya'." Mark said he would, without meaning it, and vowed never to refer to himself as a "veteran" around his father.

There were three festivals held in Lake Charles in three weeks. Friends, most of whom worked in the refinery, seemed to have been frozen in time during his absence. Zydeco, jazz and pop music filled his ears; jambalaya, etouffee, boudin and fried fish filled his guts;

young girls (none as pretty as Hang or as athletic as Qui) danced before his eyes and all of it bored him and fired his anxiety to get to Ft. Meade and back to his Greyhawk comrades.

Clemson, South Carolina

Braxton Hood returned to a very different scene than Mark Babineaux, his partner at Vung Tau Field Station. Hood had written home regularly, letters addressed to his mom that she would read aloud to his dad and in them, he had created a narrative that would leave them proud of him. Pride, honor and duty to country held a high place in his family and his town going back to the Civil War, which may have left them on the losing side but not for any lack of courage or effort. Doing one's best and giving one's all was expected by Hood's extended family, dozens of whom had worn the uniform in war and in peacetime for more than a century. This ethos was now taught to the family's young men on the football field and reinforced by older members who cheered wildly from the stands. Whether you won or lost, what mattered was giving your team everything you had.

So while not being at all specific (intelligence work requiring, as it did, discretion), Hood's letters home conveyed his dedication to his work, to defeating the Communists and winning the war. Needless to say, no mention was made of his bedroom and bath in Frank Monroe's luxurious villa in Saigon with its live-in chef, maids and guards, all paid-for by Army reimbursements for a large spy network "in Cu Chi" that didn't exist—in Saigon or Cu Chi or anywhere else—except on paper. Nor did his letters describe the way CIA agents were bilked out of $60,000 in a two-day poker game (using Hood's own strategies and facility for doing math in his head). Nor was notice taken of Monroe's much more dangerous (but profitable) currency fraud that netted a couple hundred thousand in scrip in ten frightening days. Hood's family would have been no more proud of his part in these schemes than Braxton himself was. Owning and operating a hotel/tavern/whorehouse on the beach? *God Forbid!* There was no way for him to hint at any of this that would not open the door to embarrassment, guilt and shame.

As he had painted himself gradually into a corner with Frank Monroe, he had done so as well with his letters. He had no other choice than to return as the honorable soldier of his own myth-making. The warrior he never was had come home from a war that was, for him, a beach resort.

Not only a "Welcome Home Braxton!" banner but bunting and flags as well festooned the house when he was driven into the driveway perched on the back seat of his cousin's convertible. Neighbors and family gathered around as Hood threw one of his huge arms around his mom and shook his dad's hand with the other.

"Just look at you!" his dad said, stepping back, his eyes wet with emotion. But Braxton hoped he wasn't looking too closely at his wrinkled khaki uniform blouse adorned with only a Good Conduct Ribbon, a "marksman" badge and corporal stripes that pointed more east and west than true north. He carried his envelope cap folded in his hand because he had misplaced his own and was given one by a paratrooper, so it sported a parachute insignia he didn't want to have to explain. Everybody was invited into the house, where an elaborate array of edibles was waiting, two large punch bowls (one spiked), plenty of beer and hard liquor, balloons and crepe in red, white and blue. Neighbors of all ages piled into the food and drink, everyone talking at once, treating Braxton like the bride at a wedding.

Questions flew at him about the war and his life in Vietnam. Where was he during the Tet Offensive? Did he see much action? Were the Vietnamese good fighters? Were we winning the war? Treated like an expert and eye-witness to history, Braxton did his best to satisfy their curiosity despite interference by visions floating through his head of sunsets on the South China Sea, the endless stretch of white sand beach crowded with happy people, the jabbering mobs of soldiers and sailors filling Bravo, Juliet! with laughter. He drew for them life as he had created it in his letters—with hints of dangerous spy missions to gather intelligence on enemy troops, artillery barrages and mortar attacks, his work with Australian Naval Intelligence and more.

By the time neighbors and family began to drift off, Hood was on the point of collapse. He had flown out of San Francisco on "military stand-by" early in the morning and now evening was falling in South Carolina. He had been engaging intensely with interested people for hours and he was wrung out. He dabbled with drying dishes for his mom, but she saw the fatigue in his face and sent him to bed in his old room. He needed a shower but didn't have the strength. He pulled off his clothes and slipped into bed in his underwear, the walls around him heavy with banners, ribbons and photographs that celebrated his achievements. His dad rapped twice then stuck his head in the door and told him, "It's great to have you home, Braxton. We couldn't be more proud of you!"

"Thank you," he mumbled, "Good night."

As he drifted off to sleep, a wave of panic swept through him. *How much longer can I keep this up?* he thought, *How soon can I get out of here?*

Hood's salvation arrived on Friday, 11 October, when everyone gathered to watch the launch of the Apollo 7 mission. Three crew members had died almost two years earlier when their capsule caught fire during training, which put the program on hold. Today would prove the redemption of America's space program—or it would be the disaster that would probably end it. For the first time, a Saturn 1B, originally designed to launch nuclear warheads into space and drop them as falling objects on intended targets, was being used to propel humans into earth orbit. The Saturn was the largest American rocket ever built and no one knew whether its size and power could be tamed for manned space travel. Hood had career dreams that involved NASA in some capacity that would allow his gifts as a mathematician full range. He had been reading everything available about the Apollo program and as the launch count-down proceeded, everyone gathered around the television turned to him to explain the technical aspects of what they were seeing.

Just after 3:00 in the afternoon, two boosters and three huge engines were ignited and the enormous silver silo began to move upward, so slowly at first that everyone assumed something had gone wrong. It climbed above the launch tower with great effort, a giant struggling to rip itself free of the earth, then it gained speed and rose into the sky above Cape Kennedy and began to shrink until it was a point of bright light with a trail of smoke behind it. Within minutes, they announced that Shirra, Eisele and Cunningham were in space, orbiting around the earth at 17,000 miles-per-hour. Everyone broke out into cheers and applause and tears of joy and relief. America had succeeded!

For the next eleven days, a rotating audience of family, friends and neighbors carrying food and drinks stood sentry in the living room, calling out to each other when there were live pictures from space or when they were attempting docking maneuvers and other protocols, practicing for the attempt to land men on the moon that was scheduled to follow soon, so long as things worked on this low-earth-orbit mission.

And through it all, Braxton was rarely absent. He was the center of attention as the young man who had already, he said, put his application in to NASA, who had a rare talent for mathematics and would someday be a vital member of the launch crew—hovering over a monitor, making critical decisions about missions or, who knows, perhaps an astronaut himself!

Already a war veteran, it was clear to everyone that Braxton Hood would continue to make his family and the broader community proud.

Nashville, Tennessee

Zachary Rosenzweig's homelife ran on average at 20% the volume of Babineaux's and 10% the volume of Hood's, but his family's emotions were no less powerful for being quieter. His father and mother were at the airport to greet him, along with his older sister, Ruth, and they each gave him a strong, lingering hug. His mother cried, trying not to, as they spoke their words of welcome and happiness. They went home to a dinner of fried chicken and mashed potatoes, with cherry pie for dessert—menu favorites of Zachary's that his parents found barely tolerable. During the meal, the parents took turns running interference for the guest of honor.

Sister: "So what was it like over there?"

Father: "Zachary is eating, Ruth. Let your brother eat in peace."

Sister: "I'm just curious. It's a simple question."

Mother: "Pass the gravy to him, Ben. He needs more gravy."

Sister: "Were you ever in any danger?"

Father: "Ruth, please! He just got home!"

Mother: "Zachary doesn't want to talk about that now, do you, Zachary?"

Brother: "It's OK to ask questions. I don't mind."

Mother: "Don't talk with food in your mouth, Zachary. It's impolite."

Father: "He just got home! Who needs to take an oral examination the first thing when he gets home?"

Ruth: "Did they shoot at you over there?"

Father: "OK, Ruth, that's enough! What did I just say to you?"

Mother: "He was never in any fighting, were you, Zachary? If he had been in any fighting, he would have told us in his letters. You would have told us, wouldn't you, Zachary?"

Silence.

Mother: "Not that there were that many letters."

Zachary groaned. Ruth laughed.

At 9:00, Benjamin laid aside Norman Mailer's *Armies of the Night* and Marian put down Herbert Tarr's *Heaven Help Us!* and they fetched Zachary and Ruth to watch Rowan and Martin's "Laugh In."

"When did they start letting naked girls dance on television?" Zachary asked.

"They're wearing swim suits," Father said.

"Bikinis," Ruth amended.

"And they're covered all over with painted words," Father said, "They're billboards."

"They're girls," Zachary said.

The comedy was fast-paced, unpredictable, off-beat and laugh-out-loud funny. Still Zachary found himself taken aback by the nudity and double-entendre humor and he laughed less than the others.

As they retired back to their rooms, Ruth said to him, "You've changed, little brother. I can tell."

"I'm still me," Zachary told her, "I'm no different."

"No, you're not." Ruth studied his face for a moment. "You're sadder."

He had no answer for that he could share with his sister.

"Did all your friends come back OK?"

"Sure... yeah, we all got back."

Ruth detected something hollow in his voice and sensed he was holding back. "And you are happy, then, that you didn't lose anybody... nobody that you knew."

Rosie saw that she had the scent. Once his sister got onto something, she was a bloodhound. She would bark, bay and nip at him until her curiosity was satisfied. This would not stop until she had her prey or was thrown off the trail. "I lost a colleague, someone I worked with in the office," he admitted.

"How did he die?"

"Friendly fire... there was fighting half-a-mile away and a bullet from a helicopter just found its way to him."

He hoped this would suffice, but Ruth continued to study his face in that way she had. "What was his name?" she asked.

"Nguyen... Nguyen Sang," he told her.

The next day Rosie knocked on the door of his oldest friend, Buzz O'Malley, who, after years of giving-out lectures about not being a "love slave" and warnings that females only wanted to "get their hooks into you," had married the first girl he dated, straight out of high school. There was a cooler of beer between them on the patio table behind O'Malley's big house, but they were ready to run indoors if the darkening clouds overhead produced rain.

"I thought I was the lucky one, man, getting a pass from the draft board for my knees." O'Malley downed a half can of beer on one go. "But if I was smart, I would've found some way to join up like you did."

"You've got a beautiful place here, Buzz. Susan is a doll. Looks to me like you're doing OK... lots better than me."

"Sure... Stuff!" O'Malley drained his first can and popped another. "We got a condo out at Priest Lake, two cars and a truck to haul the boat, and I'm here to tell ya', it's all a giant pain-in-the-ass. We both work overtime to maintain it all and Susan, Christ! She's got both houses crammed full and is always out lookin' for more... more stuff!" O'Malley guzzled another half-can and announced, "You're the richest guy I know, Rosenzweig... because you're free-and-clear. No wife. No houses. No responsibilities. No goddamned load of shit weighin' you down. And now what? Now Susan, she's talking about kids!" O'Malley polished off his second beer. "It's all a part of her Master Plan, Rosenzweig! First, she fills two houses to bursting with clothes and shoes enough for a small town, furniture everywhere, her piano room and art studio and another room piled up with sewing crap, then she wants kids! Where they gonna sleep? We'll need another house!"

Rosie wanted to laugh, but O'Malley gave no hint he saw a comic side to his diatribe. So he accepted his childhood friend's sense of desperation in his fate or choices, whichever it was, and he compared it with his own sense of tragedy—that he could not stay with Nguyen Sang, who needed so little, to love her and provide for her, while the O'Malleys' love for each other, such as it may have been, had suffocated under a landslide of abundance.

Rosie avoided Buzz O'Malley for the remainder of his leave time. He read and dreamt about his life in Saigon for hours on the back patio of his home, chatted pleasantly with his family, visited friends, until the evening before he was due to leave for Ft. Meade. His father dragged a patio chair over and sat close beside him. He leaned in and said in a low voice, "I need to ask you something that I can't get off my mind…"

Zachary said, "Sure… OK."

"You might have been forced to defend yourself at some time… maybe more than once… maybe never… I'm not asking about that."

"OK… then what?"

"I have to know, Zachary, did you do anything that you're sorry for? That you regret?"

The image of Lieutenant Aaronson's bloody face leapt into his mind.

"Or is your conscience clear about your conduct while you were in Vietnam?"

Zachary looked this decent, caring man in the eye and answered in all sincerity, "You can rest your mind, Father. I have great respect and affection for the Vietnamese and I conducted myself towards them as you would have wanted me to."

Harlem, New York City

After a year spent mostly on a rubber plantation, Rick felt whip-lashed by the pace of his native New York. He had forgotten what it felt like to be swept along in a sea of humanity, all of them desperately wishing that they were someplace they weren't. His someplace was a large townhouse on West 121st Street where his family was anxiously awaiting him. More and more riders crowded aboard as the ear-split-ting "A" train screamed to a halt in each station then blasted off again as though some aspiring racecar driver was at the controls and Rick struggled not to lean onto perfect strangers, but he had a duffle bag to straddle and the support bars seemed always just out of reach. No one in the ninety-minute ride from Jamaica, Queens, to 125th Street made eye-contact with this black corporal in the wrinkled uniform, as though he didn't exist for them and it was a great relief, at last, to stretch his legs along familiar sidewalks on a cool September evening. The nearer he got to the house, the more curiosity was shown him, a solitary soldier hauling a duffle instead of one face in a beehive of faces, until he arrived on his block and neighbors began to wave and call out.

"Hey, man! Yeah, I'm back for a while," he shouted and, "Good evening, Mrs. Williams. Yeah, it's me. Don't let the uniform fool ya'."

He mounted the flight of brownstone steps to the front door of the stately townhouse and looked up and down the block that had been his world, growing up. There had been many terrifying moments over the past year when he didn't expect ever to see this place again, when it was the decision of another man whether he would live or die, be taken captive or walk away. He experienced that sense of transcendent joy that lucky survivors alone can know, the knowledge that each day is a miraculous, undeserved gift. It took him some minutes now before he felt he had control of his own emotions and was ready to receive his family's welcome.

He rang the bell and waited. His teenage sisters shrieked when they saw him through the glass of the outer door and they unlocked it and threw themselves on him, shouting with delight. They pulled him and dragged his heavy duffle into the narrow hallway where his mother pushed her way into the scrum of embracing arms. Rick Singleton had known his share of fear and hardship, so the act of being enfolded into his loving family was especially emotional for him and tears of relief ran freely down his face. He smeared them away as best he could with the short sleeves of his khaki uniform shirt when his father appeared on the long stairway.

The Most Reverend John Singleton, pastor of the second largest Baptist congregation in New York, was a power to be reckoned with and an imposing physical presence. Hundreds of faithful people carried his strong baritone voice in their heads and their hearts, drawing inspiration from his message of forgiveness, redemption and love. His resolute convictions and moral authority were mainstays for his flock and for his family. But Rick almost didn't recognize the man descending the staircase, gripping one banister for support. He seemed to have lost not just weight but height as well and he had aged a decade in the year of his son's absence. His voice, as he welcomed Rick home, sounded tentative, almost frail. Rick embraced his father and felt vulnerability where overpowering strength had been. When he turned, his sisters were staring at him, wide-eyed, the unspoken question between them: "Do you see what's happening to him?"

Dinner began, as always, with grace, the family holding hands around the table while father expressed gratitude for the food, for all the blessings of this life and especially for his son's safe return. The talk was light-hearted, full of laughter, catching Rick up on all the developments in the elaborate network of his community, the neighborhood and the church-family. Rick's sisters were gently admonished whenever they wandered from the news to juicy gossip or critical judgments about other people's lives. An obligation to respect others was the ethos of the family. Rick glowed as he looked around, vowing never again to take such "normal" intimacy, abundance and security for granted.

"The death of Reverend King has been a terrible blow to him," Rick's mother whispered to him as she perched on the edge of his bed that night. "Everyone brought their grief and their anger and laid it at his feet, expecting him to shoulder it all and provide them comfort and understanding… but he had none to give. Martin was his friend and his mentor. He was in such pain, how could he reassure others of Jesus' eternal love when he couldn't feel it himself? So, Richard, you must help him every way you can. I pray that your coming home will be the spark that he needs to regain his strength and go on."

Having neither lost his religious faith nor practiced it much in recent years, Rick Singleton nevertheless prayed that night for God to help his father.

He spent much of his leave-time in his father's company and he was astounded to realize the tempo and quantity of the work that was expected of him. He answered phone calls during breakfast, juggling toast and coffee with his free hand. Then he walked to the church down sidewalks where everyone knew him and presumed he had time to hear them out. The church office had two full-time secretaries who scampered around from phone calls to paperwork to managing the stream of visitors, those with appointments and those without. A car service took Reverend Singleton to three or four meetings a day with politicians, charitable causes, and big-time donors. After dinner at home, he often went back out to lead committee meetings or prayer groups, then he worked in his study on correspondence, his sermons or other writing commitments until after midnight. That his father was working himself to death seemed apparent to Rick, but he did not see what he could do about it. The more he tried to insert himself into his father's work-load, the more he felt he was just getting in the way.

At the end of the second week home, Rick found a distraction at the 123rd Street Tavern, where friends of his youth joined the crowd watching the XIX Olympics—not pre-recorded this time but tele-cast live and in full color from Mexico City! Many in this audience had been local track celebrities themselves, winning races at the City and State meets while in high school before settling into jobs under hotel awnings or behind the wheels of limousines or cabs. Excitement mounted after the Opening Ceremonies on 12 October and the tavern was soon known in the neighborhood as the place to be for former athletes and their fans. Pride in their race stirred this all-black audience into a frenzied joy as Hines and then Miller and then Greene all qualified for the finals of the pinnacle Olympic event, the 100-meter dash. Their emotions overwhelmed them on Monday, October 14, when the Americans swept the event! Jim Hines became the first Olympian in history to officially run 100 meters in under 10 seconds. The medal podium was monopolized by Americans whose ancestors had been slaves and every man and woman in the place felt personally vindicated. "The fastest human who ever lived is a brother!" the bartender shouted.

Two days later, Tommie Smith became the first Olympic runner to cover 200 meters in under 20 seconds. When he and bronze medalist John Carlos mounted the platform to receive their medals, they bowed their heads to their flag as the National Anthem played but held gloved fists aloft in the Black Power salute to protest, they said, the continuing poverty and inequality of black Americans. The response of the crowd in the 123rd Street Tavern was one of subdued tension. There was pride in the courage of these men, whose statement was echoing around the world, but there would be inevitable consequences—punishments, wrath, death threats.

IOC Chairman Avery Brundage's condemnation was immediate. He ordered Smith and Carlos expelled from the team. Most of their teammates stood in defiant support, threatening that if they were sent home, the whole team would leave. But in the end, Brundage prevailed and the two athletes were sent home. The controversy sparked emotional debate among the fans at the 123rd Street Tavern:

Should the men have seized the moment of world attention as they had? Or might it have been better had these great athletes simply accepted their medals and used their fame to speak out later?

One afternoon, Rick found himself discussing the topic with a middle-aged man in a business suit while he was watching the qualifying heats for the high hurdles. The man was soft-spoken and seemed well educated, with an accent that was perhaps Jamaican or Trinidadian. Rick, working on his second beer, absorbed in the telecast and watching the door for his group of friends, was paying little attention to the man's assertion that Smith and Carlos had marked a crucial turning point in public awareness. When the gentleman insisted, three times in succession, "They are revolutionary heroes on the world stage," he caught Rick's full attention for the first time. He was heavy-set, with rough hands that seemed incongruous with his tailored suit—and his neatly trimmed beard and moustache were, Rick's theater experience told him, a glued-on disguise. "I am Mr. Thomas, a friend of Vo Danh's," he said quietly, "and I believe you are a friend of his too."

When Rick caught his breath, he said, "I don't recognize the name."

"Oh, I think you do, Mr. Michaels. You and he became great friends when you lived on the rubber plantation."

"I don't know what you're talking about," Rick said, sipping at his beer.

The man drew in closer and said, "Vo Danh wanted me to ask you a simple question, sir. Whose side are you on? Are you on the side of Tommie Smith or Avery Brundage? In 1936, the Germans who were given medals all gave Nazi salutes as they stood on the winner's podium. Mr. Brundage said that was OK with him. Now after throwing them off the team and sending them home in disgrace, he's trying to strip Smith and Carlos of their medals. So, it's a simple question. Tell me. Are you on his side or theirs?"

There was no hesitation. "I am squarely on the side of my people," Rick told him.

"Then we can count on you to help us…"

"That depends on who 'us' is, Mr. Thomas."

"The oppressed… our people."

Months of intellectual fencing with Vo Danh had not been in vain. Singleton had split ideological hairs for months on end while under house arrest at Xuan Song. Now he was a free man, his feet planted on his home turf, and he didn't have an AK-47 pointed at his head. Vo Danh's sophisticated challenges to his identity had left him crystal clear as to where he stood.

"With all due respect, Mr. Thomas," Rick told him, "Get lost."

The man paused, looking for a way around the finality of Singleton's command. "They murdered Dr. King… and they will lynch Smith and Carlos, disgrace them, destroy them… and you're willing to just stand aside and let it happen?"

"No, sir. I sure as hell am not willing to stand aside. Reverend King has been our guest, in my father's house, and nobody feels his loss more than I do. What he taught me is that Smith and Carlos have a right to protest because they're Americans. They'll catch hell for it, sure, but they're used to that. They've been catching hell their whole lives. Race-haters will come after them, but good people will stand by them. And my sense is, if we can't get justice and equality to work in America, then we're not going to do any better in some people's republic, where guys who stand up, like Smith and Carlos, are summarily executed."

The man was clearly losing his composure as he tried to interrupt several times. Rick remembered from his training that the "control agent" was supposed to guide his recruit, not take a lecture from him. The man sat taller on his bar stool and said, "I understand you shared a great deal of sensitive information about American military operations with Vo Danh… that you willingly collaborated with him against a combat unit of the US Army. You could be in serious trouble with your superiors, Corporal Singleton, if they were to learn of your cooperation with a North Vietnamese…"

Rick turned to face him squarely and refused to take the bait. "First off, Mr. Whoever-you-are, my superiors have my report detailing everything that happened while I was a prisoner on the Xuan Song Plantation. And further, they're going to want to hear all about you… a good physical description of you without the phony beard and fake accent… and see if they can't match that up with some file the FBI already has on you. So why don't you pay for your beer and find someplace else to be."

Singleton strolled home that night feeling much relieved. Vo Danh had given him that "recognition signal," as it was called at Greyhawk: "I am a friend of Vo Danh." And he had been working up the script he would perform if and when the time came. He felt that, like Smith and Carlos, he had struck a blow for freedom of expression and American ideals, imperfect as they may be in practice.

"Why else bother to be a soldier in the white, imperialist army?" he asked and laughed out loud on the sidewalk outside his house.

Two days later, the raucous crowd in the 123rd Street Tavern witnessed the thrill of the summer. "Would Bob Beamon have to match his previous long-jump record of 27' 4" to mount the podium ahead of Gold Medal holders Ralph Boston and Lynn Davies?" the announcer asked. The tavern audience roared as Beamon made his first attempt. It looked good but there was delay and apparent confusion in announcing his distance. Minutes passed while officials huddled in discussion. Beamon paced nervously in circles. After nine minutes of scrambling around, someone finally obtained a carpenter's tape-measure. Beamon had jumped *almost two feet* further than anyone in Olympic history—flying *completely beyond* the electronic apparatus that was designed to record his distance! The Tavern mob exploded in shouts of amazement and joy as Beamon was seen collapsing to the ground, his face in his hands.

Hours later, the Stars and Stripes climbed the center pole once again and an American athlete stood atop the podium while they played the National Anthem. Then, after the music stopped, a smiling Bob Beamon held his closed fist high in the air for all to see. But this time there would be no talk of snatching his medal or shipping him home. Mr. Brundage had been silenced. And Rick Singleton almost wished Mr. Thomas would return—because he had a few more points he wanted to make with him.

Providence, Rhode Island

From the wide, wood porch of Rene Levesque's home, he could see the Catholic high school he'd attended, which is why his parents said he didn't need a car of his own. But Providence College, the Jesuit school that was his alma mater, was a thirty-minute commute, which justified his buying a used Nash Rambler. This circumscribed little realm in the circumscribed little State of Rhode Island gave Renee a solid identity growing up, as did the many summers he spent with French-speaking relatives in the circumscribed little town of Sainte-Catherine, on the opposite bank of the Saint Lawrence from Montreal. His rich liberal arts education and being fluidly bilingual gave Levesque an appearance of sophistication that masked his essential provincialism. He enlisted in the Army for the same reason most recruits did—because his draft board was breathing down his neck—yet he found Basic Training an exciting experience, as he was surrounded for the first-time by non-Catholics, undisciplined ruffians, foul-mouthed drill instructors, and all manner of human flotsam and jetsam. He felt like a choirboy who had joined the circus and, for him, the main attraction was a "fallen-away" Catholic named Mulcahey who was irreverent, aggressive and fearless—all the things Rene Levesque was not.

It was ironic, then, that the liberation Rene felt at being released from his safe but stifling childhood had ended with his being shoved into the cassock and role of a Jesuit monk! After an exciting sojourn in Basic Training and Greyhawk Intelligence School, Rene was thrust back into the circumscribed little sphere he had briefly escaped. Still, he figured, it beat getting shot-at.

His welcome home went exactly as he had expected. Two aunts, his mother's sisters, and their husbands joined in an afternoon of sincere affection for him and relief that he was back safe. But much to his surprise, he was to find that this occasion of good cheer and solidarity was deceptive. The Vietnam War had come home even before the soldier had.

Senator Joseph McCarthy's crusade to save the government and the nation from the scourge of Communism had ended with his censure and death more than a decade earlier—but not in the hearts and minds of Rene's father and uncles. There it lived on, refreshed by every battle against the Communists of Vietnam and against their hordes of sympathizers on streets and campuses closer to home. And now proof that McCarthy was right to warn against the creeping Red Menace was staring them in the face as their wives—their staid, apolitical, acquiescent wives—had been stirred to rebellion by the Berrigan Brothers! In May, Philip and Daniel Berrigan and their followers had set fire to hundreds of draft records in Catonsville, Maryland, and as the trial of "The Catonsville Nine" drew near, sympathy for them among the three sisters had evolved from whispers in the kitchen to snippets of spoken (unwanted!) opinions to outright (outrageous!) defense of these (so-called!) Catholics (all of whom were Fifth Columnists!).

Rene Levesque had left behind a monolithic family unit in which for the two decades of his rearing not one original thought had been uttered. But he returned now shocked to find that the war in Vietnam had spilled over into his extended family! The fragile tranquility of his home was being broken to pieces by barbed comments, scoffing remarks, irreverent criticisms, mocking and sarcastic assaults that might have passed for fairly normal give-and-take in other families but were unprecedented in this household. Dissent, even from adolescents, was not acceptable under the rules of the house when Rene lived there. Disagreement was now freely expressed in rooms decorated with religious figurines and crucifixes that had previously known only consensus. Heretofore, obedience to the authority of the One, Holy, Catholic and Apostolic church as defined by orthodoxy had reigned from heaven above, interpreted by the priest and administered in-house by the father of the family. When the Berrigan's poured lamb's blood over draft files and burned piles of them, however, it resounded as a clarion call to every mother's heart to ask "Who is Christ if not the Prince of Peace?"

The three sisters of this tight-knit family had preserved the tranquility of their homes very well during the previous summer, as their growing convictions led them to action—until one day Rene's father had discovered a placard nailed to a fence slat hidden behind the

water heater in the basement. In large, black letters, it proclaimed
"END THE WAR!"—and he demanded to know how it got there. To
his surprise, his wife told him—and with no sign of shame or contrition. From there, the fabric of their staid existence unraveled (in his
view) or took an interesting new direction (in her view). The more the
three husbands tried to bring the sisters "back into line," the more
unabashedly they resisted, even appearing to enjoy their heresy (such
are the wiles of Satan!) and, in response, the husbands became more
entrenched.

When Rene discovered he had departed Eden and returned to
Gettysburg, he felt both excited and relieved: Excited that the banal
and predictable platitudes of family dinner conversations had been
replaced with an emotional thrust-and-parry debate with substantial
content—politics, philosophy, history. His family had become real
people! His sense of relief came about as he escaped having to explain
his own complicated life while he'd been gone (pretending to be a
Jesuit brother, for example) or make any mention of the two thick
stacks of letters in his duffle bag from a girl in Baltimore—and no, she
was not a Catholic. The trial of the Catonsville Nine escalated the
family dynamics as news of it took center stage on television and in
the *Providence Journal*. From quiet, insistent debate in the first week of
Rene's leave, the atmosphere of his home built into what would have
passed even in secular, blue-collar families for a full-scale argument.

"She who has ears to hear, Marie," Rene's father said firmly,
"would know that Father Donahue certainly *does not* support hooli-
gans who wear the collar setting fire to government property!"

"Has he told you that himself, Frank? Or are you speaking *ex
cathedra?*"

"What do you mean, *'ex cathedra?'*"

"I mean from the seat of your pants, Frank."

Rene asked, "May I have the potatoes, please?"

"If you had been paying attention on Sunday, Marie, Father made himself very clear on the subject."

"Unless I missed something, Francis, his sermon was about pigs... pigs going crazy and drowning themselves in the sea."

"And why did they drown themselves, Marie-Anne? Because The Lord drove the devils out of the madman and placed them in the pigs!"

Rene asked, "Would someone like more ham?"

"What kind of so-called priest goes around setting fires? A madman priest, Marie! One full of devils, like Daniel Berrigan!"

This exegesis clearly angered Rene's mother. She narrowed her eyes at her husband and put down her fork. "All I can say, Frank, is" she paused to choose her words, "if and when Rene is called, I hope he will be *exactly* the kind of priest Daniel Berrigan is!"

"What sort of son do you think we've raised?" Rene's father stared at Rene, seeking the answer to his question in his son's face. "Rene will make a perfectly honorable priest, one who will serve his people and obey the authority of Scripture and the church... not a priest-arsonist!"

They both studied him now, silently pleading for him to weigh-in on the correct side. "Would anyone like more bread or wine?" Rene asked, but neither of his parents was in the mood for comedy.

On Wednesday, 9 October, the Catonsville Nine were found guilty of destroying government property. By then, Rene had had enough. He'd spent time with friends in town, his parents were gone all day—his father at the office, his mother at meetings and rallies for the Catholic Peace Movement and the Hubert Humphrey campaign—and he was desperate to reunite with Linda, to test the bonds they had forged through a year of correspondence. Besides, after the verdict was in, the dramatic dinner conversations had given over to a silent grudge-match with his father wearing his "Nixon's The One!" button on his suit jacket at one end of the table and his mother, her "HHH" button at the other.

He loaded his duffle bag into the trunk of the Rambler along with a dozen books from his room and left a note on the kitchen table telling his parents he loved them both very much, and that the twenty dollar bill was for a lot of calls he had made to a friend in Baltimore, mostly at "Day Rates," which would appear on their next phone bill.

The Road Back to Chicago

Of them all, John Francis Mulcahey was the most anxious about returning home and, therefore, the least anxious to get there. A prolific letter-writer, he had never sent any of his letters to his home from Vietnam, so no one was expecting him anyway. He shed his uniform in San Francisco and paid cash for a flight to Salt Lake City where, after a twelve-hour layover, he caught an early morning flight on a two-engine turboprop that made short hops to Ogden, Brigham City, Logan, Pocatello, Butte and Missoula—exchanging a few passengers and mail bags in each place. Mulcahey climbed down the stairway in Missoula about noon, his ears ringing from the roar of the engines, and turned himself slowly around, prepared to be overwhelmed by the majestic mountain scenery. He was not in the least disappointed. John Steinbeck had written in *Travels with Charlie* that he was "in love with Montana," and Mulcahey wanted to know what it meant to be in love with America. What would it mean to be an American if you were no longer a Chicagoan or an ex-Catholic or a corporal in the

Army or the only son of the Mulcahey family? He had shared with no one his plan to walk through these beautiful mountains at the heart of his country seeking an answer to that question. He stood there for some minutes, letting this exotic scenery sink into all his senses, and he wondered how long it might take the Department of Defense to find him if he just hiked deep into these mountains. Forever, maybe.

He shared a taxi ride into town with two students from the University of Montana who seemed to him too young to be in college. The cab driver helped him locate a cheap motel three miles from the Lincolnwood Trailhead that led into Rattlesnake National Park. His room looked out over lush, low hills that called to him, but it was late in the day and he wasn't yet prepared for—for he wasn't sure what. He dug his Army-issue jungle boots out of the bottom of his duffle and laced them on. He'd worn them four times, a year ago at Long Binh Replacement Depot, so they needed to be broken in. He walked three miles into town and, after grabbing a bite to eat, bought a canteen and nap sack, bread, cheese, raisins and nuts.

For six days straight, he hiked the low mountain trails of Rattle-snake Park, learning several hard lessons: A man with new boots needs to pack a lot of iodine, gauze, tape and band aids; anyone, even a young person, who has spent a year behind a manual typewriter and the steering wheel of a jeep will be in terrible physical condition and will require aspirin and tubes of Ben Gay if he intends to walk many miles each day; and if you have seen one narrow path through a forest that bends up toward tall pines and down to shallow, ice-cold creeks, you've seen them all.

But the week in Missoula accomplished what he hoped it would. He got the chance to ease himself down a little from the hyper-nervous state imposed on him by his Saigon year. He was now able to endure the memories of Louis Leffanta bleeding out on the villa roof and of his image glowing on the tile floor in the dark bedroom, the sound of the bullet that buzzed past him on its path to Louis and of his final, surprised "Oh!" These became merely pictures, framed and hanging on the walls of his mind, frozen in the past tense. Less manageable for him was the persistent knowledge that he had come apart in the wake of Leffanta's and then Robert Kennedy's deaths. That he was capable of a complete break-down was not so easily contained as the memories of what caused it to happen. How men like the sergeant from the Hue battlefield could cope was beyond Mulcahey's understanding. Mulcahey had only sipped from the cup that Sergeant Hollis had drunk to the lees.

And he had—despite blistered feet and mosquito bites and getting soaked to the skin in a downpour and once getting lost when night overtook him on the trail—fallen in love with the mountains. If this was, as Steinbeck thought, the best of America, then it was worth loving.

The same taxi driver returned him to the airport and wanted to know if he'd seen any rattlesnakes or bears when he was hiking. "You were alone the whole time?" the driver asked. Trails into the mountains had seemed exciting and mysterious, but it had not occurred to Mulcahey until now that he had been in any danger on them. A chill climbed up his spine as he imagined being mauled or writhing in agony from a snake bite in the mountains he and Steinbeck loved.

"I'm from Chicago," he told the driver. "The only bears and snakes I've ever seen live in Brookfield Zoo."

Yet, he wasn't finished stalling.

He boarded the next noisy turboprop headed east, which traded passengers and mail bags in Helena, Bozeman, Billings and Bismarck before landing at Minneapolis-St. Paul, where Mulcahey climbed off. Forty minutes later a taxi dropped him at the address in Bloomington for his college roommate, Bob Schneider. Mulcahey had written dozens of letters to his best friend from college years and had received a dwindling response, but Bob had been busy starting a family and a career so occasional notes was all he had time for. Still, Mulcahey knew that all the wild times and all-night bull sessions over the years they lived together had cemented a life-long friendship between them.

Mulcahey was excited to meet Bob's wife (whose name he couldn't remember) and was nervous about it, which is probably why she seemed suspicious of him, holding the door slightly ajar while he explained who he was, Bob's best friend from the University of Chicago, his roommate for three years. Still, she didn't invite him inside to wait for Bob, who would be home any minutes, she said. He sat on the duffle bag on the porch after she'd shut the door and waited for two hours, reading a paperback, while she peeked at him through the blinds from time to time.

Bob, when he pulled in the drive, was very happy to see him indeed! They shook hands and punched each other in the shoulders and Bob invited him in to meet Elaine and see their baby daughter. The guys reminisced and drank beer in the living room while Elaine made chili and cornbread and tended the baby, then they ate together around the kitchen table. But the invitation to crash on their couch never came, as Mulcahey assumed it would. After dinner, Elaine settled the baby in the back bedroom while Bob, without discussing it, called a cab for Mulcahey, walked him out when it came, told him how happy he was to see him again, shook his hand, wished him luck and punched him on the shoulder. "Say 'Hi' to your mom," Bob said as he turned toward the house. Mulcahey spent the night on the terrazzo floor of the Minneapolis-St. Paul Airport, propped against his duffle bag.

The moment he had dreaded had to come. He mounted the

steps of the two-story brick house to which he no longer carried a key, tried the knob before ringing the bell, like a visiting stranger. His Ma greeted him with hysterical shrieks, desperate clutches, flowing tears, shouts for the Old Man, then the Old Man lumbered in with a beer can in his right hand, so there'd be no question of having to shake. "Take your stuff up to your room," he muttered, barely audible beneath his Ma's wailing "Why didn't you tell us you was comin', Johnny? Don't worry! Your bed is all made up and everything is just the way it was when you left!"

"Precisely what I feared most," Mulcahey mumbled under his breath.

True to her word, his Ma had preserved his room with all the reverence due a reliquary. The small desk was there, the sharpened pencil aslant across the spiral notebook exactly as it had been when he last closed the door. Mulcahey wondered what he had done in his life that he should be worshipped by one parent and despised by the other.

Temperamentally different as they were, his folks agreed about most everything. The family was classic blue-collar Irish Catholic—the Church, the Democratic Party and the Steelworkers Union provided the no-frills articles of faith, which Mulcahey never questioned until he was accepted into the University of Chicago and began walking to classes, a few blocks from his home. Then he *did* begin to question. "Those pinko professors," as the Old Man called them, filled his head with Commie propaganda that upset his Ma and insulted the church. In retrospect, Mulcahey admitted he could have been less aggressive in his assault on his parents' ignorance and though it would have made no sense financially, it might have made things easier on everyone if he had moved into student housing. But he had made a great effort to smooth things over at home by becoming Jack Kennedy. His parents adored JFK, whose picture graced the wall of their dining room, alongside "The Last Supper," and so Mulcahey began brushing his hair off his forehead with his fingers, diving his hands in-and-out of his jacket pockets, squinting his eyes and jabbing his index finger in the air saying, "Just let me shay thish about thayat…" This greatly amused his Ma and brought some levity into a home without much. But the price he paid was when the impersonation became his personality and then his person. John Francis Mulcahey too, in some measure, died in Dallas on 22 November 1963.

Ma came to him while he was sorting things out in his room. "You'll come to church with us tomorrow, won't you, Johnny?" she asked.

"Sure I will, Ma, of course." The truth was he enjoyed seeing his father cleaned up, dressed in a suit, sober and on his best behavior, even if the mass had become a hollow shell to him since college.

"Father Murphy will be so glad to see you! He says your name in The Prayers every week."

"That's good, Ma, OK. If Father Murphy is glad to see me, I'll be surprised, but he keeps me in his prayers, so that's good."

"I have to ask you something, Johnny. Did you get my letters?"

"Letters? What letters?"

"I wrote you every week after church."

"It was a war zone over there, Ma. Things were crazy. Guys got big batches of mail all at once, months old. So maybe yours are still coming. I'll get them at Ft. Meade, maybe."

"We didn't hear from you either, Johnny. Didn't you write to us?"

"Sure I did. That's what I mean… Army mail's all screwed up. Maybe you'll get my letters a year from now. It's lousy!"

"I worried about you, not having any word all this time!"

"I worried about you too, Ma…" Their eyes wandered to far corners of the room, as if looking for something lost. "How you been?" Mulcahey asked. "Have you been… has he been treating you right?"

Her hands began washing each other without soap or water. "Well… you know how he is. He tries his best, but he has good days and bad days, like all of us."

"Not like all of us, Ma. You've never hit anybody."

"He's getting better, Johnny. He's been talking to Father Murphy and he's been better. But big changes set him off sometimes…"

"Like me coming home?"

"This is your home. You have every right…"

"I should talk with him. Forget Father Murphy. He'd talk to me, now I've been to Vietnam. He has some respect for that."

She thought about it for some time before risking, "If you think that would be a good idea, for you to talk man-to-man with your father…"

Mulcahey pulled his shoulders back and stood up straighter. He felt she had conferred a softly spoken rite of passage on him.

Although they had come close a few times, Mulcahey and the Old Man had never come to blows. The reason they hadn't was simple: The Old Man had sixty pounds of solid muscle on him, he was a steelworker and a combat veteran, so the outcome of any fight was foreordained. The Old Man had never even threatened to strike his son. Violence against his wife, however, when he was very drunk and upset by something that had nothing to do with her was a cycle of behavior that nothing seemed to cure—not intervention by the priest or by the police nor even his own expressed contrition. Therefore, Mulcahey carefully prepared the ground for several weeks before he spoke to him.

On Sundays, Mulcahey was openly friendly and outgoing with

Father Murphy, whose face clearly showed puzzlement as he waited for the insults that never came. He made sure the Old Man witnessed these exchanges on the steps of Our Mother of Sorrows, the sustained handshakes that accompanied lavish compliments about the sermon and the church.

Further, he stopped avoiding the Old Man, breaking a habit of many years. When the Old Man sat on the screened porch after dinner with a can of beer and his cigarettes, Mulcahey dropped into the chair beside him with his own beer and a paperback book. The two spent hours at a time side-by-side, each one lost in his thoughts.

The Old Man mowed the lawn each Saturday and was surprised to see his son emerge from the garage with the rake and the edge-trimmer.

They sat together watching Jackie Gleason one night, laughing at all the same jokes, and Ed Sullivan the next, exchanging a few comments.

And in the midst of this campaign, Mulcahey came to realize how alone the Old Man had been during the years when he had avoided him. There are, he admitted, two sides to everything.

The standard rotation of Scripture readings in the Catholic church meant that Father Murphy spoke one Sunday about the madman whose devils were driven out of him and into a herd of swine—the same topic that was, simultaneously, causing much debate in the Levesque household. Mulcahey made a point of reaching across in front of the Old Man to take the priest's hand in both of his. "That sermon was the most eloquent thing I've ever heard from any pulpit, anywhere," Mulcahey told him.

"How kind of you, John," Murphy said, "It's good to have you back among…"

"I've been working with a Catholic boys' choir at the Saigon

Cathedral. If you'd like to start one here, I'd be glad to help you with it."

"Well… that is… I must say…"

"Catholics don't sing in church," the Old Man interrupted, "That's what Protestants do."

This provided a good opening for discussion, Mulcahey thought, civilized conversation instead of the usual sniping exchange between insolent adolescent and thin-skinned adult. "Why should the Protestants have all the fun," he ventured as they walked to the car.

"We tried singing in the pews last Christmas," the Old Man growled, "Sounded like someone was strangling chickens."

"Maybe we just need a few centuries of practice, like Protestants have. If they rolled a piano in there, I could play accompaniment for them."

"You play piano? Really? I didn't know that!" The Old Man unlocked the car and jumped in, leaving Mulcahey to ponder when the last time was he had played the upright that Ma kept dusted in the living room. Or played in public somewhere with the Old Man in attendance. College? No. High school? No. A recital for his last private lesson? WOW! That would have been 1954 or 1955! The driver window slid down. "You comin' or not?" the Old Man asked.

That night after supper, he found the Old Man on the screened porch with a beer in one hand and a volume of the *Reader's Digest Condensed Novels* in the other. Mulcahey pulled a chair ninety degrees off his bow, sat down and said quietly, "May I interrupt for just a minute? I'm off to Ft. Meade tomorrow and I need to set a couple of things straight." This was a tone he had never before used with his father. He did not want the speech he'd been preparing for days to be either brushed off as youthful rebellion or mistaken for a direct challenge to his father's authority. "A lot of things have happened to me in the past couple years, especially overseas," he began, "And I know now that I haven't been a very good son to you... I think you've deserved better. You provided for me... kept a roof over my head long after you could've tossed me out... and I treated you to a whole lot of disrespect."

His father gazed into his face for a long moment, waiting for him to say, "However..." before answering, "You shouldn't be so hard on yourself, Johnny. It's nothing personal between you and me. It's just that your whole God-forsaken generation of Commie-inspired misfits and bums are disrespectful to everyone and everything. You just happen to be one of them."

Mulcahey hadn't expected any sudden capitulation, but he was surprised by this cultural analysis. Without realizing it, he defended himself by confronting one father-figure with another. "Well just let me say this about that," he said, "The men I serve with in the Army are not misfits or bums and they're certainly not 'Commie-inspired'. My generation answered the call to serve our country, same as yours did, and you should be proud of us... of me."

"You went because you were drafted."

"I volunteered for three years!"

"Yeah, to avoid combat because they were about to draft your ass."

"You were drafted too."

"Sure I was. But I didn't sit behind a typewriter in an office because I didn't have a college degree, like you did. I saw a hell of a lot of fighting." He cleared his throat with a swig of beer, then he said, "My mistake with you was sending you to college. Instead of getting an education and coming out an engineer or a manager, you wasted your time with a bunch of egg-heads and came in here spouting half-baked ideas that were worthless to anybody."

"I got a good education. It taught me to think, to question things. You paid for most of it and I'm grateful to you for giving me that chance."

"Big mistake! I didn't fully realize what a big mistake until this summer. Ah! You should've been here, Johnny! We could've watched it on TV together. Mobs of gypsies and hippies… your generation of spoiled, college-educated pricks who never held down a job or supported a family… completely overran the city! Mayor Daley turned over Grant Park to 'em so they could hold their rallies and give speeches, whatever they wanted to do. But that didn't satisfy 'em. They attacked the Convention Center where our party was trying to select its candidate for president in an orderly manner. They smashed windows and injured cops and threatened the lives of delegates. The mayor had to call in the National Guard to restore order. Martial law! Right here in Chicago! And do you know what these violent, raggedy-assed hippies said they wanted? Peace! They said they wanted to end the war! If they meant that, they should've dispersed and gone home and campaigned for Humphrey instead of trashing our Democratic Convention. The goddammed idiots are gonna end up with Tricky Dick Nixon, who has no intention of letting the Commies have Indochina and I'm so mad about it, I may just go ahead and hold my nose and vote for that Republican creep myself so he can draft their asses and send 'em all to Vietnam! So much for 'learning to think'! This is where 'questioning things' gets you!"

His father ended his rant by stomping out of the porch but surprised Mulcahey by returning with two cans, one for each of them. Mulcahey took this as a sign that "man-to-man" might be working after all, despite appearances, so he reached across and "clinked" their beer cans together, raised his in tribute and drank a toast. "You feel all better now?" he asked.

For the first time in many years, Mulcahey heard his father's laughter. "Yeah… you said you wanted to get a couple of things straight, so I figured I'd take advantage," he said and both men laughed. "But let me make you a promise. They've got a few of the ring leaders from last summer's riot in jail and they're putting 'em on trial. And when the pansy-assed jury and the candy-assed judge lets 'em walk out of there free, I'll be waiting for 'em in the parking lot with a baseball bat and I'm going to beat the shit out of 'em for wrecking my city."

"It's good to know Chicago is well defended," Mulcahey said, "But look at the bright side of this. Your generation fought the Nazis and your children may be a mob of spoiled, unruly hippies but at least we're not marching around in black uniforms, saluting some American Hitler. We question authority. So, you won your war against fascism."

"One way to look at it, I guess… what else?"

"What else what?"

"You said you wanted to set things straight. Your turn."

"Yeah. While we're at it… about Ma."

"That's what I figured. Johnny, that's none of your business."

"It may surprise you to hear this from me, but I agree with you. It is none of my business, not anymore. When I was growing up, living here, it was. But now I'm gone. This is your home, not mine anymore. She's your wife and how you get along is your business. All I want to say is this…" Mulcahey unbuttoned his shirt and pulled out a narrow, black case which he handed to his father, who took it, pulled it open and studied the medal inside, a Purple Heart exactly like the two he had upstairs in his sock drawer. He unfolded and read the commendation written by Major Shimazu—which tactfully said nothing about who had shot at Corporal Mulcahey or about the corporal's stupidity—but only that he had been wounded in the line of duty and had shown courage under fire.

Mulcahey's father held the medal under his reading light and looked closely. The only sign of a response was that his hand trembled slightly. Then he gently closed it into the box and said, "Congratulations, John."

"I want you to know that things happened to me," Mulcahey said. "I met men over there, guys who had seen violence and death close-up… and that I understand now every man has his own ghosts. I've got mine. You've got yours. And I've got no right to judge you."

Mulcahey's father stared down at the black case in his hand for a long minute, then handed it back and the two men shook hands. There was nothing more to say for now, but as Mulcahey lay in his childhood bed for the last time, he examined the dark room for the ghosts that had always hovered there. But they had gone. *I'll write letters to him when I get to Ft. Meade,* he thought as he drifted off. *Ma, too.*

9

THE PATRIOT REBELS OF '68

O n the last night of their post-Vietnam leave, Hood, Babin-eaux, Mulcahey, Singleton and Rosenzweig slept on the floor of the Camden, New Jersey, apartment Linda Wilson shared with Rene Levesque. This arrangement made Rene very nervous because he didn't know Linda very well, actually, and he had himself been living in her apartment for less than two weeks. But Linda seemed not to mind having her well-ordered home turned into a flop-house, bedrolls and duffle bags scattered all over the place, at least for this one night.

She and Rene Levesque had maintained a steady correspon-dence during his year in Vietnam, the tone of her letters growing in intensity as she confessed first her affection and then her deepening love for her soldier, her "intended" as she had begun to call him. Rene, for his part, struggled to respond in kind to this Greyhawk Inn wait-ress whom he had dated a few times during his training. His sensitive, restrained nature and rigid (perhaps "frigid") Catholic upbringing ill-equipped him for any kind of torrid romance, especially with a young lady he hardly knew. He liked Linda. He liked her very much indeed. But the truth was, he didn't quite trust her. Her passion for her lover in Vietnam, the wonderful man she feared losing forever, without whom she could not imagine ever being happy in life (as she wrote in her letters) struck Rene as perhaps a young girl's fantasy. When he returned to her, his gaunt, pale, bony presence towering over her, surely she would be brought back to her senses and realize how inadequate he was beside the figment of her fevered imagination. "Oh… it's you," she'd say, turning away. This prospect made it difficult for Rene to respond to her with anything like the fervor she expressed. He didn't even have the vocabulary for it. But the moment she opened her apartment door on 12 October to find him standing there, unannounced, tall, gaunt, pale and bony—she threw herself weeping into his arms and Rene Levesque knew then that he was loved as he had never been before in his life. He too shed tears and hugged her tight to him.

Her first words to him during that passionate welcome were "Where are your bags?"

"In the trunk of my car," he said.

"Well, let's go bring them up" had settled the matter of their domestic arrangement.

Before car-pooling down to the 250th MI Company at Fort Meade on 26 October, the six friends demolished two dozen eggs, two loaves of bread and a gallon of coffee. Then they pulled on their tan uniforms with crooked stripes—ill-suited to the fall weather but the only ones they had—and profusely thanked Linda for her hospitality. They were as nervous as cats about what this new assignment would be like, and they filled the three cars with excited speculation about how they would adapt to military conformity after their otherworldly lives in Vietnam, which seemed to them now like something they must have imagined.

They need not have worried. They were about to enter a realm almost as strange as the one they had left behind.

Fortunately for them, no one suffered the fear of military routine more keenly than the commanding officer of the 250th, Major Barton Dwight. He began his Army career as a forward observer for an artillery battery in Korea, where he developed a taste for adrenaline. He re-enlisted to attend Greyhawk Intelligence School, leading to a career he found exciting—commanding a company that trained and handled agents who reported on Russian and East German military operations. The 250th MI Company had served honorably for two decades in that beehive of spy activity, West Germany, under civilian cover as the "Corporation for International Service" (CIS). But with the escalation of the war in Vietnam, personnel and resources were shifted away from the 250th until it became a skeleton—so in mid-1966 the European Command closed down the whole operation and assigned the dozen remaining operatives to Fort Meade "on temporary duty." The assumption in 1966 was that the fight for Vietnam's future would be swiftly concluded and the 250th could then be returned to Europe to resume operations against the Soviet Block.

When in August of 1966, Major Dwight was snatched from his hilltop quarters in scenic Rothenberg (with its panoramic views of rolling Bavarian countryside), assigned to Fort Meade to a tiny office (with views of a wooden barracks), and stuffed back into uniform for the first time in many years, he became the least-happy member of the 250th. He fumed behind his desk for seven interminable hours each weekday, tugging at the black cotton necktie of his uniform (which seemed to be self-tightening), shuffling meaningless paperwork from his in-box to his out-box, and reminiscing about the brave Germans whose trust he had cultivated, whom he had abandoned when he stopped showing-up at the *ratskeller* or on the park bench.

Nevertheless, the 250th ran smoothly despite the depression of Major Dwight because the *de facto* company commander was Sergeant George Conrad. Sergeant Conrad had taken (perhaps unfair) advantage of an Army screw-up that occurred during the early days of the frantic build-up of forces in Vietnam. On the day of his graduation from Greyhawk Intelligence School, three sets of orders were issued to then-PFC Conrad, all dated 4 August 1966. The first set directed him to report (like all his classmates) to San Francisco for transportation to Long Binh Replacement Depot in Vietnam, further assignment to be determined. The second set of orders awarded Conrad the Vietnam Service Ribbon, in appreciation for his service overseas, and promotion to the rank of Sergeant (E-5). The third set assigned him to the 250th MI Company at Fort Meade, Maryland, effective immediately. Following an astoundingly brief period of consideration (thanks to his having just completed weeks of Army training in deception and evasion), Conrad burned one set of orders, being careful to pulverize the ashes, as he had been taught to do, and then drove that very afternoon to Fort Meade. There, by the authority of the third set of orders, he obtained a red bumper sticker that allowed him to drive onto the post and with the second set of orders, he purchased at the Post Exchange a Vietnam Service Ribbon for his dress uniform and two pairs of sergeant's stripes, one for his fatigues.

The next morning, Sergeant Conrad spent some time driving around the enormous base before finding the 250th MI Co., two wooden buildings in an out-of-the-way corner. The small company was just arriving from Germany and bunk beds and lockers were being carried into the two-story barracks while desks and files were being arranged in the small office building. Major Dwight, in a tight new uniform, was settling into his tiny office. He returned Sergeant Conrad's salute from behind his steel desk, then looked over the orders assigning him to the company.

"We are expecting a whole flock of you 'Nam returnees to be joining this unit, sergeant," Dwight said, tugging on his necktie, "I'd appreciate it if you'd help these men out, assign each one a bunk and locker, help him get settled, report any problems that arise directly to me."

"Yessir," Conrad responded while he adjusted to being called "sergeant" and "Nam returnee."

"And that First Army insignia on your shoulder? Replace that at once with this one, see? Blue background, flaming sword." The major turned his left shoulder toward Conrad. "We're European Command with headquarters in Bonn, Germany. We're only here on temporary duty. We expect to be returning to Europe in a few months."

"Yessir."

"Remember! Any problems, skip the lieutenants and report them directly to me, got it?"

"Yessir."

"And I would appreciate it, sergeant, if there were no problems. Understand?"

"Yessir."

From that day in August 1966 onward, Sergeant Conrad saw to it that there weren't any problems—ever. Whenever the two men passed each other on company grounds, the major would ask, "Any problems, sergeant?" and Conrad would salute smartly and say, "No, sir!"

As the war dragged on in Southeast Asia, the 250th evolved

into a mere housing nest for eighty or so college-educated enlisted men, trained and experienced in deception, drifting in from Vietnam where, with virtually no supervision, they dressed as and were treated like civilians. These young men shared only faint memories of Basic Training, of wearing starched fatigues and heavy black boots, of being yelled at and marched in formation to the mess hall for meals. All the Vietnam veterans who carried orders for the 250th arrived with dread in their hearts at the prospect of being dressed as and treated like soldiers.

By the time Hood, Babineaux and the four others reported to the 250th, 26 months later, there was a very well-established routine in place. The lieutenant in the office told them, "report to Sergeant Conrad over in the barracks." They tapped on the door of Conrad's private room, heard "Come on in," and their fears of military life were greatly allayed by finding themselves in a college dorm-room: Playboy pin-ups and a Georgetown banner on the walls, curtains on the windows, an area rug on the floor, a stereo playing classical music, and a large, curly-haired young man in civvies reading a textbook on Tort Law. "Gentlemen, have a seat around the table," he said, "and I'll explain how the system works here at the two-five-zero. First, I have a welcome-home present for you. Pass the box around and help yourselves to two shoulder patches. That blue patch with the flaming sword means you are officially under European Command. If anyone accuses you of being in the United States, tell them 'I'm sorry, sir, but I'm not here… I'm in Europe.' The tailor will be here in half an hour to take your measurements for new fatigues and a dress-green uniform, he'll sew one on the left sleeve of each of your soldier-suits. Then, gentlemen, hang these uniforms in your assigned locker and wear them only when you absolutely have to… when you fly military stand-by or get in line for your paycheck at the end of the month. Then immediately duck into the nearest men's room and, like Superman, change back into Clark Kent. There are thousands of civilians on this base. Nobody bothers them. But when you're in uniform, every shave-tail second louie takes an interest in your haircut or your attitude or that smirk on your face and our *number one* job is to stay out of the First Army spotlight. If you are in uniform and get into words with any First Army personnel, show them your pretty blue shoulder patch, tell them you're just visiting for a few days and your commanding officer is in Bonn, Germany. Do not say, "Get lost" or "Screw you" but in all ways be polite. Try not to mention the two-five-zero—which they've never heard of anyway—unless you are actually in handcuffs.

"Do not go into the company office, ever. If you need something from there, ask me. You will see lieutenants come-and-go with European Command patches. Their names don't matter to you. If they see you in uniform, salute as you pass by and say 'Sir' but do not say another word. They are conditioned not to speak to you, but if they do, do not listen to them. They may order you to do something or other, but they won't expect you to do it. Pretend to listen but do not listen. When they cease talking, say "Yessir," salute smartly and walk away. Don't worry about insulting them. They are used to being ignored, and we all must work together to keep them that way. 'Yessir,' salute, walk—got it?

"Every Wednesday morning at eight o'clock sharp, you will stand formation for roll call. You will see Major Dwight at that time from a distance. Be exactly on time in clean fatigues and answer 'Present, sir' when he calls your name. The duty roster for the week will be posted on the bulletin board to the right of the office side-door. You will see our superb company clerks, Spec-4 Hanson and Spec-4 Fackenthall, hovering by the duty roster. Your name will appear on the duty roster... for enlisted man in charge-of-quarters or mail run or scrubbing the barracks floors, latrine duty, lawn maintenance, etc. etc. Very quietly ask, 'Would someone like to take my duty this week?' One of the clerks will say, 'I will.' You will place a crisp twenty-dollar bill in his hand and watch him replace your name with his on the roster. Say, 'Thank you very much, specialist.' Our company clerks work harder than anybody else on Fort Meade, but do the math. They each pull down about $800 a week—forty grand a year besides their Army pay. They make five times what you make, so show them the respect they deserve.

"If you're smart, you'll choose some roomies and find an apartment in Baltimore or College Park, where most our men live. That way, you can come onto Meade just once a week, Wednesday morning, and be gone by nine a.m. Find a full-time job, save up some money, or enroll in school like me—I'm finishing up a law degree at Georgetown. The first month, you'll be worried. You'll think some burly MPs are going to kick in your door. But you'll get over it. I've been here over two years and, believe me, you're safer staying away from here than hanging out on Meade, where only bad things can happen to you.

"OK, the tailor is here. Line up and give him your last name, your European Command patches, and twenty bucks. He'll measure you up and by this time tomorrow, your uniforms will be all ready for you with shiny new sergeant's stripes on each sleeve. Hanson and Fackenthall are typing-up your recommendations for promotion today, Major Dwight will sign them, and by next week, you're all going to be NCOs, buck sergeants, E-5. It may take a couple more months for you, PFC," he said to Rosenzweig, "but our company clerks like to be paid on Wednesdays, so they'll do whatever is necessary to increase your pay-grade. Go line up on the tailor, choose empty storage lockers and I'll come around to make sure your bunks and lockers will pass muster. If you need anything at all, my door is always open. If not, I'll see you all on Wednesday, lined up in straight files and rows at 8:00 sharp. Now put on some civilian clothes and welcome to the two-five-zero."

For the six friends, the 250th MI Company proved to be precisely the Garden of Eden George Conrad promised. Within two weeks of their arrival there, five of them were sharing a large apartment on the edge of the University of Maryland at College Park (recently promoted Corporal Rosenzweig paid a smaller percentage of the rent than his four roommates, who were all recently promoted buck sergeants). The place was a filthy, chaotic mess—piles of clothes and personal gear were heaped up beside camp cots, table lamps sat here and there on the floor, dishes and cookware piled up in the sink as the men came and went at all hours in pursuit of women and jobs and professional opportunities. They were, in short, blissfully happy and increasingly confident that burly MPs were not coming for them.

After Levesque learned from Sergeant Conrad the nature of his duties (or "duty," as it involved one Wednesday morning each week), he raced back up to Camden, two hours north, and shared the joyful news of his freedom with Linda. They embraced and she whispered in his ear, "This will be our home, not just mine, my darling! So as soon as you get your clothes hung up in the closet, see what you can do to find a job!" And Rene loved her all the more for being such a practical girl.

After each Wednesday morning routine, the Greyhawk Six placed their starched fatigues and combat boots beside their rarely-worn Class-A green uniforms in otherwise empty lockers and went off to Schrafft's Restaurant, across I-95 from the base, for a long, leisurely brunch. Amidst the usual everyone-talking-at-once exchanges, Rene took plenty of jabs about having a love-nest up in Camden.

"Why not bring your girl down to College Park and move in with us," Mulcahey jibed, "Don't ask her, tell her. Show her who wears the pants, Rene."

"Do you have any idea, Mr. Mulcahey, how much I pull down in tips at the Union League every week? You want me to give up a very lucrative position at the most exclusive club in Philadelphia and drag Linda into the squalor of your College Park pad so I can avoid a long commute once a week? Think again."

"I can fix you up with a waiter's job here at Schrafft's. I know the manager."

"I'm not a waiter at the Union League, Mulcahey. I'm a maître 'd. They always wanted one with a French accent and I'm happy to provide them with that."

"Comes the revolution," Singleton piped up, "Mad-dog and his Terrapin radicals will have all of you Philadelphia high-brows shot against the wall, isn't that right, Mulcahey?"

"The SDS aren't radicals, Rick. It just so happens they're right about the war. It's immoral! We should never have…"

"So, how come the Students for a Democratic Society think it's immoral to fight to defend a democratic society?"

Hood's powerful baritone put an end to this rancor: "Gentlemen, let us desist! We'all just devoted years of our lives to Vietnam, so let us talk about somethin' besides the goddamn war!"

"Like what?"

"Like who's gonna find Rosie a payin' job," Hood said, "He's pumpin' gas twelve hours a day at the busiest Shell Station on I-95 and barely squeezin' by on corporal's pay. We'all owe him a debt of gratitude for breakin' that smart-ass lieutenant's nose…"

"Aaronson," Rosie interrupted, "Lieutenant Aaronson's nose, and I wish I hadn't. One ten-second temper-tantrum and I'm wearing an albatross around my neck ever since."

"We pay those company clerks too damn much," Babineaux said, "Eighty bucks a month, man! What if we all give 'em ten instead of twenty next week?"

Hood pushed his chair back and stood. "We'all live as free men!" he thundered, drawing the attention of other customers. "There is no price too high to pay for freedom! Name me one price y'all wouldn't pay for your freedom!" He sat back down. "Besides, Conrad would kill us."

With Levesque and Rosenzweig working full-time jobs, Mulcahey involved in anti-war activism and chasing co-eds on the Maryland campus (though he never would be enrolled in classes), and the other three applying to masters-degree programs at the University of Maryland (Hood, engineering), American University (Babineaux, business administration) and George Washington (Singleton, political science), it seemed to them all that their eighteen remaining months of active military service would pass quickly, profitably, even enjoyably.

But The Fates had other plans. Timing is everything and, in this case, time was running out on the two-five-zero system.

On Wednesday morning, 6 November, Hubert Humphrey conceded defeat and Richard Nixon claimed victory. Phones began ringing all over the Pentagon and every other military installation as nervous predictions were made regarding the new president. He said he would support the on-going war. And he said he would halt the on-going war. Would he stand up to massive and growing anti-war demonstrations? Would Secretary McNamara stay or go? And what about many other unknowable things? Frayed nerves, especially in large, hierarchical institutions, start at the top and flow down, sizzling like electricity through every circuit of the organism. Even those men Sergeant Conrad called "shave-tail second louies" were feeling jumpy without knowing exactly why.

One such, Lieutenant Merle Hatcher, found himself anxiously roaming the back alleys of Fort Meade with nothing much to do—but gripped by a growing urge to do something. He was highly trained in an occupation every bit as obscure and freelance as "the Collection of Human Intelligence," the specialty of Hood, Babineaux and company. Lieutenant Hatcher was assigned to the largely unheralded Office of the Inspector General. The extremely broad mandate of the OTIG was to sniff out waste, fraud and abuse anywhere in US Army operations, acting as the eyes and ears of high command, in this case of First Army Headquarters.

On Friday morning, 8 November, Hatcher pulled his jeep slowly into a large gravel parking lot, his eyes, ears and nose all twitching away. Two cars, each bearing a blue "officer" tag, sat side-by-side near a single-story building in an otherwise empty lot. An enlisted man in fatigues was pushing a lawn mower between this office building and a two-story barracks. Whatever was stimulating Lt. Hatcher's investigative instincts, it took a couple minutes before he could shape it into words. Finally, he muttered to himself, "If that barracks can house seventy or eighty men, where are their cars?"

The tires of Hatcher's jeep crunched across fifty yards of gravel before coming to rest beside the two cars. He dismounted and pulled the door open under a sign that read "250th MI Co." Only two of the half-dozen desks in the office were occupied: One by a second lieutenant who was smoking a cigarette and reading *The Washington Post*; the other by another second louie who was smashing away at a typewriter with two fingers. A spec-4 in fatigues was shuffling files in the top drawer of a steel file cabinet. The newspaper so absorbed the first man that he took no notice when Hatcher passed him to take up a position behind the typist. The first words at the top of the paper sticking up from the platen, Hatcher noted, were "Dear Louise." The specialist at last became aware of the stranger in their midst. He snapped a salute in Hatcher's direction and asked, "Sir, may I help you?" Both lieutenants lumbered to their feet and stared dumbly, as though Hatcher were some forest creature who had strayed into their encampment.

"I'd like a word with your CO," Hatcher said quietly.

"Major Dwight is on a training exercise with the company, sir," the specialist said while the officers stood blinking.

"And where is this training taking place?" Hatcher asked.

"I'm sorry, sir, but that's classified on a need-to-know basis," the specialist told him, "We're military intelligence… European Command… temporary duty at Fort Meade…"

Hatcher was dying to say *And did they all drive their personal vehicles to this secret training site?* but he wanted to hold the empty parking lot up his sleeve until he could confront their commanding officer with it. It hadn't yet occurred to them to ask what business brought him to their door, so Hatcher said, "Thank you, specialist" and "Gentlemen" to the deaf and dumb lieutenants, spun on his heel and strode back outside.

Near the side door he found the company bulletin board, where "Orders for the Day" did, indeed, call for an all-day training exercise, mandatory for all enlisted personnel, location TBA.

As he turned to walk away, his eye almost missed the duty roster, of no interest to him except that it had been heavily edited with black ink. Each neatly typed name on it had been crossed out, replaced with either an "H" or an "F." Those two letters, repeated over and over, filled the page. "What the fuck?" Hatcher whispered under his breath. He squeezed the handle of the side door, drew it open and asked, "Specialist, what is your name?"

"Hanson, sir," the file clerk said.

Hatcher closed the door and ran his finger down the duty roster. "H" was there, listed as today's file clerk... and enlisted man in charge of quarters... and night clerk... and mail clerk... and two other duties. In charge of lawn maintenance and five other duties was "F." Hatcher strode past the lawn mower, snapped off a salute, and saw the name on that specialist's fatigues was "Fackenthall." Aware of the eyes staring at him from the office windows, he entered the barracks. The bunks were all neatly made, the floors polished, but when he rapped on the private room walled off at the end of the bay and George Conrad said, "Come on in," he was astounded to meet not an NCO-in-Charge but, rather, a college student. To the strains of Mozart's Second Horn Concerto, a curly-haired young man in a Georgetown sweatshirt and jeans sat at a large table stacked high with law books, his typewriter poised to add the final footnote on one page of a research paper.

"What can I do for ya'?" Conrad asked him without standing up and, since he was in civvies, not saluting either.

"My recommendations include," Hatcher's report to his superiors in the Inspector General's Office concluded, "that First Army be advised to replace the commanding officer immediately with a First Army CO from the Intelligence Corps supported by a staff of officers and NCOs all in the First Army chain-of-command to begin the work of rebuilding morale and function in this unit which has, for all intents and purposes, dissolved itself. To succeed, this task must be done with awareness of the unique composition and role of this company. It is rife with college-graduated NCOs who have served on long-term civilian status, doing intelligence work in Europe and Asia that required wide latitude and personal initiative with little direct supervision. These men have shown no interest in re-enlistment and are intent on returning to civilian life, having completed their missions abroad. Extended periods on civilian status have left them ill-prepared for military life in the ordinary sense. Duties commensurate with their training and experience and some mission with a common purpose may galvanize them into forming a cohesive and efficient unit. Conversely, barked orders followed by strict punishments, in this case, will undoubtedly result in most of these men confined to barracks or in the stockade. That should not be the goal here. With patience and persuasion, the 250th MI Company could be reconstituted as a functioning unit. Failing that, disbanding it and reassigning all personnel may be necessary."

Roll was taken on Wednesday, 13 November 1968, by a bass-voiced first lieutenant none of them had ever seen before who, it was noted, wore a First Army patch on his left shoulder. He ended with, "Stand at attention for your commanding officer, Major Weaver!" This squat fireplug of a man with a James Cagney face began, "Gentlemen! The party's over! Every one in this company collects Army pay and from this hour forward, you're going to earn it, every cent. When your name appears on the duty roster, you will personally perform that duty. If you are given an order by any officer or superior NCO, you will follow that order. Today's training schedule will begin with one hour of Physical Training conducted by Sergeant Kaiser, then you will board trucks for transportation to classroom instruction. You will then be marched in formation to the mess hall for lunch, after which you will use the afternoon to bring all your personal gear from whatever off-post domicile you have been inhabiting and arrange it neatly in your assigned lockers in the barracks, which will be your home as long as you're on active duty. Now open ranks for PT!"

Lieutenant Merle Hatcher's sage advice, it seems, had been wasted on First Army.

George Conrad called them together in the barracks at 5:00 p.m. Seventy-four buck sergeants, one corporal and two clerks formed a wide circle in the open bay on the first floor. Their fatigues were sweaty and grass-stained and their usually shiny boots were scuffed up from push-ups and squat-thrusts. "The man has a point," Conrad began, "I've been featherbedding here longer than any of you, but we've all been milking the system. I'll be discharged in a couple of months, so I'm OK with doing PT and latrine duty for that long. But you guys with more than a year left may feel differently."

There was a clamor of consensus punctuated by "They put us through a two-hour lecture about *camouflage*, for chrissakes!" and "They drove us into the woods and told us how to lay some sort of goddamn *ambush*!" and "Fourteen months like this morning, I'll need a straitjacket!" and "I'll need a hangman's noose!"

"I hear ya'!" Conrad said, "If you really mean it and there's one-hundred percent agreement, with everybody on-board, we've got one slim chance for a jail break. It could back-fire and make things worse for us, or it might get a message through to First Army... to Major Weaver's superiors... that we make bad cannon-fodder and maybe they'll rethink their approach. Higher brass is just like the rest of us... they don't want headaches. So listen up to our company clerks, then I'll ask for a show of hands."

Spec-4 Fackenthall waved a manila folder at them. "On Friday, next week's training schedule will be posted and it reads the same as the next five weeks' schedules. Each day begins with roll call and PT followed by three hours of 'Barracks Improvement,' lunch, then three more hours of 'Barracks Improvement' followed by transportation by trucks to two-hour classes in the art of warfare. This detailed plan continues over a five-week period."

Spec-4 Hanson jumped in, "You said that."

"Said what?"

"Five weeks… you already said it goes on for five weeks. I better take this. Men! We've got a plan to make a ghost town here next weekend. That's our chance to gut the whole training schedule by co-opting the 'Barracks Improvement' at the core of it. If we can do that…"

"Tell them what that means," Fackenthall interrupted.

"Tell them what, what means?"

"'Barracks Improvement,' gutting the schedule…"

"I was coming to that."

"For Chrissakes!" Conrad yelled, "Knock it off and talk straight, you-two!"

"Paint!" Fackenthall said, "For five weeks, we're scheduled to paint this barracks inside and out. We'll be closely supervised by the lieutenants, whose job it will be to impose military discipline on us, beating us over our heads with a paint brush."

"They'll stay on our asses, barking orders, harassing us," Hanson said, "Yanking us around on a short leash. Put up the ladders… move the ladders… take down the ladders… set up the paint… paint… clean up the paint. Turning us into a pack of conditioned dogs, like…"

"Get to the plan!" Conrad shouted.

Fackenthall said, "Specialist Hanson and I dug through Army Reg's about painting and they say the interior of a building may not be painted more often than once every three years."

"It's a corruption thing," Hanson added, "So paint contractors don't dig into Army pockets every year."

"Let me finish!" Fackenthall snapped. "And I'm the one who found another Reg that prohibits unqualified enlisted men from being used to paint the outside of a multi-story building."

"Ladders," Hanson said, "Falling, injuries, medical costs…"

"Right! So, what we'll have to do is paint every inch of the interior of both floors in sixty hours, ceilings included. There are forty-four double-sash windows with sixteen panes of glass each and open-frame walls with exposed two-by-four supports. That's a tremendous amount of brush work."

"And if we slop it up, with paint splashed all over the window glass and the floor and on the lockers and bunks, we may as well not have bothered."

"Yeah, the lieutenants and Sergeant Kaiser will have us scraping it up with razor blades and licking it off with our tongues. So we would have to be super-neat!"

"We've worked it out on paper and it can be done, but it will take every last one of us, full-tilt, full-time, sixty hours non-stop, Friday night at six to Monday morning at six. Lindbergh only had to concentrate for thirty-three hours, crossing the Atlantic. You'll have to go twice as long."

"Two four-man teams, one on each floor, will move bunks and lockers and tape-down edges and drop-cloths on the floors. Then four four-man teams, two on each floor, will concentrate on windows, taping glass and doing careful brush-work on the sashes and sills."

"Other teams start with the ceiling and work down the two-by-four supports over the drop-cloths. Teams will rotate like infantry, some advance while others provide support, bring paint and supplies, hold ladders, etc."

"Then roller teams will come next, fully coating the open areas, no missed spots."

"Each team will have the support of two men to monitor for any drops or spills."

"Six guys do a careful job on the latrines and shower-area and two others paint Sergeant Conrad's enclosed room."

"Two guys on each floor specialize on doors, door frames and the eight-by-eight support columns, top-to-bottom."

"Two men will tend the commissary, making sandwiches, keeping everyone fed."

"Sergeant Conrad will supervise, declaring an area dry before the drop-cloths and tape are removed and furniture gets moved back. Then final clean-up can begin."

"Hanson and I will be in charge of supplies: Paint, equipment, food and drink. The whole job will run about thirteen hundred dollars, which is twenty bucks each, counting the tip for us."

Conrad cut into the dialogue. "Take a deep breath, gentlemen. Talk it over. Then if I don't collect twenty dollars each from seventy-five willing guys, we'll just forget about the whole idea. Any questions?"

"Just one," Mark Babineaux said, "Has the place *got* to be green?"

"We are free men!" Hood boomed out, "There is no price too high for our freedom!"

The roar of approval was taken by Sergeant Conrad as a "yes" vote.

The preparation was in itself impressive. After the Officer of the Day had made his final inspection and left for his quarters on Wednesday, careful measurements determined how much was needed, which came to fourteen gallons of ceiling white, thirty-six gallons of semi-gloss "gun-metal grey" for the walls and ten gallons of a nice, complementary "thrush brown" for doors, windows and columns. Brushes of various sizes, rollers and pans, drop-cloths, masking tape, stir-sticks, rags, lamps and extension cords came next. On Friday, they bought eighty pounds of deli meats, twenty pounds of cheese, sixty loaves of bread, mustard, mayo and ketchup in quantity and, of course, twenty-five cases of soda and beer and enough ice to fill all the sinks in the latrine. Even the men who organized it were awestruck by the teamwork and energy on display. "This is like a scale-model of the Normandy Invasion!" Hood proclaimed.

When the Officer of the Day made his final inspection and drove away on Friday, Spec-4 Fackenthall called Schrafft's Restaurant and asked to talk to George Conrad. Thirty-two cars loaded to capacity with men and supplies were then released one-by-one, so the traffic-flow entering Meade through several gates would look normal to the MPs. Within an hour, the gravel lot was full of men in jeans and t-shirts hauling in supplies and Spec-4 Hanson phoned the Officers of the Day for Saturday and Sunday to tell them that Major Weaver had reassigned them to serve on Monday instead. Both lieutenants leapt at the chance for a weekend free of duty and Hanson was prepared to tell the major there had been a call from "Someone who sounded exactly like you on the phone, sir!" By Monday morning, that excuse would fit seamlessly into the size and nature of the overall conspiracy, with Spec-4 Hanson yet another hapless victim.

The work generated a carnival atmosphere, a festival of unity and common purpose. Only Conrad and the two specialists (who would vouch for each other that they were off-post all weekend) were aware that many things could go wrong with this charade, including the possibility that the whole project might collapse, that Monday would dawn with a pile of exhausted, paint-splattered soldiers lying in a heap of destruction. Or an officer or roving MP might trip across the scene sometime during the weekend. Everyone else was completely absorbed in the adventure, too excited and too busy with his assigned tasks to consider anything else. As daylight faded, lamps on extension cords provided light to the work areas and the struggle to maintain order became more challenging as men, drop-cloths, bunks, lockers, paint cans, lamps, extension cords and roller pans rotated in continuous motion, with trip-hazards everywhere for seventy-five workers on two floors. The stereo upstairs kept the work in rhythm with 45 RPM records of "Hey Jude" and "Those Were The Days My Friend" and "What a Wonderful World" repeating over and over until someone would yell, "That's enough of *that*! Put something else on!" The ground floor stereo kept them humming or singing along to Joe Crocker's "With a Little Help From My Friends" and "Mrs. Robinson" and "Sitting On The Dock Of The Bay" as the brush-work on the ceilings and in Conrad's private room and the latrine made steady progress. At 9:00, Conrad declared "radio-silence"—the stereos were shut down, voices were hushed and blankets were draped over each window to mimic a "sleeping barracks" for passers-by. The downside of this necessity was that it put the sixteen men who were just beginning to get the hang of taping and painting windows out of business and they pouted about it, drinking beer and eating sand-wiches and feeling useless. The upside was that desperately needed lighting could be shifted from the window-project to other areas. And in the tranquility of "radio silence," the painting seemed to go along more calmly, more deliberately. Coordination was getting better, communication too.

Over the course of the long night, during which bunks were moved without disturbing the men sleeping in them and Sergeant

Conrad was able to declare the first locker areas dry and complete on each floor, the 250th MI Company seemed to have become the kind of high morale, mission-oriented unit Lieutenant Hatcher of the Inspector General's Office had hoped for. Unfortunately for the chain-of-command goals of First Army, it was a headless chicken.

At dawn, Sergeant Conrad led many volunteers in a spontaneous bout of jumping jacks, to wake them up and shake off the stiffness of twelve hours tedious work in close quarters. Hanson and Fackenthall inspected the work, made suggestions for improved efficiency and declared that the project was about on schedule. Then the specialists went to the office to sleep and man the phones, the stereos came alive again (with some records moving upstairs and some down), the blankets came down and the window teams splashed water on their faces, grabbed a quick sandwich and got back to work.

There were set-backs. In full daylight, fine splatters from the rollers were discovered on lockers and floors which had been hidden in artificial lighting. Disagreements arose about whose job it should be to clean that up. There was wrangling over which ceiling team was unnecessarily hogging one of the two A-frame ladders. And in mid-morning, someone finally (inevitably) kicked over a pail of latex, thrush-brown, and cleaning up that mess required moving bunks and lockers, delaying work. But the brushes and rollers kept rolling along just like the caissons of old.

On Saturday afternoon, George Conrad grabbed a couple hours' sleep after thirty-two hours of ceaseless activity, starting Friday morning. He awoke to find that eight of the twenty bunk-areas had been completed, windows and all. His private room and the latrine were well along, which would free up those teams to join the work in the large, open bay area. Technically, the whole operation was on schedule—but something was different. A quick census, upstairs and down, found that nearly half the men were asleep, in bunks or on the floor, while small groups here and there rested, chatted, sipped beer, ate sandwiches. Just eighteen men were engaged in painting and these men had fallen into a leisurely pace with "What a Wonderful World" downstairs and "Those Were The Days My Friend" on the top floor. Gravity seemed to have increased in the barracks—and that gravity was named "exhaustion." By Conrad's assessment, they had more work to do in the next thirty-six hours than they had done in the first twenty (since painting got under way Friday evening), but they were clearly running out of steam.

"*Everybody downstairs, now!*" he bellowed on the second floor, "If they're asleep, wake 'em up! Everybody!" When he had them all together, some using columns and lockers to hold themselves up, he gave them his conclusions. "Unless we step it up right now and keep moving, we're going to look up from our work to see Major Weaver and his lieutenants standing over us! That happens, we lose! They'll have a field-day with us. Our only chance is to be in formation at 0800 hours Monday, clean fatigues and straight lines, and we don't know nuthin' about nuthin'! How the barracks got painted is a mystery… we're just as surprised as they are! But that's not gonna happen if we let ourselves fall apart over the next day-and-a-half. We've got to double-down and put the pedal to the metal right now! Go splash some water on your faces and get your butts in gear, all of you!"

"There is no price too high to pay for freedom!" Braxton Hood yelled, but this time, nobody cheered.

As they lumbered back in the direction of their work, Conrad went to his room, dug under some drop-cloths for his records and replaced the lullaby music on both stereos, turning the volume way up: "Jumpin' Jack Flash" downstairs and "Born To Be Wild" upstairs. He assigned one man to keep feeding high-energy music

onto the turntables. Then he patrolled the barracks, resolving arguments (which were on the rise), solving problems, meeting needs and
pushing anyone who was slacking. He sounded to himself like a senior
NCO ordering enlisted men around in the US Army, which he found
embarrassing, but it was, after all, his job. He just never had to do it
before.

The sun set, lamps and extension cords came back out, blankets
went back up over all the windows, lockers and bunks were shoved
around, Hanson and Fackenthall brought in more ice and just after
10:00, Conrad's private room was declared finished. The drop-cloths
and paint gear were removed from there, a flashlight inspection was
made to be certain all dribbles were scraped up and masking tape was
removed to the last and his furniture and law books were returned
to their places. Then a few at a time, men came by to marvel at the
beauty of it—white ceiling, gray walls, thrush-brown trim—and they
took encouragement from it, knowing what the finished project would
be like. "I should have done this years ago," Conrad told visitors.

Rather than reinforce the bay-area teams with the two men
who had worked on his room, he wisely put them to bed. There had
to be a rotation of some sort, even though it cost them manpower,
and his private quarters made a quiet bedroom, out of the way of the
churning bedlam in the main area. When the latrine was finished and
passed flashlight inspection, he put that small unit to rest in his room
also, with men wedged together all over his floor, too far gone to care.

Between 2:00 and 4:00 a.m., Conrad began to lose people. Some
collapsed, brush in hand. Others stood staring at the wall, asleep
standing up. No one was safe on a ladder anymore and he ordered
them taken down. One by one, he replaced the fallen. He pulled the
walking-dead along to his room and violently shook one of the men
who had slept the longest, replacing one with the other. He revived

the two-man team that had finished his private room first, then the six-man team that had finished the latrine. Each man responded differently, but no one who had worked straight-through for thirty hours and was then yanked out of a four-hour sleep could have been called "alert." However, with a soda, a sandwich, a pep-talk and a hardy slap on the back, most found it in themselves to man a brush or a roller or move drop-cloths, furniture and lamps around for a while longer.

At dawn on the Sabbath, there was no rest. The stereos came to life, blankets came down from the windows, A-frame ladders went back up and there seemed to be a second-wind blowing through the work. The need for clean-up work grew, as exhausted men showed less care and the prospect of finishing the whole project today stirred their emotions. Actual fighting nearly broke out between sloppy painters and those who caught clean-up duties. Heated words were exchanged and Conrad, who was himself slipping in-and-out of consciousness, wasn't always available to settle matters. "Jack Flash" and "Born To Be Wild" were getting on people's nerves. There was no more cheese and of the wide variety of deli-meats, only salami was left, not everybody's favorite. A few sodas remained but no beer. And the ice had run out again.

But at 5:30 p.m. on Sunday afternoon, the first-floor bay was declared finished, windows and all. Half the men pitched-in to final clean-up work while the other half went upstairs to help paint the last bunk-areas there. Before darkness set in, victory was declared. Hanson and Fackenthall had developed an order-of-battle for clean-up. Everything that would betray the conspiracy was wrapped in drop-cloths: Paint cans, full or empty, brushes, rollers, pans, salami, loaves of bread, soda and beer cans, full or empty, paint-smeared jeans, t-shirts, gym shoes—all of it was loaded into trunks and driven to the dumpsters behind the mess hall under cover of darkness. Next, the men them-selves. They shaved and showered until all the hot water was gone, then they shaved and showered in cold water. They checked each other out for paint smeared hair, ears and necks while Conrad, Fack-enthall and Hanson ran flashlights over every inch of the barracks for missed splatters or forgotten objects.

By 10:00 p.m., the barracks looked much as it had the previous Friday morning, except for a few scrapes on the floor where lockers had been carelessly shoved along and for the fact that it was now white, gun-metal gray and thrush-brown, not pale green. And then they crashed—many sleeping for the first time in bunks they had been assigned months before. There was a shared sense of wonder and pride in what they had accomplished. Each man felt an excitement from being one small part of something so grand and remarkable. They all knew it would be a life-long memory that bound together everyone who had taken part, who had given it everything he had for the good of the group, his friends. In other words, these Army Intelli-gence escapees from the military grind had at last, by default, become soldiers and the 250th MI Company was now a unit.

The moment they closed their eyes, it seemed, Conrad was yelling at them to pull themselves up and out. They pulled on fatigues and laced up boots in a fog of exhaustion.

But by 0800 hours, the floors had been swept and mopped, their bunks were made and they stood in formation, shouting "Present, sir!" crisply and clearly when their names were called. Their hour of Physical Training, however, was a pathetic performance by any standard and Sergeant Kaiser shouted himself hoarse with admonish-ments. No one managed ten push-ups in a row, most of them collapsed on the ground during squat-thrusts, and jumping jacks dissolved into most men flailing their arms around while standing still. Deciding this was willful refusal, Kaiser laced into them, face-to-face down the line, using all the profanity and threats the black-shoe Army allowed, then marched them double-file and in cadence to the mess hall for breakfast. There, they seemed cheerful and talkative—because they knew there was a confrontation in the offing when they returned to company grounds, one fraught with unpredictable consequences.

Three deuce-and-a-half trucks stood in the parking lot when they were marched back and told to fall-in. "I have a big surprise for you men!" Major Beau Weaver growled at them when they had been called to "Atten'hut!" by his second-in-command. "You will count-off-by-twos, after which all the 'ones' will unload extension ladders, paint and brushes from the trucks and under the supervision of your officers begin work on... What the hell do you want, specialist?"

There at the major's elbow stood Spec-4 Hanson with an "on-post delivery" envelope stamped "URGENT." "This just came from First Army, sir. I think you should have a look."

Major Weaver opened the envelope and read the Army Regulation that proscribed using unqualified enlisted men to paint a multi-story structure, moving his lips to form the words. "Who sent this?" he hollered at Hanson, "Where did you get it?"

"I don't know, sir. It came from First Army."

"All right, then," he barked at the company formation. "You won't count-off-by-twos. Under the supervision of your officers, you will unload those trucks and begin work painting the inside of your barracks and I will be inspecting the work on a regular... what the hell do *you* want?"

Specialist Fackenthall was at his other elbow. "This just in, sir, addressed to you, marked 'urgent'."

The stocky little fireplug of a major didn't open the envelope. He tore it apart and read with moving lips the Army Regulation prohibiting painting a building interior more often than once every thirty-six months. When he finished, he ripped the pages from top to bottom and threw the pieces on the ground. "I don't give a healthy goddamn if this barracks was painted a month ago!" he announced to no one in particular. "It's damn-well going to be painted again, starting today, by this company!"

As soon as the major had turned his officers and Sergeant Kaiser loose and they began barking orders at the men, one of the lieutenants asked to speak with him in his office. He was a First Lieutenant, his name tag said "Hatcher," and the major didn't recognize him. "I'm from the Office of the Inspector General, major," the junior officer said quietly once the office door was closed, "and I must advise against ignoring Army Regulations designed to stop waste, fraud and abuse."

Beau Weaver leaned forward and said, "I will give your advice all due consideration, LIEU-tenant, but until you outrank me, I suggest you keep any further advice to yourself."

"OTIG is advisory," Hatcher said calmly, "Giving advice is what we do. But First Army has a commitment to stopping waste, fraud and abuse whenever it happens, as in this case."

"I don't give a flying fuck about OTIG," Weaver snapped.

"You won't hear from OTIG, major. You'll hear from First Army HQ," Hatcher told him.

"So, you're threatening to get me in trouble with HQ just because I've put these men to work?" Weaver said.

"If you're in trouble with your superiors, that will be because you've ordered a barracks to be painted again that was just painted yesterday."

"Yesterday?" the major sat up straight, "Yesterday? Where do you get that?"

"One of the men in the company asked me to inspect it and the latex is still sticky in places. He told me contractors had been here this weekend and even showed me a receipt for the paint, bought last Thursday."

"Who... what man in my company?"

"I'm not at liberty to say."

"Jesus H. Christ!" Weaver smacked both his meaty fists on the desktop.

"What you've ordered to be done hits the trifecta, major," Hatcher counted off on his fingers. "It's waste... it's fraud... *and* it's abuse. It's also expressly prohibited by Army Regulations, which you not only ignored... you ripped them to shreds in front of your men."

"This is a conspiracy, goddammit! I've been set up!"

"OTIG has no interest in telling you how to run your company... within the Reg's," Hatcher said, "Call a halt to this painting project at once, and I won't report it. In the meantime, you might want to read my initial report on the 250th, which suggests assigning these men to work in keeping with their training and experience." Lieutenant Hatcher placed a folder on the steel desk containing the suggested reading. He stood and opened the office door behind him. "That's my advice, major." He saluted and went out, but the major didn't return the salute.

At 1600 hours, when the trucks came to transport the men to their warfare classes, the company grounds stood deserted. Sergeant Kaiser walked through both stories of the barracks, heavy with the scent of latex paint, but there was not a soul to be found. He swore he would see every last one of the men whose names appeared on the lockers behind bars, "especially," he muttered to himself, "the fairy who chose these colors." But by then, he, four lieutenants and a major had been sitting around the company office for seven hours with absolutely nothing to do but watch two specialists busily typing, filing, and shuffling paperwork.

"You assigned me to that hell-hole, Ed," Major Weaver said a half hour later to Colonel Edward Barkley, his immediate superior and long-time friend, "Now I'm asking you to get me out of there!"

"You're telling me not one single man showed-up for classes? Christ, Beau! Report them AWOL! A little time in the stockade will change their tunes!"

"I can't do that! I can't report the whole goddamned company AWOL! What would that make me look like as a CO? And if they all went to the stockade, who'd be left to command?! Christ, Ed! I'd be a laughing stock!"

"OK… OK, calm down. Let's think about this. I'll talk to the general in the morning and we'll figure out something that will take you off the hook. It's not your fault, Beau. That company had too many problems in the first place for any one CO to set it straight."

Major Weaver rubbed his hands over his tired face. "Truth is, Ed, that company didn't have *any* problems. We should have left them with European Command and let them just sit there and rot. They were rotting happily away for years over there in their distant corner, not bothering anybody. They had no problems and neither did we."

"They weren't a problem, Beau, but they weren't soldiers either. They were civilians, and you can't fight a war with civilians. Won't be long before we have to stop drafting civilians and make ourselves a professional military. There's growing talk of it now, with rising drug use and anti-war propaganda infiltrating the ranks. Won't be long before we keep the wheat and throw off the chaff, Beau. Meantime, we'll see what the general wants to do with this pack of loafers."

And that's how it ended for the 250th MI Company. The spirited young men of the company forged a unit, rose in revolt to get out from under the military grindstone—and won. Lieutenant Hatcher of OTIG put an end to waste and fraud—saving the Army sixty gallons of pale green paint, brushes, rollers, etc.—and kept abuse by both officers and enlisted men in check. So he won too. The Regular Army also won when conscription was ended on 27 January 1973, clearing the way for a professional military of career soldiers, sailors and airmen, ending the need to try to hammer men like Rosenzweig and Mulcahey and Levesque into soldiers. And even Major Barton Dwight won in the course of this little skirmish. Sergeant Conrad received a postcard from Germany, telling him he was "back at work in Rothenberg" and that the view from his office window was breathtaking. It was signed "Your friend, Bart" and added, "PS. I hope there are no problems to report, sergeant."

The sign over the company door was taken down, replaced with one that read "521st MI Detachment" and the new CO, a thin, young captain named Stanley Mather, was exactly what Merle Hatcher of OTIG had called for. "I am well aware that this has been a renegade outfit," he announced to them in a clear tenor voice, "I know all about the past two weeks... the fiasco of the barracks painting incident... and I want to begin by recognizing you for your initiative and teamwork. However, this is my first command and I warn you that insubordination will not be tolerated on my watch. There will be consequences! For my part, I guarantee you that you will not be asked to paint barracks or mow lawns. For your part, you men are going back out in the field to do what you were trained to do. All of you have served your country honorably as intelligence operatives and you will continue to do so in keeping with your training and experience. Like you, I attended Fort Greyhawk and I am qualified to lead you in your efforts.

"As you know, our institutions are under assault from all sides and the vital fabric of our nation is being ripped to pieces. Insidious Communist ideology has infiltrated the so-called anti-war movement and armed militants have subverted the once peaceful Civil Rights cause since Dr. King was assassinated. This has resulted in the rising use of arson and violent rioting intended to destabilize our country. This is a time when unity here at home is needed, as we fight for the freedom of the Vietnamese people and attempt to hold the line against Communist expansion into Europe. Americans have suffered through terrible times lately... assassinations, mass uprisings, rioting, heavy combat losses, a bitterly fought political election... and I am aware you may hold individual opinions about all these things. But I remind you, gentlemen, that every one of you raised your hand and took a solemn oath to defend this country against *'all enemies, foreign and domestic'* and you vowed that you would obey all orders given to you by the President of the United States and officers appointed over you... so help you God! You have kept that pledge abroad... you will continue to fulfill it now! You will repair to the barracks, store your fatigues and boots and report individually to my office in civilian clothes to receive your specific orders. Company, dismissed!"

Mark Babineaux was the first to receive his assignment and to arrive at their rendezvous at Schrafft's. He nursed a beer until Hood arrived, then greeted him loudly, "Conrad warned us this could backfire and make things worse. Looks like he had that right!"

Hood asked, "How so, pardner? Don't workin' the streets in civvies beat all hell outta PT and warfare classes?"

"I can sleep through Army lectures, Braxton. Hunting down subversives is bound to be an exercise in frustration involving a lot of wasted shoe-leather, wait and see."

Hood ordered a soda, three hamburgers and fries. When the waitress left he said, "Trouble with you, Mark, is Co Bich spoiled you rotten in Vung Tau. She did all the work while you drank and chased au dais. 'bout time somebody put the halter on ya'. All things bein' equal…"

"Which they never are."

"This could all work out for the best."

Mulcahey dropped into a seat between them and asked, "What did he assign you guys?"

Hood: "Let's wait for the others."

Babineaux: "Braxton thinks this will all work out fine. I say we're screwed."

Mulcahey: "That captain said to expect long hours, that I should never be asleep unless my targets were, so I'd have to side with you, Mark. We're screwed."

An hour later, all six were squeezed around a small table and the waitress was kept busy by them. Then Hood said, "OK, what'd y'all draw for assignments?"

Mulcahey: "I told him I knew some guys who were active in SDS on the Maryland campus, that I could keep an eye on them. He jumped all over me! He wanted photographs and complete biographies of all the leaders, who was funding them, how much did they receive, what were their personal and organizational affiliations, how did they communicate. Jesus! I started to say, 'They're just a bunch of college kids who hang out and talk a-mile-a-minute,' but that captain was going ape on me so I let him blow off steam."

Babineaux: "Did you mention that you were the president of SDS and chairman of the board?"

Mulcahey: "There isn't any board and their president is a guy named Bobby-something. They asked me to be treasurer because I have more spending money than they do, so I chip in more. And I have an honest face."

Babineaux: "So you're their funding source and one of the leaders Captain Mather wants a photo of. I can't wait to see his face when you turn yourself in."

Mulcahey: "I may not get around to mentioning any of that to him."

Rosenzweig: "We'll be working the same turf, Mad-dog. Mather wants me to build a file on all the other student groups at Maryland beside SDS… same deal with photos and bios and affiliates on student government and political clubs and, also, I should take down verbatim anything I hear from students or professors that may be 'subversive,' any threat against the government or military 'for possible criminal prosecutions' he said."

Mulcahey: "He told me that too."

Levesque, beaming: "I lucked out big time! I told him I had infiltrated a secret society, men who had money and influence who may be plotting something."

Hood: "You dog! You're keepin' your job at the Union League? Really?"

Levesque: "He's going to set me up with a miniature camera and a recording device. Meantime, I guess I may as well move back in with a pretty young lady I know so I can be near my work."

Mulcahey: "Did Mather say he wanted at least two Information Reports a week? How you gonna string him along for months like you did Cardenas? Will you 'build liaison' endlessly with nothing to report, like you did with the Catholics in Saigon?"

Levesque: "I don't know. I wonder if the Union League could use a boys' choir."

Hood: "He wants at least two IRs a week from us too. I told him Babineaux and I'd worked together in Vietnam and make a good team, so he assigned us to keep an eye on activities around The Mall and Federal Government buildings in D.C. 'Operation Commando Hunt' was announced by LBJ last week, to bomb the crap out of the Ho Chi Minh Trail network, and it's got the hippies and yippies firin' on all cylinders. Any organized activity, we're supposed to file an IR with photos, IDs, verbatim quotes, all the same stuff you guys are doin'... plus put out any misinformation that could screw 'em up or make 'em look bad... that too. He promised that whatever we report will be analyzed at Fort Holabird in Baltimore in three hours and if it's gonna require action, it'll be on a desk at the Pentagon within twelve hours."

Silent until now, Singleton said, "This all makes me sick to my stomach."

Hood: "Why? What'd he assign you?"

Singleton: "What difference does that make? Look at us! We're being ordered to collect information on people who are organizing protests and marching in the streets just like they've always done in our country... for unions, for women's right to vote, for an end to war, for civil rights. Since when did marching in protest become 'subversive' in a democracy?"

Rosenzweig: "Since forever! George the Third to The Bonus Army to this summer in Chicago, protests are always put down with troops. All the ones you mentioned were repressed, Rick."

Hood: "That's not what this is all about. This is about puttin' a lid on this stuff before it turns into arson and violence and armed militias."

Singleton: "The right to petition the government..."

Hood: "... doesn't include settin' fires and breakin' shop

windows."

Singleton: "There are laws against arson and vandalism. So the cops should arrest arsonists and vandals, but what we're doing here, building files on students and protesters, turning their pictures over to the Pentagon and listening for 'subversive' statements, that's what the KGB does in Russia."

Hood: "Soldiers are always used to keep order, push come to shove. They burned down half the cities in the country when Reverend King was murdered… without the National Guard…"

Singleton: "Go ahead and say it! 'They'… meaning black guys like me… would've burned down the other half. Goddammit, Braxton, I risked my life in Vietnam to serve my country and now, if I say I think it's immoral, maybe even illegal, to use soldiers as spies against civilians, it's your duty to take down my words verbatim and report me to the Pentagon like I'm some kind of criminal!"

Everyone at the table looked on as Hood made a long, piercing study of Singleton's face. Then he said quietly, "What did Captain Mather ask you to do, Rick?"

"He called me 'the gem of the company'. They've been looking for some way to infiltrate the black churches in D.C. because that's where, as he put it, 'those people gather and organize'. I smiled and told him he could count on me without telling him who my father is."

Hood said, "Man… I don't know what to say, Rick. That is so…"

Mulcahey: "You should'a called him 'Massah' like in *Gone with the Wind*."

Babineaux: "Shut up, Mulcahey!"

Mulcahey: "If I'd been you, I would'a said, "Sho'nough, Massah Cap'm…"

"Shut up, Mulcahey!!" everyone shouted together.

The five roommates all moved their gear, except for their uniforms and black boots, back into the College Park apartment, a final vindication for the five-two-zero's plan of rebellion. The apartment was better organized this time, with a plan for keeping food and beer on hand, for taking turns at cooking and clean-up, which they recognized was also a result of Sergeant Conrad's molding them into a unit. However, the way they carried out their duties defined their generation's response to post-consensus America, a society now riven into factions by clashes over race and the Vietnam war.

Mulcahey and Levesque reported back to the 521st MI Detachment in some detail, although everything they typed was fabricated or intentionally distorted. One example from many pages filed by Sergeant Mulcahey read, in part:

"The Students for a Democratic Society meeting on Monday evening, 2 December 1968, was attended by forty-seven young people, all claiming to be students enrolled at the University of Maryland. The first names of thirty-six of them appear in the table below. This Agent is working to determine their last names on an on-going basis. Bob, their president, called the meeting, scheduled for 1800 hours, to order at 1825 hours because John, the treasurer, was late. A directive received from the National Council of SDS was read aloud proclaiming that local chapters could decide on a case-by-case basis whether or not to send representatives to the National Council's Annual Meeting in Ann Arbor 26-31 December. Susan noted that the Ann Arbor chapter of SDS had recently split into two factions over the issue of white privilege and she wanted to know which faction was sponsoring the National Meeting. She said, 'If the wealthy white kids who don't want poor kids who are not students to join SDS, then

I'm not going. But if it's sponsored by the wealthy white kids who DO want poor non-students to join, then I will consider going, if my travel is reimbursed.' John, the treasurer, advised Susan that $104.66 was on hand, currently, which might cover one round-trip bus ticket to Ann Arbor and a couple of meals, but that would empty the treasury. 'Then forget it,' Susan said. This agent is determined to obtain Susan's last name and contact information."

The IR neglected to mention that the last name of the SDS treasurer was "Mulcahey" and that he had been altogether absent from this meeting because he was with a woman he'd met in the Student Union named Susan something, who turned out to be a disappointment because their courtship lasted an eternity, compared to shantytown. The truth was Mulcahey had skipped the last three SDS meetings because they were no longer pleasant. Bright, decent young people made up the core group and they were fun to be around because they were endlessly hopeful about not being drafted, their main concern. When around them, Mulcahey looked to the future— just as they did—and forgot for a time the loss of Louis Leffanta, of Jack and Bobby Kennedy, and the trauma of having his jeep shot to pieces at Tan Son Nhut. But their group had been invaded recently by a half-dozen angry, misguided half-wits from the People's Labor Party who bullied and intimidated the SDS kids and Mad-dog could barely hold back the urge to pick up something heavy and kick their asses. Furthermore, he knew these were exactly the type of extremists Captain Mather had sent him out to find and if he started reporting on them, it would make him a pawn in the anti-war versus Wehrmacht chess match and ruin his social life. He was the wrong man for the right job. He called Bob later to ask what had happened at the meeting and based his IR—which ended with a random list of thirty-six first names—on that phone call.

Photographs taken by Sergeant Levesque with his minicamera were rarely useful, since the lighting in the Union League was subdued. An analyst at Fort Holabird concluded that they may very well show men who were planning conspiracies, as Levesque reported, but the evidence was inconclusive and the men were not identified. Audio recordings made by Levesque were often garbled, though a Fort Holabird analyst did extract from one of the tapes the information that stock in a Mexican mining company was going to rise on an announcement not yet made public, and that analyst was able to open an account with Merrill Lynch in time to make a nice little bundle for himself. Biweekly IRs filed by Levesque consisted largely, like Mulcahey's, of invented or useless "facts" and promises that the agent was working hard to obtain more of the same.

Rosenzweig and Singleton were hard-working and dedicated, though their dedication was not to the task assigned. Their Information Reports, in contrast to Mulcahey's and Levesque's, lacked even the appearance of reporting anything. Zachary Rosenzweig enrolled full-time in the history department's graduate program at the University of Maryland. His ambition was to win his Ph.D. and teach his favorite subject at the college level, so he could not afford mediocre grades or tepid recommendations from his professors. He set out from the start to be the best student in his class. The reading load, especially in modern European history, was challenging, but the lectures were stimulating, and he burned the midnight oil in the library or at the nearby apartment he shared with four others. Once weekly, he drove up to Fort Meade to say hello to Hanson and Fackenthall and to type one very brief IR on student political organizations based on information he copied from various fliers and brochures that were handed out on campus. He had met the president of the Young Republicans Club once but forgot to ask for his name, so he omitted any mention of it.

If Rosenzweig ignored his assigned mission by default, Singleton did so with intent. He made the rounds of every black or integrated church in Washington's city limits and offered to volunteer in whatever community activities they sponsored. Many of the clergy knew his father or knew of him. Singleton took copious notes on each of the people he met, including verbatim quotes, with the intent of serving as a witness for the defense if any of them was accused of disloyalty or subversive activities. Offering oneself as a volunteer to any church, anywhere, however, can open the door to bottomless demands on one's time and energy. Doing so at a dozen churches all at once is a foolish thing to do! Soon, Singleton had an itinerary of meetings and activities that would choke a horse. He gave up driving, since parking at most locations was a nightmare, and began taking cabs from one place to another, wherever they needed him to work in a soup kitchen or tutor children in an after-school reading program or improve the landscaping or haul canned goods into a food pantry. He considered the irony of being asked to go hunting for Communist agents when, if he'd been recruited by Vo Danh, he'd be one himself. He went about his work in a state of quiet rage, that he was expected to make reports to the military on decent people who cared for children and the poor. He assumed that a government spy, his counterpart, was tailing his father around in New York, watching for any sign of disloyalty, and he fought the urge to take the train home, ferret out the informant and put him in the hospital. For now, his revenge was to file IRs that praised the work of the churches but did not name any of the names he kept in his personal notes, only the names of the churches. He wrote letters to investigative reporters at *The Washington Post* informing them that soldiers were being ordered to spy on civilians but, wishing to avoid a long stay in the prison at Fort Leavenworth, he didn't sign his name to them.

Hood and Babineaux, unlike the others, worked in good faith to execute their orders. The whole truth is Hood felt a patriotic duty to do so, while Babineaux followed after him out of friendship. After some experiments, they found that posing as tourists gave them better cover than mixing-in with demonstrators. A war protester didn't usually carry a Nikon camera with a telephoto lens and a note-book for taking down the names of his fellow protesters. Someone doing so might be mistaken for a spy. They asked for directions, went in-and-out of museums, took pictures of the Capitol that happened to include a group of chanting protesters carrying signs. Rare was the hour when no one was protesting something along the Federal Mall, usually outside the White House or Congress, but it so happened that this was a lag-period for such activity. President Johnson had mere weeks left in office, bombing of North Vietnam had been halted because Peace Talks were beginning in Paris (which gave Babineaux the weird feeling that the fairy-tale of his "White Paper" was coming true), Richard Nixon's Inauguration in January would bring to office a president who had promised "peace with honor" and word was out that he had a "secret plan" to end the war. Thanksgiving came and went, winter was in the air, and even the radical masses had Christmas shopping to do. So as diligent as Hood and Babineaux were in sniffing out threats to the civil order, they had hit upon an ebb tide in such activities. Their reports were detailed and accurate, with names of individuals and groups, photographs of their activities and verbatim quotes from speakers. But the newspapers reported the same events in more detail than Hood and Babineaux did, with better pictures too.

"I warned you, Braxton," Babineaux complained one cold, windy day as they crossed the Mall for the tenth time, "this would turn out to be an exercise in frustration wasting a lot of shoe leather! Let's go pick up a couple of hippie chicks and get inside where it's warm."

But Hood, who felt himself a traitor of sorts for the acts of perfidy and larceny that Frank Monroe had led him to in Vietnam, insisted they stick to doing their duty, following the orders they had been given, until one startling day outside the White House fence. Babineaux was taking pictures of a young man with a bullhorn shouting angry words at passers-by while Hood recorded his words on a steno-pad he kept hidden inside a city map. Hood suddenly folded the map and said, "Mark, listen up to this."

"During my time over there," the speaker shouted, "they had me crawl into hidden tunnels in the Cu Chi area… a flashlight in one hand and a .45 in the other. If I heard any movement in there, in that dark hole in the ground, I crawled out and reported it and they tossed explosives down there and killed whoever was in there! Could've been some mother with her children, hiding from the war. They didn't care. That's what turned me around. So I'm asking you…" He locked eyes with Braxton Hood and pointed the bullhorn at him. "If you know any veterans who feel as I do, tell them to contact the Vietnam Veterans Against the War and help us put a stop to this needless killing NOW!"

"Before I came down to Vung Tau, I was with the Cu Chi Station," Hood said, "That guy was crawling into those tunnels to follow up on my reports." He reached over and gently took the camera out of Babineaux's hands. He popped it open and exposed the film, then wrapped film, cartridge and all, into pages he tore from his steno pad and stuffed the whole wad into a trash barrel.

"Where you going?" Babineaux called after him.

"That guy's a combat veteran," Hood muttered, "I'm nobody to rat-out a combat veteran."

After that day, reports filed by Hood and Babineaux detailed the activities of tourists, mostly pretty young women, in the area of the Mall, with hundreds of random pictures of them. And each roll of film they turned in ended with a close up shot of a marble wall where words were carved-out: "-- That to secure these rights, Governments are instituted among Men, deriving their just powers from the consent of the governed.—That whenever any Form of Government becomes destructive of these ends, it is the Right of the People to alter or abolish it..." The analysts at Fort Holabird developed this photograph and sent it to the Pentagon for its obvious subversive content.

As for Captain Mather, he concluded after some weeks of reading reports from sixty-two individual agents or small teams as they worked every college campus and political organization in a five-state area that *all* of them fell into the same patterns, more or less, as the Greyhawk Six. This generation of citizen-soldier, he decided, had no intention of hunting down extremists. "What in the hell is happening here?" he barked across an office where four lieutenants and two specialists languished in an idleness they could not hide. "This goddamned company is trained to do intelligence work, but when somebody orders them to paint a barracks, they go nuts! They work like wild animals for three straight days and nights doing something they are not trained to do. Then you assign them to do what they *are* trained to do... what they enlisted to do... and they fall apart at the seams! If they showed one-tenth the dedication they did to barracks-painting, we'd have identified every disloyal son-of-a-bitch within fifty miles of Meade by now! But has anyone here seen *one... lousy... IR? ONE? that is worth the paper it's printed on?!*"

No one answered the captain, so he stomped back into his office and slammed the door behind him with all his might.

"He's right, Hanson," one specialist whispered to the other, "With real dedication, we could have every heretic in a fifty-mile radius burning at the stake by now."

"That," Hanson whispered back, "is a very sobering thought."

10

20-21 December 1968

OUR GENERATION

"Pull over here," Hood said, "We'll go in for a burger break, then I'll drive."

"You had your turn," Mulcahey said, "Let somebody drive who hasn't done it yet."

"Hey! Anybody not driven?" Hood barked.

"Rosie shook Levesque awake in the back seat and asked, "Have you driven yet?"

Levesque rubbed his eyes. "Don't you remember? I drove from Fayetteville to Florence and every time somebody said 'Florence,' Mad-dog said 'Henderson?'"

"I must have slept through that," Rosie said.

"Lucky you!"

Babineaux signaled a left turn with his arm out the window and pulled Singleton's (Singleton's father's, actually) platinum blue Lincoln Continental into the parking lot of the McDonald's. They climbed out and stretched, shaking blood back into their limbs after twelve hours of continuous travel from Fort Meade to Jacksonville, pausing only for pit-stops and to change drivers every two hours. They had lived on bread, cheese, apples and thermos bottles of coffee and water to this point, in part to save money and time, and in part because Braxton Hood didn't trust restaurants in the small towns of the Carolinas and Georgia to follow the new Federal laws mandating that Rick Singleton be allowed to enter through the same doors, sit at the same table and be treated in the same manner as his white companions. Already Singleton had made it abundantly clear that he did *not* want to spend his Christmas leave in Florida, even if it had the very special beach with "the most glorious sunrise you've ever seen," as Hood had promised. Singleton wanted to go home to New York to visit his family and perhaps to have a heart-to-heart talk with any creep who was tailing his father around, showing great interest in him and taking notes and pictures. But Hood had prevailed. Patiently but persistently, he sold Singleton on the idea of driving out of the snow and ice, into sunny, warm days on a Florida beach. And besides, Rick's Lincoln was the only car that was big enough to fit in all six of them. "We'll have plenty of room if we take your car," Hood said, but that was, as it turned out, a lie. They were squashed in together, three to a seat, like sardines in a can.

Nobody was in a good mood even before Hood told them, "Take a seat inside, hit the can and unwind, but we need to get through Jacksonville before rush hour so we arrive at the beach before dark. We'll grab a bite here, order one to go too, and be back on the road by 4:00."

"I'll wait here," Singleton muttered, "Bring me something."

"It's a McDonald's, Rick," Hood said.

"I can see that, Braxton, and I'm still not going in."

"We still got three, four more hours. So c'mon in and stretch out. Any Cracker so much as looks your way, I'll rip his head off, how'd you like that?"

"That's not it… I'm not worried about that. I just feel like I should've gone home over Christmas. What the hell am I doing here anyway?"

"Hang in there, man," Hood said, "I promise when you get out of the service, you can spend every holiday with your folks. This year, you got this unruly mob for family, you and I, so we may as well do stuff together before we scatter in the wind, each his separate way." He put his big hand on Singleton's shoulder. "Let's go in before Mad-dog says somethin' gets us all kicked out of the place."

They beat rush hour out of Jacksonville, but an hour later the traffic on I-95 grew heavy and they inched forward in a stop-and-go jam.

"Must be an accident up ahead," Babineaux guessed.

"Sure looks that way," Hood answered from behind the wheel, but he knew better and his heart beat faster in anticipation.

They crawled ahead, moving so intermittently that at one point Hood and Singleton switched behind the wheel without pulling off. Hood studied the Rand McNally map book in the last fading light of the day and suggested they get off I-95 at Titusville. The traffic on Route 1 was no better, though, so after another hour of crawling down local roads in the dark with Hood holding a flashlight over the map book, they agreed they'd had enough. They pulled off the road and unloaded bed-rolls from the trunk. Hood and Babineaux had the only flashlights and led the way for the line of exhausted friends. They trudged several miles along the roadway before turning inland, following a path up the side of a low dune, slogging through soft, deep sand to the top. All but Braxton Hood were surprised to find a gathering of other campers crowded along the ridgeline of the dune and spread out on the beach below. Many had vans and trailers, others small tents. To the east, across a wide body of water, a little town with bright lights glittered in the night.

"Howdy," Hood greeted a group of shadowy figures gathered around a small fire, "Mind if we set up beside y'all?" There seemed just enough open space between other campers for the Greyhawk band to lay-out their bedrolls. They heard Hood say in the pitch-dark, "Beautiful night, ain't it?" to someone who answered, "Sure is. Should be a perfect morning for it." Then, within minutes, every last exhausted one of the men who had spent seventeen hours packed shoulder-to-shoulder in a moving car dropped off to sleep, all except Braxton Hood, who was too excited to sleep and sat on the sand, looking up at the stars.

Hood was still awake, standing up with one hand on his hip, the other shading his eyes against the morning sun, a scale model of the Colossus of Rhodes, when Singleton stirred awake. "Godammit, Braxton," he growled, "you dragged us all this way to see a spectac-ular sunrise, then you didn't even wake us up for it!"

"Good mornin', pardner," Hood said cheerfully, "you haven't missed a thing, don't worry." He moved around the small area, gently shaking each of his friends awake, bidding them to rise. For as far as they could see, all down the dune-side and across the wide beach, campers were in motion and wonderful smells of bacon and coffee filled the air.

Mulcahey said, brushing sand out of his hair, "I'm starved. What's for breakfast?"

Hood said, "A special treat." He lifted a heavy pair of steel binoc-ulars off his neck and handed it around. "See the tower stickin' up on that island? What is it?"

"Oil refinery?" Babineaux guessed.

"It's a blast furnace, like the one at Republic Steel in South

Chicago," Mulcahey said.

Singleton, who was squinting through the binoculars said, "It's a rocket!"

Hood said, "Nope. It's not a rocket. The V-2 the Germans used in World War II, that was a rocket. The Saturn 1B that blasted three astronauts into earth orbit in October, that was a rocket too. They're gonna need some kind'a new name for that creature over yonder. That, gentlemen, is the first Saturn V the world's ever seen. It's 363 feet tall, near *triple* the size of the little ole Saturn 1B used in October. It's perched on top of five F-1 engines, each of 'em two stories tall and when they light 'em up, a couple hours from now, god willin', those engines and the boosters will burn through three thousand gallons of fuel every second, so the men riding on top will be thirty-six miles above the earth and fifty miles downrange from here two and a half minutes after lift-off. If everythin' works… and nobody guarantees it will… those three men will be in orbit around the goddamn moon itself in a few days' time. The *moon*, gentlemen! And we'll have been here to see 'em off!"

"President Kennedy said we could do this."

Hood smiled. "That's right, Mulcahey. He did. Americans can do whatever we'all set our minds to doin'."

They stood on the ridgeline of the dune, passing the binoculars from one to the other and squinting against the rising sun. They were tired, hungry, sand-covered, and mosquito-chewed, but they were feeling happy and lucky to be here, together, soldiers on leave, friends.

At 8:51 a.m., the campers around them who had transistor radios began to chant in unison "5… 4… 3… 2… 1… ZERO!" and a white cloud exploded beside the Saturn V. When the sound reached them across the water, seconds later, it vibrated in their chests as well as in their ears. Then what Hood had called that creature slowly climbed up, filling the air with the sound of a giant canvas sail being ripped from end to end. The craft itself was soon dwarfed by the enormous and growing plume upon which it rode. It doubled in acceleration, doubled again and again until it was gone, with just the contrail to look up at, and the cheers of the campers melted away.

Much Deserved Thanks

None of the characters who came to life for me in *There Comes a Time* and in *Vietnam Remix* would exist without life-long friends I have treasured since the 1960's. Charlie Lambert, David Jones, Ronnie Ray Fontenot, George Wolfson, Ken Drolet and Keith Konajeski have each contributed pieces of themselves to the Greyhawk Six and I need only close my eyes while writing to hear their voices.

As a graduate student at Columbia University, I found it wise not to mention US Army Intelligence or Vietnam. The campus was in full-throated debate about Vietnam, and I had already devoted three years to that topic and wished to learn about other things from remarkable teachers like Robert McClintock, Maxine Greene, Harold Fruchtbaum and Douglas Sloan. After six intense years of study, my discretion had become a habit which might never have been broken without my fellowship in the Guiness Book Club of Warren, Rhode Island. Over a decade of lively engagement and sharing in-common hundreds of books, these friends learned of my youthful adventures and insisted, "You've got to write about that!" So I broke a half-century of silence and did. I am grateful to each one of these remarkable men: Paul Abrahamson, Rick Bensusan, Kevin Blanchard, Jeff Bullock, Ralph Caruso, Andy Crellin, Bill Goneau, Bob Marshall, Jack McCarthy, Brian Power and Ken Sharpe.

There Comes a Time owes a great deal to the encouragement, candid criticism and attention received by *Vietnam Remix* from many book-lovers who devoted their time to reading it. We are afloat in an ocean of good books, so I am always grateful and deeply honored when a reader choses mine. Thank you all.

Finally, throughout Patricia Nolan's remarkable career in public health, she has brought equal energy and devotion to being a great mother to Kathleen and Heather and a great wife, unfailingly supportive and loving. Books require a living writer and, given my wild youth, especially after returning from Vietnam, that was never foreordained in the present case. I owe Pat everything.

About the Author

Jack Nolan in 1968

Reared in Northern Indiana, Jack Nolan worked for a time at US Steel Corporation, Gary Works, as did his father and grandfather.

He was graduated by Ball State University in 1965 and taught for a year before serving three years in Army Intelligence. From 1967 to 1970, he was stationed at Fort Holabird Intelligence School in Baltimore and then with bilateral operations in Can Tho and Saigon before returning stateside. He was assigned to the 531st MI Company, Fort Meade, but lived with his friends in College Park, near the University of Maryland campus.

He was awarded a doctorate in history by Columbia University in 1976, then enjoyed teaching great students at University High School in Tucson, Arizona.

Jack lives with his wife, Pat, in Providence, Rhode Island, where he is happy to receive e-mails from readers, friends, former students, daughters Kathleen and Heather, grandsons Ian, Ben and Django and studio-heads at vietnam.remix.1968@gmail.com.

Made in the USA
Monee, IL
25 January 2020

20827034R00178